NEMESIS

ROSAMOND SMITH

NEMESIS

BARRIE & JENKINS
LONDON

First published in Great Britain in 1991 by
Barrie & Jenkins Ltd,
Random Century House, 20 Vauxhall Bridge Road
London SW1V 2SA

BRITISH LIBRARY CATALOGUING IN PUBLICATION DATA

Smith, Rosamond
Nemesis.
I. Title
823 [F]

ISBN 0-7126-4927-1

Phototypeset by SX Composing Ltd, Rayleigh, Essex

Printed and bound in Great Britain by
Mackays of Chatham PLC, Chatham, Kent

FOR EMORY AND GEORGIA ELLIOTT

It is not my fault if I am like a mushroom which seems edible but which poisons you if you pick it up and taste it, taking it to be something else.

Chopin, in a letter, 1839

Part I

One

Years later, looking back to that occasion, Maggie Blackburn would not have wished to pose the question to herself, whether, knowing what would come of it – *all* that would come of it – she would have given that party, on that particular date, and invited those particular guests.

For circumstances are all, and circumstances determine fate as, on a certain level of perception, a concatenation of minutes constitutes a life, relentless as middle C struck endlessly – no music, merely sound.

No. Maggie Blackburn, a person of the highest integrity, would not have wished to pose the question.

Two

Maggie Blackburn was a transparency to herself but something of an enigma to others. Of this fact she had not the slightest suspicion.

At the age of thirty-four she lived alone: unmarried, seemingly unattached. She was a gifted pianist yet, fatally, she lacked confidence in her abilities and had chosen to direct most of the energy of her young adulthood into teaching: first at the Curtis Institute of Music in Philadelphia, then, for the past six years, at the Forest Park Conservatory of Music in Forest Park, Connecticut. Administrative work bewildered and fatigued her, yet she found herself accepting more and more of it and had recently been appointed director of the Music Education Programme for Advanced Students, a position no one wanted, yet certain of her colleagues resented it being offered to her. They murmured to one another, not quite meaning it, 'Who would have thought that Maggie Blackburn was ambitious – for such a petty sort of power?' Maggie was tall, five feet ten, and carried herself in a forthright manner that was mistaken for pride, when in truth it was a continual rebuke to her instinctive desire to shrink, to slouch, to make herself less visible; for she'd grown to her full height by the age of sixteen, and the terror of her life, at that time, was that she might never stop growing. Her mother, who had died of cancer when Maggie was still in high school, had often regarded her with loving yet worried eyes, and Maggie could not fail to detect a note of tense maternal solicitude in her voice: 'Maggie, you *are* pretty. But you must stand up straight.'

Of course, Maggie was not pretty.

By the age of thirty, however, she seemed to have grown at last into her bones and to have acquired an austere, Nordic sort of beauty, a beauty that largely escaped her own eye. She did not *see* herself and had no vanity. Conscious of so much else, and warmly if haphazardly empathic with others, she seemed dispossessed of a consciousness of herself. Her hair was a rapidly fading gold and would have fallen nearly to her waist, but of course she wore it up, neatly plaited in girlhood braids and wound, not always neatly, about her head, coronet-fashion. In public, at the piano, in a long black dress, her hair so fashioned, she did look striking – but that was not, perhaps, her intention. In fact she had no intention at all; she supposed herself in the service of the music, 'her' music only by grammatical usage. She seemed not exactly sexless but unaware of her sex, still less her sexuality, like a beautifully executed sculpted figure whose folds of stony clothing overlaid merely stone.

There did indeed seem to be something wrong with Maggie Blackburn, but what? And who would save her from it?

Like many music-minded people she had a tendency, at times, to become abstract: distracted. Certainly her slender, tapered fingers, like any pianist's fingers, often depressed the keys of an invisible keyboard; but in a fiercely musical community like Forest Park, such mannerisms were hardly considered eccentricities. Maggie Blackburn, perhaps because she was a woman – and after all she *was* a woman, unmarried, seemingly unattached – was perceived as less professionally committed than her male colleagues, even those colleagues who were less talented than she; it was believed that she must, for all her pose of independence and self-assurance, hope to marry, or at least to fall in love.

But she dressed so strangely or, if not strangely, unimaginatively. Tasteful clothes, though not many of them – a single good suit in dove-grey tweed, crisp shirtwaister dresses interchangeable except for colour, linen slacks that fitted her loosely but had perfect creases, Icelandic wool sweaters, a cashmere coat so well worn at the cuffs it might well have been (indeed, it was) a

5

remnant from college days: all in neutral colours, grey, black, off-white, soft dull beiges, greens so pebbly-pale as to be indistinguishable from grey. 'Maggie Blackburn dresses like a nun,' one or another of her friends observed. 'Can't anyone make some suggestions to her?' Her closest friend, Portia MacLeod, a teacher of voice at the Conservatory and the school's most distinguished female singer (soprano), had several times taken Maggie shopping, a schoolgirl sort of expedition both women had enjoyed, but the lovely reds, yellows, blues, and lavenders of those expeditions were rarely seen afterward. When Portia demanded where her new clothes were and why she wasn't wearing them, Maggie could only reply haltingly, 'I do wear them – I *have*. I'm sure I have.' Portia supposed her friend hopeless but did not intend to give up on her.

Maggie did frequently wear eye-catching jewellery, inherited by way of her mother and her mother's family. (They were Swedes who had emigrated to the United States in the 1880s, settling in northern Minnesota.) These finely wrought items were so clearly valuable they did not fail to signal to observers the possession of wealth in their bearer, or a familial connection to it. In fact, like so much else about Maggie Blackburn, this was quite erroneous: the Blackburns were near-destitute, for Maggie's father's protracted dying had exhausted all their savings and more. By the time Maggie was in her early thirties the Blackburns as a family had virtually ceased to exist.

Maggie Blackburn had been named after a beloved young aunt who died of leukaemia years before Maggie was born: by all accounts a gentle, saintly, beautiful girl. The original Margaret Louise Blackburn was only nineteen at the time of her death, a pianist and a harpist, blessed also with a 'crystal-clear' soprano voice, and though she had died six years before Maggie's birth she was kept alive in the family as a touchstone, a presence, a theme. Maggie had grown up as an embodiment of that theme, for she too was musically talented, but she was a lesser embodiment, of course – how, being dead, could the original Margaret Louise be surpassed? It was as if the ghostly aunt were living and

6

the living girl were a kind of ghost. Maggie told herself scrupulously that she did not mind how, in praising her piano playing, her father was clearly remembering the other Margaret Louise, that beloved older sister; she told herself that praise after all is praise. Love is love.

By the age of fifteen she had articulated these insights:

If I cannot be loved as myself, I can be loved as another.

If I cannot be loved even as another, I have, in any case, the piano.

She was wise enough to think of it not as *my* but *the*.

Maggie won a scholarship to the Boston Conservatory of Music and after graduation made her professional debut, like so many other young pianists, in the Carnegie Recital Hall; she was taken up by kindly elders, who perceived in her a genuine if narrow talent, and no threat to them or to the music – decidedly *not* atonal, iconoclastic, 'experimental' – to which they had given their lives. Indeed there was, and is, a revolution in music, but it is possible to live as if there were not; as if Debussy, Beethoven, Chopin, Mozart, Bach, even Vivaldi were our contemporaries, speaking to an unchanged world. Small but appreciative audiences applauded young Margaret Louise Blackburn's playing of familiar and semifamiliar piano pieces because it confirmed what they already knew: great music is beautiful, and technically demanding.

Thus, Maggie embarked upon a career as an occasional soloist, a more frequent accompanist; she taught here and there, was given an instructorship at Curtis, then hired, as an assistant professor, at the Forest Park Conservatory, where she acquitted herself well, was much admired by her students, and held in generally high esteem by those colleagues who troubled to think of her at all. She was, in a community sometimes split by rival factions, dominated by prominent individuals (foremost among them the composer-in-residence Rolfe Christensen), a good, reliable citizen, an unattached woman who might be expected to give more of her time, her extracurricular time, than other faculty members. 'Let's ask Maggie Blackburn to chair this committee,'

her colleagues said. 'No one can do as good a job as Maggie.'
And so it was.

Maggie worked hard, and harder still, though not long after joining the Forest Park staff she began to disappear at weekends. Where was she going? Why was she cutting back on her solo performances? Friends inquired, and Maggie murmured vaguely, 'Visiting relatives,' and changed the subject. Or, if pressed, 'Research.' Her expression was chill; her eyes invited no further scrutiny. It was remarked that she drove away in her metallic-grey Volvo with a single suitcase in the back seat and a stack of music, papers and magazines in the seat beside her. Women acquaintances speculated – might there be a romantic mystery? – but, on Mondays, those colleagues who saw Maggie at school remarked on her air of distraction, melancholy. If there was love, it was not flourishing. It was not a healthy love.

In fact, Maggie was visiting her father, a patient in a nursing home in suburban Long Island. She left Forest Park on Saturday morning, stayed overnight in a motel near the nursing home, and returned early Sunday evening. Matters were complicated in Maggie's relationship with her father because he had been estranged from the family for years: he'd divorced Maggie's mother when Maggie was thirteen; he'd remarried and re-divorced and now, in his final illness, had settled into a defensive attitude toward his actions, maintaining old quarrels of which Maggie was grateful to know nothing. These complications were enhanced because Mr Blackburn confused times and quarrels and seemed as emotionally involved with relatives long since gone as with those only recently deceased. Moreover, he believed himself financially independent, at times as mythically wealthy as Nelson Rockefeller and Howard Hughes (both of whom he claimed to know), when in fact he was, except for barely adequate insurance payments and Maggie's support, penniless. Such a state of affairs had to be kept secret from him, to prevent another 'cerebral episode'; thus, entering the room Mr Blackburn shared with a Mr Ackley, a fellow stroke victim, Maggie never knew who she was supposed to be or which era of Mr Blackburn's past she represented. When he stared at her and demanded, 'Is it *you?*' she hardly knew how to answer.

Daughter and father at such times regarded each other over an abyss of sticky linoleum.

Mr Blackburn had been successively a trial lawyer in Manhattan; an assistant district attorney; a judge. He'd had a wide and combative circle of acquaintances, a manly and, over all, gratifying career; and he did not accept that it was ended. He was seventy-nine years old, which was not, he argued, old. Age is a matter of mental ability, not physical debility. True, he was partly paralysed; true, the vision in both his eyes had deteriorated; he suffered from spells of agnosia – total forgetfulness and incoherence – and was subject to an array of tics, twitches, spasms, stammerings. He considered Maggie's role in his confinement a betrayal. He considered the nursing home – a private home in Old Westbury that was in fact his own choice – a preposterous but temporary place he had no need to take seriously. Thus, he ignored the moribund Mr Ackley, who suffered from severe aphasia in any case, and kept himself aloof from the nursing staff, spending much of his time in a sullen, stony silence. On good, more active days he listened to music (Bach, Vivaldi, Palestrina; Maggie brought him tapes); worked on elaborate jigsaw puzzles spread out on a card table (fussy reproductions of Old Master oils which, too, Maggie supplied); scribbled notes, sometimes in code, in preparation for writing his life's story. Mr Blackburn's mental life was, as his doctor told Maggie, a shifting in and out of coherence – coherence being a kindly word for sanity – and it was not a phenomenon Mr Blackburn could control or for which he was responsible.

Maggie came to Old Westbury on weekends. Not every weekend, but most. She brought this strange elderly accusing man who was her father chocolates, flowers, magazines, news of her life and her career, should he be in a receptive mood. Sometimes he was, and sometimes he was not. No one was responsible. Maggie understood that when she was not present to her father, she ceased to exist for him. Perhaps this was best. When she was present, smiling and speaking in a loud, unnatural voice so that he could hear her, she did exist – but how? In which category? He confused her with her mother and perhaps with her aunt Margaret Louise. Perhaps with other women. Did he perceive her, through his gauzy vision, as simply female? Mr Blackburn was a judge still, with many questions to ask of Maggie: '*Where* did you say you were living? What *is* your life? Teaching? Teaching *what*? Where is your husband? Did he leave you? Where are your children? Why are you *here*? *When* are you going to take me home? *What do you want of me*?' In the lucidity of his madness Mr Blackburn struck Maggie as an embodiment of that monstrous wisdom of which, in archetypal form, Shakespeare's King Lear is so famously the embodiment; the elderly, doomed men shared a common theme.

And Mr Blackburn in one of his excited, raving states much resembled popular likenesses of Lear, hair white as churned froth, noble face creased, and lapidary, mad eyes shining with a basilisk's glare. Maggie the smiling visitor, the hopeful and dutiful daughter, was sometimes stopped dead in her tracks.

After several such visits, when the strain was nearly unbearable, Maggie found herself unaccountably afoot, walking, walking aimlessly, in unfamiliar surroundings – urban, semi-rural. Was she in Old Westbury? In Mineola? In a neighbouring suburb of Forest Park? Where? And why? Once she woke to the tinny but terrifying clatter of a beer can rolling across the pavement in her direction, tossed from a speeding car amid boys' derisive yells: she was walking along a busy highway, at early evening, in an area of fast-food restaurants and gas stations. It was a windy autumnal day: a plait of her hair had come undone; her face was damp with tears. She stumbled drunkenly, though she was not drunk, and there was a smear of grease on her coat sleeve. Waking in quick startled degrees she took charge of herself – *You are all right, you are going to be all right* – and managed to locate her Volvo parked behind a Roy Rogers restaurant a mile behind her. Driving back to Forest Park and to her quiet home, to the Cape Cod cottage on Acacia Drive, Maggie Blackburn recalled her father's doctor's carefully chosen words: *These are not matters we can control or for which we are responsible.*

She did not designate these fugues of forgetfulness as 'blackouts', as if the very term, suggestive of alcoholism, were a blow to her pride. Nor did she think of them as amnesiac spells, though of course they were. Her strategy in dealing with them, as, over the years, she dealt with minor or seemingly minor physical problems (a pea-sized lump in a breast? an odd ringing in the ears? constipation? diarrhoea? migraine? or were these all her imagination?), was simply not to think of them, to give no name to them. The frightening amnesiac spells were swallowed up in a larger ocean of amnesia.

And no one need know. Not about any of it.

Because she did not want pity from her friends, or even an intrusive sort of sympathy, Maggie Blackburn chose not to tell anyone about her father; thus the mystery of her weekend disappearances. She had no idea that people speculated and would have been astonished to learn that they did.

At the time of her father's death, in May 1986, Maggie was seeing a man named Springer, Matt Springer: a Forest Park businessman who was divorced, in his mid-forties, a self-professed avid lover of music. She chose not to tell Matt Springer about her father either, for she was not certain of his feelings for her, or of her feelings for him. He was an attractive man, and seemingly good-tempered. It was not clear whether his divorce had shaken him or restored a portion of his youth to him. He'd been impressed with a piano recital Maggie had given at the Conservatory and subsequently made her acquaintance. His first words to her were both romantic and aggressive: 'How beautifully you play Chopin, Miss Blackburn! And how beautiful *you* are!' Matt Springer had the air of a man who requires marriage, at least as a matter of identity and pride.

Yet he was, too, the sort of man whose interest in a woman escalates in inverse proportion to her accessibility; and though Maggie did not know this, inexperienced as she was, not with men, precisely, but with coolly analysing their motives, she quickly realized that, if she presented herself available on a certain date, Springer's response was guarded and tentative; and if she presented herself as unavailable, Springer's response was one of curiosity, even hurt. 'But I'd hoped to see you on Saturday,' he would say. 'Where are you going?'

Was he considering marriage? There had been intimacies of a kind between them. They were, in a way, lovers; in other ways, not. For much went unspoken, including information about Matt Springer's ex-wife and three children, and Maggie could not after all interrogate her friend as her father so briskly interrogated her.

To Matt Springer, Margaret Louise Blackburn the concert pianist, this tall, slender, self-assured woman who wore her silvery-blonde hair in so studied and elegant a style, Margaret Louise Blackburn of the prestigious Forest Park Conservatory of Music, represented an ideal, even an iconographic image: a woman whom, were she his wife, other men could not fail to covet. She was not pretty, but she was beautiful; she was not conventional in any way, but she was wholly reliable in her 'womanly' moods, never emotional, any more than Matt Springer was emotional, and never demanding – unlike the overly eager and self-betraying 'eligible' women of a divorced man's acquaintance.

Over the eight months of their romance Springer was intrigued, and teased, by the fact that Maggie kept a certain distance between them; gracefully disarmed his questions; did not so much as hint that she might like their relationship to become more permanent, or even more defined. Asked where she had gone over a weekend, Maggie might murmur vaguely, 'Oh, visiting relatives,' and change the subject. Or, her forehead lightly creased, her bluish-grey eyes opened wide in an expression of sincerity, yet evasive in their gaze, 'Oh, doing research.' She was writing an essay on Schoenberg's *Piano Pieces*, op. 19, experimental works for which, as she said, she felt no temperamental kinship yet hoped to understand. Such detachment Matt Springer found, for a time, irresistible.

Then, abruptly, it was over. Maggie simply went too far. Two weeks before her father died she'd returned to her house on Acacia Drive to discover, prominently taped to her front door, a letter from Springer chiding her – teasingly, bullyingly – for having neglected to tell him she was going away; he'd been telephoning for days, out of worry and stubbornness, had even called colleagues of Maggie's to see if they knew her whereabouts. Reading this, Maggie burst into tears and tore the letter to bits; and, a half hour later, when Springer called, his tone both charming and importunate, Maggie interrupted. 'I won't be spied upon! How dare you! What right do you have! I'm not a woman' – and here wild words tumbled from her mouth, wholly unbidden, irrevocable – 'I'm not a woman who is spied upon!'

Matt Springer heard her out but made certain he had the final crushing word: 'In my opinion, Maggie, you're hardly a woman at all.'

Three

It was at Maggie Blackburn's house on Acacia Drive, on the evening of 17 September 1988, at the large party Maggie gave to introduce new faculty and graduate fellows to the Conservatory community, that Rolfe Christensen and Brendan Bauer met; thus, this innocent occasion, an annual, semi-official gathering hosted by Maggie in her capacity as director of the Music Education Programme for Advanced Students, would generally be considered, in Forest Park, the catalyst for all that followed.

Maggie Blackburn's fatal party.

Not that the two radically different composers – the 59-year-old Pulitzer Prize-winner Christensen and the wholly unknown 27-year-old novice Bauer – would not have met eventually but that, at another time, in other, more sober circumstances, Christensen would surely not have behaved as he did. Nor would the young man from Idaho, having by then heard something of Christensen's reputation, have gone off so unquestioningly with him.

Maggie was in her second year as director of the programme, and this was the second time she was to give the party. Yet the prospect still rather unnerved her, for she was an inexperienced hostess and swung between dread and euphoria in planning it. Like many deeply introverted people she imagined herself 'most herself' in gay, festive, noisy, gregarious, unthinking surroundings; she imagined too, though she rarely practised it, that she possessed some special talent for bringing like-minded individuals together and providing an atmosphere that might allow them to become friends. And there was the more selfish hope too that she, who spent so much time alone, in her head and in her music, might establish some new, unexpected rapport with another person.

(Indeed there was one individual, a man, a colleague and a friendly acquaintance, among the sixty or so invited guests whom Maggie did await with special anticipation: anticipation and apprehension. This man's presence in her home, to which he rarely came – for he was married, and his wife disliked social evenings – would give to her ordeal as hostess a powerful secret purpose; whatever the party yielded for others, its emotional centre, for Maggie Blackburn, would reside in this man.)

September 17th, a Saturday, was prematurely chill and autumnal; a glassily bright day of high, sporadic winds. Preparing food for her guests, far too much food, as, the previous year, energized by nerves, she'd prepared far too much, Maggie drifted into one of her intense but undefined states: there was a hallucinatory vividness to all that she saw, heard, tasted, smelled. The friendly near-constant chirping and tittering of her canary pair in their smart bamboo cage, the occasional exuberant arias of the male, seemed to her fraught with musical meaning. And such beauty! And consolation! The very wind in the trees behind the house and along the house's gutters had an eerie melodic sound ... oboes, bassoons – the bassoon in its yearning upper register, the very start of Stravinsky's *Rite of Spring*. Maggie's heart filled with longing. She did not now regret having been cajoled, perhaps coerced, into her time-consuming administrative position. It was healthy for her to do such things. Since Matt Springer there had been no other man, no romance. And, since the death of her father, no 'mystery'.

An hour before the party was to begin, and Maggie was upstairs changing her clothes, the telephone rang; she lifted the receiver with apprehension, knowing it could only be one of her guests saying he wouldn't be able to make it after all, and through the sudden suffocating pounding of her heart she heard a familiar voice. 'Naomi seems not to be feeling well, I'm afraid ...

15

won't be able to . . . tonight . . . But *I* can . . . I hope that's agreeable?' and Maggie quickly murmured, faint with relief, 'Oh, yes, Calvin, yes of course,' happening to catch sight of her white face in a mirror close by, ghastly white, and the eyes swimming with panic, grateful that Calvin Gould could not see it. For that face revealed all. Maggie Blackburn's soul, tremulous in her eyes, revealed all.

Maggie hung up the receiver, and her hands were shaking.

His voice. In that fraction of an instant before Calvin Gould explained the reason for his call Maggie had gazed in sick helplessness down the long tunnel of an arduous social evening to no purpose except its own execution. 'But he is coming,' she whispered aloud. 'He *is* coming.' She recalled that, the previous year, shortly before her party was scheduled to begin, Calvin had telephoned with a similar excuse; and she knew by way of Portia MacLeod and others that such last-minute cancellations for the reclusive Mrs Gould, always made with an air of sincere regret, were pro forma in Forest Park. ('It isn't clear whether Naomi Gould is agoraphobic,' Portia said, 'or whether the woman simply dislikes *us*.' But Maggie had rarely seen Mrs Gould at any Conservatory function, even concerts of exceptional interest. Though Calvin Gould was provost of the school and a highly regarded musicologist who frequently lectured at universities and music conservatories, his wife simply declined to accompany him.)

Downstairs, Maggie checked her generous supply of food and drink another time and removed the canaries' cage from its place in a bay window of her dining room, to carry it into a room at the rear of the house, out of harm's way. The canaries fluttered their wings and scolded, immediately alert. They were tropical birds, thus delicate, for all their tireless energy, and a blast of cold air could kill them within minutes; the noise of a party would badly agitate them. Maggie had named the male Rex – he was a flamey-orange red-factor from Germany and an extraordinary singer; the female, whose melodic titterings could not be called singing, Maggie had named Sweetpea: she was an American canary, pale yellow, a lovely hue, with subtle, near-invisible white gradations on her wings and tail feathers. The canaries were a mated pair but had thus far produced no offspring; Maggie, who had never before owned birds and would not have supposed she would be interested in owning birds, had bought them for herself, impulsively, in the summer of 1986. After the death of her father and the abrupt defection of Matt Springer.

The two events were blended in her imagination, like disparate notes struck on a vibrating, pedal-depressed piano.

By degrees the pace quickened.

For a time Maggie stationed herself at her front door, welcoming her guests, smiling so hard it seemed her brittle face must break. She was wearing black – why? A silken black wool dress with long sleeves, loose in the bodice and waist as if it belonged to another person, and its skirt awkwardly cut: too formal for the occasion and not, despite its quality, very flattering: Portia MacLeod sighed, seeing.

After a while Portia brought her friend a glass of wine and urged her away from the door and into the party. 'Do you think things are going well enough?' Maggie asked anxiously. 'Shouldn't I be making more of an effort to introduce people?'

'It's a lovely party,' Portia said. 'People can introduce themselves perfectly well. Why don't you relax, Maggie?'

Maggie's enormous eyes appeared glazed and her face was unevenly flushed, a hectic ruddiness imposed upon its pallor. She said, 'Oh, I am, Portia – I *am*. Relaxed.'

One of the early arrivals, amid a carload of graduate fellows, was Brendan Bauer, a new student whom Maggie had registered a few days previously and with whom, in her office at school, she'd had a lengthy conversation. Shy, thin, fidgety, his eyes round behind round, rather thick lenses, he stepped into Maggie Blackburn's front hall and thrust a bouquet of flowers at her, stammering hello and thanking her for inviting him, as if, in the midst of so many others, he could imagine himself singularly honoured. He wore a crudely cut brown suit with boxy shoulders; black loafers; a narrow, dead-black necktie of – was it simulated leather? He'd come to Forest Park by a circuitous route: a Catholic seminary in St Louis, before that an incomplete year in law school in Seattle, before that musical studies (theory, composition, musicology) at Indiana University, with some interruptions. Maggie Blackburn, in her official role, considering his application, had caught him out in a minor falsification of his record, perhaps an inadvertent error (involving credits and dates), and for this Brendan Bauer had apologized, profusely. His hometown was Boise, Idaho, and he'd never been in the East. His stammer was mild yet it seemed to embarrass, even to anger, him. In Maggie's office, where they had discussed the courses Brendan would be taking, the opportunities he would have to work, as a composer, with vocalists, but also with computers and synthesizers, he'd squirmed miserably in his seat as several times his voice failed; and Maggie, who knew that one must never upset or insult a stammerer by supplying a word for him or assuring him, 'That's all right, I know what you mean,' sat silent, waiting for the young man to continue. There is a subtle tyranny exerted by some seemingly handicapped persons, and Maggie Blackburn was not the sort to resist.

At her party, Brendan clung close to her for a time, before easing out, as if into treacherous waters, into the crowded living room and dining room. Talking with other guests, Maggie found herself watching the young man in his ill-chosen clothes, knowing why, as others spoke so readily, and asked questions of one another, and burst into peals of laughter, he stood more or less silent, guarded. Though Brendan Bauer was twenty-seven he was a very young twenty-seven: from a short distance he might well have been mistaken for a boy of sixteen or seventeen. He had a narrow fox face with intelligent if squinty features, fox-coloured hair that grew limply over his shirt collar; when finally he ventured into speech, within Maggie's hearing, in a conversation with Maggie's colleague Nicholas Reickmann and the twenty-year-old soprano prodigy Cecilia Ch'en, a beautiful Chinese-American from Hong Kong, his manner was excitably grim, yet in its way charming. Maggie liked Brendan Bauer though she was relieved he'd left her side. She saw in him, in his eager yet retreating attitude, in his sombre, plain, intense face, even in the slope of his thin shoulders, something of herself: he might have been a younger brother of hers, a distant cousin. She seemed to perceive that he would prove a problem to the school, as, now and then, with a sort of statistical regularity, students did, yet of this, in the noise and gaiety and distraction of her party, she certainly did not think.

'Great party, Maggie! First rate!' Nicholas Reickmann slipped an arm, gallant, fleeting, around Maggie's shoulders as he eased past, drink in hand. 'Very decent wine!' Rolfe Christensen muttered, close behind Nicholas. Maggie glanced up at Christensen in surprise: she had assumed he wasn't coming tonight, since he hadn't troubled (as he had not troubled the previous year, when he'd stayed away) to respond to her invitation. Christensen was a big burly figure in a plaid sports coat; his silvery-grey hair grew thick above his forehead, with a metallic brilliance; sober, he was coldly gentlemanly; after a few drinks he cultivated a glamorous-thuggish style and could be enormously, if sometimes cruelly, entertaining. Approaching sixty, with a large, heavy, red-veined face, Christensen had lost the attractiveness of his youth yet was empowered with the jaunty, slightly overbearing manner of one whom nature has privileged. Usually, Rolfe Christensen ignored Maggie Blackburn or looked pointedly through her; now, in passing, drink in one hand and cigar in the other, he winked at her and gave her a sliding sort of smile, or grimace – smiling at people with whom he did not want to waste time was difficult for him.

'Whatever else might be said of me,' Christensen had once boasted, at a Forest Park dinner party, 'I am not a hypocrite.'

Maggie watched Nicholas Reickmann and Rolfe Christensen make their way, elegantly shoulder their way, through the crowded living room, with the intention apparently of talking with Christensen's longtime friend Bill Queller. Nicholas Reickmann was a young woodwind instructor in his early thirties, tonight, as always, vividly dressed; he wore a turquoise suede jacket, a red and white polka-dot shirt open at the throat, oyster-white trousers, glossy shoes with a Cuban heel. Despite certain excesses of behaviour, Nicholas was a very nice young man: warm, courteous, amusing; an excellent musician and a reliable teacher; and unfailingly friendly to Maggie Blackburn, with whom, on committees, he was often an ally. When Nicholas first joined the faculty at Forest Park several years ago it was Rolfe Christensen who had immediately and somewhat jealously befriended him – an intense sort of friendship, as Portia MacLeod observed, that would soon burn itself out. And so seemingly it had: its intensity, at least. Yet the two men remained amicable; in a way, at such gatherings, allies of a kind.

A warm hand descended on Maggie's shoulder and her cheek was kissed – Jamie Katz. And here, with a hug and another kiss, was Barbara Katz. And Si Lichtman and his wife. And Andrew Woodbridge. And Stanley Spalding. And Katherine Nash. And Morley Nash. And Maggie Blackburn, sipping wine, in a euphoric haze, heard her own laughter erupting in peals, startled and girlish. She found herself the recipient of so many animated greetings, so many handshakes, embraces, kisses, it seemed that she might be, despite her self-doubts, a well-liked woman, perhaps even a very well-liked woman: a fact she must file away for serious consideration at another time.

She saw him, at the far end of the living room, deep in conversation with the beautiful soprano Cecilia Ch'en, and her heart went cold.

But no, it was not he; it was Stanley Spalding, who, from a certain angle, resembled him. Dark hair, profile. A way of leaning his elbow against the wall.

He was not coming after all.

Yet in her strange invulnerable state, giddiness bubbling along her veins, she did not mind.

How extraordinary: to realize *she did not mind*.

Why, she was invulnerable as the hide of one of those scaly

reptilian mammals, ugly little devils . . . armadillos, were they?

'What on earth are you laughing at, Maggie?' Portia asked.

'Armadillo,' Maggie Blackburn said, weak with hilarity. 'So *funny.*'

Suppose Maggie suffered one of her amnesiac fugues at her own party, beneath her own roof, and woke dazed and uncomprehending after everyone had gone home? Maggie laughed, wiped at her eyes, then at something peculiar that had dribbled down the front of her tasteful black dress (caviar off a Finn Crisp cracker?), and vowed through gritted teeth *that would not be.*

She accepted a damp goodbye kiss from one of her colleagues Fritzie Krill, with the scratchy shoeshine-black whiskers and the pirate's gold stud in his left ear, laughing, vowing *that would not be.*

Seeing Maggie in the front hall waving after her guests who were leaving early, Byron MacLeod said to Portia, 'Maggie really *is* a fine woman, isn't she,' as if the issue were debatable, and there was a maddening condescension in his tone; thus Portia said, 'Oh, Christ! You men!' and turned away. And Byron, who meant only well, stared in astonishment after her.

Maggie Blackburn was not drunk, nor was she consumed with anxiety that one of her guests had failed to arrive. Not at all. In fact she no longer checked the time. Her wristwatch went unconsulted, twisted around her wrist and upside down.

Talking perfectly coherently, indeed very intelligently, about the difficult Beethoven piece she and her colleague William Queller, the cellist, were scheduled to perform together in the chapel, in December, 'A beautiful, beautiful piece of music,' Maggie said, her eyes misting over. Bill Queller, smooth bald head, amused eyes, nasal voice like a woodwind, said, '*I* think of it as a problem to be solved, and suggest that you think of it that way too. If we want to get on together.'

Bill was a friend of Rolfe Christensen's, one of the composer's few intimates in Forest Park. It occurred to Maggie that, yes, probably yes, these men shared a common disdain for her . . . for which she was not to blame? Or was?

The party was scheduled to begin at six and end at eight.

At seven-forty, when it was almost too late, and indeed Maggie had given up, Calvin Gould did arrive – breathless, with an air of impatience – an important man: Provost of the Conservatory, highly regarded musicologist. He did not kiss Maggie's burning cheek, too formal a man for such a gesture, but he did squeeze her hand, harder than might have been necessary, pressing one of her outsized antique rings into her flesh. But Maggie did not wince. Her eyes shone in simple girlish joy. Calvin Gould, who'd shaved hurriedly, dressed hurriedly, for a social event to which perhaps he had not much wanted to come, apologized to his hostess for being late, and for his wife's absence, and smiled one of his tense twitchy smiles, saying, as his eyes dropped to take in the whole of her dress, 'How lovely you look tonight, Maggie!'

Maggie's cheeks burned brighter. She stammered vague happy words. Thinking, Oh, God, what a pity, she could not say in turn, careless, reckless, even in the guise of semi-drunken palaver, that Calvin too looked lovely, that is to say beautiful, for indeed in Maggie's eyes the man *was* beautiful: blunt-boned, with deep-set intelligent eyes, an olive-pale and somewhat roughened skin. He was tall, taller even than Maggie Blackburn in her black medium-heeled pumps; his posture had a military correctness, an air of pride. He retained strong traces of his Maine accent – he'd been born in Bangor but had not lived there since boyhood – and Maggie could not help but associate some core of masculinity, or intransigence, with that distinctive accent, those cool nasal vowels and consonants. 'May I get you a drink, Calvin?' Maggie asked, walking with her friend into the kitchen where a bar had been set up. So seemingly at ease, Maggie Blackburn, tall, poised, and calm amid the giddy roaring in her ears: *He has come. He is here. In my house.*

Eyeing the display of bottles, Calvin Gould, ever public-minded, said, 'Don't forget to send a bill to the school, Maggie; this *is* an official function.'

Maggie protested, 'Oh, no, Calvin, really – I think of this as my own party. Mine.' But the words sounded wrong, not at all what she had intended.

Shortly afterward, to her disappointment, Maggie was separated from Calvin, for the Lichtmans were leaving – so soon? – and Maggie saw them to the door; and once it was known that Calvin Gould had arrived guests drifted in his direction . . . for, as provost, serving with an ailing and generally ineffective president, Calvin was the most politically powerful person at Maggie Blackburn's party. Even Portia, who would have said she scorned the pettiness of Conservatory politics, murmured, sighting Calvin Gould, 'Ah, Calvin is here! I have a bone to pick with that man.' And moved grandly upon him.

It was frustrating for Maggie, caught up in her duties as a hostess, to be able to catch little more than snippets of Calvin's conversations with her guests; she too had things she might have said to him, and surely, for they shared many musical interests, he had things to say to her.

Over the years, like many other residents of Forest Park, Maggie had had few occasions to meet Calvin's wife, Naomi, for the woman was eccentric, reclusive, stubbornly unsociable . . . an artist of a kind, though it was not really known what kind; it was said that Calvin had married his wife when they were both quite young, college or even high school sweethearts in Maine. Seeing Mrs Gould, Maggie had had to resist the impulse to stare, to stare hard; for, yes, she was . . . not jealous exactly, or even envious . . . rather more curious. *Why her and not me? What are her qualities that I so sadly lack?* Maggie's sense of Mrs Gould was that of a strong-willed individual, dark as Calvin Gould was dark, resembling him slightly, but restless, sceptical, somehow intractable. Once Maggie had seen the woman in, of all places, a public park, lying on the grass sleeping; another time Maggie had seen her, at a short distance, at a Conservatory function where she had coolly but unmistakably rebuffed all attempts to befriend her: a tall, slope-shouldered, harshly handsome woman wearing make-up for the occasion as if in parody of the occasion and of the other, more clearly feminine faculty wives: bright crimson lipstick, rouge prominent on her cheeks, eyebrow pencil applied with a dramatic hand. Mrs Gould's hair coiled in a frizzled tangle on her shoulders; oversized white-framed sun-glasses hid half her small face: a striking presence, but rather intimidating. For an ambitious administrator Naomi Gould was hardly an ideal wife, but the liberalism of the Forest Park Conservatory of Music, conjoined with the high worth of her husband, seemed to excuse the liability.

Of course, not everyone agreed on the 'high worth' of Calvin Gould. He was, to Maggie's surprise, a controversial figure, admired by the majority of the faculty but disliked and distrusted by others. He was perceived to be overly ambitious, demonically driven, a fanatic for work, and exacting in his demands of others' work; ruthless, at times, in his dealings with colleagues – some of whom, especially the older ones, resented being manipulated by a 39-year-old provost. Yet Calvin had been a tireless fund-raiser, especially dedicated to improving scholarship programmes for students; he had helped to secure, for the composer-in-residence Rolfe Christensen, an endowed chair that brought with it a salary rumoured to be the highest at any music institution in the world; he had hired any number of gifted younger faculty, including Maggie Blackburn, defying a ninety-year tradition of exclusively male instructors in her department. For these reasons, and for countless others, Maggie would be Calvin Gould's partisan for life.

She would hear no ill of the man. *Could* hear no ill. If forced to she turned very pale, or blushed fiercely, or leapt to defend him, often indiscreetly. After an incident at a dinner party some months before, at the Nashes', when Calvin Gould's 'ambition' had been an issue and Maggie had been unable to sit in silence, hearing the man wrongly attacked, Portia MacLeod had taken her aside and advised, gently, that she be more . . . circumspect. 'Do you want people to begin to talk about you, Maggie?' Portia asked. 'Do you want it to get back to *him*?' Deeply embarrassed, Maggie had not known what to say. 'It was a principle I was defending,' she said finally. 'Not a person.' Maggie was one of those people who lie so awkwardly, to whom the most rudimentary sort of subterfuge is a foreign language, the effort seems, to others, almost touching. So Portia felt, contemplating her friend.

How much more suitable Maggie Blackburn would have been for Calvin Gould than that impossible woman he married.

It was 8.10. So quickly.

In Maggie's living room there erupted a keyboard crescendo: Charles Ives – Henry Cowell tone clusters, or a riotous parody thereof. But can such music be parodied, seeing it *is* parody?

Rolfe Christensen, Distinguished Professor of Music and Composer-in-Residence at the Forest Park Conservatory of Music since 1977, who owned a concert-grand Steinway, muttered a rude assessment of his hostess's mere Knabe – eight-foot, of 'insufficient' resonance – as he got up from the piano. His little gathering of listeners laughed.

In the foyer, at the front door, stood Maggie Blackburn, whose beauty – tonight, yes, and always – seemed somehow, in the crush of voices, eyes, handshakes, witticisms, egos burning and winking like fireflies, beside the point: saying goodbye to guests who (it seemed) had only just arrived.

'Is my party ending . . . so soon?'

In the dining room someone surprised in careless laughter swung an arm, thus spilling red wine on the heirloom Chinese rug of creamy-yellow wool threaded with pale pink roses, but 'Oh, don't bother,' Maggie insisted, 'please, it's nothing,' as Morley Nash, squatting, swabbed away with a damp paper napkin shredding gradually to bits.

She recalled other parties, other years.

That sense of loss, of something draining away.

So soon?

A waterfall of plumbing in his wake, there appeared, in the hall, Rolfe Christensen, burly and magisterial, adjusting his hunter-green sports slacks, making his swaying way, as if to a musical beat, back from the rear of his hostess's house . . . from the neat little bathroom where he'd left a damp towel twisted from a rack as if its neck had been wrung and the lid of the toilet seat splashed with his pungent urine; and before that, it isn't unlikely, the composer had been poking about in the rear rooms, as was his custom at parties, drink in one hand, cigar trailing smoke in the other. *I am Rolfe Christensen; I do what I do. A creature of impulse.* The music in his head was one of his own old compositions, a shrewd employment of a musical theme of Milhaud's, some percussive tricks of Stravinsky's, *genius and impulse in electric cohabitation.* Sighting the rather priggish Calvin Gould in one room he steered himself, as if steering a bulky boat in narrow waters, in another direction, and there was Bill Queller in the kitchen doorway, Bill Q who was, to Christensen, an old, old story but a trusted story, yes, and the great man's literary executor too, for though Rolfe Christensen certainly did not intend to die for a very long time it isn't ever too early to make preparations, so many of his acquaintances dying lately (of illnesses too foul and too depressing, yes, and too contagious to be named).

So Christensen advanced upon Bill Q, winking what felt to him a neon-greenish eye, and curled his upper lip, a lip precisely the colour of Cohoe salmon, and murmured, 'Mmmmmmmm, sweetie, move your ass and let me by.' And Bill Q, the really quite talented cellist, the gentlemanly bald bachelor of whom it was said always, *Isn't it strange he hasn't been more successful,* was torn between a fit of laughter and a more proper response of chagrin, if not horror, for there was Andrew Woodbridge the Conservatory attorney close by, possibly listening . . . and there appeared Calvin Gould the provost, both married men, presumably straight men made to feel distinctly uncomfortable overhearing their gay colleagues' banter.

Bill Queller, a man of strong conservative upbringing, overcome rather more by chagrin and horror than by hilarity, succumbed to a spasm of coughing.

Rolfe Christensen, his eye on some young graduate students in

26

the other room, pounded his friend on the back in passing. 'Cough it up, cough it up! *Don't* swallow!'

The party was waning. Guests were slipping steadily away. Maggie Blackburn, perspiration shining on her upper lip and fore- head, eyes bright, smiled a happy-sad smile, the smile of an un- married hostess: How nice of you to come, thank you so much for coming, must you really leave so soon? A spirited little crew of graduate students, male and female both, Maggie's particular friends, were carrying things out into the kitchen, running water in the sink, making motions toward tidying up. It was kind of them but Maggie watched with melancholy eyes. So soon? Everything ending so soon? And where was Calvin, surely he'd meant to take Maggie aside to talk with her; there was in fact something she'd been intending to ask him but it seemed to have slipped her mind. 'Thank you, Maggie – lovely party!' the MacLeods cried, on their way out, and Portia kissed Maggie on her burning cheek, and Maggie's heart ached at the ease of her friend's walking off arm in arm with her husband, Byron, out to the street, to their car, and home.

Maggie caught sight of roses lying atop a bookcase as if flung down, Brendan Bauer's thoughtful gift, long-stemmed white roses and how had she forgotten them? – she took them up and hurried into the kitchen seeking a vase. And, there, became involved in an emotional debate among the graduate fellows regarding the foreign language (German or Italian) requirement in the advanced degree programme at the Conservatory; thus she was prevented from joining Calvin Gould in the other room, and then others were leaving, calling out goodbye, and thanks, and Maggie hurried to the front door, feeling a heavy plait of hair beginning to uncoil, and there were half-moons of perspiration beneath her arms, and in the wintry chill at the door she seemed to feel herself becoming in- visible – as she'd felt, frequently, at the Old Westbury Convales- cent Centre and Nursing Home – as her guests backed away into the night waving goodbye to her, *goodbye goodbye Maggie Blackburn*.

So soon.

By the time Maggie returned to the living room, only a few of her guests remained. The piano was now silent, with a look of abandonment. Maggie was smiling, though no one glanced in her direction. A frieze of images leapt forward like a Bosch dreamscape: Rolfe Christensen in his red-green plaid sports coat, metallic hair rising in tufts, engaged in an animated conversation with – was it young Brendan Bauer, backed against a bookshelf? – Brendan's childlike round eyeglasses winking in mirth and his lower lip caught in his teeth in a shy, or sly, smile; there was handsome Nicholas Reickmann, hair becomingly dishevelled, engaged in a hilarious conversation with the Nashes; there was, in his tailored pinstripe suit, mahogany-dark hair crisp and gleaming as if lacquered, Calvin Gould in conversation with – yes, it was Cecilia Ch'en, she of the straight jet-black hair, flawless camellia skin, and limpid black eyes – the young Chinese-American soprano whose voice in its upper register was so eerily beautiful Maggie never heard it without wanting to weep.

By nine-fifteen they were all gone. Maggie's two-bedroom house on Acacia Drive, the charming little 1940s Cape Cod, was restored to its usual quiet.

Belatedly, as they were going out the door, Maggie's graduate students asked would she like to join them? They were going out for pizza and beer at Aldo's, on Route 1. Maggie was aware of their kindness, for of course they could not possibly want her, an elder and a teacher. 'Another time!' she said, smiling.

In parting, Rolfe Christensen had been almost cordial. It was said that a moderate dosage of alcohol brought out in him, sometimes, an unexpected warmth – though he could be volatile and bad-tempered too. But he smiled at Maggie, even winked, as if there were some bemused understanding between them, thanked her and called her 'Margaret Louise' with a quaint lilting of his voice. It seemed he was going to drive Brendan Bauer home in his white BMW; and Brendan, thin cheeks glowing as if pinched, said, with virtually no hint of a stammer, 'Thank you so much, Miss Blackstone – excuse me, I mean Black*burn*.' And Calvin was warm and smiling, thanking Maggie too, shaking her hand briskly in parting, saying she must certainly send the bill for the party to accounting services. There beside him stood Cecilia Ch'en with her gleaming straight curtains of hair, her rosebud mouth, petite and perfect and murmuring thank you to Miss Blackburn, whom she scarcely knew except as a semi-public figure. It seemed that Calvin had volunteered to drive Cecilia back to her residence hall on campus – 'No trouble, it's hardly out of my way,' Calvin said.

And now the utterly silent house.

Maggie kicked off her tight shoes; headachey and exhausted she went from room to room, gathering up party refuse her students had overlooked. There was a partly eaten jumbo shrimp lodged between the strings of her Knabe and, underfoot, mashed into the carpet, the remains of a devilled egg. Crumpled paper napkins, discarded plastic forks. In the kitchen she leaned against the refrigerator to steady herself, the overhead lights were so bright. That terrible clarity always so much more blinding after guests have departed, after we are restored to ourselves. But what was she hearing, a faint sound of music? Piccolo-like music? Could it be Rex singing, at this time of day?

Maggie went to her study to investigate, drawn by the cascade of lovely liquid warbling notes, and knew at once, opening the door, that something was wrong: the room was cold and draughty, and there was an acrid odour of cigar smoke. Someone had been in here, smoking, and he'd opened a window a full foot high. A damp chill wind blew in.

Still Rex sang, with a terrible sort of deliberation and urgency Maggie had never before heard in him. His tiny red-orange body quivered; he stood on the perch closest to Maggie, feathers pressed against the bars of his cage. On the floor of the cage amid the shredded bits of corncob, Sweetpea lay dead: on her side, an eye partway closed, utterly still, stiff.

Maggie could not believe it. She fumbled, opening the cage, reached inside, picked up the small lifeless body. The external feathers were cold but the body itself felt warm. 'Sweetpea? *Sweetpea?*' she said. Still, she could not believe it.

Four

This much is known and, in time, would become a matter of public record: from approximately nine o'clock in the evening of Saturday, 17 September 1988, until approximately six-thirty in the morning of Sunday, 18 September 1988, 27-year-old Brendan Bauer, a newly enrolled graduate student in the Forest Park Conservatory of Music, was in the company of 59-year-old Rolfe Christensen, Distinguished Professor of Music and Composer-in-Residence at the Conservatory, in Christensen's house at 2283 Littlebrook Road, Forest Park, Connecticut: whether Bauer was a guest, a 'freely consenting adult', a 'willing and active participant' in what occurred, or a captive, 'held against his will', 'terrified into submission' by force and threats against his life, would be a matter of debate.

Where genius and impulse cohabit, none dares legislate.
　　Consider the old French proverb, *Erotic love is a mystery which, once solved, is at once forgotten.*
　　Mmmmmmm. Sweet.
　　Just don't provoke me.
　　DON'T make me angry.
　　DON'T MAKE ME ANGRY.
　　AND DON'T PLAY GAMES WITH ME.
　　Rolfe Christensen wasn't the sort to use force, for with his powerful charms of persuasion he had no need. Nor was he the sort to 'take advantage of' students in his tutelage, for, again, he had no need.

He was no seducer, surely no rapist ... though certain prac-
tices, undeniably, gave pleasure.

To subdue another against his wish *and to make that very wish
yield.*

Oh. Undeniably.

Down the evolutionary slope from gentleman to grovelling beast
the Pulitzer Prize-winning American composer Rolfe Christensen happily descended when he drank, and he drank frequently,
though not always excessively, at least in public; true, Christensen behaved sometimes eccentrically in public depending upon
the liberality of 'public', but there were things the man clearly
would not do in public because they were things you did (if, indeed, you did them) exclusively in private.

Meaning: no witnesses.

Or, at the most, one.

As the white BMW turned on to Juniper Road bordering the
eastern edge of the Conservatory campus, Rolfe Christensen inquired of his passenger Brendan Bauer, casually, as if he'd only
now thought of it, 'Would you like to drop by my house, Brendan, for a nightcap or a bite to eat? It seems to be rather early.'

'I- I- –' A pause. A seeming-sincere look of uncertainty,
hesitation.

'You mentioned earlier having admired my "Adagio for Piano
and Strings": I have a tape of the only really decent performance
of the piece, done at the Santa Fe music festival in 1983, and if
you're interested I'd be happy to play it for you.'

Still that look. Thick-lashed eyes blinking behind the round
eyeglasses. 'I-I'd like that very much, Mr Christensen, b-but
tonight I'm – '

Playing coy? Or truly shy? Intimidated?

'Unless of course you were simply being polite? Courteous to
one of your elders? A sort of *jeunesse oblige?*'

'Oh, n-no, Mr – '

'It's hardly a secret that young composers are more intrigued

31

by the pablum of Philip Glass et al. than by the "strenuous neo-classicism of Rolfe Christensen" – smiling a crooked dimpled smile, flushed face radiating good humour and resignation in equal measure – 'but I try not to be discouraged. After all, our only judge is posterity.'

'Oh, but I t-truly admire your work, Mr – '

'Do please call me Rolfe, will you, Brendan? My tutorial students at the Conservatory, my favoured students, always call me Rolfe.'

'. . . Rolfe.'

The response was hardly more than a murmur, coquettish-shy but immediate.

Thus Brendan Bauer went of his own free will with Rolfe Christensen to his stately red-brick Georgian home on Little-brook Road, and admired with unfeigned sincerity the house and its eighteenth-century furnishings, and seemed virtually struck into silence by the handsome A-frame addition at the rear made of walnut, fieldstone, and pigmented glass, the elder composer's music studio containing a splendid Steinway concert grand and thousands of dollars' worth of stereo equipment, records, tapes, compact discs, and the like; a white lamb's-wool rug from Peru; Ming vases, Etruscan figures, a couch and chairs in kidskin; a liquor cabinet and a wet bar; ingeniously recessed lighting that suggested a stage; and an entire wall of framed photographs, citations, plaques and mementoes. Though saying in his soft stammering voice that, really, he would have to go home soon, Brendan accepted a glass of aquavit from his host, which he claimed he'd never before tasted and found rather . . . over-powering. Indeed he made a show of coughing, wiping at his eyes, gasping. 'It's like an acetylene torch going up my nostrils and into my sk-sk-skull.'

Christensen, who had taken off his sports coat and loosened his tie, regarded his young visitor with a look of frank fond interest and said, screwing up one side of his face into a genial wink, 'Really, Brendan! And do you know what an acetylene torch feels like going up your nostrils and into your sk-sk-skull?'

But Brendan Bauer was still coughing and gasping, and the little joke passed unnoticed.

Brendan went to examine the wall of memorabilia, artlessly wide-eyed, exclaiming. 'Is this Leonard Bernstein with you, Mr Christensen? Is this . . . P-Poulenc? And . . . President Reagan? Mrs Reagan? And w-who is . . . ?'

Brendan Bauer, drawn to Rolfe Christensen's display of Rolfe Christensen as a moth to a flame; or, indeed, as many another young ambitious musician, male, had been drawn to the same wall, the same dazzling display. Very likely thinking, with the crude ingenuousness of youth, *There someday go I.*

This pair of tight buttocks from Omaha, or was it Oklahoma City, or Boise, or Missoula – more recently from a Catholic seminary in St Louis – in an ill-fitting cheap brown suit that looked as if it had been bought off the rack at Sears. Oddly coarse brown hair growing over his shirt collar, a slightly pimply skin, a suggestion of buck teeth – beautiful buck teeth – beautiful eyes too behind the round owlish plastic-framed glasses, grammar school circa 1951: *charming.* Brendan Bauer was precisely the type Rolfe Christensen found himself attracted to, not the big husky sort of fellow (like Christensen himself) but the skinny sparrow-boned sort, muscle that might be hard and lean but no larger, in the upper arm for instance, than an apple. There was something too in the fact that he wore glasses, such boys always wore glasses, and once the glasses were taken from them they blinked in that strangely trusting way of myopia . . .

Electrical cord is, on the whole, gentler than rope: leaves fewer abrasive red marks.

Consider the old French proverb, *Tears too can be a lubricant.*

Not stealthily, but quietly, and with a measure of grace, despite the pulse and throb of alcohol in his veins and the mounting excitement, so familiar, yet exotic, in his groin, Rolfe Christensen came up behind his young visitor and laid a warm heavy hand on his shoulder, the unexpected weight of which caused the young visitor to stiffen for a moment but not (did he fear the gesture might be perceived as impolite?) to edge away.

'Yes, that's Lenny Bernstein and me, 1973, the world première of my "Suite for Orchestra" at Lincoln Centre; Lenny is a third-rate composer himself but a first-rate interpreter of others' work. . . . Yes that's the late Poulenc – dear Francis! *le voleur suprême* – we were lunching at his château in Touraine the very year of his death, 1963. Along with Ned Rorem, I was the only American composer Poulenc admired: an ambiguous honour, isn't it? . . . Of course I'm very, very fond of Ned, I don't consider the rivalry between us quite so pitiless as he does, in fact this is Ned and me – Ned looking rather striking, indeed – the occasion was a luncheon at his place on Nantucket. Isn't it a deliciously provoking thing Ned is doing, excluding me from his diary entirely! Fearing a libel suit, perhaps. Fearing who knows what. As if Rolfe Christensen doesn't exist . . . Yes, this was taken in the White House, one of those large public occasions honouring American 'artists'. You glance around and your heart sinks, seeing the others. Of course the Reagans are absolutely tone-deaf, he is such a vulgarian, but d'you know I rather liked the man: I *did* vote for him, both times . . . This was taken at the Pulitzer Prize ceremony – again, a somewhat diminished occasion when I discovered who the other winners were – but I *do* look rather trim, don't I, a bit younger then . . . This commemorates my belated induction into the American Academy and Institute of Arts and Letters – the old gent shaking my hand is none other than Milton Babbitt, one of the chancellors of that august society – everyone congratulated me, expected me to grovel with gratitude when in fact I was inwardly seething: Rolfe Christensen had to wait until the age of fifty-four to be elected to the society when I should have been elected at the age of thirty-four, or younger; I will never forgive them, the spiteful egomaniac bastards . . . And here, at Tanglewood, Aaron Copland presenting me with a "promising young composer" award, a long time ago, when we were still on speaking terms . . . And here, at the Aspen Music Festival in 1967, Virgil Thomson and me . . . And here, at the Spoleto Festival, Gian Carlo Menotti and me . . . And here – '

34

It was a familiar litany but by no means an unpleasant one, for Rolfe Christensen even in his sixtieth year remained fascinated by the history of Rolfe Christensen, particularly when recounted for youth's rapt ear.

Six feet of electrical cord twined like a drowsy household snake in a cavity behind the liquor cabinet.

As Proust said, *Without nervous disorder there can be no great art.*

Christensen never employed force for rarely was there need JUST DON'T PROVOKE ME DON'T MAKE ME ANGRY; thus the evidence of blood-speckled or -stained sheets (or, the previous winter in London, in the Mayfair flat, so puzzlingly, stained stairs after a fifteen-hour visit by an importunate young man) was always an astonishment JUST DON'T PLAY GAMES: I WARN YOU.

It was ten-thirty, and it was eleven o'clock, and Rolfe Christensen provided his young visitor with food, drink, conversation – a happy interlude of Bavarian chocolates, chocolate-covered truffles, richly salted Brazil nuts, Scotch on the rocks for both – though Brendan Bauer, seemingly unaccustomed to such quantities of alcohol, showed by his sleepy puffy eyes and slack cherry-red mouth that he was nearing a state of what's called inebriation. Several times the young man murmured in his charming stammery voice that he really should go home, and several times Christensen assured him yes, soon, he'd play the tape for him and drive him home soon, yes.

Rolfe Christensen, too restless to remain seated, paced about the studio, eyes aglow, face flushed, chattering . . . chattering. Now and then he stooped over the piano and played chords, joyous excited crashing chords. He was smoking one of his fragrant cigars, a fine Havana blend, gripping the cigar tight between his teeth, smiling around the cigar, exhaling smoke in luxurious curving tusks. Brendan Bauer, silly boy, began to choke and gasp, and Christensen flailed his arms about to wave the smoke away. 'You haven't ever had a cigar, Brendan? Would you like to try one of mine?'

Brendan was sitting in one of the low kidskin chairs, his thin knees awkwardly raised and his head and torso thrown back, a disadvantageous position. He smiled wanly. Wiped at his eyes. Shook his head to clear it. 'N-no, thank you, Mr Chris – I mean Rolfe. M-m-maybe some other time – ' His voice faltered in a suppressed spasm of coughing.

Rolfe Christensen stood gazing down at him with a little curl of a smile. 'So you believe, Brendan, Bren dan, that there will be an "other time"?'

The young man stared up as if perplexed.

There is a point at which coyness and audacity converge, and this point young Bauer was quickly approaching. He shook his head again, like a puppy, and giggled, and said, '. . . time *is* it? . . . should be g-g-going . . .'

'And where, dear Bren dan, do you think you should be g-g-going?'

Another perplexed look.

Gently, Christensen chided the young man for wanting to go home without having heard the 'Adagio'. 'Or have you forgotten? It was the ostensible purpose of your visit, after all.'

Now Brendan tried to rouse himself, looking a bit chagrined, guilty. Saying quickly, 'Oh I d-d-do want to hear your composition, Rolfe,' smiling, clumsily lying, 'I didn't forget.'

Rolfe Christensen smiled down at the young man around the cigar clamped between his teeth. 'Didn't you!'

There followed then, at about midnight, the playing of a tape of Christensen's 1972 composition, 'Adagio for Piano and Strings', op.26; since the piece was only eighteen minutes long and structurally intricate, the composer played it a second time. During these highly charged thirty-six minutes Christensen continued to pace about the room, observing his young guest, who was seemingly trying to impress him by following the score, frowning, nodding, tapping his foot, trying to keep his eyes open and his mouth from going soft and slack. An opportunistic young man, yet transparent in his motives: Christensen recalled himself at that age, seeking out elder composers, Aaron Copland,

William Schuman, to flatter and impress. No doubt this Bauer secretly imagined himself a genius, a Mozartian prodigy perhaps – he looked as if he were about twenty years old, possibly younger. Possibly virginal.

Earlier in the evening young Bauer had mentioned to Christensen (and Nicholas Reickmann) that coming to Forest Park was the 'fulfilment of a lifetime' for him; the opportunity to work with a composer of the stature of Rolfe Christensen was 'the answer to my prayers'; in fact, coming to Forest Park was a milestone in his life since this was his first time in the East, his first time, almost, east of the Mississippi River. Saying 'first time in the East' he'd lowered his eyes, seemingly blushing, as if the words were a signal in code.

Later, as the party was nearing its close, Christensen had said to him, 'So: this is your first time east of the Mississippi?' and Brendan had laughed as if embarrassed and said, 'Oh, al-al-almost.'

Which left the matter tantalizingly ambiguous.

Just don't make me angry Bren dan. Don't play the cocktease Bren dan.

Down the evolutionary slope Rolfe Christensen descended, and what relief in it, and joy, and anger too – a mysterious surge of anger, a pinch and a pulse in the groin. In the blood-swollen fruit of the groin. For he was bored, bored nearly to madness, by being forever the gentleman, the genius, the aristocrat from 'an old and revered New England family'; weary of plaudits of his 'long and distinguished and much-honoured career' sounding in his ears like a ceaseless Gregorian chant even as he knew well that others withheld their praise. He was weary of casting his pearls before swine; indeed, he was furious, for what did Rolfe Christensen care of his music colleagues' judgement at Forest Park or elsewhere? What did he care of the judgement of his fellow composers, devoured by envy and spite as they surely were, the contemptible sons of bitches? What did he care about the ignorant, indifferent, slothful audiences that season after season trooped into music halls to hear Beethoven, Mozart, Brahms, the

New World symphony, the Nutcracker suite, anything and everything by Mozart no matter how facile, anything and everything by
Liszt no matter how turgid, anything and everything that was of
the past and not 'modern', and then, most infuriating of all, the
fatuous young musicians, the generations of new composers
coolly ignoring Rolfe Christensen but idolizing claptrap by Philip
Glass, John Cage, Terry Riley, entranced by serial music, syn-
thesizer music, anything that was considered 'experimental'. And
here, astonishingly, was one of those young composers in
Christensen's very house; in his very music studio; slouched
semi-drunkenly in the low-slung chair, musical score on his lap,
pretending to be listening with painstaking scrutiny to one of the
most challenging and beautiful of twentieth-century American
compositions . . . the callow little hypocrite.

Bren dan. Bren dan Bau er.

Don't provoke.

Now Christensen was perspiring, now the bulldog began to
push his way forward, panting in anticipation: the hot flushed
skin, the small damp red eyes, the snout, and the folds of flesh
bracketing the snout . . . and the lower jaw protruding.

The 'Adagio' came to its exquisitely irresolute conclusion for
the second time. A dramatic silence followed.

After a seemingly respectful moment Brendan Bauer said,
clearing his throat, 'Very i-i-interesting, Mr Christensen, very
fine' – as Christensen stood a few feet behind him, staring at the
back of his head, meaty breath quickened, cigar clamped between his teeth – 'it sort of reminded me, that brief phrase in the
second movement, of a theme of Poulenc's . . . *Dialogues*? And
certain of the straight triads near the end . . . Fauré? And back
through Fauré maybe to . . . Chopin?'

There was a long, painful pause, a beat of several seconds. As
if unable to comprehend what he'd heard, Christensen remained
motionless, staring at the back of his young visitor's head. Then,
the cigar still clamped between his teeth, he said, calmly, though
shivering, 'You *are* trying to provoke me, Bren dan, aren't you.
You conniving little cunt.'

Brendan Bauer turned a stricken, dead-white face to the man who was standing close behind him, smiling down at him, twin tusks of smoke curving up around his head: a man not immediately recognizable as Rolfe Christensen the Pulitzer Prize-winning American composer. And again there was a pause. Profound, paralysing silence.

Five

We are the creation of some famous maker, in his way a Stradivarius, who is no longer there to mend us. In clumsy hands we cannot give forth new sounds and we stifle within ourselves all those things which no one will ever draw from us ... These rather pessimistic and alarming words, from a letter of Frédéric Chopin to his friend Fontana in 1848, had imprinted themselves on Maggie Blackburn's consciousness when she first read them as a young girl, in an early stage of that extreme vulnerability to others that constitutes, for some, the essence of the romantic predicament; since meeting Calvin Gould, with whom she believed herself in love, however distantly, she found in them an added piquancy.

In clumsy hands ... we stifle within ... things which no one will ever draw from us.

Is this a tragic dilemma? Maggie wondered quite seriously. Or is it, in its way, nothing more than a simple fact of life? A fact which, if one were mature, one would accept with the same equanimity with which one accepted one's hair and eye colour, bone structure, genetic destiny – assuming of course that one accepted these things with equanimity.

Sunday following Saturday: the aftermath of a party, thus susceptible to melancholy, fatigue, a futile reimagining of how things might have gone. From prior experience Maggie knew that such days were dangerous unless navigated briskly and without sentiment. This she meant to do.

'Above all,' she instructed herself, 'no self-pity.'

Burying Sweetpea was the day's first task. The night before, she had wrapped the canary in a linen napkin and laid her on a kitchen shelf; now she carried her outside, into the rear yard, to bury her beneath a rosebush. During the night Sweetpea had stiffened, and her body, near weightless, was now decidedly cold; she looked ornamental, a work of artifice. Maggie's eyes flooded with tears even as she recognized that the death was a small one, as deaths go, and would readily be forgotten. She did not want to think that anyone might be to blame and refused to allow herself the resentful luxury of puzzling out how or why the window of her study had been left open, who the intruder might be.

Of course, she had a good idea. But it was pointless to think along such lines, wasn't it.

On one of her visits to the nursing home, Maggie's father had eyed her with a bitter sort of envy, mumbling, 'Walk out of here don't you and . . . drive away . . . forget,' losing track of what he meant to say even as he spoke. He'd meant that Maggie had the freedom to walk out of his life and to forget him even as he could never walk out of it himself, still less forget; and though the accusation was unfair, Maggie had been struck by its possibility. And by the revelation that the person closest to her of all living human beings in terms of blood relations saw her as coolly independent and unsentimental.

Sweetpea's grave was shallow, a token sort of grave, made in the dry crumbly earth with a few swipes of a kitchen spoon. Laying the dazzling-white linen shroud inside, Maggie had to resist the impulse to unwrap it another time and see if the bird really was there.

Back inside the house, the solitary male was singing. He'd begun at dawn, or before. Never in the two years Maggie had had the canary pair had the male sung so urgently and so persistently, alone now, flitting from perch to perch in his smart bamboo cage.

The canary's singing hadn't woken Maggie, she'd already been awake. A night of intermittent sleep, confusing dreams. She'd been jarred into full consciousness by the thought that, if Calvin Gould were miraculously unmarried, a free man, it would hardly mean that he might reciprocate her feeling for him; or even that he might put himself into the intimate position of becoming aware of that feeling.

So utterly simple a thought, it might have been overlooked.

Wiping at her eyes, Maggie spooned earth back into and on the miniature grave. My first task of the day is done, she thought.

Maggie Blackburn's house stood on an acre and a half of land in a residential area of Forest Park of older single-family homes; to the rear was undeveloped property, trees, outcroppings of rock, a deep meandering stream about the size of a ditch. It was a place of birds: jays, cardinals, starlings, red-winged blackbirds, crows: the luminous air of morning was filled with the sounds of their calling and singing, of which Maggie became only gradually aware. And then she could hear little else.

So many birds, a seemingly inexhaustible supply!

Yes, it was the wisest strategy, to drive all sentiment from her heart.

By midday, in any case, her spirits had lifted. She'd played the piano for two hours: Chopin mazurkas, preludes, impromptus, Bach two-part inventions, miscellaneous pieces by Ravel that gave the unsettling impression of having neither beginnings nor endings but of having existed, always.

Mid-afternoon, just as Maggie was about to go out the door, the telephone rang; but when she went to answer it, no one spoke. 'Hello?' she said. She could hear, or believed she could hear, someone at the other end of the line; she seemed to feel a rippling or shuddering, a very nearly convulsive agitation, as of a person trying to speak but unable. 'Hello? Who is it? Is someone there?' Maggie asked. She hung up the receiver and waited for the phone to ring again, but it did not.

In Philadelphia, when Maggie had taught at the Curtis Institute and lived in an apartment close by the University of Pennsylvania, she'd been troubled from time to time by mysterious, somewhat threatening telephone calls; since moving to Forest Park she'd had fewer of these, though her name was listed in the telephone directory, as *M. Blackburn*. The most upsetting episode had involved a former piano student of hers, an enormously gifted but emotionally unstable fifteen-year-old boy who had had to drop out of the Conservatory for reasons of health; he'd moved back home with his family but telephoned Maggie at regular intervals, talking incoherently, once informing her that he was going to slash his wrists with a razor while she was on the phone with him . . . She had had to break the connection and call the police, and though the boy hadn't been serious about slashing his wrists, in fact denied to police that he'd threatened to do so, Maggie was involved, caught up in the emergency, agitated and insomniac for weeks afterward. Yet she had not, as friends urged her, changed her telephone to an unlisted number; she hadn't wanted, as she thought of it, to become anonymous. Thus there remained the neuter *M. Blackburn* in the Forest Park, Connecticut, telephone directory for anyone to call who wished to call. And when the phone at that number was answered, the voice there was unfailingly light and melodic, lifted in hope.

It was a two-mile walk to the Conservatory, a walk which, on Sundays especially, Maggie Blackburn very much enjoyed. At such times she wasn't required to hurry (though she always walked swiftly – she loved the pump of blood to her heart, the sensation of leg muscles, tendons, sinews springing into startled life); there were no classes and no students and few colleagues; she was free to spend a lazy, pleasurable hour or two in her office answering mail, writing memos, planning the upcoming week's work. Going to the Conservatory she took a route along Acacia to Juniper; on her way home she took a slightly longer, hillier route by way of Juniper, Littlebrook, and a stretch of beautiful wooded parkland . . . Littlebrook, past the handsome Georgian house owned by Rolfe Christensen that was said to be exquisitely if eccentrically furnished (Maggie had never been invited to one of Christensen's infrequent soirées: the composer did not like her, seemed to have decided before they met that he would not like her, though he was courteous enough to Portia and others in Maggie's circle). This afternoon, nearing five-thirty, in the wanly coppery autumn sunshine, the house at 2283 Littlebrook looked particularly impressive and remote; the venetian blinds on the front windows, upstairs and down, were drawn, and Christensen's white BMW was not in the drive. Maggie passed on the far side of the street, for she felt shy in the very vicinity of the house.

What had Christensen muttered in her ear the evening before, in jest, as, at one point during the party, he'd passed close by her, his blood-heavy face screwed up into a wink? 'Don't look so fearful, dear: I'm not infectious!' Had he really said those words, or had Maggie imagined them? It was Christensen's social style to utter such things, outrageous, sometimes obscene, sometimes nonsensical, in such a low voice that his listeners blinked, bewildered, never certain they'd heard what apparently they'd heard and usually too intimidated by the man to ask him to repeat himself. So Maggie hadn't known and had not remembered the teasing remark until now.

She thought, hurt, Why does he dislike me, despise me? I've done him no harm.

(In fact, Maggie Blackburn had probably done him harm, or had in any case insulted him, simply by concentrating her piano performances on traditional 'great' composers and never having once played a work by Rolfe Christensen.)

The much-publicized appointment of Rolfe Christensen to the Forest Park Conservatory of Music had not been in itself controversial, but controversy had certainly arisen when, in 1984, the school gave Christensen a highly endowed chair at a yearly salary rumoured to be above $150,000 for teaching a single master's class in composing each semester. Christensen's adversaries on the faculty argued that, as a composer, he was decidedly of the second rank; he'd done some good early work but that was far behind him now, and students often complained of his indifference to them, his high-handedness and contempt. Christensen's powerful supporters (among them the president, the provost of the Conservatory, and the Board of Trustees) insisted that he was an important contemporary American composer of the stature of Copland, Thomson and Barber and that numerous students over the years had expressed great admiration for him and gratitude at being allowed to come in contact with a man of his reputation. After all, Rolfe Christensen had won the Pulitzer Prize, hadn't he?

In the end, after months of subterranean quarrelling, Christensen was installed in his chair, and the event garnered a good deal of publicity for the Conservatory. Since Calvin Gould had been involved, Maggie would not have thought to criticize the appointment. She supposed, yes, people were probably jealous of Christensen, certainly of his reputation, and no one among his contemporaries could be objective about him.

Maggie left Littlebrook and entered the park, so inwardly absorbed that if, from time to time, passers by waved to her or called out her name, she rarely heard. Her piano students, sighting her at such times, her forehead creased, her eyes scanning the ground, assumed she was hearing music in her head, ceaseless music, mesmerized by a dream keyboard and by the skilful manoeuvrings of her fingers. Sometimes they were correct.

There was a figure near a rear corner of Maggie Blackburn's house, on the paved walk between the house and the garage: it looked as if whoever it was might be hiding from the street. Maggie turned hesitantly up the driveway, staring. The visitor, or trespasser, was not yet aware of her approach and was behaving strangely, as if agitated or deranged – walking with exaggerated stiffness in a tight circle, head deeply bowed, thin shoulders hunched. His movements were jerky and uncoordinated, and he appeared to be talking to himself, muttering. Without thinking that this person might be dangerous, Maggie called out, 'Yes? Who is it?'

The young man turned, and she saw to her amazement that it was Brendan Bauer, to whom she hadn't given a thought since he'd left her house the evening before in the company of Rolfe Christensen.

'Brendan? What on earth has happened to you?' Maggie cried.

It was evident that something extreme had happened. Brendan Bauer, staring and blinking at her as if, for a confused moment, he didn't know who she was, had the dazed, cringing, yet unfocused look of a man who has been in an accident. He appeared to have aged years. His skin was of the colour and texture of curdled milk, yet reddened, as if scraped raw in several places; there was an ugly bruise above his left eye; his glasses had been broken and were somewhat comically mended at the bridge with adhesive tape. He was wearing not the proper brown suit of the previous day but a baggy blue jersey with sleeves that fell to his knuckles and nondescript trousers also baggy at the knees. His stammer was so severe that when he first tried to speak his head and the upper part of his torso were involved in a gagging, convulsive sort of movement. 'M-Miss Blackburn, c-c-can I talk with y-you?' he asked, not meeting Maggie's eye. 'For j-j-just a few m-minutes?'

'Of course,' Maggie said. She would have taken his arm to steady him and lead him into the house, but she sensed that he would not want to be touched.

Inside, Maggie invited Brendan to sit down. But it seemed he could not, or would not, be seated. He walked about gawky and stiff-legged, running his hands swiftly through his spiky hair. There was a curious sheen to his eyes, and the flesh about them was puffy as if he'd been crying. But when Maggie asked, 'Did you hurt yourself, Brendan? Are you in pain?' he made an impatient noise meant to indicate no.

For some minutes he wandered about the living room, peering at bookshelves, then at the music on the piano. While Maggie stood in the doorway not knowing what to do or to say, Brendan leafed through her piano books nodding and murmuring to himself, as if this were a social visit and he, the brash young composer, was behaving just a bit eccentrically.

He leaned over the keyboard and very deliberately struck a single note: C two octaves above middle C.

'N-n-nice t-tone,' he said.

He played chords with both hands, not well, rather clumsily. 'P-p-pure like c-crystal,' he said.

Maggie said, a little more forcibly, 'You look terrible, Brendan. Please – what has happened?'

Brendan Bauer seemed not to hear. Or, hearing, he chose to ignore her.

He was bent stiffly over the keyboard depressing chords, bass and treble, up and down the keyboard, stridently. Maggie thought, He is mad. Something has driven him mad.

Aloud she said, 'Shall I call a doctor? Shall I take you to the emergency room?'

Without glancing around he said, 'N-n-no. *No.*

Maggie paused. Then, inspired, she said, 'Shall I make us some coffee?'

Brendan murmured what sounded like 'Yes.'

Maggie fled to the kitchen to prepare coffee – instant coffee, out of a tin – while the young composer played chords, seemingly at random, in varying tempos. Yet there was a logic to the chords' succession, an echo of Charles Ives; perhaps this was one of Brendan Bauer's original compositions.

The sound of Maggie's own piano being played apart from her was disorienting, as if she were herself in two places. The effect was uncanny and made her hands shake.

When she returned to the living room with the coffee things and a plate of macaroons, Brendan appeared more subdued. He thanked her. He said he wouldn't stay long. Again he declined to take a seat, as if sitting might pain him or place him at a dis- advantage; he stood beside the piano, leaning an elbow on it. Maggie could not help staring at the lurid bruise above his left eye and the raw red scratches on his cheeks.

In the baggy long-sleeved jersey, his hair lifting in tufts from his head, Brendan looked both childlike and violated, and Maggie's heart went out to him. She recalled his somewhat clumsy attempt to revise minor details of his academic history, and his intense embarrassment upon being found out. Now she resisted the impulse to question him, for she saw that his eyes

47

behind his thick lenses were reddened with hurt and outrage.

He was surprisingly hungry – eating up all the macaroons Maggie offered him and drinking coffee heavily sweetened with sugar and cream. Maggie provided him with leftover canapes from the party, which he ate voraciously as well. His hands visibly shook.

For approximately a half hour, as if this were indeed a casual social visit, or as if he had forgotten its specific purpose, the young composer spoke ramblingly yet excitedly of various subjects. His stammer was less severe and sometimes vanished altogether. Composers he admired, Schoenberg, Stockhausen, Janáček; his current work on a 'cycle of anti-art songs'; his parents' bewilderment with him, and their tacit dismay; an experience he'd had in the seminary in St Louis when in the midst of a period of intense fasting and prayer he'd suddenly heard music, distinctly *heard* music, so beautiful and powerful he'd burst into tears.

'Because I knew the music was God,' Brendan said, looking hopefully at Maggie. 'I mean, G-G-God was the music.'

Maggie recalled that long ago, in another lifetime, it seemed, she had had a similar experience, during a Lutheran church service in St Paul. She must have been about eleven years old at the time, and very much caught up in her piano lessons. While the congregation prayed aloud a bubble of sound had seemed to emerge from the very air, a cascade of infinitely beautiful piano notes, which the child Maggie had been convinced others must hear but did not acknowledge. Until this moment she had not recalled that curious incident in years.

Mistaking her expression for one of doubt, Brendan said defensively, a bit sullenly, 'I suppose you think I'm c-crazy, huh?'

Maggie said, 'Oh, no! No, I don't.'

Brendan smiled, or smirked. 'But maybe I *am* crazy.'

There was a brief silence. Brendan had set his coffee cup down, brushed crumbs from his mouth and the front of his jersey, as if preparing to leave. Maggie said, suddenly, 'Was that you who telephoned, a few hours ago?'

Quickly he said, 'N-no,' not meeting Maggie's eye.

She supposed he was lying. But he would have to be granted the lie.

There was another silence. In the bay window of Maggie's little dining-room her canary, Rex, began to sing. The young composer listened and said, 'One of my aunts had a c-canary too. It's amazing, isn't it. It's' – he pressed his mended glasses against the bridge of his nose and looked for a moment merely baffled – 'amazing. Of course,' he said, almost derisively, or self-mockingly, '*they* can't vary their song.'

Maggie let the remark pass and said, 'Shall I take you to a doctor, after all? The emergency room of the Medical Centre?'

'N-no. I told you *no*.'

'Then why have you come here?'

'To inform you that I-I-I'm n-n-n-not' – and here Brendan Bauer's stammer overcame him for several convulsive seconds, until, virtually spitting, he managed to get the words out – 'starting classes tomorrow. I'm thinking of g-g-going back h-h-h-h – '

Maggie cried, 'Brendan, what? But why?'

'M-m-made a m-m-m-mistake – '

'But *why*?'

These many minutes the young composer had been on his feet, slouching beside the piano, leaning an elbow against it, shifting his weight nervously from leg to leg, from one side of his body to the other. Now and then he winced with pain. His curdled skin was damp with an oily perspiration, and the edges of his pale grim mouth glittered with saliva. He looked, to Maggie's alarmed eye, not mad precisely but maddened; barely restraining his rage; yet at the same time frightened, cringing, broken, on the humiliating edge of tears. But now he laughed harshly and spat the words at her as if somehow she were to blame: 'I-I-I've been r-r-r-raped.'

'Raped!'

And that possibility, not simply that Brendan Bauer blamed Maggie Blackburn for the horror perpetrated upon his body but that she was, in part, however unintentionally, to blame, Maggie

49

was never to forget. It would be one of the profound shocks of her life.

'I should k-k-kill myself for letting it happen . . . it was m-m-my own fault . . . let the bastard do it . . . c-c-couldn't stop him . . . he was so strong, he was a m-maniac . . . tied me up . . . I was terrified he'd k-k-kill me . . . strangle me . . . he threatened . . . said he'd ruin my c-c-career if . . . if I . . . oh Christ I'm so ashamed . . . I want to die . . . why didn't I fight him harder . . . *why didn't I kill him* . . . now it's too late!'

Stiff-legged, grimacing with pain, Brendan Bauer paced about Maggie Blackburn's living-room. He would not allow Maggie to comfort him; not even to touch him when, like an aggrieved child, he burst into tears. Maggie protested, 'Don't say such things, Brendan,' but he ignored her, waved her off. She said, 'If you've been injured, Brendan, if you're in need of medical care – '

'N-no. *No.*'

'Rape is a serious criminal offence, the police will have to be - '

'*No.*' He screamed at her to silence her, and Maggie acquiesced.

She thought, I must not persecute him further, he has suffered enough.

She was also somewhat fearful that, in the frenzied state the young man was in, he might turn violent against *her*.

For the next several hours, suppressing much of what she felt of shock, anger, disgust, incredulity, and an immediate wish that Rolfe Christensen be publicly exposed and punished, Maggie Blackburn gently coaxed out of Brendan Bauer an account of what had happened to him the night before; a disjointed, rambling, frequently incoherent and interrupted narrative, as if the distraught young man could not bear to tell his story outright but had to circle it, and back away, and circle it again, and approach it, yet again back away, shuddering with rage, frustration, self-loathing. Repeatedly he broke off his story to say, 'I'm so ashamed,' and 'Why didn't I f-fight him harder?' and 'I wish I was dead,' and '*Why didn't I kill him*!'

Maggie regarded him with anxious sympathy. Tears formed in her own eyes, and her heart knocked hard in her chest. It seemed to her that she had never witnessed another person so upset, so consumed by passion; there was a kind of perverse grandeur in it, of which, she was sure, she would never herself be capable. At the same time she reasoned that, when this wave of hysteria subsided, Brendan would be more tractable and allow her to get him professional help. He would certainly have to be examined by a doctor; he would certainly have to go to the police. The loathsome Rolfe Christensen must be exposed, publicly tried, punished . . . And to think that he had approached young Brendan Bauer in Maggie's own house, at a social gathering she herself had devised!

He is a monster, Maggie thought, trembling. And I never guessed.

In all, Brendan had been a 'captive' of Christensen's for approximately six and a half hours. The assault began suddenly, with no warning, at about midnight; the actual rape (the details of which Brendan did not supply) must have taken place an hour later, in Christensen's bedroom, on his king-sized bed with its 'grey, rubberized sheet'; though Brendan pleaded, begged, wept, screamed, Christensen refused to let him go, and through the night there were subsequent assaults, sadistic episodes, numberless threats of torture, death . . . for the man was a madman, a sexual maniac.

'He did th-things I can't say . . . I'd never t-t-tell anyone . . . he hurt me, bad . . . he's very strong . . . he's big, heavy . . . must weigh t-t-two hundred th-thirty pounds . . . played at strangling me . . . laughed at me . . . said I wanted it too . . . I'd led him on . . . saying I knew . . . knew what . . . what would happen . . . saying I was a . . . c-c-c-c-cocktease . . . laughed at me the more t-terrified I was . . . I was so scared . . . paralysed . . . like all the strength was gone . . . I was sure I was going to die . . . I begged him . . . I told him . . . *I've never done anything like this before* I told him *I'm not gay* I told him . . . he didn't listen . . . it was all *him*, what *he* wanted . . . grunting and drunk and . . . a maniac . . . in his bed . . . in the bathroom . . . I passed out I guess . . . I don't k-know all that happened . . . I was drunk too . . . he got me drunk . . . at one point he made me drink . . . forced whisky down my throat . . . roaring and laughing . . . pretended I wasn't hurt . . . or scared . . . like the bleeding too . . . was a joke . . . "Tears too are a lubricant", he said . . . "Blood too" . . . like it was all a joke . . . I was vomiting in the bed . . . he didn't like that . . . he s-s-straddled my . . . hips . . . he yanked at my . . . hair . . . grunting and screaming . . . a pig, a hog . . . I started vomiting . . . he dragged me into the bathroom . . . he pushed my head down to the toilet . . . banged my head on the porcelain rim . . . he was furious with me . . . hit and kicked me . . . then dragged me somewhere else . . . collapsed on top of me . . . he'd black out I guess then wake up again . . . sometimes just a few seconds he'd be out . . . I tried to crawl out from under him . . . but he'd wake up . . . not fully awake but enough to stop me . . . I couldn't get my hands free . . . I c-c-couldn't get free . . . then in the morning he woke up and seemed almost sober . . . like he was sorry or worried . . . not repentant but worried . . . real worried . . . guilty . . . tried to behave as if it was just . . . what happened was just . . . a . . . something mutual . . . I didn't challenge him . . . I just wanted to . . . get away . . . all I thought about was getting away with my . . . life . . . he saw I was hurt gave me something for the b-b-bleeding . . . said it was my own fault . . . driving me to my apartment he started th-th-threatening me again . . . "I wouldn't tell anyone about this, Brendan," except the bastard, the filthy son of a bitch, he'd always say "Bren dan", like my name was funny . . . *Bren dan* . . . "I wouldn't tell anyone about last night Bren dan or you'll regret it you little cocktease you'll be out of here so fast you won't know what happened conniving little cunt Bren dan" . . . so he let me out . . . I went to my place . . . collapsed . . . it was about six-thirty in the morning . . . I fainted . . . I guess I fainted . . . I didn't know where I was, thought I was back in . . . the seminary . . . bells ringing . . . thought I heard the master of novices t-talking to me . . . I couldn't get up for p-p-prayer . . . I dragged myself to the bathroom at one point . . . I took some aspirin . . . ran some bathwater . . . tried to soak in it . . . the pain was . . . it's . . . I'm ashamed . . . so ashamed . . . my life is over . . . I want to die . . . I couldn't stop him . . . *why couldn't I stop him?* . . . I was so weak, so . . . scared . . . he threw himself on me . . . just . . . like an animal . . . he'd played the tape of his "Adagio for Piano and Strings" and . . . I looked up at him . . . and . . . it wasn't just he was drunk . . . he was . . . he . . . oh Jesus if I'd known . . . if I'd acted fast enough . . . but I didn't know . . . didn't know . . . nobody warned me . . . I don't want to live . . . I don't deserve to live . . . the pig! The filthy pig! *why didn't I kill him when I had the chance*!'

Maggie was on her feet, pleading. 'Brendan, you must let me drive you to the Medical Centre – you've been injured! And you *must* let me call the police!'

'N-no.'

'I think I will have to insist. You came to me, and I will have to act. For your own good. This is a serious, criminal – '

'I said *no*.'

Beginning to lose patience, Maggie said, 'Rolfe Christensen tied you up, didn't he? Kept you captive? Assaulted you? Repeatedly? And you don't want to press charges against him?'

'He – he didn't tie me up,' Brendan said. 'Did I say that? I didn't say that.'

He stepped back from Maggie. She saw how the long loose sleeves of his cotton jersey covered his wrists, fell nearly to his fingers. 'Your wrists?' she said. 'Your ankles? With rope?'

'It was my own fault, I'll l-l-live with it. I – I'm not staying here.'

'But we can't let that terrible man, that monster, get off freely, go on to victimize others – '

'What do I care about others?' Brendan Bauer said bitterly. 'Nobody cared about *me*.'

'What do you mean, Brendan?'

'Inviting me here! Inviting students here! And *him* – here!'

'But I didn't know – '

'God damn you! God damn you all! You must have known! *Why didn't somebody warn me!*'

Later that evening Maggie prepared a meal for Brendan and herself and invited the stricken young man to spend the night in her guest room if he wished, but Brendan preferred to return home – 'home' being his two-room service apartment in a building on Route 1, on the outermost edge of affluent Forest Park. Though Maggie continued to argue her case, he refused to allow her to drive him to the Medical Centre, nor would he allow Maggie to call the police. *No. Anything but that.*

'If you change your mind about pressing charges . . . it would be helpful to have been examined by a doctor,' Maggie said gently. 'And you might, you know, change your mind.'

Brendan Bauer was staring at a vase of white roses on one of Maggie's tables without seeming to recognize them. He said shuddering, 'I'm too h-h-humiliated.'

And: 'I can't risk anyone knowing, back h-h-home – my family – relatives – in Boise. They'd never understand. They'd never forgive me. They never approved of my studying music at Indiana and they'd never believe that I'm not h-h-h-h-' – and here his stammer became a physical struggle – '*homosexual.*'

Carefully Maggie said, 'Morally and legally, it should not make the slightest difference, should it – whether Rolfe Christensen assaulted a gay man or not? Surely the law protects us all equally?'

Brendan gave a groan, hid his face in his hands, and began to sob.

Maggie Blackburn quickly retreated to her kitchen.

I must not persecute him further, she thought.

And she supposed it was so, that, in the impersonal judgement of the police and of the criminal justice system, even, no doubt, in the eyes of Rolfe Christensen himself, a sexual assault upon a gay victim would seem less criminal than the identical assault upon a straight victim.

While Maggie prepared one of her frequent meals, an ome-

54

lette stuffed with stir-fried vegetables and sprinkled with basil, the young composer leaned over her piano striking chords: affectless near-inaudible chords reminiscent of Satie: his rage was temporarily quelled. Maggie was thinking of Calvin Gould, who must be notified as quickly as possible of this terrible incident ... though perhaps she should wait to see him in the morning. The school would have to be informed that one of its tenured faculty members had not only violated regulations forbidding sexual relationships between faculty and students but had committed a criminal act, or acts; if Brendan Bauer would not consent to file the complaint, perhaps Maggie Blackburn could do it in his place? She felt as if she herself had been violated, or had barely escaped violation; she certainly felt soiled.

What had Christensen said to her, stretching his fleshy lips in a mock smile: *Don't look so fearful, dear: I'm not infectious!*

It made Maggie Blackburn feel slightly ill, that he should have joked, so coarsely, of AIDS.

For perhaps Rolfe Christensen *was* infected ... ?

When Maggie and Brendan sat down to Maggie's hastily prepared little meal, which she served at the kitchen table, in an alcove of her small, attractive, old-fashioned kitchen, neither spoke of what was uppermost in their minds, as if by tacit consent. They talked instead of neutral matters, or of music; or were silent. And after an initial hesitancy Brendan ate the meal with appetite ... with, Maggie was thinking, a boyish appetite, ducking his head toward his plate.

The young man *was* a boy, in his manner, in his lack of experience. Only close up, studying his eyes, might one guess he was an adult man in his late twenties; an adult man who gave the appearance of being clumsily at odds with his body.

Of course, Maggie thought, he has been a seminarian: he'd intended to become a Catholic priest. Did they not take vows of poverty, chastity, obedience? Was it not their wish to remain celibate for life?

Later, when Maggie drove Brendan to his apartment building

55

several miles away, he sat stiffly in the seat beside her, leaning his weight, subtly, to one side of his buttocks; of which Maggie was well aware, and suffused with sympathy for him, and anger, and a sense of powerlessness. She understood that many rape victims refuse to report having been raped; she believed she would not behave in so self-defeating a way, but perhaps she wasn't in a position to judge – for how does one know what one will do, with what desperation one might behave, in such extreme circumstances? in such circumstances for which nothing in one's life has been an adequate preparation?

Gently, for she did not wish to provoke him, still less to torment him, Maggie asked, as they approached the neighbourhood of his apartment, 'Shall I telephone you in the morning, Brendan? And we'll go to the Provost or the Dean together?'

He shrugged wearily, as if the entire subject was suddenly of little interest to him.

He said, 'I shouldn't be troubling you, Miss Blackburn. It's my own fault; it's *my* l-l-life.'

His voice was so flat, Maggie had to resist the impulse to reach out and squeeze his hand.

Maggie stopped her car in front of the apartment building in which Brendan lived; into which, only a week before, he'd moved. It was an absolutely featureless building of five storeys constructed flush to the sidewalk. For a moment Maggie and the young composer sat motionless, silent, as if there were more to say; but both were dazed with exhaustion. Maggie saw that his face visibly sagged and that the white adhesive tape on the bridge of his glasses glowed smudgily, like a blind third eye.

She said softly, 'If – if you want to, telephone me at any time. If – '

'Thank you, Miss Blackburn,' Brendan said, stirring to get out, loosening his long legs, 'I don't deserve anybody being so n-n-nice to me.' Before Maggie could protest he went on, in an almost bemused voice, 'Shouldn't have come here, I guess – '

Maggie had not quite heard, and misunderstood. 'But why? I'm your faculty adviser, Brendan, I'm your friend; where else should you have gone?'

'I mean,' Brendan said miserably, 'I shouldn't have left the seminary. I'm being p-p-punished for leaving.'

Maggie did not protest this statement, though she wanted to. Instead she asked a question which, in ordinary circumstances, she would not have been bold enough to ask of someone she knew so slightly. 'Why *did* you leave, Brendan?'

'I . . . I ceased to believe.'

'In God?'

'In . . . all of it.'

'I see.'

Brendan Bauer was poised stiffly, his hand on the car door-knob. Outside on Route 1 traffic passed in a steady yet capricious stream. In a voice vague and rambling with exhaustion he said, 'But I believed in something still . . . like God. But not . . . their God. Myself as a p-p-priest of that God. I believed, though; I believe . . . in something. Like a brick wall. The way a brick wall if it's there is *there*. It stops you d-d-dead whether you believe in it or not.'

Maggie Blackburn would wonder, afterwards, at the certitude with which she said, so simply, 'Yes.'

Six

'Assaulted? Do you mean . . . sexually?'

'Yes, I'm afraid I – '

'*Raped?*'

'Yes, I – '

'Rolfe Christensen raped one of our graduate students?'

'Yes, he came to me . . . his name is . . .'

'Are you serious? Is this so? *Rolfe Christensen raped one of our graduate students?*'

'. . . Brendan Bauer, the composition student . . . from Idaho – '

'How could he! Christensen! After all the school has done for him! After all *I've* done for him!'

It was Monday morning, shortly after nine o'clock. Maggie was standing in Calvin Gould's office, the door shut, contemplating her friend's stricken face, forced by his extreme reaction to realize how rarely in her life she found herself the bearer of dramatic, let alone shocking, news . . . how rarely she had so pronounced an effect upon another's emotions. Never before had she seen Calvin Gould, that poised, even guarded man, display such surprise and dismay; never had she heard his voice so angry. His accent seemed more emphatic, as if it were a function of his anger. He said, 'If what this young man Bauer says is true, we have a very serious situation here.'

Maggie said, 'It must be true. Brendan certainly isn't lying.'

She told Calvin of Bauer's visit the day before; summarized his remarks; described his appearance and behaviour. That morning too at four o'clock he'd telephoned her – to tell her that he wanted to withdraw immediately from the Conservatory, and would his tuition and fees be refunded? – and Maggie had tried to reason with him, advising him not to act rashly. 'Before he hung up he said, "One thing I won't do: I won't commit suicide!" He was stammering so I almost couldn't make out his words.'

Calvin Gould, having drawn a handkerchief out of his pocket, began to wipe his face slowly with it, staring at Maggie. He said, 'Is he the one who stammers so badly? Brendan Bauer? I remember speaking with him, briefly, at your party.'

He paused. He shivered with disgust.

'Isn't it just like a . . . a man like Christensen . . . to pick on someone weak . . . like *him*.'

Maggie said, 'After we talked on the phone I was so worried about him, I called him back, and we talked quite a while longer . . . at least an hour. Once or twice Brendan burst into tears but he kept assuring me he wasn't going to hurt himself: he wouldn't give that bastard the satisfaction, he said. I tried to convince him that even if he withdrew from the Conservatory temporarily, he should remain in the area so that he could make use of the school's resources; even if he refused to go to the police or the Medical Centre, he should file an official complaint with the administration. I offered to pick him up this morning and bring him here, to talk with you, but he said he couldn't . . . he couldn't talk with anyone until he was ready.'

'He hasn't seen a doctor? He hasn't been examined?'

'Not yet.'

'Or the police?'

'He seems terrified of going to the police.'

Calvin paced about his office, his handkerchief crumpled in his fist. He said, 'Sometimes in such cases the complainant simply withdraws, and the case evaporates. There isn't any case, really, without testimony.'

'We can't let that happen,' Maggie said.

'No, we can't. We can't.'

'If you knew how distraught Brendan is . . .'

'I can imagine.'

Like the majority of his fellow senior administrators and executives, Calvin Gould had all but inured himself to revelations of a startling nature; to problems, indeed emergencies, which he was expected to resolve without disagreeable publicity. It was rumoured of him that his Vietnam War experience had well prepared him for such civilian occasions and that his marine training had carried over into his professional life: he was deft, canny and unsentimental. (In fact, Maggie Blackburn knew that Calvin Gould had been in the marine corps for less than two years – he'd signed up, impetuously, aged nineteen, but had been allowed an honourable discharge for unspecified reasons; he had never served in Vietnam at all, in any capacity.) But Calvin was genuinely distressed, even agitated, by Maggie's news, as Maggie would afterwards recall; his immediate response was one of intense sympathy. He said, 'The danger is that something more could happen: Bauer might try to hurt himself. If he insists he isn't suicidal that might mean the reverse.'

So, at Calvin's suggestion, Maggie telephoned Brendan Bauer from his office. At first, as the phone rang at the other end of the line, Maggie thought it was already too late. Then Brendan answered, cautiously; his voice was raw and frightened, his stammer subdued. Maggie said, 'I'm here in the provost's office, Brendan, and Mr Gould and I are both very concerned. We think you should come to talk with him . . . file a complaint . . . Everything will be kept strictly confidential, we promise.'

There was a brief silence. Then Brendan said, to Maggie's surprise, 'I . . . I w-will. I've been thinking it over. Maybe I'll go to the p-police too. *I hate that filthy bastard's guts.*'

Arrangements were made for Brendan to come, by taxi, to Calvin Gould's office, at noon; by early afternoon, Calvin would have summoned the Conservatory's committee on ethics and faculty responsibility and would have contacted Andrew Woodbridge, the school attorney, so that he could sit in on the interview. 'So you can go home, Maggie, if you want,' Calvin said. 'You look as if . . . this has been a considerable strain on you.' He smiled at her, uncertainly. What did he see in her face, in her eyes? Maggie Blackburn was a beautiful woman whom intense feeling made more beautiful still.

'We must see to it,' Maggie said passionately, 'that that terrible man is exposed and punished. Rape is a criminal felony, after all, and Rolfe Christensen is a rapist.'

Maggie had no intention of going home – for she had a senior honours seminar to teach, and a luncheon meeting, and an arduous afternoon of piano instruction, two students per hour from three o'clock until six – but she was relieved that Calvin was going to take charge; she knew now that justice would be done.

Calvin Gould, his necktie loosened, his expression grim, walked Maggie Blackburn through his secretary's office and out into the hall. The administration building was housed in a former private home, an English Tudor mansion built by a multi-millionaire industrialist in the early 1900s and donated, along with two hundred acres of wooded land, to the Conservatory; at the end of every hallway in the house, and on staircase landings, stained-glass windows gave to the atmosphere a churchly yet exotic tone. Walking Maggie towards one of these windows, Calvin was saying in a low voice, as if he were thinking aloud, 'I'm shocked by this but not, I suppose, entirely surprised . . . considering Rolfe Christensen's reputation.'

Seeing Maggie's expression, Calvin said quickly, 'Not that he has done anything of this magnitude before, that I know of. Certainly not with – or to – a Conservatory student.'

'But he has done . . . things?'

Calvin chose his words carefully. 'He has been complained of now and then. And there have been rumours of . . . rather ugly episodes . . . in London, and at the Salzburg Festival . . . and when I was a scholarship student at Interlaken, in 1967 I think – did you know I was a serious pianist then, Maggie? – Christensen had been there the summer before, and there were tales told of him, his drinking, his behaviour, a story of an incident being hushed up, something fairly serious involving a young man. But of course things like that are unsubstantiated. No formal charges, no arrests. Nothing official. You can't judge a man of Christensen's stature by way of rumours.' Calvin was frowning hard, and Maggie saw that one of his eyelids had begun to twitch. His eyes were a deep wary brown, so dark that pupil and iris were one. 'Can't judge without evidence. And he *is* gifted, or was. He *is* Rolfe Christensen. People dislike him, then come around to liking him: "Isn't he a character!" they say. "Isn't he something!" As if genius is allowed anything, and Christensen is a genius. Remember how Nick Reickmann came around to defending him, after that early trouble between them?'

Early trouble? Maggie Blackburn was again perplexed. 'But the men are such good friends now, aren't they?'

'They're ... friends, of a kind. I don't know how good, or how intimate. Of course, Christensen can have intimates who aren't friends. But when Nick first came here he complained that Christensen was harassing him; he went so far as to bring a formal complaint of "sexual harassment" to our committee. We had some closed hearings, and things were smoothed out, and I'd assumed that everyone knew, more or less; Nick wasn't exactly secretive about it himself. He was very angry. He isn't after all a natural victim like this poor Bauer boy.'

Maggie was sorry that Brendan Bauer should be so casually defined, or dismissed, but she let the remark pass, for she was quite shaken, and in a way ashamed, that she seemed so unaware of what was taking place in her own community, among her colleagues. She wondered if people shielded her from upsetting news or whether they did in fact inform her, or spoke of such things in her presence, but she somehow failed to hear. She passed a hand over her face and asked Calvin, 'Should I have known of these things? Of Rolfe Christensen's reputation? In order to protect students from him?'

As if taking pity on her, or moved to sudden sympathy with her limited perspective, Calvin Gould laughed and squeezed Maggie's hand in parting and said, 'For God's sake, Maggie, *no*: don't start blaming yourself. You have, after all, your own life.'

Walking away, out of the building and into silvery autumn sunshine, Maggie tried to think what Calvin could possibly mean by those words.

You have, after all, your own life.

The first time Maggie Blackburn had seen Calvin Gould was on the occasion of a lecture he gave at the Curtis Institute of Music, years before. At that time Calvin was a youngish man in his early thirties with hair trimmed short and wiry like a terrier's; he'd stood ramrod straight behind the lectern, tense yet not exuding nervousness; a deck of note cards between his fingers from which he took cues, speaking lucidly, always smoothly, shifting each card to the back of the deck as he progressed. His delivery was assured but not complacent, and he seemed to know virtually everything about his subject, which was Franz Schubert. (Maggie was particularly struck by the observation that Schubert was a 'born composer', a genius who required no development: thus his death at age thirty-one was not premature in the way that, for instance, Verdi's death would have been premature at age eighty.) After the lecture she had been drawn forwards irresistibly to meet Calvin Gould; to confront something the man embodied, or which shone through him.

Sometimes, recollecting that day, Maggie distinctly remembered the presence of the elusive Naomi Gould, dark-haired and frowning, who sat at the rear of the auditorium during Calvin's lecture; sometimes Maggie had no memory of the woman at all.

There must be a deep erotic bond between husband and wife, Maggie thought, resigned. For there seemed so little else, of companionship, or sympathy.

'Please tell us what happened between you and Rolfe Christensen,' Calvin Gould instructed Brendan Bauer, who was sitting, ill at ease, shamefaced, deathly pale, in Calvin's office, at one end of a conference table facing Calvin, the Conservatory's attorney, Andrew Woodbridge, and the five-member committee on ethics and faculty responsibility. 'Everything you say will be held in strictest confidence.'

63

So Brendan Bauer told his story another time. It was less dis-jointed than it had been in the telling to Maggie Blackburn, but still the young composer was subject to brief stammering lapses, and his mood swung between anger and despair, lucidity and in-coherence, certainty and defensiveness. He had shaved that morning with a badly shaking hand and in the process had nicked his jaw in several blood-stippled places; the bruise above his left eye, a rich plum-purple, pulsed with hurt and indignation.

Brendan Bauer told his story and endured questions.

These seven men and women, strangers to him, *were* sym-pathetic . . . or so it seemed.

The precise nature of the sexual assault?

'R-r-rape.'

But could he . . . elaborate?

'M-m-male r-rape.'

Meaning . . . forcible anal penetration?

Eyes shut, Brendan Bauer nodded. 'That is . . . the clinical term.'

And did he try to escape, during those six and a half hours of captivity?

'I was too t-t-terrified, thought he would . . . k-kill me.'

And Christensen had no idea that Brendan Bauer was . . . re-sistant? In these circumstances, after having been drinking, there was no possibility of . . . a misunderstanding?

'N-no. *No.*'

So Brendan Bauer told his ugly story through that afternoon, told and retold it. Doubled back on himself. Repeated himself. Excused himself to use a men's lavatory. Several times he seemed unable to continue, but he did continue, grim and resolute. He blew his nose, he sighed, he yawned, he hunched forward and hid his face in his hands. His little audience of two women and five men exchanged quick glances of alarm and pity from time to time, for it was clear to them that he had suffered a considerable trauma.

Only at the end of the afternoon, however, did Brendan seriously lose control.

'*Why?* To hear one of his c-c-compositions. "Adagio for Piano and Strings." I didn't want to go . . . but I wanted to . . . wanted to go . . . I was f-f-flattered . . . sure I was. Serves me right, doesn't it? Drinking and I don't know how to drink, and he fed me chocolates . . . chocolate-covered truffles, my God . . . I'd never seen anything like them before . . . vomited up, later. Aquavit and Scotch. I was drunk. "You like pain, don't you, Bren dan?" he said. Twisted my arm till I screamed. Took off my clothes, s-s-straddled me on the . . . bed. Hurt me. Pounded himself in me. When I screamed he pushed my face in the pillow . . . *he* screamed . . . I was s-s-suffocating . . . then the vomiting began. "I'll kill you, cocktease," he said. So strong. Angry. Why did he h-hate me? Why . . . want to hurt me? My punishment for leaving the s-s-seminary . . . cemetery . . . "sin of pride" . . . "pride of intellect" . . . he joked about graves out back . . . "Do you want to be buried out back with the other cockteases?" he said . . . I fainted . . . didn't have any strength . . . things he did like in a . . . dream . . . things I'll never tell anyone. Then in the morning he drove me home, anxious to get r-r-rid of me. He was wearing a fresh shirt, a necktie . . . hat on his head . . . like nothing was wrong. "I wouldn't tell anyone about this, Bren dan" . . . thought I was bleeding inside . . . up inside . . . couldn't look at him . . . those dead eyes . . . "I can help you with your career, Bren dan," he said, "or I can squash you flat like a . . ." *Why didn't I kill him when I had the chance? Why didn't I –*'

Quickly, as if to silence him, Calvin Gould laid a hand on Brendan Bauer's narrow shoulder, as the others stared. Calvin said, 'You'll be all right now, Brendan. You're safe, now.'

Those several hours, telephone calls were being placed at regular intervals to Rolfe Christensen's home and to his office at the Conservatory; every half-hour Calvin Gould's administrative assistant, Mrs Mills, would knock at his door to inform him that Christensen hadn't yet been located. Stanley Spalding, the chairman of Christensen's department, reported that he hadn't seen Christensen yet that day; neither had Bill Queller, nor Nicholas

Reickmann, nor Si Lichtman, with whom he sometimes had lunch in the faculty dining-room. 'Mr Queller thinks Rolfe Christensen might be out of town,' Mrs Mills said. 'But he doesn't know where he is or when he might be back.'

Flushed with anger, Calvin Gould said, 'We'll send Christensen a letter, then, registered mail, and instruct him to contact us as quickly as possible.'

Calvin Gould offered to drive Brendan Bauer home after the meeting. At first, Brendan declined, with thanks, saying he'd rather walk; then, ruefully, he said, yes maybe he'd better accept a ride. He wasn't in any condition to walk two or three miles and though he'd been in Forest Park, Connecticut, for a week – 'It s-s-seems more like six months!' – he didn't yet know his way around. He had no idea in which direction was his 'home'.

Andrew Woodbridge accompanied Calvin and Brendan as they walked across campus to Calvin's parking lot. He was urging Brendan, as he'd urged him intermittently that afternoon, to go to the campus infirmary, at least, if he was still reluctant to be examined at the Medical Centre; it would be in Brendan's best interests, if his charges against his assailant were to be fully validated. 'We certainly believe your account,' Woodbridge said, in his even, impassive voice, 'but it would be helpful, from a more clinical standpoint, to have a medical report with which Christensen might be confronted. You were saying earlier you might even press criminal charges?'

After his brief breakdown, Brendan had hidden himself away in a men's lavatory and seemed to have washed his face, wetted and combed his stiff unruly hair, adjusted his clothing. His face was still parchment-pale and he carried himself with only the slightest suggestion of pain, but his eyes behind the thick lenses were darting rapidly about as if, in the open air, in the midst of young men and women students who were strangers to him, he expected to be pointed out, curiously stared at.

Vaguely Brendan said, 'I . . . don't know.'

'About the criminal charges?'

66

'About a-a-anything.'

Calvin Gould joined Andrew Woodbridge in urging Brendan to be examined; he'd be happy to drive him to the infirmary, he said, and to accompany him inside, if . . . if Brendan should so wish. And there was the matter of psychological counselling too: 'In such cases,' Calvin said, choosing his words carefully, 'I believe that psychological counselling is always recommended.'

'Yes,' Woodbridge said, with paternal energy, 'yes, it certainly *is*.'

But Brendan Bauer was not to be persuaded.

After a moment he said sharply, 'Look: I don't want to be *touched*. By any doctor or . . . *anybody*. And I don't need any damn "psychological counselling" because I'm not crazy, I'm not un-balanced, *I'm not suicidal*. Got it?'

The older men fell apologetically silent and did not persist.

After Woodbridge parted from them, Brendan said to Calvin Gould, with a sardonic smile, 'Hah! Just like the others, up in your office! *I* caught that.'

Calvin Gould asked, 'Yes? What?'

'He – him – I don't remember his name – he walked away without shaking hands with me. Like the rest of them. They fear I am *infected*,' Brendan said, laughing bitterly, 'and that it can be transmitted by *hand*.'

Calvin Gould protested weakly, 'I really don't think . . . I don't think that's it, at all.'

Brendan merely laughed.

They walked to Calvin's car, and Calvin was intensely aware of the young man: this tall gangling slope-shouldered youth, with a schoolboy seminarian's prim face, ill-fitting clothes, and glasses crudely mended with adhesive tape: how was it possible that another man, even so presumably decadent and reckless a man as Rolfe Christensen, should be attracted . . . sexually, violently . . . to *him*?

He must have been unknowingly regarding Brendan with a look of fascination, loathing wondering fascination, for the young man said, grinning, 'Hey, don't worry, Mr Gould: *you* won't have to t-t-t-t-touch me either.'

Which meant, of course, when Calvin dropped Brendan off at his apartment building, that he certainly did shake hands with him: briskly, warmly, without an instant's hesitation.

Seven

Where had Rolfe Christensen disappeared to? No one knew, not even his closest and presumably most intimate friend, the cellist Bill Queller, whom so many people telephoned, or sought out, to inquire after Christensen's whereabouts that he quickly cultivated a neutral, guarded tone: 'I'm afraid I have no idea where Rolfe is. I'm sorry – I simply don't.'

After a day or two adding, with the slightest edge of defensiveness, 'And I *am* telling the truth.'

Nicholas Reickmann too had to contend with queries, which made him distinctly uncomfortable. Perhaps he was remembering how, as they'd all left Maggie's party on Saturday evening, he watched Rolfe lead that sweet-faced stammering young graduate student off in the direction of his car, had a thought, a warning thought blunted by alcohol, and in the next instant dismissed it. Nicholas said, 'Certainly *I* have no idea where Christensen is: why would I?'

By this time, though all involved had been sworn to the strictest confidentiality, a tale had begun to spread in Forest Park – and even in some quarters in Manhattan – that something extreme had happened involving the composer Rolfe Christensen. In one version of the story Christensen was the aggressor, in another the victim. Who can explain the genesis of such stories – rumours wispy and insubstantial as vapour at the start, rapidly broadening, deepening, taking strength until the entire landscape is obscured by smoke and the air fevered with crackling flame? Each of the members of the committee on ethics and faculty responsibility was the sort of person who respected confidentiality and could not conceivably have told anyone about Brendan Bauer and his accusations; neither Calvin Gould nor Andrew Woodbridge, fearful of scandal, would have told a living soul; Maggie Blackburn certainly did not tell anyone; and it was inconceivable too that Brendan Bauer, in a state of dread of being found out and identified as the victim of a rapist, would have told anyone. Yet within forty-eight hours of Maggie Blackburn's initial conversation with Calvin Gould, rudiments of the scandal were known in Forest Park.

Monday evening at eight o'clock the telephone rang in Maggie's home, and it was her friend Portia: 'Maggie, my God, have you *heard* – about Rolfe Christensen and one of our new graduate fellows?'

The registered letter sent to Rolfe Christensen at his Littlebrook address could not be delivered; and even after Christensen finally returned home, late in the evening of September 26, and learned, by way of a quick telephone call to Bill Queller, what the situation was, how grim, how grave, how seemingly inescapable, the composer would haughtily refuse to sign for it. Discovering several postal notices in his mailbox, along with his regular mail, Christensen tore them to bits in a fury.

All of September 27, a Tuesday, and September 28, Rolfe Christensen spent incommunicado in his home, unplugging his telephone and refusing to answer his doorbell. By now it was known in Forest Park that he had returned, but how could he be forced to speak with the Conservatory administration? Then, boldly, with theatrical extravagance, Rolfe Christensen drove to campus in a Bond Street-tailored grey flannel suit worn with an emerald silk ascot tie, his dove-grey fedora riding the crest of his large head, calmly ignoring the stares of students as he passed. (Did they know already? Had that lying little wretch Bower or Bowen or Brauer spread tales of him already? Or were these young people simply acknowledging Rolfe Christensen's admired presence in their midst, driving along the curving lanes of the

70

Conservatory campus in his familiar white BMW?)

Except for a token glass of wine or two, Rolfe Christensen had
had no alcohol that day; but he showed a seasoned drinker's
flushed, damply swollen face as he stormed ('stormed' was the
only adequate word) into the administration building and into the
provost's office, without so much as a glance at the provost's
secretary. He yanked open the door to Calvin Gould's inner
office and, paying no mind to the fact that Calvin had a visitor, he
loudly demanded, 'Just what is going on here, Gould? *Just what
the hell are you people saying about me behind my back?*'

After several more days of angry resistance, Rolfe Christensen
finally consented to meet with the seven men and women who
had heard Brendan Bauer's confidential testimony; but brought
along with him, unexpectedly, an attorney named Steadman, a
trim, muscular man in his forties with shiny dark eyes and a
moustache that looked as if it had been pencilled in lightly on his
upper lip. Steadman's manner was knowing, sardonic and brisk;
he seemed very much at home with this case, as he called it, of
'crude character assassination and attempted blackmail'.

Steadman said, singling out Calvin Gould and Andrew Woodbridge for his particular attention, '*We* will establish what the evidence is here, and *we* will consider whether grounds for slander
or libel exist.'

For it was Rolfe Christensen's contention that there had been
no sexual assault against Brendan Bauer: no rape: only an 'innocent erotic interlude' following an evening of companionable
drinking, an interlude of a familiar, unexceptional sort indulged
in by two mutually consenting adults.

After, all, the complainant was hardly a child, or even an
undergraduate. 'We've learned that he isn't nearly so young as he
pretends to be,' Steadman said, 'but is in fact pushing thirty.'

'Brendan Bauer is twenty-seven years old,' Woodbridge said,
as if conceding a point. 'He *is* an adult by the statute. But that
doesn't exempt him from protection against physical assault, as
you well know. And even if "rape" were not the issue here, the

Forest Park Conservatory of Music adopted strict guidelines in 1984 regarding sexual harassment of students by members of the faculty. The student in question contends – '

'He is a liar,' Christensen said. 'A liar, an opportunist, a conniving little' – he shuddered and reconsidered his words and said – 'nonentity.'

Rolfe Christensen's account of the evening and night of September 17 conformed to Brendan Bauer's in certain general ways but differed radically in others. Christensen did acknowledge that he had met, and befriended, the young composer at Maggie Blackburn's party; that they had gone to Christensen's house together, primarily to listen to a tape of Christensen's 'Adagio for Piano and Strings'; yes, there had been some drinking – but not an excessive amount; yes there had been the 'erotic interlude' – but Bauer had initiated it, and Bauer had extended it, and Bauer had all but confessed, in the morning, when Christensen was driving him home, that he did such things now and then to punish himself, for he was one of those who took pleasure from pain and had had to leave the seminary for this reason.

Andrew Woodbridge said sceptically, but politely, 'Why, then, did the young man go to the home of one of our faculty members and tell her in a state of hysteria what had happened to him? Why has he come to *us*?'

Rolfe Christensen drew breath to speak, but his attorney Steadman spoke for him. 'That isn't a question my client is bound to answer. The burden of proof is on you. This is not a trial, or even a hearing, and if serious accusations are made against Mr Christensen please be advised that we will respond with serious counter-measures.' He paused, and smiled, and with a glance at Rolfe Christensen, who sat grim and impassive beside him, said, 'And if Mr Christensen's public reputation is damaged by any of this, for instance by slanderous rumours emanating from this office, the measures *will* be serious.'

'Surprised to feel these fingertips on my arm . . . turned to see a fey sort of youngish man . . . smiling . . . pressing rather close . . .

no mistake about his intention and of course we'd both been drinking . . . flattered me I suppose talking about my music but I didn't really sense it . . . not by nature a suspicious, still less a paranoid sort of personality. So I invited this – Brower, is it? – Bauer . . . back to the house with me . . . he wanted to see my music studio . . . wanted to hear my "Adagio for Piano and Strings" . . . we got along rather well I was thinking . . . he was most affectionate . . . I see now in retrospect that it was the most crass sort of . . . the most cold-blooded sort of . . . hypocrisy . . . opportunism . . . but at the time how did I know! how did I know! . . . though I might have guessed, considering the way he stood marvelling at my photographs . . . my citations, awards, and such . . . hands on his hips rather suggestively . . . cockily . . . his eyes practically aglow with excitement I seem to have mistakenly imagined was for *me* . . . for my work . . . though in fact he did praise the "Adagio" effusively . . . a work of genius he called it . . . he *was* high . . . spoke of having smoked some hashish before coming to the reception . . . pushing himself on to me rather aggressively but how did I know, how did I know! I seem to have been a victim of my own . . . failure to be suspicious. And so this Brower, or Bauer, is it . . . well, naturally . . . I do have certain in-clinations . . . tastes . . . I *am* human . . . I don't apologize for myself . . . see no need to defend myself . . . this Bauer was cer-tainly forthright . . . fey and simpering as if butter wouldn't melt in his mouth, in public . . . and then in private *very* different . . . *very* different . . . I've witnessed such transformations in the past but I am always surprised when they occur. And so we . . . there was . . . as I've said there was this "erotic interlude" . . . in the young man's insistence upon it I was overcome . . . lost my sense of . . . propriety you might say . . . for he wasn't identified quite yet in my mind with being a student . . . yes, he was enrolled in my seminar, true, but at the time I didn't know that . . . the first class hadn't met . . . I admit I was susceptible . . . I *was* drinking . . . I *am* human . . . I simply lost all track of what was happening, lost all track of time, and even where we were . . . it must have been hours . . . I was unconscious for some of the time . . . I believe he did it deliberately, urged me to exhaust myself . . . expend myself . . . later after he was gone I discovered he'd been prowling through the house . . . going through drawers . . . my personal correspondence . . . my financial records, jewellery . . . a tie clip seems to be missing . . . an inscribed copy of a book by Lenny Bernstein . . . some trinkets and mementoes from travel . . . so humiliating! outrageous! But at the time I had no idea of course, not the slightest . . . he'd encouraged me to "play rough" as he called it . . . *he* was certainly rough . . . uninhibited . . . shameless. Not at all the way he advertises himself . . . hardly! But then in the morning . . . when the giddiness had worn off . . . when he was inspecting his bruises . . . the devious little hypocrite claimed he couldn't remember most of what had happened . . . claimed I'd gotten him drunk . . . began to rant and sob about sin . . . leaving the seminary . . . the *s-s-s-seminary*. And being punished by God.'

Only at the end did Rolfe Christensen betray some of the emotion he was feeling as, cruelly, yet with a ferocious sort of humour, he mimicked Brendan Bauer's stammer and glanced at his male colleagues with a wink of complicity, as if confident they wouldn't be able to resist laughing.

But there was silence. A startled silence. One of the women rose to leave, with the excuse that her migraine headache was so painful she could no longer see or hear or think clearly.

In that heartless fashion, unsurprising in retrospect but wholly unanticipated at the time, thus deeply upsetting to Calvin Gould and the others, Rolfe Christensen defended himself against the charges that were to be brought against him.

Even during a ninety-minute interrogative period Christensen managed to speak with restraint and conviction. Though it was clear that he and his attorney had rehearsed their salient points, down to the precise phrasing of certain key sentences, Christensen seemed to grow increasingly sincere; he was the very image of a vain, ageing man, susceptible to flattery, both humiliated and outraged by what had befallen him at the hands of a manipulative young person. 'If Rolfe Christensen is lying,' Calvin Gould said, marvelling, to Andrew Woodbridge, after the session was adjourned, 'he gives the uncanny impression of not knowing he is lying.'

Said Woodbridge, grimly, wiping his face with a tissue, 'The man is mad. Sick and mad. He creates a sort of madness around him.'

No one believed Christensen, of course. For he *was* the man he was; his colleagues knew him; his shadowy reputation preceded him.

At the same time, his account of the 'innocent erotic interlude' was quite convincing. He told it, and retold it, and insisted upon it, exactly as he would have done were it true. And he *was* Rolfe Christensen, after all: the Pulitzer Prize-winning composer and the most distinguished faculty member of the Forest Park Conservatory of Music.

Eight

Through her life, beginning as a young girl in St Paul, Minnesota, expected to perform flawlessly at the piano for the admiration (and gratification) of her family, Maggie Blackburn had been susceptible to feelings of unreality. All this is happening, she might think, but it is not happening to me. Such thoughts assailed her during piano recitals; and afterwards, when she had to face out into an audience of applauding strangers; and during intimate conversations, with men in particular, which always took her by surprise. These incursions of unreality had the effect of dream remnants incompletely recalled during the day: they were haunting, at times very much so; they could not be confronted head on (for dreams, the products of unconsciousness, resist definition by consciousness), yet they were undeniably present.

For some reason Maggie began to feel this way about the Christensen – Bauer case, as it came quickly to be known in Forest Park. The numerous hearings – meetings – negotiations taking place in October seemed to her mysteriously, and disagreeably, involved with her own life, though for the most part they occurred at a considerable remove from it. She was asked to attend a single session, to give her testimony about Brendan Bauer's visit, but apart from that she had nothing to do with the committee's protracted discussions and knew only what Brendan reported to her (though with the passage of weeks Brendan himself did not know a good deal, for the official committee met in secret, and it was rumoured that negotiations were a matter of the two attorneys determining some sort of decision), and what tales, lurid, airy, improbable, contradictory, circulated in Forest Park. 'These things are happening,' Maggie instructed herself, 'but they are *not* happening to me.'

Still, Maggie could not shake off the conviction that, in coming to her home that afternoon, in appealing to her for help, Brendan Bauer had not so much initiated a bond between them as confirmed one. From the first, when the tall self-conscious stammering young man had come into her office at the Conservatory, Maggie had felt there was something special – fated? – about him. It was not that she liked him – for, indeed, Maggie Blackburn was one of those teachers who feel a good deal of affection for their students, as if in a way they were all nieces or nephews, thus all special; she did not like Brendan Bauer nearly so much as she'd come to like other students over the years, her devoted and industrious piano students. 'I feel responsible for Brendan,' Maggie told people who wondered why, apart from the general outrage the community felt at Christensen's unconscionable behaviour, Maggie should care so much, be so emotionally involved. 'I feel as if ... I might have prevented it somehow,' she said. At such times her forehead creased into worry lines and her large pale eyes appeared unfocused.

Said Portia MacLeod, drily, 'The only certain way of preventing Rolfe Christensen from misbehaving is to take an axe to him.'

Portia's remark was meant to be both amusing and shocking, as many of Portia's more extreme remarks were meant, and the intimate gathering of like-minded friends before whom she had uttered it responded with appropriate laughter.

Except, pointedly, for Maggie Blackburn – who stared off worriedly into space, fists bunching her oyster-white linen slacks at the knees, clearly not having heard.

What had really happened between the two men?

And what action, if any, would the Conservatory take against its most prominent figure?

Because of the seriousness of the Christensen – Bauer

incident, which still threatened to become a criminal case, thus involving the school in what would surely be an ugly public scenario, the original seven-member committee on ethics and faculty responsibility had been expanded to include the Dean of Faculty, the Dean of Students, the Director of Humanities, the Composition Department Chairman, the Head of Psychological Services, and two students – one a graduate student, the other an undergraduate. This unwieldy group met several times a week through much of the autumn, their meetings closed, and conducted without the presence of either Rolfe Christensen or Brendan Bauer. Negotiating in tandem with the committee, but conferring too in private, the attorneys Woodbridge and Steadman were also involved, and their protracted deliberations too were in strictest confidence. Yet men and women in Forest Park talked of little else.

In theory, no one was supposed to know about the incident at all. Members of the committee were awkwardly obliged to pretend that their committee did not exist; or, if it did exist, that it possessed no agenda. And though Brendan had been repeatedly assured from the first that his name would not be released, somehow, who knows how, within days of his initial meeting with the committee, the name Brendan Bauer was known by virtually everyone in the Forest Park community and freely batted about. Was this faceless and anonymous composition student who was in fact not a student (Brendan had temporarily withdrawn from the Conservatory with a vague hope of registering again in January) a rapist's victim? A blackmail-minded troublemaker? A disgruntled boyfriend of Rolfe Christensen's? A total stranger to Rolfe Christensen? One of Rolfe Christensen's 'most brilliant, most promising' composition students? Was he a rawboned farm-boy from Iowa or Nebraska or a seminarian from Montana? A Gay Rights advocate from New York City? Even those few people who had actually met and spoken with the young graduate student speculated extravagantly about him and about *what had really happened between the two men* in Rolfe Christensen's house.

Hearing these rumours and being, in fact, asked to verify some

78

of them, Maggie felt sickened, helpless, trapped into suggesting, by the vehemence with which she denied them, that she knew the true story – a story so lurid and scandalous she dared not speak of it. 'It's in everyone's best interests not to spread rumours,' Maggie said earnestly. 'The poor young man –' And she stopped, forced herself to stop. For she was already too closely associated with the case, and with Brendan's accusations against Christensen, to risk involving herself still further.

In some quarters – misogynist rather than gay – it was believed that Maggie Blackburn was a militant feminist who had launched a personal vendetta against Rolfe Christensen; with the complicity of one of her students, she had manoeuvred the elder composer into being suspended from his job. (The fact was, Rolfe Christensen had been suspended from his teaching duties for the autumn term, pending the decision of the committee – but he had been suspended on full pay.) Friends in Forest Park shielded Maggie from such preposterous rumours, but friends and acquaintances elsewhere began to telephone her to ask what was happening. One evening Maggie's undergraduate roommate, now a professor of musicology at Stanford, telephoned to ask, in alarm, 'Maggie, do you have any idea what people are saying about you?'

Feeling suddenly faint, Maggie said, stammering, 'About m-me?'

Brendan Bauer finally, if belatedly, consented to be examined by a doctor, a private physician with an office on Route 1 of whom no one had heard, and his medical report was made available to the committee, for whatever worth it provided. Consequently the rumour began to spread anew – it was mid-October now – that Rolfe Christensen's victim was going to go to the police; yet a counter-rumour immediately followed, surely initiated by Christensen's attorney, Steadman, that Rolfe Christensen intended to bring a civil suit against both Brendan Bauer and the Conservatory for slander, defamation of character and breach of contract. On the morning that Maggie appeared before the committee, this

79

issue appeared to be uppermost in their minds; no one said so explicitly, but Maggie sensed that her colleagues, even Calvin Gould and Andrew Woodbridge, even the somewhat abrasive Dean of Faculty Peter Fisher, were beginning to be intimidated by Steadman (who had a history, it was learned, of winning large lawsuits for his clients) and had become, however subtly, less sympathetic to Brendan Bauer. She said, her voice trembling, 'But we know – we all *know* – what happened. I've told you exactly what Brendan told me, as much as I remember of it, and I – I'm morally certain – I'm absolutely convinced that everything he says is true, that there are things Brendan has not even wanted to say that would add to his – to the case. And we must not' – here Maggie's voice shook almost painfully – 'abandon him.'

Maggie Blackburn spoke with such uncharacteristic passion, there seemed a sort of pale, radiant flame about her; her fine-boned, beautiful face was luminous, her normally colourless eyes alert and shining. As if empowered by conviction – by a right-eousness that was in fact *right* – she seemed even to take no special notice of Calvin Gould, in whose presence she was custo-marily subdued and self-effacing. And, indeed, Calvin regarded Maggie with an expression of extreme interest, as if he had never seen her before; as if she were a woman entirely new to him.

Maggie went on, 'I've counselled Brendan to go to the police. He's fearful of the publicity and a possible trial – but he knows he should go through with it, he says he *knows* what he should do. I realize that you are all concerned with the reputation of the school, but it seems to me wrong, it seems to me unconscionable, it seems to me *criminal*, that Rolfe Christensen, because of his stature, should be absolved from charges of rape, and assault, and God knows what all else – keeping that terrorized young man captive in his house, threatening his life.'

So Maggie Blackburn spoke, and she did not know if it was a good sign, or a troubling one, that the members of the com-mittee, most of them well known to her, did not argue; sat listen-ing respectfully, even grimly, to her; asked only a few questions and seemed satisfied with her answers, as if everything she had to say, everything she knew, were already known to them.

Only afterwards did she recollect how Calvin Gould had looked at her. He was, himself, rather more the worse for wear – fatigued, unusually taciturn, remote. As the most powerful member in that little assemblage he had seemed, for the time at least, to have abdicated his role; others spoke, others asked questions, while Calvin sat with his elbows on the table, turning an inexpensive ballpoint pen between his fingers, frowning, staring at her. She thought, *He* will see to it that justice is done.

Only once in five weeks, and that by chance, did Maggie Blackburn happen to see Rolfe Christensen – at a performance, in November, in the conservatory's concert hall, of the Amsterdam String Quartet. Christensen was stylishly dressed in a russet-red sports coat, black silk ascot tie, checked trousers; with no suggestion of self-consciousness, or even defiance, he loomed tall, bigheaded, at ease amid the crowd, and afterwards at the reception talked at length, very cheerfully, with the Amsterdam players, whom he seemed to know fairly well. His complexion was redmottled and his eyes rather puffy, his hair whiter than Maggie recalled but handsomely brushed, with a sheen as of metal; he was aware of people looking frankly at him, surely whispering of him, but then people had always done so, there was a sort of creaturely satisfaction in being the cynosure of interest and speculation, and in a way Maggie envied him: for in his place, so exposed, so shamed, she could never make a public appearance: the very thought was inconceivable.

A tale had recently made the rounds that Rolfe Christensen had had a 'nervous collapse' – that, in fact, both Brendan Bauer and Rolfe Christensen had had 'nervous collapses' – but Christensen's appearance that evening dramatically contradicted such gossip; and Maggie happened to know that Christensen had been in Paris for a week, in late October, attending a performance of one of his early symphonies, after which he'd flown somewhere southerly and exotic – Tangier, maybe, or Casablanca. (Brendan Bauer, though he'd had no nervous collapse either, was ravaged-looking most days, solitary and obsessed with the case, but meeting twice weekly with a campus psychologist for what was called crisis therapy.)

During the concert Maggie had found herself, despite her effort to concentrate, repeatedly distracted by the figure of Rolfe Christensen seated several rows in front of her; at the crowded reception she had to fight an impulse to slip away early, and unseen by him, as if believing the two of them could not share the same space, breathe the same air. Maggie had particular reason to think of Rolfe Christensen because, a few days before, her red canary had died at last, of an apparent respiratory infection, and her house was deathly silent. (Since his mate's death, poor Rex had outdone himself in song, waking Maggie at dawn each day and accompanying her in urgent trills and warbles and prolonged piccolo-like flights as she practised the piano. His outburst of energy had been explained to Maggie as a natural, instinctive response to his mate's disappearance, which Maggie had guessed must be the case; there was a melancholy logic to it.) But Maggie had no spirit to replace the canary and had hidden the bamboo cage away in the basement.

'It's like a t-t-tomb in here,' Brendan had unthinkingly remarked, when he'd dropped by as he did once or twice a week.

At the reception Maggie could not fail to note with a shiver how Rolfe Christensen's gaze skimmed over, passed through with the icy finesse of a razor blade, *her*. But she was not to be daunted and remained with a little group of friends and colleagues, her head high, her silvery-blonde hair wound in braided coils and fastened in place with large tortoiseshell clips. She wore a pewter-grey jersey dress just slightly too long in the waist, and her slender neck appeared burdened by several chunky heirloom necklaces, but she was relaxed, even festive, or gave that impression. Said Portia in a laughing undertone, 'You really have to admire Rolfe Christensen, don't you, the man is so without shame', and Maggie said rather tartly, 'Isn't shame what makes us human?'

Later, in the cloakroom, as Maggie was putting on her coat,

she felt someone help her, and thinking it was one of her friends turned her smiling face upwards – to see that it was Christensen himself, smiling down at her mockingly. When Maggie shrank involuntarily from him he smiled more broadly, and said, 'I haven't seen you, Maggie, in a long time, since that lovely party of yours. I hope you've been well?'

'Y-yes,' Maggie said weakly. 'I've been well.'

'And so have I,' Rolfe Christensen said, staring. 'And so have I.'

Nine

And then, on November 19, the tension of weeks was resolved, though not as Maggie Blackburn had expected.

She was surprised to receive a telephone call at home in the early evening from Peter Fisher, informing her of the committee's decision based upon an agreement drawn up, after countless hours of deliberation, by the attorneys Woodbridge and Steadman: Brendan Bauer had consented not to press criminal charges, but Rolfe Christensen would never again teach any students at the Conservatory. His teaching duties were permanently suspended. He would, however, retain his office on campus, his rights and privileges as a faculty member, his rank as Distinguished Professor and Composer-in-Residence.

Quickly, Maggie said, 'And his salary?'

'I'm afraid so, yes.'

'His *salary*?'

'Yes. His salary.'

There was a moment's silence.

Peter Fisher went on to say that they hadn't much choice really, for reasons he couldn't divulge, but Maggie wasn't listening. Several times she said, 'I don't understand, Peter,' and 'I can't ... believe it,' and, dazed, perplexed, 'His *salary*, you say? Rolfe Christensen's *full salary*?'

After they hung up Maggie sat for many minutes listening to the ringing silence of her house, too weak even to feel as if she had been betrayed.

In recent weeks it had indeed been advanced, as one of the

more outrageous and cowardly options open to the Conservatory, that the administration would settle with Rolfe Christensen by relieving him of his teaching duties, hence the man's direct, presumably contaminating contact with students, but maintaining him at his enormous salary; Maggie Blackburn had impatiently dismissed such cynicism, for it reflected ill upon the administration, prominent among whom was Calvin Gould. *He* would not consent to such a legal expediency. And now it had come about – and now it was so.

Her enemy was not to be punished at all. He was in fact to be rewarded for having raped a student.

Maggie Blackburn had not known how furious she was with Brendan, for whom, she'd thought, she felt such sympathy and pity . . . but when, the next evening, the young man rang her doorbell, grim and sullen, his plastic schoolboy glasses still mended with adhesive tape, she had an impulse to slam the door in his face.

But she invited him inside of course, made him one of her absentminded but nourishing little meals, and the two of them sat together in her kitchen, humbled by events, bewildered, not quite knowing what to say. 'But how could you have consented to such a thing, Brendan, how could *you*?' Maggie said, regarding the young man as if she'd never seen him clearly before. 'The most shameful sort of . . . legal expediency.'

Brendan shrugged his narrow shoulders, wiped his nose roughly with the edge of his hand. He was wearing a frayed corduroy jacket, nondescript trousers, soiled running shoes. The bruise above his eye had faded, but his skin had a raw, abraded look, as if it had been rubbed with sandpaper. Since beginning psychological therapy he spoke with a mockingly eerie, measured detachment about himself, and though he still stammered he did so, Maggie thought, with an air almost of deliberation.

Maggie repeated her words, for Brendan seemed scarcely to have heard, and again he shrugged, an overgrown sullen adolescent, and said he hadn't had any choice; there had been no witnesses to the assault; it could be reduced to one man's testimony against another's, as both lawyers insisted upon saying repeatedly. If he went to the police, and if the issue came to trial, the publicity would be devastating for everyone, Brendan Bauer included. And there would be other problems too, for Brendan. 'Could *I* be c-c-cross-examined – on the witness stand, by a hostile attorney? – with my gifts of l-l-language?' he said, sneering.

Maggie said impatiently, 'You might have tried. There might not have been any trial; there might have been a settlement out of court.'

'There *is* a s-s-settlement out of court.'

'But in Rolfe Christensen's favour! In that terrible man's favour!'

'He isn't just t-terrible, he's – Rolfe Chr-Chr-Christensen.'

Suddenly they were quarrelling, like a sister and a brother who have lived together too long, tried each other's nerves too systematically. Maggie Blackburn, that most gentle and premeditated of women, lifted her hands in frustration, made a gesture of clamping her palms over her ears. 'How *could* you, Brendan! You! After coming to me, after all we've talked of it! After finally going to a doctor! After being brave enough to give your testimony, make your charges, and now you've capitulated – '

'I didn't have any *choice*, they were nice to me and s-s-sorry and want me to s-study here, my God they t-t-talked to me for hours, I was worn out, I'd c-c-capitulate to anything; what do *you* know, Miss Blackburn, M-Maggie, *you* weren't there, *you* weren't the v-victim, *you* have a job and a place in the god-damned w-w-world; who are *you* to tell me what to do!'

'But now that man is free to do it again and again – he has been rewarded for – '

'I don't give a damn if he does it again! Leave me alone!'

Furiously Maggie said, 'You don't? Truly – you don't?'

Brendan Bauer drew the edge of his hand beneath his nose and said, not quite so vehemently, 'Why should I? – every man for h-h-h-himself.'

Maggie was on her feet. 'Please leave this house.'

Brendan stared up at her, squinting, as if he hadn't quite heard. 'What?'

'Please. Just leave.'

He rose slowly, uncurving his spine from the wicker-backed kitchen chair, blinking, making an almost visible effort to recover his pride. At first it seemed that Maggie was too upset even to walk him to the door, but her good manners prevailed and she accompanied him, her heart pounding in her chest, her fingers shut into fists, and Brendan said, not contritely or even defensively but as if he were offering a simple, belated explanation, 'The person who counselled me most, in private, was the P-P-Provost, Mr Gould. He's right: I'd never be able to endure a t-t-trial, my family would know, everyone would know, even if I w-won I'd l-l-lose, that's how "sexual harassment" cases always are: if you win you lose, nobody w-w-wants you around, nobody will hire you, you're f-f-fouled, you're *disgusting*, it's true. I'm not going to give up my m-music though, I've been writing all this time, I've been working all this time, Mr Gould promised that when I came back –'

Maggie Blackburn ushered her guest out the door and without ceremony shut it after him.

All this is happening but it is not happening to me.

The remainder of that night would be a puzzle to Maggie, for she must have entered one of her fugue states, her amnesiac states, within minutes of getting into her car and driving in pursuit of Brendan Bauer. She repented of her harshness, her inhospitality to a guest, she could not comprehend her anger at the young man and felt she must apologize at once, bring him back if possible; he was after all the victim of a brutal assault, *he* was entirely innocent and required her sympathy; so there was Maggie driving her car rather erratically along Acacia Drive . . . down the long hill to Grandview, then to Meridian . . . in the direction Brendan Bauer must surely have gone on his way home. She bit her lower lip; her eyes welled with tears. How could she of all people have been so cruel! It was not like Maggie Blackburn, was it? It *was* not Maggie Blackburn, was it? Already she had begun to forget the shocking words Brendan had uttered before leaving her house, the world was becoming blurred and muffled as if seen through pigmented glass, her nerves were taut as a half-dozen times she was convinced she saw the young man walking ahead on the sidewalk, a tall thin hurrying figure, yet each time to her keen disappointment it was not Brendan but a stranger, in one case a young black man who grinned derisively at her, and as she drove along Meridian to busy, brightly lit State Street she felt the onset of the amnesiac fugue as a high humming in her skull while at the same time (and this was the peculiar thing, this was the mysterious thing) she continued to recognize herself as the agent of action, the core of consciousness, as if seeing herself from a comfortable distance, without emotion, even as, as Maggie Blackburn with her fingers clenched hard about the steering wheel of her Volvo, her face creased with worry, she was feeling the strange empowerment of rage, her blood beat with it, a righteousness deep in her bones, for she was in fact furious with Brendan Bauer without knowing exactly why, she was furious with Maggie Blackburn without knowing exactly why, and driving in the direction of Route 1 she intended to go to Brendan's apartment building to await him thinking that she would apologize for her rudeness, perhaps she hadn't irrevocably insulted the young man, but somehow she lost the thread of her concentration and an hour or so later she was driving north on the turnpike seeing signs for New Rochelle and still later she was in a brightly glaring turnpike restaurant drinking a glass of water, swallowing aspirin tablets, 'Yes, thank you, I'm all right, I'm certainly all right,' she said, and at another time she saw someone approaching her, emerging from beneath a ragged awning, but she turned quickly away, she was wearing flat-heeled shoes thus could walk swiftly, and in her car on the turnpike she saw lights rising and passing her with an ease that made her sigh for she *was* safe after all, no one could touch or harm her.

All this is happening but it is not happening to me.

She was thinking of that Sunday afternoon several years before, following a recital at the Conservatory when she had given a pinched, inadequate performance of Chopin's *Preludes* and had had to confront an audience transformed by delight, friendly smiling faces, rows of applauding hands, and she'd endured the shame of it but slipped away desperate to be gone and later that afternoon – it was late spring, damply warm and sunny – she'd gone to walk in the parkland near the Conservatory, desperate to escape from even her own house, and there in the park she saw, surprised, a figure lying in an open grassy space that might have been a derelict except there were no derelicts in this suburban village, were there? – a young or youngish woman in a khaki jacket, shapeless trousers with a front zipper carelessly zipped so that a corner of a white shirt-tail peeked through, frizzy dark hair like a cloud about her head, and as Maggie drew forwards fascinated she saw that the woman asleep on the grass was of all people Naomi Gould. She had a small triangular face, a lean flat-chested body, strong cheekbones and heavy brows, and a fleshy attractive mouth. Was she sleeping? Or was she slyly watching Maggie approach through her part-closed eyes? Embarrassed, Maggie said, 'Hello? Is it . . . Mrs Gould? I'm Maggie Blackburn, a colleague of your husband's. I believe we've never met, but . . . ' and with an irritated gesture the woman who was so very improbably Naomi Gould raised herself on one elbow and said, 'Yes,' in a flat chill voice, 'we've never met,' and turned over lazily as if she were in bed, as if she were indeed a person accustomed to sleeping in public places, and there stood Maggie Blackburn staring down at her beginning to feel how she herself was obliterated, as if erased, as, by degrees, the woman known as Naomi Gould fell back asleep.

Part II

Ten

Some time in the late afternoon of November 29, 1988, a young woman sales clerk for Heidi's Imported Chocolates, 522 East 60th Street, Manhattan, sold two boxes of Austrian gourmet chocolates to a customer who made a distinct impression on her: the customer was a woman of indeterminate age, tall, heavily made up, wearing dark, oversized glasses and a lavender turban that completely covered her head, and a bulky leather coat, and dark leather gloves. She had applied make-up to her face with a theatrical flair, or compulsiveness, so that her very skin looked encrusted; her lips were ruby-red and appeared enlarged. She moved stiffly, even awkwardly, as if she were unaccustomed to her leather boots with their two-inch heel.

Watching the customer, the young woman sales clerk felt a momentary stirring of the hairs on the nape of her neck. 'My first thought was – maybe this was a crazy thought but it went through my head this might be a man impersonating a woman.'

After some minutes spent critically examining the displays of elegantly packaged candies, the customer drew the sales clerk's attention by loudly clearing her throat and then making a gesture of an apparently practised sort, fingers twirled toward her throat or mouth as if to indicate that she was incapable of speaking (was she a deaf-mute or suffering from some sort of illness? had her vocal cords been damaged or removed?) but that she could communicate by way of sign language, which in fact was the case, for the sales clerk had no difficulty determining which boxes of chocolates she was indicating inside the glass display case, nor

93

was there any difficulty in ringing up the sale since the customer paid cash.

In all, the transaction probably required less than ten minutes, and the young woman sales clerk for Heidi's Imported Chocolates would surely have forgotten it for ever, except for subsequent events.

Eleven

'What *is* it, Maggie? We've all been so curious.'

Maggie Blackburn found herself eagerly awaited in the departmental office on the morning of Monday, December 5, since an intriguingly large package had come for her in the mail that seemed (or so the secretaries had determined) *not* to be merely another book. The package was too oddly shaped to fit in Maggie's narrow mailbox; it was fastidiously wrapped in stiff brown paper with an excessive amount of crisscrossing transparent tape and string; MS MARGARET BLACKBURN and the address of the Forest Park Conservatory were printed in large block letters, in black ink, on two sides. Quite by chance – for Maggie Blackburn was hardly the sort of person to notice such details – Maggie happened to see that the zip code of the Conservatory was inaccurate by a single digit and that the package was postmarked New York City.

Gladys Moyer, the administrative assistant, and Louise and Jody, the office secretaries, helped Maggie open the package, for it was like a puzzle, so elaborately tied and taped. Then, amid exclamations, Maggie unwrapped what appeared to be a Valentine's Day present: a glossy red satin heart-shaped box of chocolates, three dozen in all, in a double-tiered arrangement. Some of the candies were wrapped in gold foil, and each was exquisite as a jewel. Maggie's immediate thought was that the gift must have come from Matt Springer – for whom else did she know, what other man had there been in recent years who might have so much as considered sending her a romantic gift like this? – but the little card inside the box suggested otherwise. *From one of those many grateful pupils of M.B. over the years, J.*

At least the letter resembled *J*; it was slightly smudged.

Mrs Moyer said, marvelling, 'Isn't this lovely! *Isn't* it a surprise! Do you know who *J* is, Maggie? He – or she; I suppose it could be "she" – is certainly fond of you.'

Not fond, Maggie thought. Grateful.

She turned the card in her fingers, trying to think who *J* could be, and feeling her cheeks, cool from the out-of-doors, rapidly heat. So much attention embarrassed her (for others were coming into the office, colleagues and students; at this time of the morning the departmental office was a cheerful much-trafficked place); yet of course she was pleased, and touched; at the same time (though she managed to hide this) she could not fail to feel a keen ache of disappointment, for a luxurious box of chocolates from a piano pupil is not quite the same thing as a luxurious box of chocolates from a lover, even a former lover. Maggie thought, Of course it couldn't be Matt Springer; he has forgotten me entirely as I've almost forgotten him.

The thought struck her: 'It's probably Jennifer Lehman – you all remember Jenny, don't you? – I got a very nice card from her weeks ago, from London. She said she was coming home for the holidays.'

So it seemed established, on such slender evidence, that the mysterious *J* was a 1986 graduate of the Forest Park Conservatory, a gifted young woman pianist currently teaching and studying in London.

Maggie passed her gift box liberally about, and some eight or ten or twelve people sampled the chocolates, pronouncing them delicious; she would have left the box with Mrs Moyer and the others, for the rich gourmet chocolates were simply too much for her – she'd inherited from her mother a vague moral disapproval of such extravagant foods – but Mrs Moyer vehemently protested. She was one of those older, well-intentioned female presences in Maggie's life who believed that Maggie slighted herself; less intrusive than Portia MacLeod, for she was after all

96

not nearly so close to Maggie, she shared with Portia a conviction that, in her unmarried and presumably loveless state, Maggie had an obligation to reward herself more visibly. 'You must take the present home; it's for *you*,' Mrs Moyer said, shutting up the red satin heart and giving it to her. 'It wasn't sent to *strangers*.'

Maggie did not see the logic of this but would not quarrel and, chastised, carried the box back with her to her office, where she set it prominently on her desk so that students and colleagues could sample the candies. Maggie's office, too, as a consequence of her administrative duties, was a much-trafficked place; within a day or so all the chocolates – milk chocolates and bittersweet chocolates and chocolate-covered Brazil nuts and nougats and cherries and creams and liqueurs – were safely gone.

Rarely did Maggie eat sweets, which she associated with childish, even infantile tastes and desires; but in a weak moment (when dusk had deepened to night, and the wind was blowing icy particles of snow against her office window, and she was still at her desk doing paperwork, answering memos, letters, graduate applications, there being no compelling reason for her to return to her silent, empty house, and the thought, *Oh why?* passed over her like a shadow) – in a weak moment she ate a single chocolate, one of the plainer ones, a dark rich solid chocolate, chewier than she might have expected, and extremely sweet. Sugar assailed the inside of her mouth as if it were a sort of acid or poison, achingly delicious.

The taste, which seemed to her faintly obscene, remained with her for hours.

'We know what that is, Mr Christensen, at least we *think* we do!'

On the afternoon of Thursday, December 8, Rolfe Christensen in his handsome sealskin coat, looking quite rested, even invigorated, dropped by his departmental office to pick up his mail (which accumulated in his absence, often taking up much of a table adjoining the faculty mailboxes); and there awaited him, delivered priority mail that morning, an oblong box of the size and approximate shape of a necktie box but with slightly more

97

thickness. It was heavier than one might have expected and was fastidiously wrapped in stiff brown paper with an excessive amount of crisscrossing transparent tape and string; MR ROLFE CHRISTENSEN, COMPOSER-IN-RESIDENCE and the address of the Forest Park Conservatory were printed in large block letters, in black ink, on two sides. Whether the zip code for the Conservatory was inaccurate by a digit or not Rolfe Christensen took no time to notice, nor did he trouble to open the intricately secured package himself; Mrs Moyer, who liked him so much, was happy to open it for him.

(Though Christensen was certainly the object of jealousy and rancour on the part of certain colleagues, he was unfailingly popular with the female departmental staff, expecially with white-haired Mrs Moyer, whom he effortlessly charmed. Christensen was one of those men, monumental in his own vision, like Wagner or Balzac, who enjoyed his own magnanimity of spirit as it applied to underlings in no way competitive with or even critical of him. Thus good-hearted Mrs Moyer, fond as she was of Maggie Blackburn, was fonder still of the distinguished Rolfe Christensen and would hear no evil of him from any quarter).

While Christensen bemusedly glanced through his other pieces of mail, flipping some envelopes directly into the waste-paper basket without troubling to open them and humming cheerfully under his breath – one of his own, freshly imagined compositions, to be worked into a tone poem cleverly built upon an inverted phrase of Mahler's – Mrs Moyer struggled with the package, using scissors, and tore away the paper, crying, 'Ah, look! It *is*! Just what we thought!'

But this gift was different from Maggie Blackburn's: an elegant little candy box resembling an old-fashioned jewel box, made of finely engraved lightweight aluminium and filled with one dozen chocolate-covered white truffles, imported from Vienna.

Rolfe Christensen quickly set aside his other items of mail and took up the candy box, his face radiating childlike pleasure. It was not simply that he had a weakness for chocolate; he had a weakness for quality, especially ostentatious quality, in any form. But what if the gift was a trick of some kind? What if the chocolates had been tampered with? He examined the little card that accompanied it and read aloud, '*From one of those countless grateful former students and devotees of R.C., without question the most brilliant composer of our time. Yours for ever, J.*'

'Isn't that thoughtful! Isn't that generous!' Mrs Moyer exclaimed. Her tone was nearly vehement as if, these many weeks, she had been defending the Conservatory's most prominent faculty member against certain of his detractors and would have liked them to see what he was holding so triumphantly now in his hand. 'If you can't guess who *J* is, Mr Christensen, there's a way you can find out.'

'What do you mean?'

'Well – maybe I shouldn't spoil the fun for you, and let you guess –'

'You know who sent this?'

'It's a piano student who graduated two years ago; she's studying now in London, and –'

'But how do you know that?'

'Because Maggie Blackburn received a gift box of chocolates from her the other day too, wrapped up exactly like yours. Not such fancy chocolates as yours, and not in such a beautiful box, but –' Rolfe Christensen's expression had stiffened, and he no longer appeared quite so delighted. 'I see,' he said. 'The Blackburn woman – too.'

'You must have had a student in common: Jennifer Lehman? Do you remember Jennifer? A very sweet young woman, a very talented young pianist.'

'Oh I'm sure I remember her – I'm sure I will,' Rolfe Christensen said carelessly. 'As long as the chocolates are all right.'

'They're absolutely delicious. Maggie passed her box around, and we all had some.'

'Well,' said Rolfe Christensen. 'Good.'

It was clear that the composer was losing interest in his present surroundings. He made no more effort to recall his former student and apparent devotee 'Jennifer Lehman' and gathered up his things, preparing to leave. A gentleman of impulsive charitable gestures, he certainly wished it were the case that his gift box was larger, so that he too could pass it around the office or at least offer a chocolate to Mrs Moyer, who was always doing him so many small favours; but it was not, and such delicacies were too precious to be squandered on anyone excepting a particular friend or houseguest.

As Rolfe Christensen, burly, kingly, silvery-haired, swept out of the office, Mrs Moyer said to her assistant, Louise, 'Isn't he a fine figure of a man! I don't care what jealous people say about him – I don't even *listen*.'

'Small consolation.'

Rolfe Christensen was often secretly angry when, in others' eyes, he appeared most pleased: for life was not a matter of mere surfaces to him, and each gift or award or honour or good notice he received brought with it a fresh and humiliating reminder that such boons came more readily to certain of his rivals; that they came, often, belatedly and even grudgingly to Rolfe Christensen; that they were in fact small consolations for the vaster, less tangible rewards certain of his contemporaries enjoyed – the genuine admiration of the young, the attention of music critics and theorists, the respect of performing artists. It seemed to Christensen a surpassing insult that no major performing artist had ever asked to play a composition of his. 'Why then should *I* go to hear Horowitz, Menuhin, Entremont, Pavarotti? Why should *I* buy their records?' His friends had long since learned to change the subject.

So far as the Conservatory was concerned, Christensen felt somewhat more at ease, though still ambivalent. The school was his home, so to speak, when he was in the States. (He spent a good deal of his time each year in Paris, Rome, Tangier.) He was proud of his position – and of his gratifyingly high salary – and would have been mortified to lose them. Thus – perversely, as it seemed to some observers, yet quite naturally, as it seemed to others and to Christensen himself – the composer was in the habit of visiting campus more frequently than ever since the controversial decision of the committee on ethics and faculty responsibility suspending his 'teaching duties' but maintaining him as composer-in-residence. He knew that community opinion was divided; he had a vague awareness that there had been several short-lived protests organized – one of them a petition signed by a number of faculty members and sent to President Babcock; another a spontaneous demonstration in front of the administration building, led by graduate students in support of Brendan Bauer (whom most of them had never met) – Bill Queller had even mentioned an unsigned letter sent to the *New York Times* charging the Conservatory with a cover-up and inviting the newspaper to do an investigative report on the case. ('Let anyone talk who wants to talk,' Christensen said excitedly. 'If it gets into print, Steadman and I will slap them with defamation suits.') He understood that mean-spirited people would always gossip about him, yet that filled him, in a way, with a sense of purpose, even of elation. For Rolfe Christensen was not so easily defeated.

Since giving his testimony to the committee, and reiterating portions of it countless times, Christensen remembered not what had happened on the night of September 17 between him and young Brendan Bauer but what he'd testified; even within a day or two of the episode he was beginning to forget, as he often did in such situations. (There had been a few such, over the course of Christensen's varied and vigorous career.) Yes, he supposed he'd played rough with Bauer, or Brower, or Blower, whatever the young man's foolish name, and perhaps he regretted it, in retrospect at least, not for the hurt he'd caused (in which he did not much believe) but for the hurt he'd experienced and all the hypocritical rant of 'ethics' and 'responsibility'.

Yet the fact remained, he and the young man were mutually consenting adults. There had been no crime committed – surely!

One evening, his friend Bill Queller had surprised him by saying, out of nowhere, 'This poor boy – *must* you persecute him too?' Christensen had been incredulous. 'What do you mean, persecute him, persecute him *too*?' And Queller said, with a forcefulness unusual in him, 'Haven't you been telling the committee he's a liar, trying to blackmail you?' and Christensen retorted, 'How do you know what my defence is? The hearings are closed,' and Bill Queller said, 'Just answer my question, Rolfe: must you defame the poor boy too, in addition to having – well, injured him?' And so the men had argued, one of their very worst arguments, and Rolfe Christensen had sent his importunate friend home, and it was weeks before they were on speaking terms again. But Christensen felt he could never again trust Bill Queller, for what is friendship if it is not predicated upon loyalty?

Calvin Gould was not, strictly speaking, a friend of Rolfe Christensen's. But the man was *loyal*.

As were others, at the Forest Park Conservatory and elsewhere. For Christensen had had indeed a varied and vigorous career.

'And here I am, still.'

He was thinking of these matters, smiling to himself, as he strolled in the wintry sunshine, in no hurry, in the direction of his BMW, illegally parked behind the concert hall. Taking note of the wondering eyes of students – the frank stares of some – yet there were invariably those who brightened at the sight of him, the distinguished composer-in-residence, grinning – 'H'lo, Mr Christensen!' – favoured students of his of past semesters whose names he might have forgotten but whose attractive faces he had not. And there was Fritzie Krill with his piratical black beard and irreverent eyes, who should have been an ally surely? – yet with a clumsy pretence of being in a hurry, no time for more than a mumbled greeting as he passed, the contemptible little bastard.

Did Rolfe Christensen's colleagues think he would, however persecuted, simply *go away*?

Did the fools think that, if they chose to ignore him, he would not therefore *exist*?

In the BMW, as the motor roared and warmed, Christensen impulsively removed one of the chocolate-covered truffles from the box, unwrapped the gold foil, and tossed it, crumpled, out of the window; as he drove along the central campus road he chewed the delicacy, inner concentration intense. He was not addicted to chocolate, of course, but chocolate was an early and abiding love of his.

Where human beings have failed us, the pleasures of the stomach remain.

So Christensen devoured one of the chocolate-covered truffles and would, in a sudden rush of appetite, have unwrapped and devoured a second, but there came within moments an eerie counter-sensation, as of the earth shifting on its axis, or of infinite regret.

Not nausea but a violent and melancholy absence of nausea – an incapability of vomiting.

A sudden constriction of the chest. Something flamelike, rippling, in his throat, in his chest. And his mouth too, belatedly, though flooded with saliva, began to burn.

'Help! H-help me!'

Even as the BMW drifted off the road before the astonished eyes of onlookers, Christensen managed to get the door open, managed to stagger out, and fell to his knees on the snow-stubbled grass, crying for help. He tore at the collar of the seal-skin coat; he was gagging, choking, gracelessly heaving, and then, as passers by stared in horror, he began to writhe and convulse on the ground, no longer screaming but only gagging and grunting. He knew then that he had made an irrevocable error, but even as he knew he was incapable of comprehension, for the violent clawing and scalding and scouring pain that illuminated his body from within was beyond comprehension; he had not even the language to think *I have been poisoned* or *I am going to die*, nor could he hear the soft terrified cries of witnesses: 'It's Rolfe Christensen, isn't it?' and 'Oh, it's Mr Christensen!' and 'Oh, my God – is it Rolfe *Christensen?*'

In this convulsive agony, his face red and swollen as a tomato about to burst, his eyes bulging in their sockets, Rolfe Christensen no longer resembled himself or any person he had ever imagined he might be.

By the time an ambulance from the Forest Park Medical Centre arrived, Christensen was no longer conscious; by the time the ambulance delivered him to the emergency room of the Medical Centre, he had sunk into a deep coma.

And by the time Maggie learned of the episode, at 6.45 p.m. – she had been rehearsing, with Bill Queller, the Beethoven sonata for cello and piano they were scheduled to perform at a Conservatory recital in two weeks, the two of them hidden away in one of the soundproof practice rooms in Phillips Hall – Christensen was dead. His heart had stopped during the emergency room procedure and no effort of resuscitation could bring it back.

Hearing the astounding news, Maggie whispered, 'Oh – oh, *no*,' and for a moment seemed to lose consciousness, though she was able to remain on her feet. Her first sensation was not one of horror but of simple incredulity laced with guilt, as in a child who cannot comprehend that his deepest wish may have been granted, because it is his wish, and because it lies lodged so deep.

Twelve

I did not do it.

I did not calculatingly inject a dozen chocolate-covered truffles with poison and mail them to Rolfe Christensen with the intention of killing him.

I might have said I wanted to kill him. But I don't remember.

I might have said I wanted to kill him but I don't remember, and if I said those words I didn't mean them and if in the madness of saying them before witnesses I seem to have meant them I didn't commit the murder. I did not.

For hours he'd been waiting for the footsteps in the corridor and the knock on his door, and when at last, shortly before midnight, the police came for him, he gave himself up unprotestingly to their authority, grown exhausted by that time, physically depleted, broken. His limbs were trembling and his teeth faintly chattering and his stammer was bad . . . very bad . . . so like a muscular spasm that the police officers regarded him with looks of frank alarm. Was Brendan Bauer an epileptic, was he about to have a convulsion? He meant only to say, to explain, Yes I am Brendan Bauer, yes I know you have my name, yes I'll go with you and answer your questions but I am innocent, *I am the victim and this is a mistake and I am innocent*, but the helpless gagging sounds that issued from his mouth were scarcely recognizable as words.

'That's all right, son,' the eldest policeman said. 'You'll be all right.' Laying a hand on Brendan's shoulder not to coerce but to give comfort as, to his shame, Brendan burst into hot splashing tears.

He'd known they were coming because, earlier that evening, Maggie had called to tell him of the shocking news, the really quite incredible news: Rolfe Christensen was dead!

He had just come home from eating a distracted, tasteless meal in a diner within walking distance on Route 1 when the telephone rang. His heart lifted in hope – a friend? a friendly call? – even as he knew there could be no friendly call, for he had no friends in Forest Park. He'd shunned the company of the music students who might have befriended him and he had no promising acquaintance among the staff of the Book Mark (a new and used bookstore in the village of Forest Park, at which he'd recently begun work) and he knew that Maggie was unhappy about him and no longer cared to see him, yet he lifted the receiver hopefully, and indeed it was Maggie, but she sounded upset, extremely upset, for a brief while he was incapable of absorbing her words: something had happened to that bastard Christensen, someone had done something to that bastard Christensen? 'I think you should know, Brendan,' Maggie was saying, 'and be prepared.' He asked her to repeat her words. He was so surprised he didn't even stammer at first.

So Maggie in a low urgent voice told Brendan all she knew at that time, early evening of December 8, 1988, of the death of Rolfe Christensen: that he had died in the emergency room of the Forest Park Medical Centre at approximately 5.30 p.m.; that he had collapsed on the Conservatory campus, while driving his car; that it was believed he'd been poisoned by eating a piece of contaminated chocolate candy. Forest Park police were already making inquiries, Maggie had been told, and it was unavoidable that they would be given his name, Brendan Bauer's name, and told of the assault case hearings. 'I had to call you, Brendan, to warn you: you must be prepared.'

Numbly, Brendan said, 'Let me see if I understand all this. Rolfe Chr – Christensen died? Today? He's dead? He was poisoned?' Brendan swallowed hard. 'He was *m-m-murdered*?'

Maggie said softly that she thought it must be so: for it was not likely that he would have poisoned himself or that a box of chocolate-covered truffles would be accidentally laced with a lethal poison.

Brendan whispered, '*Murdered*,' in so low an undertone Maggie did not hear.

Brendan was bracing himself against a doorframe but he had no clear conception of where the doorframe was in the physical world, what the rooms were it divided. There was a murmurous swelling of sound inside his head like hundreds of kettledrums struck in unison.

His enemy – dead? So abruptly, and irrevocably, dead?

And he, Brendan Bauer – how was he implicated?

At this time, Maggie did not know precisely what sort of poison had killed Christensen; the forensic laboratory results would not be available for another day or two. She knew only by way of several friends, including Nicholas Reickmann, whom, as she told Brendan, she'd encountered on the steps of Phillips Hall, a look of astonishment on his face, that Rolfe Christensen had been poisoned and that the poison had been somehow embedded in a box of gift chocolates. As Maggie excitedly amplified the account, Brendan became more and more confused until finally he had the idea that Maggie too had received a gift box of poisoned chocolates in the mail – from a former student or from someone she'd erroneously presumed to be a former student. His head swam. 'But *you* weren't poisoned, Maggie, were you?' he asked. '*You* weren't?'

There was a moment's perplexed silence. Then Maggie said, 'Of course I wasn't, Brendan. If I had been, I wouldn't be alive now.'

As they talked, Brendan removed his glasses (which were still clumsily mended with soiled adhesive tape) and rubbed at his eyes. If since that terrible night in September he had frequently envisioned Rolfe Christensen dead – if in his most shameless and childish dreams of vengeance he had imagined himself the agent of his rapist's death – this sudden fulfilment of his wish gave him

107

no pleasure. For now the drama between them was over: Christensen could never be suitably exposed, punished, and forgiven; Brendan, who had been humiliatingly bound, wrists and ankles, and scorned, and abused, and assaulted, and reduced to the object, the receptacle, of another's grunting heedless lust, could never triumph over the circumstances of his degradation. And there was more: 'I – I didn't do it, Maggie, I didn't – you believe me, don't you?'

At once Maggie said, 'Of course I believe you, Brendan. Don't even say such things.'

Still bracing himself against the doorframe, as in a strong gale, Brendan said numbly, 'But I – I *didn't*. Please believe me.'

There was another brief pause. Brendan could imagine Maggie's face: the pale skin warm with feeling, animation; the eyes alight. She said, 'Maybe the police won't even question you, Brendan – maybe I've called you and worried you to no purpose.'

Brendan Bauer laughed bitterly.

After they hung up he began his wait, his vigil, for he knew of course they would come: it was not yet eight o'clock and he would have supposed they might come within the hour, at any moment; he prayed only that they would not speak with the building superintendent or any of the other tenants, his very bowels writhed in agony of more, and yet more cruel, public exposure. Since that terrible night in September – these were the terms in which Brendan thought of the incident: *that terrible night* – he was well aware of people looking at him covertly; well aware of talk behind his back, of irresponsible speculation. And he could not control it! He could not make the truth known!

And now the police were coming for him, now he must prepare to defend himself: *I might have said I wanted to kill him. But I don't remember.*

He heated up a pot of instant coffee and paced about in his tiny room-and-a-half drinking cup after cup of scalding bitter-black coffee; not minding, or not noticing, how the inside of his tender mouth was being burnt. The loathsome acts he'd been forced to perform with his mouth, in service to Rolfe Christensen: no scalding, no scouring, could ever be cleansing enough. *But don't think of that. Not now.* And his anus, tender too, and lacerated, and partially ruptured, and bruised ... and his genitals, his terrified penis in its soft, so vulnerable envelope of skin, an emblem, as he'd been taught for so many years in his Catholic schools, of sin, of shame, of that-which-must-be-overcome. *But don't think of that now. Don't think.*

Even as, in preparation for the police, Brendan cleaned his dirt-ridged fingernails with the prong of a fork, and washed his face energetically, and shaved, steadying his right hand by gripping his right elbow hard, he was thinking of flight: a bus to the Manhattan terminal where he might lose himself in humanity, hide, disappear, the wild notion of *forty days and forty nights in the wilderness* came to him, and certain hypnotic phrases of Varèse's *Ionisation* sounded piercingly in his head. Those orgasmic cries, howls, grunts of his rapist – his enemy! How could he, Brendan Bauer, who was so shy, so courteous, so stammering and ineffectual, hope to expunge them from his memory?

These past few months, he'd learned to shave without looking himself in the eyes.

What beautiful eyes those are Bren dan ... long-lashed like a girl's. And those tears! Sparkling tears! Jewels of tears! D'you know that tears too are a lubricant?

That morning in the Book Mark when Brendan was sorting a begrimed carton of used textbooks the store manager, a man named Pollock, fortyish, straggly-haired, greying, in a plaid flannel shirt with sleeves too short for his long arms, ambled by to chat and hinted strongly that he knew something of what had happened to Brendan that autumn, and Brendan had continued working, head bowed, eyes averted from Pollock's seemingly sympathetic face, and at last Pollock said, as if unable to resist a big-brotherly slyness, 'Look, Brendan – everybody knows. It's no secret.'

Everybody knows. It's no secret.

'And what I heard,' Pollock continued, 'is that the Conservatory gave you a raw deal. A truly raw deal. Am I right?'

Brendan Bauer shook his head mutely and shut his eyes.

Everybody knows. It's no secret.

But what do they know?

And what would they think they knew now, now that Rolfe Christensen had been murdered?

Shaving, Brendan Bauer's hand slipped. A tiny nick in his chin began to bleed. Still, he did not look himself in the eyes; he reasoned there was no need.

Blood too is a lubricant. Not too much – not too little.

Don't move! Don't.

Mmmmmmmmmmmmm Bren dan: sweet!

He could hear voices in the corridor outside his door, he could hear footsteps approaching his door and his heart stopped but there was – nothing. No one and nothing.

Nine-thirty. His enemy had been dead for four hours, yet he, Brendan Bauer, was still free.

How feeble and unconvincing his voice over the telephone, *I – I didn't do it*, how suddenly childlike, raw, *You believe me, Maggie, don't you?* What choice had Maggie Blackburn but to assure him *yes*?

He'd lied to her, hadn't he. About a few small matters.

Oh, he couldn't help lying: just a little, now and then; not lying so much as fabricating, embellishing . . . making himself more interesting. A habit he'd had since childhood. The youngest of four boys, the two eldest big husky strapping guys, good-looking and no-nonsense and athletic and uncontaminated (he'd thought, meanly) by intelligence, thus how was little Brendan to distinguish himself – in school; at the piano; as an altar boy, Sunday mornings at high mass? He'd lied to Maggie Blackburn about things too trivial to set right; that was the nature of most of Brendan Bauer's innocent fabrications, for which he'd castigated himself in the seminary, spent a good deal of time in self-analysis, examination of conscience, *Why do you lie, Brendan, isn't the truth enough?*

Never. Never enough.

Which was why he composed his music too ... or made the effort.

Maggie believed him, though. She trusted him, seemed to like him: sisterly, sweetly ... unquestioningly. A woman of such poise and elegance and beauty, an intimidating sort of beauty, like the girl singers with their crystalline heartbreaking voices, sopranos, mezzo-sopranos, velvety-throated contraltos, several of them at Indiana, in the music school; you kept your distance and regarded them with the proper detachment of irony, wrote your 'art' songs as 'anti-art' in order to spurn them. And Maggie herself he'd managed at last, that night in November, after the committee had made its decision, to exasperate ... to disgust. She'd politely asked him to leave her house, and he'd crept away like a dog with its tail between its legs.

He'd been shocked, yet acquiescent. Of course Maggie had been right: the rapist's victim is degraded, damned; it is pain to look into his face.

And what would they think they knew now, now that Rolfe Christensen had been murdered?

Not lies so much as falsifications ... subtle innocent-seeming misrepresentations. The Church defines such clever ruses as sins of omission. For instance, in order to whet Maggie's natural sympathy for him, Brendan had indicated to her how friendless he was in Forest Park, how scorned, lonely ... when in truth it was he, through the autumn, who had systematically avoided certain of his fellow graduate students, male and female, who had made overtures of friendship; attractive and clearly bright and talented young people whom in other circumstances Brendan would have liked enormously but in these perverse circumstances found himself disliking ... yes, he'd been chill, haughty, abrupt ... partly this was sheer nerves but partly (and the Master of Novices had shrewdly seen this in his behaviour in the seminary) it was a self-lacerating pride, a neurotic pleasure in hurting others by which one is spared the possibility of being hurt oneself. *Don't stimulate me to like you. To love you. I can't take that risk, I am not strong enough.*

III

By way of clever omission Brendan had also misled Maggie into thinking him rather more ill-treated by the Conservatory than he was. He had been disappointed by the committee's final decision, but he'd been fully prepared for it, having had lengthy conversations with individuals on the committee, among them the school attorney, Mr Woodbridge, and the provost, Mr Gould, and the Dean of the Faculty, and the Dean of Students, and there was the psychologist who'd been so patient and kind with him, and there was Nicholas Reickmann, who'd called him up one evening and asked if they could have dinner together and talk, and so Brendan had consented, suspicious at first (for was not Nicholas Reickmann a friend of Christensen's, if not an ally) and then quite pleased, flattered, grateful for Nicholas's concern, for though he *was* a friend of sorts of Christensen's, he was also a very decent and fair-minded young man and seemed simply to want to know the truth of what had happened, or had not happened, between Christensen and Brendan. So Brendan had confided in him, to a degree. Not so thoroughly as he had confided in the doctor who'd examined him, or the psychologist, or Mr Gould, but more than he'd been able to bring himself to tell the committee, or Maggie Blackburn, whom he had not wanted to shock and disgust ... though he wanted to enlist her pity and sympathy and support. And at the end of the evening, after paying for Brendan's dinner, Nicholas had said thoughtfully, clearly from the perspective of one who knew the way of the world, or at least the way of a certain corner of the world, 'Look, Brendan: I know it's been hell. I know – I can guess – something of what you've gone through. But in your place, considering circumstances, your own future, I guess I'd try to accommodate myself to what happened, as people accommodate themselves to accidents, diseases, 'acts of God' – yes, certainly I know that Rolfe Christensen isn't exactly an 'act of God'; he *should* be made to pay for his behaviour – but, Brendan, there's another side to the man: he can be generous, he can be helpful ... if you don't press your advantage – don't look so surprised: I mean it: your advantage – you might discover that something valuable can still come of . . . of this mess. But if you become obsessed with him, if you try to make trouble for him, for instance by going to the police, it will only hurt you even more in the end . . . as I suppose Andrew Woodbridge counselled you? And Calvin Gould? Your music should come first – your music, and your career. So if Rolfe Christensen has behaved monstrously towards you, if the man is a monster: so be it. You'll outlive him.' And Nicholas smiled a lovely dazzling assured smile. 'We all will.'

None of this had Brendan Bauer told Maggie Blackburn.

Everybody knows. It's no secret.
   But what do they know?

By eleven o'clock the police had not yet arrived and Brendan was becoming exhausted by his vigil. He was playing a tape of a Bach toccata and fugue, music of a rhythm and a speed to match his quickened heartbeat. He'd wetted his hair and combed it flat against his head but, drying, it lifted in wry little tufts, like field grass. From so much bitter-black coffee his nerves were like wires strung tight – he could hear in the distance strangers' voices lifting derisively (*'Bren dan, Bren dan'*) but the voices refused to define themselves and remained teasing, taunting.

Bren dan? Don't make me angry.
   Bren dan don't play games with me!

Like a sacrificial victim he changed his clothes: fresh underwear, fresh shirt, clean trousers, necktie, the brown tweed coat frayed at the sleeves but still his 'good', his 'public' outfit . . . for at the age of twenty-seven Brendan Bauer was very poor and could afford nothing better.

This too was a part of his shame. *He could afford nothing better.*

Years ago when Brendan was seventeen, and still in Boise Consolidated Senior High School, and dreaming of going away to college to study music, his father warned him, 'Remember we're not poor – we just don't have any money.'

Mr Bauer was a plumber but for all his skill and industry his income fluctuated, and not one of his sons cared to learn his trade. His life was money – notes of demeaningly small denominations, methodically counted change. Yet he had, upon occasion, a strange careless flair for the piano; he could improvise songs without seeming to know what he did or how he did it; like magic the right notes came, his broad stubby fingers ranging up and down the keyboard. Rarely did Mr Bauer play the piano, however, without being mildly drunk, and his playing was thus qualified, subtly polluted, by the association. He loved music, he *was* musical, and yet wasn't it a kind of weakness, a waste of time, a 'feminine' inclination no responsible father should encourage in a son, let alone subsidize?

Brendan's piano lessons, twice weekly, were paid for by his grandmother, his father's mother, who'd had, it was said, a lovely mezzo-soprano voice as a girl. And before his voice changed Brendan too had a lovely singing voice, a sweet clear tenor, a girl's voice of which he was alternately proud and deeply, complexly, ashamed.

Fortunately, this voice coarsened, became transformed into a slightly strident and high-pitched but recognizably 'masculine' voice.

Brendan went away to study music and to learn that he had not the talent for piano that others – so many others! – had, nor had he the requisite patience. He wanted to *compose* new sounds, not be trained to *imitate* sounds already known. His family did not understand, and he sensed their subtle disappointment in him: for where, in his secret pride, he believed himself talented, they saw deformity of a kind; where he saw the possibility of his being freed of home, of a merely local, parochial life, they saw the possibility of his being unfit for that life, in a way unworthy. *Remember we're not poor – we just don't have any money.* Poverty was like dust and grime, ingrained in the very texture of one's life.

The Bauers were Catholic – Brendan's mother's family was of solidly Irish Catholic stock – thus the priesthood was a better idea, or seemed so. In any case, in the priesthood, weakness and 'femininity' were elevated to a higher, more respectable plane. Wasn't there something invulnerable in the dark-clad figure of a

Roman Catholic priest, something of dignity, of secrecy and power? Christian love had little to do with it, for the priests most respected were stern no-nonsense authoritarian personalities, masculine yet stubbornly sexless, neutered. Yet no sooner had Mr and Mrs Bauer adjusted to the astonishment of their youngest son, Brendan (the 'odd' one), studying to be a priest at the Precious Blood Seminary in St Louis, no sooner had they fallen into the innocent custom of bragging about him, than he'd decided to quit: decided he hadn't a vocation after all, decided he couldn't bear a life so deprived. (There were health problems too, 'nervous' problems, of which no one cared to speak and which were not indicated on any of Brendan Bauer's records or applications.)

And so it was back to music.

'Music must be my salvation.'

Brendan was thinking of these things when at last, at a quarter to midnight, the Forest Park police arrived.

He was thinking of these things while listening to the Bach toccata and fugue for the third, perhaps the fourth, consecutive time, stiffly seated in one of his beige vinyl-covered chairs (his little apartment came furnished: he had two such chairs), waiting. To a neutral observer he might have appeared drugged or catatonic: a long-boned boyish young man with large, startled, yet sleepy-looking eyes, unruly hair, twitchy mannerisms. One of the shaving cuts had bled anew and had dribbled down over his chin. His Adam's apple protruded painfully over his tight shirt collar and the lumpy knot of his woollen necktie. The waterfall brilliance of the Bach piece so transfixed him he might not have remembered where he was, or why. For was not Bach a prayer – a secular prayer – a fierce declaration of a world of logic, sunlight, and sanity, however remote from this world?

Though he'd been awaiting the knock on the door for so many hours, Brendan seemed not to hear it when it came; so it was repeated, louder, and louder still.

Police! Open up! Police! Open up!

Like a sleepwalker, Brendan went to the door and opened it, fumbling with the lock. 'Y-yes? Wh-wh-what do you w-want?' he asked. His pose of innocent surprise laced with terror must have assured the police officers (there were three of them – why *three*?) that he was of no possible danger; thus they were courteous with him and did not lay a hand on him.

In a nightmare trance Brendan Bauer was taken to police headquarters in the village of Forest Park for questioning regarding the death of Rolfe Christensen. He was not arrested – he was not, seemingly, under suspicion – but they had questions to put to him. Many questions.

Thirteen

This much was known generally within forty-eight hours of Rolfe Christensen's death: the composer had died as a consequence of having eaten a chocolate-covered truffle injected (apparently with a syringe) with a powerful dose of the poisonous compound sodium cyanide; each of the twelve candies in the box he had received on the day of his death had been similarly injected, and the candy itself had been traced to a gourmet chocolate shop in Manhattan – where, fortuitously, a sales clerk claimed to remember the purchaser and was able to supply police with a detailed description of the woman.

A second gift box of chocolates, bought at the same time as the truffles, had been sent to one of Christensen's colleagues at the Conservatory, the pianist Maggie Blackburn, but these chocolates had not, evidently, been poisoned.

It was the first known instance of homicide in the ninety-year history of the Forest Park Conservatory of Music. Indeed, acts of homicide – or aggravated assault, rape, armed robbery, suicide – were rarities in the residential community of Forest Park, where the local weekly, the *Forest Park Packet*, headlined perennial debates over tax assessments, zoning, sewer and road repairs, and the like. The jarring bold-black headlines POLICE INVESTIGATE CYANIDE DEATH OF COMPOSER ROLFE CHRISTENSEN and HOMICIDE BELIEVED CAUSE OF DEATH OF FAMED CONSERVATORY PROFESSOR seemed incongruous with the newspaper's genteel format.

The story was picked up by other newspapers, of course, and

sent out over the country by way of the AP and UP wire services. Maggie Blackburn, who had so recently, and so unhappily, received telephone calls and notes from far-flung friends, concerning her involvement in a scandal precipitated by Rolfe Christensen, now received more calls and notes, most of them from the same far-flung friends. *What on earth is happening there? You must have some idea who killed R.C. – don't you?*

When a photograph accompanied one of the news stories about Christensen's death, it was likely to be an old photograph, showing the composer as a stolid but handsome man of youthful middle age, regarding the camera with a small measured smile of lapidary dignity or derision; the caption beneath was invariable: *Rolfe Christensen, Pulitzer Prize-winning composer.* Christensen was revealed as one of those contemporary American artists of whom there are legions, minor celebrities of a kind whose work is wholly unknown to most Americans even as their names have a teasingly familiar ring.

No one more famous than Rolfe Christensen had died on December 8, 1988, so the *New York Times* featured Christensen's obituary on their obituary page on the morning of December 9, with the attractive photograph, and the caption, and two columns of respectful print. Reading this obituary numerous times as if unable to comprehend it, the inexorable bedrock of reality of which these words were but the emanation, Bill Queller, Christensen's friend and colleague of years, was, as he told friends subsequently, so shaken and confused that he found himself half thinking that Rolfe would be pleased with the piece since it was, overall, a decent, perceptive notice, and the *Times*'s music critic had sometimes been a bit bitchy about his work, and the photograph *was* flattering. 'Then I realized that Rolfe would never see the piece, to be pleased, or possibly offended, you know how he is – was – how vain and unpredictable and easily wounded; and the fact of it, the horror of it, washed over me: Rolfe is *dead*, and *dead* in such a terrible way.'

Unquestionably, the cellist William Queller was the most upset of Christensen's circle of acquaintances at the Conservatory in the week following the composer's death; after it was revealed by Christensen's attorney that Nicholas Reickmann, and not Queller (as everyone, including Queller, had been led to believe), was to be Christensen's literary executor, he was no less upset, but the nature of his upset took a decidedly different turn.

'How could he betray me – *me*? *When I did so much for him*?'

Maggie Blackburn had never seemed to herself an obsessive person, except for brief, intense periods in regard to piano performances and some preparations for teaching, yet in the days and weeks following Rolfe Christensen's murder (though 'murder' was not an expression Maggie used, 'mysterious death' was her preference) she found herself caught up in the near-ceaseless community speculation: uncharacteristically opinionated; almost, at times, quarrelsome. And, alone, even when at the piano or listening to music closely, she found that her concentration shifted free of its ostensible object and that she was thinking of Christensen's death.

The man had been Maggie's enemy, her adversary: she was reasonably certain he had wished her ill, and would have done her harm, at least professional harm, had he had the opportunity. (Though very likely he would not have gone out of his way to do her harm – it was said of Christensen that he was too lazy, or too indifferent, to be actively troublesome.) At the same time, Maggie did not really want to believe such things and told herself, with an impatient gesture of both hands as if she were silencing some heedlessly outspoken person, that she was being foolish, small-minded, and paranoid.

'Paranoid': an ugly clinical word, a cliché of contemporary usage.

'I have got to think of Rolfe Christensen's death as nothing more and nothing less than it is, with no reference to me,' Maggie instructed herself, her eyes filling with tears of dismay. 'It's just that, until the mystery is solved, I don't know what it *is*.'

Surely she was exaggerating to consider Rolfe Christensen her enemy – even her adversary? Surely it was more rational to think of him as a colleague with whom she'd had some difficulty getting along, as others at the Conservatory, no less congenial and fair-minded, had had difficulty getting along with him?

Fritzie Krill said half-seriously, or was it half-jokingly, one evening at the Spaldings', 'I wonder: Do any of the rest of you feel the kind of guilty relief, the almost pleasurable remorse, the . . . childish gloating and vindication . . . that I feel? Because he's dead, and he seems to have deserved it? But a strange kind of sorrow too, a sense of fright, and loss . . . since, though I disliked the man intensely, I won't ever see him again even to dislike him?'

Others murmured vague embarrassed assents, but Maggie shivered, and laughed nervously, and said not a word. The pupils of her eyes seemed to have shrunk to mere pinpricks, as if a powerful beam of light were being shown into them, and her pale lips were set hard. I must not incriminate myself, she thought. Even here, among friends.

For what if, by a careless word of Maggie Blackburn's, Brendan Bauer were drawn into it?

Night following night, as Christmas approached in that dark uncharted December of 1988, the most turbulent winter solstice of Maggie Blackburn's psychic life, she lay sleepless in her bed listening to the utter silence of her house, her empty house, her house vacant and dead of even remembered music, and she thought of Calvin Gould, who would never love her and whom, in time, most likely, she would cease to love; she thought of her father, who had looked through her, not recognizing her, as if no one, daughter or stranger, had stood in her place; she thought of that man . . . a lover of a kind . . . who had in fact looked at her and uttered the most damning of judgements: 'In my opinion, Maggie, you're hardly a woman at all.'

Quickly, almost stealthily, Maggie ran her hands over her body, the soft contours of her body, the sharp-defined bones of pelvis, ribs, shoulders that separated these contours, and could think of no defence. If breasts and female genitalia constituted 'woman' Maggie was a woman, but if something more, something rather more mysterious and hidden, were involved, then perhaps she was not a woman and had no words for what, in the world's or her own imagination, she might be.

Intermittently through her adult life, men had told her she was beautiful. She had felt the force of their fleshly desire for her – she'd shared in desire, at least to a degree – but, apart from their sexual feeling, apart from their physicality altogether, she seemed to lapse to something *other*. She had no doubt it must be something *lesser*.

There was a tangible absence in her. But can one be defined in terms of absence? She thought of her canary Rex, who had sung so urgently, for weeks, for the return of his dead mate, Sweetpea. Or was Rex simply a male bird singing for a female, any female; then, as time passed, simply a living creature singing out of creaturely loneliness and isolation, for any sort of company at all? Then, abruptly, he'd stopped singing altogether and died a few days later.

For which no one could possibly blame Rolfe Christensen: the very idea was absurd.

Maggie wondered, however, at the baffling connection between her and Christensen, about which the Forest Park police had asked her; the fact that whoever had poisoned the chocolates meant for him had sent a box of chocolates from the same store to her a few days earlier. But why? Did people think of the two as somehow linked? Was it because of Brendan Bauer?

But Maggie had done all she could to detach herself publicly from the dispute. So far as she knew, only a few people were aware that Brendan had come to her first.

Vividly she recalled the luxurious red-satin box of expensive chocolates. The velvety fragrance as the cover was lifted. Something very nearly erotic . . . illicit . . . in the mere fact of such rich candies: the smell, the appearance, the texture, the overpoweringly sweet chocolate taste in the mouth.

For some reason, as Maggie had opened the mysterious package, she'd seemed to know that the chocolates were not exactly for her.

You must take it home, it's for you . . . it wasn't sent to strangers.

She recalled with eidetic precision the outward appearance of the package. The meticulous hand-printed name and address (and the small error in the zip code, which she'd remembered to mention to the police – the error was repeated on Christensen's package); the crisscrossing lengths of tape and string; the exaggerated way Mrs Moyer and the secretaries had fussed over the gift, and over Maggie Blackburn, laughing in girlish delight, congratulating her, as if suspecting that the 'romantic' gift must be quite an event in Maggie's life.

And so it was, indeed. But it had not been a romantic gift after all.

How alarming, after the fact, to think that she had passed the box around the office, offering the chocolates to anyone who happened by, with never a thought (for why would she have had such a thought?) that the chocolates might have been tampered with. And how trusting people were, overall.

Alarming too how carelessly she had assumed the gift was from her former student Jennifer Lehman, on the slender evidence of the initial *J*. (When Maggie more closely examined the card afterwards, she'd thought the *J* might easily have been an *I*.)

A long time ago when she'd been a girl still in her teens and her father was a youthful and vigorous and, it was said, ambitious assistant district attorney on Long Island, he'd told her in a rare moment of expansiveness that the human mind works to draw quick conclusions from virtually no evidence at all – calculating recklessly, yet persuasively, with the aim of *making sense out of senselessness*.

Out of a flood of inchoate material, selecting randomly, yet persuasively, to create *a narrative with a quality of self-justification*.

As an assistant prosecutor, Mr Blackburn had been, at least at a remove or two, a kind of police investigator: he'd enjoyed cases, the more puzzling the better, for the solving of puzzles gave him a distinct pleasure. Maggie wondered how he would have dealt with the mystery of Christensen's death, in his prime.

Though of course the police probably had evidence – leads – of which Maggie knew nothing.

To her horror – but it was impossible for her to prevent this, since Mrs Moyer had been immediately questioned by police, and had naturally, unthinkingly, provided them with Jennifer Lehman's name – the Lehman family had actually been contacted. Jennifer was still in London; even had the young woman wanted to send the fatal chocolates she could not have done so. Maggie apologized to the Lehmans, and she apologized to the police, for her misleading assumption. Her manner following the poisoning, the mysterious death, was oddly apologetic, as perhaps others noticed; she felt somehow (but how?) involved; it had been so careless of her to pass *her* gift box of chocolates about ... hadn't it?

'It was a wrong idea of mine. I ... I was wrong.'

So Maggie had told the investigating detective for the Forest Park police department when, on the afternoon of December 10, he'd come to speak with her in her office at the Conservatory. The man's name was Miles; his rank was detective sergeant; he was in his forties, perhaps, or younger – his hair thin, grey, his manner courteous but brisk, even clerical. Maggie found herself relating to him as, half-consciously, she had always, through her life, related to figures of authority, no matter their actual power or significance in the world. She tried to answer his questions as truthfully and as succinctly as possible, but there was an undercurrent of anxiety to her words and her eyes continually misted over. For the previous two nights she'd slept miserably; since the shock of Christensen's death and her not very coherent telephone call to Brendan Bauer. From her look of wan distress Detective Sergeant David Miles – as he formally introduced himself – might have thought Maggie Blackburn a close friend of the murdered man or one of his devoted admirers.

Miles asked Maggie questions of a kind he had surely been asking others, and Maggie answered as, she supposed, others had answered. She told him of her mistaken idea that she'd known who had sent her the gift box of chocolates – 'It was a wrong idea of mine.' When he asked who she thought might have sent it, and the box of poisoned chocolates, she hesitated for what seemed a very long time, gripping her hands together, almost wringing them . . . thinking, in the interstices of more urgent thought, of how poor Schumann had tried a finger-stretching machine and ruined his fingers for the keyboard for ever. Her own reach was just a little longer than one might have expected: an octave plus one in the left hand, an octave plus two in the right. Faintly she said, 'I . . . I have no idea.'

Maggie knew well that Brendan's name was known to the police and that they had already questioned him, perhaps even interrogated him, at length. (She did not want to think which of her colleagues or which Conservatory administrator had provided police with his name.) Yet, with Detective Sergeant Miles staring at her and taking notes on a little pad, with everything seeming so very crucial and so weighted, Maggie could not bring herself to utter Brendan's name even to state that, in her opinion, the young man could not possibly have sent poisoned chocolates to Rolfe Christensen. She did not want to utter his name in this man's presence at all.

More emphatically, she said, 'I have no idea. I can't believe it's anyone I know, or anyone connected with the Conservatory.'

Miles asked, 'And why do you think, Miss Blackburn, you were sent a box of chocolates three days before the victim received his?'

The victim! Maggie had not heard this term before, in reference to Rolfe Christensen, and was struck by it. She wiped at her eyes with her fingertips.

The answer to the detective's question seemed to Maggie self-evident: the murderer had hoped to make people believe that the poisoned chocolates Rolfe Christensen was to receive would be as harmless, as delicious, as Maggie Blackburn's had been. But she was not sure whether she wanted to say this. Did she want Detective Sergeant Miles to be impressed with her intelligence (if, indeed, he would be impressed), or did she want him to have no particular impression at all of her? Which was wiser, more expedient? She said, 'I – I'm not sure.'

'And why *you*, Miss Blackburn? Why did the potential killer single out *you*? Were you close to the victim; was there any special reason for you and him to be coupled together?'

Coupled together! Maggie Blackburn was struck too by this expression and for a moment could not speak.

The detective had asked his question in a matter-of-fact, even perfunctory voice, and the question was certainly logical; yet it made Maggie strangely nervous, and she stammered slightly as she replied. 'I – I don't know. I'm afraid I – I don't know.'

And truly she did not. She had no idea.

Next, the detective asked Maggie to tell him anything she could about Rolfe Christensen that might be helpful: what she knew of him, what her relationship with him had been, what enemies he might have had. Maggie spoke hesitantly, even shyly, in starts and stops; she shrank from saying anything critical of the dead man for it all seemed, now, beside the point. When pressed by Miles to be more specific, she said, reluctantly, 'He had the reputation here of being 'difficult'. I didn't know him well, I'm afraid. I don't believe we'd ever had a single conversation in all the years I've been here. I . . . I wasn't a member of the Christensen circle.' This was misleading and not at all what Maggie meant to say. She added vaguely, 'He was a sort of mystery to me, I suppose.' But neither was this what she meant to say.

'A mystery? In what way?'

But Maggie had no idea what she meant.

So the interview, rather awkwardly, continued.

From time to time Detective Sergeant Miles offered Maggie – 'Professor Margaret Blackburn, Dept of Piano' in his notes – a measured little half-smile. He must have sensed her anxiety, and something perhaps deeper, set in opposition to him and his investigation. On her side, Maggie saw the policeman in the deceptive mode of Dr Rayburn, an early dentist of hers back in St Paul. *Please sit still, no pain, just relax, dear, I promise no pain.* But in fact there was always pain. There was only the matter of when it would come.

Then abruptly Miles was asking Maggie about Brendan Bauer: hadn't the graduate student reported having been sexually assaulted by Rolfe Christensen some weeks ago; hadn't he in fact come to Maggie herself? Reluctantly, wincing, Maggie admitted it was so. Then added, 'I'm director of the Music Education Programme. All the graduate students in the programme come to me for registration and counselling.' She felt a sick sort of despair, for she saw where the detective's questions must lead.

As Maggie should have known, Miles knew a good deal about what had happened. He knew that Brendan had come first to Maggie, that she'd counselled him to go to the Conservatory administration, and that the hearings were closed – 'Kept under cover, right?'

'The hearings were private; I wasn't a part of them. You'll have to ask –'

'Yes,' Miles said curtly, 'we will. We have. Where murder has been committed, that sort of confidentiality no longer holds.' The detective was not discourteous, but he looked at Maggie Blackburn with a measure of irony. 'It might have been better if the assault had been reported to the police. Bauer has told us he was counselled not to report it.'

Maggie said quickly, her face warm, 'But not by me. I told Brendan he should go to the police – to you. He should have pressed charges. He spoke of what Christensen had done to him as rape and said he was terrified he'd be killed; he may even have been tied up for part of the time – it was outrageous. It *was* a crime.'

'Yes,' Miles said emphatically. 'It was a crime, if it happened the way he described it.'

'Certainly it happened,' Maggie said. 'I saw Brendan the next day. I was the first person who saw him. He'd been beaten – battered. There was a large bruise over his left eye, he walked wincing with pain, even his glasses had been broken. At first he could hardly bring himself to tell me what Christensen had done to him – I don't think he really told me everything. He –'

'This was back in September? September the eighteenth?'

'Yes. He didn't want to report the assault to the Conservatory at first, but I encouraged him, and so he did, and after that it was out of my hands and, as I've said, private. I think for a while Brendan had intended to go to the police but he was dissuaded by the administration. By the school's attorney.' Maggie spoke rapidly, impassioned. 'I can't blame the administration for hoping to avoid unfavourable publicity, but I do blame them for putting their own interests above those of one of their students. Brendan Bauer was too trusting; he seems to have trusted everyone! I gather you've spoken with him, Mr Miles? Then you know how sensitive he is, how young, a shy, innocent, delicate sort of person . . .'

Miles appeared to be agreeing with Maggie, at least in theory. But he said, 'Brendan Bauer is a name a number of your colleagues have suggested as someone who might have had a strong motive to kill Christensen. It seems to us fairly reasonable. He has denied it, and no one has accused him, and there isn't as yet any evidence to link him with the poisoning, but the motive is certainly there. In fact, we know that Bauer made threats to kill Christensen in front of witnesses.'

Maggie Blackburn stared at the detective as if neither hearing nor comprehending.

She said, 'I'd thought – wasn't the person who bought the chocolates a woman? In the newspaper –'

Miles said guardedly, 'The description we have is of a woman, yes. But it's a description that could also fit a man – a man in disguise. The sales clerk stressed that. And there are other details that aren't incongruous with Bauer . . . And even if the person who bought the chocolates were someone other than Bauer, Bauer could still have prepared them for mailing. He might have had help. He's the one with the obvious motive.'

Half-pleadingly Maggie said, 'Oh, but there may be many people, countless people, with motives . . . I'm sure my colleagues have told you, Mr Miles, that Rolfe Christensen was a much disliked man.'

'But Bauer is actually on record, on tape in fact, as saying he'd have liked to kill Christensen, only a few weeks ago. The tape we heard reveals him as quite emotional.' Miles paused, regarding Maggie with his encouraging little smile. 'But he seems not to have said such things in your hearing, Miss Blackburn?'

'I . . . I don't remember.'

'Threats against Christensen, remarks like that? "I'm sorry I didn't kill him when I had the chance"?'

Maggie shook her head adamantly. 'I would remember if he had, and I don't remember.'

'Others seem to remember.'

Again Maggie shook her head, perplexed and despairing.

Miles said patiently, 'You appear to be very protective of this student, Miss Blackburn. Do you know him well? Can you attest to his character? He's new to Forest Park, isn't he?'

'I think I am a fairly good judge of character,' Maggie said. 'I . . . I believe that I am.'

'But he *is* new to Forest Park, isn't he? An ex-seminary student from St Louis, who had been advised to quit because of emotional problems?'

'"Emotional problems"? I hadn't heard that.' Maggie pressed her fingertips against her eyes. She said almost desperately, 'This is so cruel! Such a nightmare! First, a student is savagely victimized by the very man he'd come two thousand miles to study with – then he's victimized, in another way, by the school in which he has enrolled – and his rapist is *rewarded*. And now through no fault of his own he is being victimized by –'

'This young man Bauer isn't being "victimized" by police, Miss Blackburn, I assure you. We've talked to him. He could have engaged a lawyer, but he declined – he isn't under arrest – we've asked him not to leave the area without notifying us, that's all. As I said, no one has accused him – none of your colleagues has seriously suggested he might have committed the poisoning – and so far there isn't any evidence linking him with the crime.'

Maggie shook her head slowly. Her thoughts were racing, but to no purpose.

Miles persisted. 'You are convinced that Bauer couldn't have had anything to do with the poisoning of Rolfe Christensen, Miss Blackburn?'

'Of course I'm convinced,' Maggie said. Her voice was surprisingly shrill in her own ears. 'In fact, there is no one in Forest Park less likely to have killed Rolfe Christensen than Brendan Bauer.'

No sooner had she uttered these extravagant words than Maggie wondered why she'd done so; such dramatic hyperbole was more in the style of Portia MacLeod than of Maggie Blackburn.

Miles said, smiling, 'Yes? Really?'

He asked Maggie several more questions before at last closing his notepad and preparing to leave. On his feet, he seemed less imposing; he was scarcely Maggie's height: a small, compact man with an air of equanimity. He wore a suit of an ordinary fit, neither inexpensive nor expensive. His skin was rough, slightly pitted, perhaps by acne scars. Afterwards, thinking over the interview and not at all happy with her performance, Maggie would recall Detective Sergeant David Miles's practised, professional ease; the lack of surprise he'd shown when, with no warning, Maggie had begun speaking recklessly. *Why did I say such things? Why did I become so emotional?*

Of course, Miles was a policeman. A member of the general species to which Maggie's father had once belonged. Evoking emotion in others, they took care not to betray it in themselves, for that was hardly to their advantage.

When, in parting, they shook hands – shaking hands was a ritual Maggie Blackburn took care to cultivate in her dealings with men; she knew it a ritual men took seriously – Maggie made an effort to soften the effect of her strong opinions. She smiled apologetically. She reiterated her certainty that Brendan was wholly unconnected with the poisoning; that she hoped police would not trouble him further, since he'd gone through such a wretched period these past few months. In fact she'd been worried, for a while, that he might be despondent, even suicidal;

fortunately he'd gone to a psychotherapist on campus. She said pleadingly, 'Brendan isn't the type for any kind of violence, though. I know. I know he isn't. I'd swear to it, Mr Miles – he simply isn't the type.'

Detective Miles, leaving, said, not sarcastically, or even ironically, but merely as a statement of fact, as if it were a matter Maggie Blackburn ought to know, 'Poison is the weapon of choice, Miss Blackburn, for exactly that type of personality: the kind that can't bear violence.'

Maggie had been planning to spend part of the holidays in Key West with a friend, a pianist and teacher, and the friend's businessman husband, both of whom she had known in graduate school in Boston; but, as the date of her flight approached, she decided she could not leave Forest Park with so much undecided, the police investigation unresolved, and Brendan Bauer, the sole suspect, alone and friendless.

Fourteen

'It's an honour, yes. An honour I had not expected.'

So Nicholas Reickmann, choosing his words carefully, his expression grave, spoke of having been named Rolfe Christensen's literary executor: the overseer of the composer's voluminous files, both in his home and in his Conservatory office, containing thousands of pages of notes, drafts of compositions, manuscripts, journals, letters both personal and professional (letters written to Christensen and carbon copies of letters written by Christensen, the earliest dating back to 1944), tapes of musical performances of Christensen's work, photographs, reviews, articles on Christensen, tapes of conversations with distinguished people (Christensen talking to Stravinsky, Britten, Pablo Casals, numerous others), and tapes of interviews (Christensen being interviewed, for instance, by National Public Radio, virtually every year since 1971). There were perhaps forty cartons of such materials, Nicholas said – apart from the files, which Christensen had kept religiously up to date. There were bureau, desk and kitchen drawers stuffed with memorabilia; there were papers, including programme notes, stuffed into books on shelves; there was even, apparently, a special archive kept by the composer in a safety deposit box in a Bridgeport bank, which Nicholas had not yet seen. Most of these materials, which constituted Rolfe Christensen's literary estate, Nicholas Reickmann had not had the opportunity, by the time of his death in mid-January 1989, to examine.

Among the younger instructors at the Forest Park Conservatory, Nicholas Reickmann, swarthy-skinned, dark-haired, unfailingly self-dramatizing, was one of the most admired and emulated, by students at least; and yet, in the community, the most controversial. He was 'Nicholas Reickmann' in public, 'Nicky R.' in private. (In the hastily drawn-up document dated November 15, 1988, in which, in effect, Rolfe Christensen repudiated his old friend Bill Queller and named Nicholas Reickmann his literary executor in Queller's place, Reickmann was referred to somewhat flirtatiously as 'Nicky Reickmann' and 'Nicky R.') He was an accomplished clarinettist and played for the Forest Park Woodwind Quintet and for the Conservatory Orchestra and the Connecticut Symphony Orchestra, and he shared with that instrument a certain enigmatic tone: to some observers his manner was coolly and impeccably stylized and impenetrable; to others it was direct, intimate, seductive. He had no single lover but it was rumoured he had lovers; he was careful not to encourage disciples among the young; he accepted social invitations – he was, of course, extremely popular – but rarely reciprocated except to send, now and then, enormous bouquets of flowers to his hostess friends (like Portia MacLeod, who was very fond of him). His older colleagues tended to distrust him; his contemporaries were drawn to him yet frequently rebuffed, not by actual words, or even gestures, but by the young man's calm cool studied façade. 'It's complained of you, Nicky, that you are *inaccessible*,' Rolfe Christensen once observed, and Nicholas Reickmann said happily, 'Oh, yes!'

Of course, Nicholas dressed beautifully and expensively; he owned, he confessed, more than two hundred neckties – 'and each a work of art'. He collected novelty wristwatches, oversized rings, hand-tooled leather boots. If at times his clothes looked slapdash, even jarring, if now and then they had the thrown-together appearance of an ensemble of mismatched instruments, this was precisely the look Nicholas Reickmann strove to achieve, the look currently fashionable on West Broadway, SoHo. Nicholas had very dark eyes set wide in his face, and an olive-dark skin, a full sensuous mouth, features that seemed to some observers as Arabic, exotic – though in fact he had been born, in 1956, in

Westchester County, New York; his severely styled hair with its maroon-red-synthetic sheen lifted from his forehead in quills that appeared waxed, and he wore a tiny diamond in his left ear-lobe, sparkling as a tear. Like many flamboyantly handsome men he exerted himself in gestures or mannerisms of simple kindness; so gifted by nature (and by art: Nicholas was a superb musician) he had no need for vanity but believed it his obligation to spread himself about, however impersonally, multi-tiered as a wedding cake. Thus to attractive young women like Maggie Blackburn, Nicholas behaved no differently than he behaved, for instance, to elderly women or to most men. Maggie was not immune to the young man's charismatic charm and would have been somewhat overwhelmed by him – except of course she knew better – when Nicholas Reickmann sought her out, clasped her hand, stared into her eyes, and said breathlessly, 'Maggie, dear, where have you *been*? I've been *missing* you!' It was no less a performance than his clarinet playing, and no less practised.

As local legend had it, the first time Rolfe Christensen heard Nicholas Reickmann play his clarinet, in a scintillating Mozart quintet for clarinet and strings performed at the Conservatory, he'd had to shut his eyes hard to concentrate on the music – otherwise, he said, he'd have been too 'actively aroused'.

Christensen told of his uncomfortable experience in bawdy, comical, anecdotal terms, crude in some ears but rather endearing in others. When, as Christensen surely intended it, the anecdote was repeated to Nicholas, the young clarinettist had been both deeply embarrassed and excited. But he'd said, his cheeks tinged with scarlet, 'Doesn't he know that lacks *finesse*!'

For weeks during Nicholas Reickmann's first year at the Conservatory, Rolfe Christensen had pursued him openly – as well as clandestinely. There was a good deal of bemused talk, some fear of scandal, yet finally – no one beyond Christensen's select circle knew on quite what terms – the men became friends. For ever afterwards Christensen was 'Rolfe' to Nicholas Reickmann, and Reickmann was 'Nicky' to Rolfe Christensen. They were not lovers, but there was between them an air of something settled, sated. And Nicholas Reickmann's career at the Conservatory prospered.

Nicholas was, however, for all his provocative behaviour, a truly congenial young man. He had a horror of making enemies – the very antithesis, in fact, of Rolfe Christensen, who was given to say that it was enemies, not friends, who kept him on his toes – and tried very hard not to stir displeasure or disapproval in others. After the astounding revelation that he, and not Bill Queller, was to be Rolfe Christensen's executor – a role and a burden Nicholas Reickmann, in secret, did not at all covet – he went immediately to the older man, whose much-abraded affection for Christensen had endured for more than twenty years, and said, with genuine regret, 'Bill, I can't explain it, I won't try, but I'm damned sorry. Will you – *can* you – forgive me?' and Bill Queller sniffed and cast a cold, hurt eye on young Nicky R., and said with dignity, 'Oh, of course I'll forgive *you* – but never *him*.'

The men remained friends. In a time in which, in certain melancholy circles, the ravages of AIDS had depleted their population of friends, acquaintances, admirable and irreplaceable contemporaries, neither Nicholas Reickmann nor Bill Queller could afford to cast each other off. Nicholas assured Bill that Rolfe Christensen would certainly have changed his mind and tossed out that hastily concocted document, for he was a man of mercurial moods and far too thin-skinned for his own good. 'You criticized him for what he'd done to the Bauer boy,' Nicholas said, 'and he felt you betrayed him. You know how he needed constant unflagging support from his friends.'

Bill Queller said, sighing, 'I suppose that was the case, yes. But I felt sorry for Bauer, and I don't regret telling Rolfe what I did. There *is* a point beyond which even genius must be held to account.'

Nicholas Reickmann said quickly, 'Oh, yes. I agree. But I thought, you know, it might be more politic simply to tell the young man.'

Fifteen

'I am here, Maggie. So that you'll be less lonely.

These words sounded out of the very air, calm, impersonal, yet consoling, in a dream of wintry chill; and Maggie Blackburn, the dreamer, glanced hopefully upward – to see, of all people, Calvin Gould. The man stood above her, a step or two above her, but smiling; he lifted her to him and kissed her lightly on the lips and, almost at once, released her. How extraordinary, that kiss! – how Maggie's heart swelled! – though in the next instant Calvin Gould was gone, the entire dream had faded, and only the wintry chill remained.

And Maggie Blackburn woke alone in her bed to a snowy January morning and cold yet stale air that meant – oh, unmistakably – that her oil-burning furnace had gone out for the third time that winter.

How swiftly it had been Christmas 1988, and then New Year 1989, and though the police investigation into the poisoning death of Rolfe Christensen surely continued, and Christensen's death remained the focus of social conversations in Forest Park, there were, so far as anyone knew, no significant new developments; there were no arrests or even any leading suspects except the luckless Brendan Bauer – whom most people believed had committed the crime, whether police would ever succeed in linking him to it or not.

(By now it was known that the purchaser of the chocolates, of ambiguous gender, had not spoken a single time during the entire transaction, but had made herself – himself? – known by way of hand signals. 'Exactly the strategy for a stammerer,' people said; and if Maggie were present she would counter, at once, 'Exactly the strategy for someone who wants to suggest a stammerer!' Her friends had learned not to discuss the case, or Brendan's probable involvement in it, in Maggie's presence.)

Whether innocent, as he insisted, or guilty, as others suspected, Brendan Bauer, miserable with the new, yet crueller aura of notoriety attached to him, had quit his job at the Book Mark (where, he believed, customers stared openly at him) and moved from his shabby apartment on the outermost periphery of Forest Park to another, even shabbier apartment three miles north on Route 1 in the scrappy industrial-suburban town of Waldrop. There, he was wholly dependent upon bus transportation – 'God, how I hate buses!' – but at least, as he told Maggie, with whom he spoke frequently on the telephone, he could lead an anonymous life in Waldrop, where he knew no one, and no one knew him, and where he had an 'outdoor, healthy' job working in a car wash alongside robust, well-muscled high-school youths who knew him only as Bren and took not the slightest interest in him. Hardly the life he'd envisioned for himself a few months before when he'd come east to study at the prestigious Forest Park Conservatory of Music, but he supposed he dared not complain. 'After all, the police haven't arrested me for murder yet, and I haven't been sexually assaulted for months, and I *am* alive.'

Hearing Brendan so sardonic, so brash, so oddly energetic, Maggie Blackburn was amazed; did not know whether to pity him, for the quivering edge of mania in his voice, or to be relieved that he seemed no longer despondent. She knew that, under duress, some personalities strengthen, perversely – perhaps she was of that type herself? – she had not been tested. But it seemed to her (though she did not mention it to him) that in a way Brendan was maturing, for his self-pity was laced with humour and irony, and his stammer was becoming infrequent.

She told him, 'I'm confident that the police will find whoever poisoned Christensen soon – I have a good deal of faith in the detective I met, David Miles – and that things in Forest Park will return to normal. And then you can move back, close to campus, and start classes, and – everything will be all right.'

'Oh, s-sure!' Brendan laughed.

Oddly, as he reported to Maggie, he was beginning to be able to write music again, after being blocked for weeks. He had no piano, so maybe when he actually got to a piano he'd be disappointed with what he had, but he was composing in his head during the day, at the car wash; then in the evening the pent-up music tumbled out on to sheets and sheets of paper – all kinds of music. Weird experimental sounds with much silence separating them, traditional music with a hope of symmetry and beauty, some of it for voice, for soprano. And he was writing a series of brief piano pieces Schoenberg-style: 'If they turn out halfway interesting, Maggie, I intend to dedicate them to you!'

Maggie hesitated, perhaps not perceptibly, then said, 'How kind of you, Brendan. Thank you.'

Now with the enormously public fact of death – of murder – it had been revealed that the Forest Park Conservatory of Music had tried to conceal a scandal some months before: an act or acts of aggravated sexual assault committed by a senior faculty member against a student. Thus the Conservatory administration was often in the news locally, and Maggie steeled herself when she opened the weekly *Packet*, or the student paper *The Chronicle*, preparing to see yet another photograph of Provost Calvin Gould, or Attorney Andrew Woodbridge, or Dean of the Faculty Peter Fisher, or another of her chagrined colleagues and to read yet more about the attempted cover-up and its consequences. By early January the President of the Conservatory, Mr Babcock, a gentleman in his late sixties who had had a coronary bypass operation two years before, was given out to be in poor health and was rarely available for comment; he would resign at the end of the academic term, so it was pointless, and cruel, to harass him about the Christensen case. His successor would very likely be Calvin Gould, who was now President *de facto* – if, in the wake of so much unfortunate controversy, the Board of Trustees had not revised their high opinion of him.

As the man most in the spotlight, Calvin handled the protracted crisis with admirable authority. He told the press no more and no less than he was obliged to tell them, explaining that, since the victim of the alleged sexual assault had declined to press formal charges with the police, the Conservatory had no case with which to dismiss Rolfe Christensen from its staff; there was only the heated testimony of one man against another. As Andrew Woodbridge was frequently quoted, 'Our hands were tied.'

Maggie winced at this expression, which seemed to her singularly ill-chosen.

But she supposed they were right – and now that Rolfe Christensen was dead, the terrible fact of his death took precedence over even his alleged crime.

The police investigation was making public a number of odd, disparate facts, which Maggie believed must be parts of an enormous jigsaw puzzle, to be fitted together by someone (Detective Sergeant Miles?) at a future time. Or perhaps they were simply odd, disparate facts. For instance, on a suggestion made to them by an unnamed source (in fact, Maggie knew the source was Brendan), police had secured a warrant authorizing them to search Christensen's house and property for evidence of other, earlier assaults, the 'shallow graves' of which Christensen had boasted in order to intimidate Bauer. No corpses were unearthed, however. (Was Maggie disappointed at this? She surely hoped not; she was hardly so vindictive!)

Rolfe Christensen had been involved, however, in as many as a dozen reported incidents involving sexual assaults or offences of one kind or another, at music schools, music festivals, colleges and universities – from Oberlin College in 1955 through the Interlaken Music Festival in 1966 to the Salzburg Festival in 1974. Nearly always there had been settlements out of court. Twice there were lawsuits and countersuits. The only actual arrest had taken place in Miami, in 1981, when the 52-year-old composer was charged with the sexual molestation of a 14-year-old boy: he had been sentenced to sixty days in jail with a fine of 500 dollars and the proviso that, if he enrolled in a sex therapy programme, the sixty-day sentence would be suspended. (It was.) The most recent incident had occurred in 1986, in New York City, but there charges of sexual assault against a student enrolled in the New York University Institute of Fine Arts had simply been dropped when the victim declined to press them.

So that evil man was passed along, Maggie Blackburn thought, almost bitterly, to Brendan Bauer: to *us*.

Yet there were facts that mitigated so negative a portrait of the deceased, for, in investigating certain gay circles in Manhattan with which Christensen had been associated, police discovered that he had helped establish a foundation to provide funds for AIDS victims and had contributed 20,000 dollars anonymously; he had established a composers' scholarship fund at his former school, Juilliard, as well as here at Forest Park (of which Maggie had naturally known); he had set up a trust to provide an annual award ('The Rolfe Christensen Award for Distinguished Musical Composition') at the American Academy and Institute of Arts and Letters. While a number of Christensen's acquaintances and associates spoke openly of his 'troubling' or 'disagreeable' personality to police, there were those who insisted he'd been a 'good, generous man', a 'true eccentric but a genius', a 'man incapable of inflicting any real harm upon another person'.

One man spoke of Rolfe Christensen as 'impulsive, yes, as a child is impulsive – but he was never *intentionally* cruel.'

Reading such things in the newspaper (in fact it was the *New York Times*, which had printed several stories on the Christensen case), Maggie had the sudden thought that it was just such innocent-sounding parties whom Detective Miles should investigate, those who put themselves conspicuously on record as having not the slightest dislike of the deceased. Whereas a suspect like Brendan Bauer was – simply too obvious.

'Unless Brendan is emotionally unbalanced. And I can't believe he is.'

This mode of reasoning struck Maggie as typical not of her but of her father. Mr Blackburn had been by instinct a shrewd, suspicious man, quick to puzzle out motives where others saw nothing but surfaces; in his dealings with law-breakers, however middle- and upper-middle-class, he had learned to suspect duplicity, even among his own clients. Of course criminals lied. Of course human beings lied. How obvious a truth – so obvious it was often overlooked.

Maggie halfway wondered if she should drop a note to the detective to alert him to this possibility. But perhaps it was self-evident to him. Perhaps he suspected everyone, even Maggie Blackburn herself?

What had David Miles said, fixing her with his tight little smile, 'Poison is the weapon of choice, Miss Blackburn, for people like you'? Or had it been, more reasonably, 'Poison is the weapon of choice . . . for that type of personality that can't bear violence'?

In her brooding on the case Maggie had also wondered if the inaccurate zip code address on both packages might have been intentional. For if the chocolates had been mailed by a resident of Forest Park, by way of a Manhattan post office, it would be a clever distraction to get the address just slightly wrong. That would appear to indicate that whoever sent the chocolates was not a native or was (like Brendan Bauer?) new to Forest Park. For no long-term resident of any community gets his zip code address wrong.

Like her telephone number, Maggie Blackburn's zip code number was permanently impressed upon her memory: 06545. Whereas on both her package and Christensen's the zip code had been 06540.

She felt convinced the error *was* intentional.

For part of an excited evening Maggie fantasized contacting Detective Miles about these matters; then, sobering abruptly, she realized she was being ridiculous. The last thing a professional policeman wanted to receive was advice from an amateur. And a woman.

In any case, Maggie Blackburn was far too shy for such an intrusion.

(And what did it mean, that someone *might* have had a motive and *might* have committed the murder?

Surely there were many, an infinite many, in this category; and very few of them – of us – could be seriously suspected, let alone investigated. So Maggie was compelled to think, soberly, one morning when, rummaging through a kitchen drawer, she came upon a ball of string – ordinary white durable string, the kind with which the killer had wrapped his or her packages of gift chocolates – at the back of the drawer.)

Sunday afternoon of January 8, 1989. Maggie Blackburn was attending, alone, a cocktail reception in a newly opened gallery in New Haven, an hour's drive from Forest Park; and there, by chance, she caught sight of Calvin Gould amid the crowd – Calvin and a woman with a dark dense cloud of hair who must have been his wife, Naomi.

Her heart beat absurdly. She had heard that the reclusive and eccentric Mrs Gould was an amateur artist of a kind and that she sometimes attended events of this sort, by herself or with her husband, so long as the events were not in Forest Park, but Maggie had never run into the couple in such a context and was undecided what to do. She felt a childlike impulse simply to turn away, to avoid a meeting ... but it was too late, for Calvin had seen her, apparently, and raised a hand in greeting. Or *was* it too late? – for Calvin made no further effort to acknowledge Maggie and showed no signs of approaching her.

Maggie Blackburn, tall, in a navy-blue wool suit and a white silk blouse, her silver-blonde hair braided and wound about her head, felt rather more relieved than rebuffed. She returned her colleague's casual gesture and continued on her way.

The new museum was a splendid bold structure of open spaces, dazzling white surfaces, plate glass, stone and brick, ramps and open staircases and white wire mesh; the première exhibit, no less striking, was of gigantic antediluvian-looking figures by a woman sculptor from West Germany. How strong, how assured these images, part animal and part human, and the imaginative new building that housed them – Maggie found herself wandering wide-eyed, wholly uncritical. For months, since that terrible Sunday in September when Brendan had come to her house, she had rarely been of a frame of mind to respond to aesthetic experiences of any kind; but now an impersonal happiness flooded through her. Her fingers twitched with pleasure as if seeking an imaginary keyboard. I am an artist too, she thought. A sort of artist.

Though lately her experience at the piano was frustrating. When she concentrated on the interior life of a piece, not merely its notes, she played with something of her old feeling; but much of the time she was distracted, even anxious. As if, while she immersed herself in the piano, something urgent, even fatal, were happening elsewhere. *This intolerable mystery must be solved!* The Beethoven recital had been rescheduled for February, but Maggie was having difficulty getting Bill Queller to rehearse with her. The last time she'd seen the cellist, at a New Year's Day open house at the Lichtmans', he had seemed to be trying to avoid her until at last Maggie approached him directly; but he'd been vague about making plans – 'My concentration isn't quite back to normal.' Maggie was struck by the man's sallow skin, an air of something both sickly and sullen in his face. Near-bald for years, Bill Queller had yet had a certain youthful manner; he had cultivated not the roguish-puckish humour of his friend Rolfe Christensen, but another quieter, more assured, sort of public persona. Now that stance was gone. The cellist looked middle-aged, defeated, yet angry too. The thought came to Maggie – and was at once rejected – that here was Rolfe Christensen's murderer: his oldest friend in Forest Park.

She'd said, clumsily, 'I – I know you've taken – this all so – hard –'

Bill had said, with a mean little smile, 'Some of us, yes – *we* have. Taken it hard.'

142

Now, in the museum, contemplating an earthen-coloured six-foot-tall stylized fossil, part humanoid, part leaf, Maggie Blackburn again considered the possibility of Bill Queller as the killer – and rejected the idea a second time. For Bill, who played the cello so beautifully, whose life was his cello playing, any act of violence, however indirect, would be unthinkable. Only in the abstract can we suspect people, Maggie thought; people, at least, whom we know as friends, colleagues, like-minded men and women. She knew Bill was bitter (and publicly embarrassed) over the fact that Nicholas Reickmann, and not he, had been named Rolfe Christensen's literary executor; but he had not known of this until after Christensen's death. It had been a posthumous slap of a kind, very likely devised by Christensen in a moment of pique.

Staring at the six-foot fossil, a thing of beauty possessed of a crude, primitive power, Maggie felt someone touch her shoulder; it was Calvin Gould. He was smiling his sociable smile and said warmly, 'Why, hello, Maggie! I was sure it must be you.' His words were perhaps not quite sincere, but Maggie understood their purpose. (For Naomi Gould, indifferent to Maggie Blackburn, very likely not knowing or caring who Maggie Blackburn was, continued to stroll at the far end of the gallery, her back to them.)

As they spoke together – initially, of the museum and the exhibit – Maggie felt her face burn, thinking, He knows. For surely her love of this man shone in her eyes, exposed and helpless.

Calvin Gould was standing rather close to Maggie, it seemed. He was regarding her rather closely. And smiling – smiling hard. She saw that the irises of his eyes were hazel-brown, rimmed with black distinctive as crayon; the whites were faintly threaded with blood. Though, as always, Maggie was confused in this man's very presence, happy and scattered, prone to nervous laughter, uncertain speech, as if her vision of herself had suddenly lost its focus, she could see that Calvin too was sallow-skinned; if not defeated, he was tired; despite his animation there was a current of something strained and apprehensive in his manner, worry lines in his forehead, the hairs at his temples touched with grey, like frost. His mouth appeared thinner, tighter, than Maggie recalled. Poor Calvin! The pressure of the past several months had exhausted him. Maggie felt a stab of sympathy and anger that his detractors were deriving satisfaction from his predicament. Maggie had long since reconciled Calvin's politic advice to Brendan Bauer with what she knew of the man's essential integrity.

Calvin continued to praise the museum, the exhibit. 'I wouldn't have driven up here, I'm afraid, except for Naomi's insisting, and now I'm certainly glad that I did' – words that seemed to Maggie purposefully ambiguous: for he was looking so intently at her.

Maggie said, laughing, 'I'm grateful sometimes just to get away from home. From – certain obsessive thoughts.'

Thus they began to speak of the subject uppermost in both their minds. Like a magnet, its attraction was irresistible.

In an undertone, as if he believed someone in the gallery might be listening, Calvin told Maggie that he had reason to believe, from something Detective Miles had said the other day – 'We keep in frequent contact; he's a good, reliable man I think' – that the case might soon be resolved; an arrest might soon be made.

Maggie said, 'An arrest?'

'Possibly.'

'But who?'

'I don't believe I can say.'

Maggie stared at him searchingly. 'I certainly hope so,' she said, slowly, 'for Brendan Bauer's sake.'

'Ah, yes – for Brendan Bauer's sake.'

'It would be such a relief to him. To be truly free.'

Calvin was regarding Maggie attentively, with a look she could not interpret. This was not, she realized, the Calvin Gould of old, but a man both uneasy and expectant, frowning, smiling, tense with feeling. Did he feel concern for her? Even, in his somewhat stiff way, a kind of affectionate worry? But why?

He touched her arm: Maggie felt the subtle shock of it radiate through her.

He said hesitantly, as if to spare her feelings, 'Maggie, you've been wonderfully kind to that young man, and supportive of him. But –'

'Yes?'

'Brendan Bauer may not be after all the person you think he is.'

'What do you mean?' Maggie smiled, perplexed. Her tone was disbelieving and frightened.

Calvin seemed reluctant to continue, embarrassed. He sighed and drew a hand rapidly through his hair, in a gesture of distraction and frustration Maggie had often seen him make, in faculty meetings for which he was chair, when confronted with obtuse or obfuscatory persons. He said, 'It's just that, Maggie, some of us – your friends – think you should be prepared for the possibility of – a disappointment.'

'I – I don't understand.'

'Don't you?'

'I don't understand.'

Patiently, kindly, his fingers still on her arm, exerting a pressure almost of constraint, Calvin was saying extraordinary things, things not to be absorbed, though Maggie stood tall and calm, at her full height, listening attentively. It was as if – a detached sort of delirium! – she were hearing jarring notes, incomprehensible errors in rhythm, even as her fingers continued to play flawlessly, precisely, at the outermost limits of their skill. 'We all know how generous you've been to Brendan, and how he has depended upon you. You seem to have felt personally responsible for him. But from the first, when he came to me that morning, with his account of having been mistreated by Rolfe Christensen, I seemed to sense that something wasn't quite right. I don't mean, of course, that I didn't believe that something had happened to him – certainly, it was obvious that something had happened. But there are such things as sado-masochistic affairs. And self-inflicted injuries. And what might be called an almost wilful hysteria, if that isn't somehow a contradiction in terms. The capacity, in any case, for somehow not knowing what one clearly *knows*.'

Still Maggie continued to stare at Calvin. Her heart beat slow and hard and heavy in her chest.

When she spoke her voice was hoarse, almost harsh. 'But Calvin – you did believe him. You did. I know you did. You believed *me*. And you were angry too. When we first spoke, on that Monday morning –'

Calvin shook his head impatiently. 'But since then many things have come to light. His death threats, for instance. Before witnesses. His history of emotional instability. His habit of exacting revenge.'

'Exacting revenge? But how? Where?'

Calvin removed a handkerchief from his coat pocket and wiped at his upper lip fastidiously. Maggie saw now that he was warm – perspiring. 'There is a history. There are facts. I am not supposed to be repeating them.'

'But Calvin, you must tell me.'

He glanced around as if, in this place of affable strolling strangers, he might be purposefully overheard. But no one was close by; the dark-haired woman in the black cloth coat who was his wife was nowhere near and, for the moment, obscured from Calvin and Maggie by gallery visitors. If from time to time people glanced at them, in passing, it was perhaps because they were an attractive yet enigmatic couple: with their air of being lovers confounded by the fact of each other, utterly stymied. An observer might have believed them lovers who had inadvertently fallen into an intense conversation in a public place, in a place of extreme impropriety, without yet knowing how to extricate themselves from the issue between them, or from each other. Almost miserably, with an intimacy Maggie had never before heard in him, Calvin said, 'I – I'm violating confidentiality, Maggie, by telling you these things. At least – before the arrest is made. If it *is* made. You must know – of course you know, yet it is so easy to forget – that not all crimes are successfully prosecuted, for want of evidence; not all crimes are even charged against criminals, though it's known by police that they are guilty. Unless there is enough solid, substantial evidence to bring before a grand jury, it's pointless for a district attorney to take steps. This you know, surely? Didn't you tell me once that your father had been a public prosecutor?'

Maggie made an effort to keep her voice low. But she was trembling badly. 'Please, Calvin, you must tell me. What kind of revenge?'

'At the seminary, in St Louis. There were accidents. Including a fire of suspicious origin.'

'Oh, but I can't believe –'

'Bauer was a suspect – that is, *the* suspect. Yet not a formal, official suspect – there is nothing on any official record. No charges were ever made against him, and naturally he denied everything, and in the end it was enough for the seminary to simply expel him. He has no record anywhere. David Miles has made a thorough investigation, and each time it was seemingly the same – no official record.'

'What do you mean, each time? Have there been other times? Where?' Maggie asked.

By degrees Calvin had been edging backward; and by degrees Maggie had been following him, unconsciously, gazing up into his face with her immense, wondering eyes. She had taken hold of his arm – her fingers bunching the material of his sleeve – and seemed about to tug at him in desperation, or in anger.

'Revenge? Where? What kind of revenge? What do you mean?'

Calvin said grimly, 'I am not at liberty to tell you, Maggie. All that I've told you already, it was – it is – unconscionable on my part. But I like you too much to allow you to continue to risk yourself. I – I like you much too much – to allow anything to happen to you.'

At this statement, surely unanticipated on both sides, Calvin Gould and Maggie Blackburn fell abruptly, confusedly silent, for in the context of Calvin's customary demeanour, the undercurrent of powerful feeling in his words, very nearly anguish, was the more extraordinary. Does he love me? Maggie wondered,

147

astonished. But why – now? For she was so dazed, so genuinely confused, she could not think: as if having absorbed the shock of one blow to the head she could not summon her strength, or yet her vision of herself, to absorb, or even to acknowledge, the fact of a second.

All this while, seemingly oblivious to them, Naomi Gould remained at the far end of the gallery, about forty feet away, contemplating one or another of the tall sculpted figures. Afterwards Maggie would recall, unless in recalling she imagined, how the woman – her high-held head, her defiant back in the black cloth coat – exerted an unmistakable pressure upon them; so that even as Calvin appealed to Maggie Blackburn, even as, so uncharacteristically, he touched her, he was all the while glancing in Naomi's direction – all the while nervously, even fearfully, aware of her. But Naomi Gould did not so much as once look around.

As Calvin was about to leave Maggie, he said, as if incidentally, 'I . . . I'm under a bit of a strain in another way too. And this too is confidential . . . though it's surely not important to very many people. Naomi is entering the Medical Centre for surgery next week, next Monday, the sixteenth. The doctor has been encouraging; he has said that it – the growth – is probably benign . . . chances are no more than one in one hundred that it would not be benign. But . . .' His words faded; Maggie could see his mouth tremble.

She said, 'I'm so sorry, Calvin!'

'Yes. Well. We – she has been putting it off, I'm afraid. The surgery. She's fearful of hospitals . . . doctors. She had a bad time, once. As a girl of twelve. I didn't know her then, of course. I . . . I don't know what happened to her precisely because she refuses to talk about it, but it was a trauma of some kind and it affected her memory for a while. I've tried to assure her that this time things will be much different,' Calvin said. Again he glanced in his wife's direction. 'But of course we're under a bit of a strain.'

'Is there anything I can do?'

'Thank you, Maggie, but I don't think so.'

'Has Naomi spoken with anyone who has had surgery of this kind, any woman? I assume it's a –'

'No,' Calvin said quickly. 'No, Naomi isn't that sort. She dreads the very idea of people talking about her, even in sympathy. She has always been that way; very proud, you might say intransigent. It *is*, yes, a gynaecological problem, but we're hoping not a serious one; she'll enter the Medical Centre on the morning of the sixteenth and if all goes well, as our doctor seems to think it will, she'll be home again by the eighteenth; possibly even sooner.'

Maggie said, not very effectually, 'Well, if you or she need any –'

'It's kind of you, Maggie, but I don't think so, thank you,' Calvin said. He smiled, narrowing his eyes as if there were something in Maggie Blackburn's face almost too bright, or too raw and unmediated, to be confronted directly. 'I must leave now, but may I call you? Soon? And the things I've told you – please don't repeat them. Naomi's upcoming surgery is a minor item, I don't suppose we can really keep it a secret in a place so intimate as Forest Park, but the other, about Brendan Bauer: please don't speak of it to anyone, at least not yet. Above all, don't tell him! Bauer should be considered dangerous even to people who are his friends, but all we can do, I'm afraid, is wait. In the meantime, Maggie, can you keep your distance from him? Will you promise?'

Calvin spoke earnestly, almost pleadingly. He took Maggie's hand as if to shake it, in parting; but simply held it instead, squeezing the fingers. Maggie, in a transport of emotion, found herself returning the pressure. Do you love me, Calvin? she wondered, staring at him with her glistening eyes. And if you do – what will come of it?

Even at this precarious moment, Maggie managed to maintain some of her usual composure. She said, apologetically, 'I . . . I can't promise, Calvin. I don't know.' Seeing her friend's look of disappointment, she added, 'I *am* Brendan's friend, after all – his only friend, I think, in this part of the world.'

'Yes,' Calvin said, backing off, with a wincing smile, 'I'm afraid that must be true.'

He turned quickly and walked away, and Maggie Blackburn, deeply agitated, could scarcely bear to watch him – could scarcely bear to watch him make his way to *her*.

I am not jealous of her, I do not even envy her.

I would not want to be her . . . except to stand in her place.

Then Maggie Blackburn was herself walking hurriedly, blindly, climbing one of the steep ramps to the second level of the building, gripping a railing in each hand. She had only the most general sense of where she was, for white (white walls, white ramp, white wire mesh railings) is the hue of amnesia, yet this was not (she was certain – she was *determined*) one of her amnesiac fugues. Not at this most crucial hour of her life.

Whether by instinct or calculation, Maggie found herself, a minute later, from a vantage point on the first floor, able to observe Calvin and Naomi Gould as they left the museum and crossed the pavement to their car. She saw that Naomi walked ahead of Calvin by a foot or so and that they were not speaking to each other; seemed, strangely, not very much aware of each other, though they maintained the same pace, carried themselves in virtually the same posture. *I don't mean to spy upon these unsuspecting people; I am not the sort of person to spy upon another person – am I?* Naomi Gould was wearing, not a black cloth coat of a conventional cut, but a black cape with a skirt that fell past mid-calf. She was bare-headed; her lavish, dense hair whipped heedless in the January wind – she wore no gloves; her small pale hands were balled into fists. From this angle Maggie could not see Naomi's face, which she remembered as triangular, with a small, strong chin and a fleshy determined mouth; but she could see the woman's profile, foreshortened from above.

And then, as he passed below, Maggie could see the top and the side of Calvin's head, his profile foreshortened as well, and the bizarre thought ran through her with the force of an electric shock – *weren't their profiles identical?*

Subtracting from Calvin Gould and Naomi Gould the most obvious distractions – their hair, their clothing, the superficial characteristics of their respective genders – *weren't their profiles identical?*

The Goulds continued on their way, unaware of Maggie's scrutiny, headed for Calvin's metallic-green Mercedes in the parking lot. Maggie stepped back from the window and drew a hand shakily over her eyes. It was absurd, of course – it was bizarre and unacceptable. She had not possibly seen what she believed she had seen; unless, so distressingly, it was the case that she had seen what she was not quite able to believe she *had* seen.

Part III

Sixteen

For years afterwards, speaking of his friend Nicholas Reickmann's death, and so hideous a death, Rory Carter would shut his eyes and shudder and say, 'The frightful thing was, Nicky had no *premonition* of what was to come. He prided himself on his powers of intuition, as he called them, his ability to read others' souls, and those of us who knew him well – let's say those of us who Nicky in his sweet, dear but rather princely manner allowed to know him well – were continually struck by his ability, yes, almost to read us; it was more than just sympathy, it was *empathy*, that strange, mysterious gift given to some, a very few, and altogether alien to others. So to think that Nicky Reickmann of all people entertained his killer after we left, that night – that the poor man didn't sense, in the other, what *his* purpose was! – it's really quite unsettling, it leaves me bewildered, yes, rather vexed, and cross, about the intuitive powers of the sensitives among us, of whom Nicky Reickmann was decidedly one. Ah, to hear him play his clarinet, to hear him play the piano, to hear him (when he could be coaxed into doing so, among friends) *sing*: what a privilege! We all have our talents, of course, of course of course, but Nicky Reickmann was *the real thing*. Yet Nicky *didn't know* and *couldn't escape*. Wouldn't you have thought he might have had a premonition?

'But there we were, Nicky and Dabney Sloane and me, having an uproarious time, a few drinks, a joint or two – of course we did feel, at least initially, some awkwardness, some reserve, about being in Rolfe Christensen's house (that is, Dabney and I felt that way: we'd never set foot in it before, but Nicky had been spending a good deal of time over there, sometimes spent the night, sorting through Christensen's papers and such, trying to catalogue things – 'My Augean stables!' Nicky would say, screwing up his pretty face as if smelling a foul odour, but Nicky didn't mean it truly; Nicky didn't mean it *entirely*, I'm sure; he was fond of the old boy, as he'd say, and Nicky Reickmann of all people was no *hypocrite*), but we – well, I must confess, it seems a bit shameless of us, doesn't it, we did enjoy ourselves as we invariably did in one another's company, for what are close dear friends but the persons in all the world with whom you can relax and make an absolute fool of yourself should you so wish, knowing they won't be *critical*, and won't *judge*. So Nicky served us drinks, and we smoked a bit and sat there in the great man's music studio listening to these extraordinary tapes Nicky had discovered among Christensen's things, of which I suppose I should not speak: the tapes weren't of music, or weren't of music primarily, but had – well, how shall I put it, other elements, vocal elements – unrehearsed, 'aleatory', you had to listen closely to figure out what in heaven's name was going on – it seems that Christensen, the sly old fox, recorded certain of his amorous sessions – or *bouts* – but oh dear I'd better not drift off on to *that* subject right now.

'In any case, Nicky was quintessentially himself that night. Perhaps he knew another friend was coming over to see him later in the evening and that was why he didn't care to join us for dinner and eased us out around ten o'clock but I can't be sure; I mean, how could I know? I simply don't *know*. Or perhaps the killer just showed up and Nicky let him in, knowing him, indeed being on quite friendly terms with him, so it was unplanned, an accident – poor Nicky had no suspicion, I gather, at *all*. If you didn't know Nicholas Reickmann I don't believe I can describe him adequately; even his photographs don't do him justice. Though there's one of him holding his clarinet, his big moony thick-lashed eyes, his mouth, that sort of shivery Arabic look to him he'd have sometimes; I can't bring myself to look at it and then, if I do, I can't bring myself to look away. Nicky was – *princely*. Yet at the same time *sweet*, and *generous*, and yes *modest*; some thought him coy and manipulative, and very very cold behind that dazzling smile, but I never did, and *I* knew Nicky like a brother. Now I don't mean to suggest that Nicky Reickmann, our Nicky, was a world-class musician, for of course he wasn't – he'd gone to Juilliard at thirteen and very quickly, as he said, sized up the competition and knew he'd never be great, or even almost great; he'd say, making a joke of it, 'You miss greatness like you miss a train: you glance up and it's *gone*' – but he *was* gifted, damned gifted, and hearing him play you'd absolutely fall in love with him, and half his students were mad for him; it wasn't just his musical ability, or even his exotic good looks, but his gift of empathy, as I've said, his ability to "intuit" others' motives, as he used to boast, and was justified in boasting, for a man of such spectacular charisma must be very very cautious whom he allows near, not just in his bed but, simply, *near*; and Nicky Reickmann did seem to have that ability – or so we thought.

'Poor sweet Nicky: so unsuspecting, when we left him, of what was to come: the last glimpse I had of him, saying goodbye to Dabney and me, he was smiling, his eyes were shining – I must confess we'd been a bit rowdy, laughing till tears ran down our cheeks at naughty old Rolfe's cavortings on tape, and Nicky showed us some porno mags he'd discovered in a drawer, I mean *tacky*, I mean *tacky tacky tacky* but *so* funny. So Nicky was a bit gig-gly still, and a bit high, hugging Dabney and me good night, wav-ing at us from the door, I swear he didn't look twenty-one years old; he was wearing a turtle-neck sweater, I forget the exact colour but it was very attractive, and there was the little diamond in his ear, his sort of Nicky trademark, he'd had his hair cut the day before in SoHo at this place where the hairdresser was alleg-edly in love with him, and his hair looked – well, it was the kind of hair, razor-cut at the sides of the head, tufted and full on top, and this bold shiny-plum shade, the kind of hair, you know, that makes a *statement*. And Nicky Reickmann, over all, was the kind of personality who makes a *statement*. So to think of him, poor Nicky, the most alive and the most electric and the most spectacular of anyone at that proper old dull old Conservatory of Music, to think of him surprised and betrayed by someone he trusted, by a sort of friend, and his throat cut – *slashed* in that dreadful way – to think of him, of it, just leaves me faint: and all I can hope is that at the end, when he saw it was inevitable and he couldn't escape, Nicky Reickmann lost consciousness and just never *revived*. And just never, ever *revived*.'

Seventeen

'Oh, Maggie – what on earth have you done to yourself?'

The first person to remark upon the severe change in Maggie Blackburn's appearance, at least to Maggie Blackburn's face (for others had seen her walking across campus and may have expressed their opinions, blessedly out of earshot), was Mrs Moyer, the administrative assistant, who exclaimed unthinkingly, as Maggie entered the office, and stared at her with a look of dismay and disbelief and something almost of a mother's disapproval: 'Your hair, your lovely *hair*, oh, *why?*' Even the secretaries, Louise and Jody, who were much younger than Mrs Moyer and whose hair too was cut fairly short (Jody's in particular: it was growing out from a brutally stylish cut so abbreviated as to have resembled, weeks ago, a marine crewcut), were visibly restrained in their enthusiasm; though, loyally, they said that they preferred Maggie's hair so much shorter – it looked 'great', it looked '*young*'.

Maggie laughed, though deeply embarrassed and confused, and said, 'I – I thought it was time,' and, not much liking so many rude, assessing eyes upon her, 'time for a change.' Her tone was an odd commingling of apology, regret, excitement, even defiance.

She got her mail from her mailbox and turned to leave, her cheeks flushed scarlet, and poor Gladys Moyer, realizing how tactless she'd been, followed her out into the corridor (for after all, the extraordinary plaited hair, the silvery-gold hair that must have fallen to Maggie's waist and had not been cut for years, *was* gone, irrevocably), and said, trying to smile, this kindest of women, 'You're right, dear, it is a change, and it's very attractive really and, and – it will certainly be less trouble to care for than the other.'

Again Maggie laughed, rather tartly. She said, 'Yes, I'm counting on that.'

But when, later that day, Portia MacLeod saw Maggie Blackburn, Portia gasped audibly and cried, 'Oh, my God, Maggie! *You*' – as if, unknown to her, Maggie were a 'you' of comic dimensions, a being widely known for eccentric if not self-damaging behaviour: perhaps even a public responsibility, like a wandering idiot. For it was not simply the case that Maggie Blackburn's hair was extremely short but that, apparently, she had cut it herself, with scissors.

Portia MacLeod, another kindly woman but far more importunate than Gladys Moyer, insisted on arranging for Maggie to have her hair cut properly, by Portia's own hairdresser, whom she telephoned immediately and so pleaded with and bullied – 'Henri: if I say this is an emergency, *this is an emergency*' – that by six o'clock that evening Maggie looked, yet again, different: her mutilated hair now a graceful, sunnily gleaming cap curved about her head like a cloche; her high pale forehead no longer exposed but partly hidden beneath a wing of silvery-gold hair. And now her large limpid bluish-grey eyes appeared to distinct advantage, and her neck was long, columnar, striking – the proverbial swan's neck. So pleased was Portia with this transformation, as if it were her own handiwork – which, in a way, it was – she refused to allow Maggie to pay the hairdresser herself. She waved away Maggie's protests and said, 'Now you *do* look lovely. Not quite like yourself of course but – lovely.'

Maggie turned her head from side to side, regarding herself critically in the mirror. She said, 'But this *is* me, isn't it?' Portia would recall afterwards that her friend asked this question not in jest but as if hopeful of an answer.

As the women were parting, Portia happened to remark that

she'd heard, from Calvin Gould, that his wife had been scheduled for surgery that morning (this was Monday, January 16), and she wondered how it had turned out and how serious the surgery was? Maggie said she didn't know but that she was surprised (she *was* surprised) that Calvin had mentioned it to Portia, since he had seemed to want to keep the information confidential. 'Calvin told me,' Maggie said, not quite liking how these words sounded in her mouth, 'that Naomi dreads the possibility of people talking about her.'

Portia said carelessly, 'Oh, I think Cal has mentioned this to a number of people. The surgery, I mean. It must be that he's anxious. In fact, he has seemed anxious lately – not really his usual self. Since that – that terrible murder. I suppose, as provost, he deals with pressures we don't know about, and it *is* all so public, we've all been so exposed.'

Hesitantly, Maggie said, 'Do you know much about Naomi Gould? Have you ever met her?'

Portia said, 'I did actually shake the woman's hand, once. At a dinner at the Babcocks', years ago. She was very quiet all evening – stubbornly quiet, I thought – hiding away behind dark glasses, and her hair all frizzed and in her face, hardly trying to disguise the fact that she was bored with us all. Cal has said vaguely that she's an artist, but I've never seen anything of her work, have you? No one has! After the Babcocks' dinner Byron told me (you know Byron has a brother who'd had a cerebral haemorrhage at the age of twenty?) he thinks Mrs Gould must have some sort of neurological impairment, or maybe it's biochemical. It's more than simply psychological. For instance, she said so little at dinner, and when she did it seemed very studied, deliberate as if she has to concentrate on each of her words separately; speech doesn't come naturally to her. And her eyes – there seems to be something unfocused about her vision – or maybe it's just that one eye is slightly out of alignment with the other. This might help to explain why the woman is so reclusive and indifferent to us all – to our invitations. But she *is* attractive in her strange way, I've always thought. Like someone not wholly domesticated, though there's that edge of cynicism to her too. Actually, I haven't seen Naomi for years. Have you seen her recently, Maggie?'

Maggie said, 'No.' And then added vaguely, 'Not close up.'

Portia went on speculatively, 'I was wondering if Cal happened to mention that she was spending a night or two in the Medical Centre so that I might be inclined to send flowers or a card, or even call. But I don't think that would be appropriate since we aren't friends; we aren't even acquaintances. I have the idea that Naomi would resent well-wishers, don't you, Maggie? She'd think us simply inquisitive. But did you send anything?'

Maggie had certainly not sent anything to Naomi Gould in the hospital; she had not so much as thought of it.

Embarrassed, she told Portia, 'I – I'm sure you're right, Portia. It wouldn't be appropriate, under the circumstances.'

Why had Maggie Blackburn cut off most of her splendid hair, residents of Forest Park wondered: why so abruptly, and why *now*? Though few of them were forward enough to ask her point-blank.

When they did, Maggie said, 'Oh, it was time. For a change.'

In fact, Maggie did not know why she'd done anything so extreme and so out of character. Though she was by nature a deeply introspective person, susceptible to long periods of brooding, and worrying, and rehearsing, and revising, there was a sort of potent emptiness at the core of her vision, or perhaps it was a blinding light; and this impairment (if that was what it was) allowed her to think obsessively, often futilely, around the margins of one of her actions, yet prevented her from seeing it directly. Or from seeing herself.

Years ago, as an undergraduate, Maggie had been astounded to be told, by a friendly roommate, that she, Maggie Blackburn, was a person of 'absolute integrity': in fact, Maggie had always known herself weak, vacillating and malleable.

And when from time to time her undergraduate students wrote of her, on their course evaluation sheets, that Miss Blackburn was 'an excellent teacher, but cold and aloof', she wanted to protest; she was too modest to conceive of herself as an 'excellent' teacher, but surely she wasn't 'cold and aloof'.

Maggie had never made any rational decision to cut her hair or to do something irrevocable to it. But on the Friday following the Sunday of her meeting with Calvin Gould in the art museum, she was lecturing on Erik Satie in her 'Contemporary European Music' course, and sitting at the piano to demonstrate, for her class of eighty students, certain principles of parodic repetition in Satie's work, when, though she was more or less at ease in her teacherly role (for which she dressed scrupulously in a grey jersey suit, a silk scarf at her throat, her hair as always plaited and wound about her head), she felt a braid of her hair begin to uncoil and shift, slow and heavy as a snake. How had the pins and the mother-of-pearl combs, so fastidiously positioned, come loose? Maggie ignored the slipping braid and hoped that her students (who invariably stared at her when she sat at the piano to demonstrate points of her lecture, as if the musical notes issued not from the piano as an instrument to reproduce sound, nor yet from Maggie Blackburn's well-practised fingers, but in some mysterious way from Maggie Blackburn herself) would ignore it too; she continued to play and then rose, with no haste, and secured the braid in place and continued with the lecture; and that night while undressing for bed she felt a flame pass swiftly over her of sheer frustration, and rage, and a wish to do injury, and before she quite realized what she was doing she had taken up a pair of scissors and lifted a handful of her long thick hair and begun cutting.

Throwing down the first shredded handful, Maggie heard herself sob, 'There! Done! Can't be *undone*!'

Maggie had not heard from Calvin Gould since Sunday, since their disturbing conversation, but then she had not realistically expected to hear from him, and deliberately – discreetly – stayed away from a lecture-recital on campus, on Wednesday evening, that Calvin Gould would have attended. But she thought of his strange, shocking words a good deal, in fact, obsessively; and though she remained convinced that Calvin must be mistaken about Brendan Bauer (what had Calvin said of poor Brendan? The young man might be considered 'dangerous'?), she did not telephone Brendan to ask after him, nor did she invite him to her house for a casual meal, as she sometimes did, sensing his loneliness. She filled the week – days, evenings, waking hours – with work: for is not work, of all human occupations, the most satisfying, the most narcotic? The elder, deaf Beethoven, cocooned in a world of silence that was yet a world of sound – *his* sound – was the paradigm of all artists, Maggie thought. His genius had perhaps little to do with the transcendental effort of his being.

So Maggie worked through most of that long week and stayed home, alone, every evening; and though, on Monday, by way of her dear friend's kindness, she looked eminently presentable, she declined an invitation to go out to dinner with friends to a local restaurant, preferring to work. So the day and the night of January 16 passed without event in Maggie Blackburn's life, even as its catastrophic events, for others, would forever alter her life; and it was not until the morning of January 17 – unnervingly early: 6.45 a.m. – that the call came from Brendan Bauer.

The young man did not identify himself, for there was hardly any need.

'M-M-Maggie? I-I-I-I've been arrested!'

Sleepy-headed, rather more annoyed initially than surprised, Maggie asked, 'Brendan? What do you mean? Why? What on earth has happened?'

(She was thinking, What bad luck he is! Though surely she must have meant, What bad luck he *has*!)

Brendan's stammer had not been so pronounced since that Sunday in September; he seemed very nearly to be choking, gagging. It was excruciating simply to hear him. In the interstices of his struggle Maggie could hear others' voices, even distinct words. Shouts. Was Brendan in police custody? Had David Miles assembled enough evidence to arrest him? Maggie had two immediate and contradictory thoughts: if that was so, Calvin must love her, for having warned her that Brendan was a murderer; if that was so, Brendan was surely innocent, and Maggie must help him.

She said, 'Excuse me? Brendan? I can't quite understand. *What* has happened? *Who* has been killed?'

And then, finally, his words wetly explosive in her ears, Brendan Bauer told her.

Eighteen

That day – Monday, January 16, 1989 – had been, for Brendan, one of his days of 'strangeness'. But not until nearly midnight had it defined itself as the very worst of such days.

Since boyhood, Brendan had occasionally experienced pockets of time he called, for lack of a better term, 'strange'. He spoke of them to no one, certainly not to his parents or his parish priest; he seemed to know that such experiences were not common to others and that it might be to his disadvantage to share them. They were dreamlike both in the sense of being unreal and yet of being painfully vivid; characterized by an almost unbearable lucidity and an excitement verging upon euphoria, an underlying conviction of *the arbitrariness of all things* – which stimulated in him, like certain hallucinogenic drugs, both horror and ecstasy. At such times Brendan stared hard at everything he could see, people, objects, gradations of light and shadow, and listened yet harder, to the ceaseless waterfall of sound, sound, sound dinning in his ears, and he would shiver, and swallow hard, and think, But why this? Why *this*? And why *now*?

For all things could so very easily be other than they were. Or, in fact, be extinguished into nothing – nothingness.

At times such revelations made him mildly ill, but at other times they had the curious effect of being inspiring, stimulating – in a way very nearly erotic, visceral – so that Brendan wanted – how *yearningly*! – to compose music; whether in acknowledgement of or in defiance of such revelations, he did not know. In his early twenties he had come across a quotation in George Orwell's

1984 that he felt described this condition: *The landscape that he was looking at recurred so often in his dreams that he was never fully certain whether or not he had seen it in the real world.*

Thought Brendan Bauer, shuddering, yes.

That afternoon, for instance, he happened to witness an accident on Route 1: a spectacular four-car collision almost directly in front of Ajax Car Wash, where he was working. One instant the highway traffic was moving at its customary rhythms; the next there came the sounds of horns, brakes, screeching tyres – as one car passing another somehow side-swiped that car, and ricocheted, and skidded across two lanes of traffic into another car, and there was a sensation as of fabric violently rent, the surface of the physical world torn away and the stark white bones of what lay beyond exposed. And so suddenly! And so without warning! Along with several of his co-workers Brendan ran out to see if he could be of help, there were injured people in at least two of the cars, the vehicles were smashed fairly badly, and Brendan found himself comforting a youngish woman in a fleece-lined parka splashed with blood as, weeping hysterically, she staggered to the side of the road, spitting blood, her fingers in her mouth working at something until she pried loose a tooth and removed it from its bloody socket to stare at it – and Brendan stared too – held like a miniature trophy in the palm of her hand.

Police and emergency vehicles arrived within minutes, fortunately. The injured were borne off amid a jubilation of sirens. The mutilated automobiles were hauled away. The accident had occurred at 4.15 p.m., and by 5.15 p.m. traffic on Route 1 was moving with its usual jagged smoothness, and the strangeness of the day, though Brendan knew it was there, was no longer visibly evident.

A light, feathery snowfall began, at dusk.

Brendan Bauer, that tall gawky schoolboy of twenty-seven, thin-limbed, myopic behind his thick-lensed glasses, had astonished himself by not only liking his job at Ajax Car Wash (this first manual labour of his life) but by proving competent at it. He who had never dared or even wished to participate in

167

school sports, since earliest memory a figure of physical uncertainty, an emblem of masculine weakness, had learned to hook cars to jerkily moving conveyor belts to be borne into the car wash; had learned to wield wads of paper towels and chamois cloths for cleaning windshields, and large stiff-bristled brushes for cleaning the filthy undersides of cars, and powerful hoses squirming in his hands like snakes – all in the often-freezing air and without (as his high school co-workers would say) fucking up that much. So competent and intelligent was Brendan that the car wash manager entrusted him with cash and credit card transactions, and there was even talk of promoting him to managerial rank if and when the present manager moved on. The work, the repetitiveness of the work, the brainlessness underlying it – human beings, flesh, blood and bone, assisting a largely automated process, primarily metal – and the jets of water! and the spray! and the steaming air! – percussive noises, hisses, occasional horns, his young co-workers' near-constant mutterings ('Fuck it!' 'Hey man – fuck that shit!' 'Whadja fucking *do*?') that might be affable, or furious, or neutral, a kind of rude music but music nonetheless, and in the background, always in the background, never not in the background through all the hours of the day, the pitiless sounds of a Hartford radio station playing Top Ten singles and albums with a brass-voiced disc jockey and strident and endlessly repeated advertisements – all this in its strangeness was somehow exhilarating to the young composer, as if it were proof of a world, *the* world, that might have obliterated him but had not. At Ajax Car Wash it was always present tense. Customers came in, and customers were served. And customers paid. And customers drove away, their cars now splendidly gleaming. You did your work and you were paid and next day you returned at the same time and you were paid (and occasionally there were tips) and so the hours passed, and the days, and though his muscles and joints and very bones sometimes ached, and he had a perpetual head cold, Brendan found that he could lose himself happily in such mechanized labour as he had never been able in other jobs (at the Book Mark, for instance) apparently more suitable for him; he could detach himself from the cacophony of noises on all sides and think his own thoughts and compose his own music, a counter-music to the other, and supremely *his*.

After work and on Thursdays, his day off from the car wash, Brendan jotted down what he had composed in his imagination; when he could he went to a rehearsal room at the Conservatory where he had the use of a piano. (Several times, Maggie had been kind enough to offer him the use of her piano, but Brendan had not wanted to impose himself further upon her generosity. He dreaded becoming a nuisance to her and halfway feared he *was*.) As he'd told her, boasting a bit, he seemed to be writing more music, and more interesting music, than he had ever written before in his life.

So Rolfe Christensen had done that much for him, at least.

How could the police prove that Brendan Bauer had committed the murder? For, in fact, *Brendan Bauer had not committed the murder.*

He had not. He had voluntarily taken a lie detector test, and though the results (as a consequence of his extreme nervousness) were inconclusive, there was no evidence that he was lying because in insisting upon his innocence *he was not lying but telling the truth.*

Voluntarily, even cheerfully, he had provided police with numberless samples of his handwriting: primer block letters done carefully, in black ink. Perhaps they resembled the letters inked on to the wrapping paper containing the package of poisoned chocolates but, if so, that was hardly proof that Brendan had hand-lettered the address on that package (or on the other package, sent to Maggie Blackburn), let alone poisoned the chocolates that killed Rolfe Christensen. That cruel filthy-minded unconscionable pervert Rolfe Christensen whom he had loathed and of whom he could not even now think without emitting a sob of fury and disgust and grief. That man whom, yes, Brendan might have wished dead but had not in fact killed.

Thus, how could they prove he had done so?

Thus, how could Detective Sergeant Miles, for all the man's dogged industry, build a case against Brendan linking him with even so much as the innocent purchase of two boxes of chocolates from Heidi's Imported Chocolates in Manhattan, on the afternoon of November 29, 1988? How could he, when Brendan had never glimpsed the façade of that shop, or even appeared in its vicinity, in the neighbourhood of East 60th Street, in his entire life? And when, for most of the afternoon of November 29, 1988, Brendan had been working at the Book Mark, at 44 South Main Street, Forest Park, Connecticut? How link agent to action in that instance, let alone agent to action in the calculated poisoning of one of the boxes of chocolates? And how could Detective Miles link Brendan with the purchase or acquisition of several ounces of the toxic compound sodium cyanide when thus far he had failed to determine where, or when, the sodium cyanide had been purchased? He could not, since in fact Brendan had not bought the chocolates, or poisoned the chocolates, or mailed the chocolates to Rolfe Christensen with the intention of killing him. *He had not.*

It was said that the police investigation, five weeks after the victim's death, was still 'in progress'. Which might or might not mean 'progressing'.

The few people in Forest Park who knew Brendan Bauer, and who must have, therefore, believed in his innocence, urged him to continue with a normal life: to begin classes at the Conservatory with the summer session (when the composer-in-residence was to be Ned Rorem, whose work, in fact, Brendan much admired), or at the very least in the autumn. To these well-intentioned people Brendan would say quietly, 'Yes, but until the actual m-m-m-murderer is found . . . who exactly am *I*?'

On Monday, January 16, 1989, Brendan Bauer left Ajax Car Wash at his usual time of 6 p.m.; rode with one of his co-workers to the intersection of Route 1 and Trimble Avenue, North Waldrop; walked a block or so to Ollie's, a popular local restaurant, where he had a quick evening meal; returned to his apartment, 5-B, in the Highgate Arms, a building on the corner of Highgate Avenue and Stadium Drive; and remained there until the telephone call came that summoned him out, to Forest Park, and to that place he had cause to dread and to loathe above any place on earth, 2283 Littlebrook Road.

This telephone call came at approximately 11.10 p.m., and it was from Nicholas Reickmann.

According to Brendan's sworn testimony, the young composer had spent the hours from 7.30 p.m. to the time of Reickmann's call alone in his apartment. He telephoned no one during this interim, and no one telephoned him. He was working on a composition first envisioned as a string quartet that had grown into a piece for a small orchestra. During breaks from the intensity of composing he'd tried to read and to listen to a classical music station broadcast out of New York City; he'd even tried to write a letter long owed to a young woman friend in Seattle. Since his experience with Rolfe Christensen, Brendan had virtually cut himself off from his former friends, even from members of his immediate family. He reasoned that he could not call them or write to them to report that he was well; he could not report to them, even, that he was studying at the Conservatory as he'd planned; and he could hardly report that he had been sexually assaulted by a madman and was now a prime suspect in that madman's murder.

The Bauers were not, in any case, a very close-linked, communicative family. Were he to be interviewed upon some future occasion, as the recipient of, say, a Young Composer's Award or, indeed, Christensen's much bragged-of Pulitzer Prize, Brendan Bauer could truthfully say that he had been moved to create music in order to replace silence; he'd learned to sing because he had not been much encouraged to talk. Through his undergraduate years at Indiana, and even more markedly since then, he had often been out of touch with his parents for months at a time. He could not escape the unhappy thought that, fundamentally, his father did not *like* him . . . though as a dutiful Catholic father Mr

Bauer *loved* his youngest son. Mrs Bauer, being a woman, was more forthcoming because (Brendan could not escape thinking) she was less critical. Yet even Mrs Bauer was not very demonstrative in her affection for him, or for any of her sons. Stiffly, she embraced Brendan, kissed him on the cheek; stiffly, he embraced her in return and allowed himself to be kissed. During that period of intoxication when he had believed it was his fate to become a Roman Catholic priest, Brendan had not touched his mother at all. *Noli me tangere.*

His relations with women other than his mother were equally uncomfortable. There had been girlfriends, and there had been intimacies of varying degrees of consummation; certainly, from early adolescence, he had suffered pangs of sexual desire – but the 'desire' was often objectless, arising from his body's mere need. How then to attach romance to it, and why?

Of course, Brendan had romantic interludes. They had all ended, not in bitterness and recriminations but in friendship – a sort of slow waning away. His former girlfriends married, became wives and mothers, or disappeared into the rigours of professional careers. The frequency with which he found himself thinking of Maggie Blackburn, and the pinpricks of hurt, anxiety, even jealousy he felt over the fact (by January 16 it *was* a fact) that she seemed to have cooled in her regard for him – telephoned him less often, hadn't invited him over for dinner since before Christmas – suggested that he was developing a romantic attachment for her; if he was not careful he would end by falling in love with her. Like many seemingly artistic people, Brendan tended to crave what could not be his – could not, in these particular circumstances, ever be his.

As if any normal woman, let alone a woman of Maggie Blackburn's poise, beauty and professional achievement, could care for *him*.

As if any normal woman, let alone a fastidious, high-minded woman like Maggie Blackburn, knowing of Brendan's treatment at the hands (and not only the hands) of a sexual pervert, could care for *him*.

And wasn't he too young for her, in any case, six or seven years too young?

Immature, unmanly. Unworthy.

(He wondered how, seeing Maggie less frequently now, and transfixed with shyness at the mere thought of bringing up such a subject, he could allow her to know – casually, undramatically – that he had learned, by way of Nicholas Reickmann, that about a month before his death Rolfe Christensen had tested negative for HIV.)

'Of course, I don't really love her. I don't love anyone.'

These words startled him. He'd spoken aloud; having left off writing his dull uninspired letter to the young woman in Seattle. It was 11.05 p.m. He was exhausted suddenly; he needed to sleep. Tomorrow was Tuesday, another workday. He had to sleep, and he had to sleep hard. Already jets of harsh cleansing water were shooting on to cars' roofs and bonnets and windows, already the rowdy high-school boys were shouting good-natured obscenities at one another. Brendan Bauer was of the working class and could no longer afford the middle-class luxury of over-much thinking, brooding, grieving.

But then the telephone, silent for days – weeks? – rang.

The telephone rang: and, by one of those coincidences that cannot bear examination, the caller was Nicholas Reickmann himself.

Though Nicholas sounded strange. His voice was faint and wooden and he repeatedly cleared his throat.

'Wonder if you could . . . come over here, Brendan? Tonight? Right now?'

'*Now*? But it's so – '

'Crucial. Must talk to you.'

Brendan was fully awake, now, and astonished.

'C-can't it wait until . . . ?'

Though in the past several weeks Nicholas Reickmann had been friendly toward Brendan, out of sympathy or pity perhaps, the men were hardly on intimate terms: Brendan was not one who would ever be invited to call Reickmann 'Nicky'.

'I . . . have material. His diary. Tapes. I . . . I know who his killer is. It will exonerate you . . . completely.'

'W-w-what?'

'Diary. Names names. Everyone. And there's a tape . . . *you* are recorded.'

'His k-k-killer? You *know*?'

Such a flood of relief and happiness rose in Brendan, he feared he might burst into tears. He cried, 'Oh, you *know*? Oh, do you? Oh – ' He gripped the receiver hard in sudden apprehension that Nicholas Reickmann would hang up. 'W-w-who is it?'

There was a pause. Brendan thought, Is someone there with Nicholas? but he was envisioning Nicholas Reickmann in Nicholas's condominium apartment, a stylish sparely furnished white-walled place with an interior courtyard, and the idea could not retain itself, for he was on his feet, breathing quickly, his eyes moistening behind his glasses. On the other end of the line Nicholas cleared his throat and said, 'I . . . will have to show you. In person. You'll see why. Can you come? Now?'

It was eleven-fifteen by the clock at Brendan's bedside.

Did the buses run at this hour? He had no idea.

'I'll have to get a b-b-bus, Nicholas, but I'll be there!'

'I'm not at home. I'm . . . at his house.'

'His?' For an instant Brendan thought the other must mean the killer's house.

'And don't take a bus, take a taxi.'

'Oh . . . I can't exactly afford a – '

'I'll reimburse you later.'

'I mean, I *can* pay, I've got at least ten d-d-dollars, but – '

'Just come here . . . at once. Hurry.'

'Yes, but – who is the k-k-killer? You have actual *proof*? I told everyone it wasn't m-m-me! I told the police, I *swore*! And nobody b-b-b-believed!'

'His house. You know where?'

'Chr-Chr-Christensen's?' Brendan swallowed hard. He halfway wondered if he could bring himself to enter that house another time. He said, in a near whisper, 'Oh, Nicholas – I don't kn-kn-know.'

But Nicholas Reickmann seemed not to hear. He was saying in his slow, strange, mechanical voice, 'Crucial to come at once. The address is 2283 Littlebrook Road. Take a taxi . . . tell no one. Brendan?'

'Y-yes?'

'*Tell no one.*'

The Christensen house was a twenty-minute taxi ride from the Highgate Arms, a trip of gradual ascensions, for Forest Park was on a higher plane than working-class Waldrop; and Littlebrook itself was steeper than Brendan had recalled. That nightmare of a street! That house of infamy, of degradation and pain! Not in his most deranged, self-lacerating fantasies could Brendan have anticipated voluntarily returning to it, yet here he was. So eager to hurry to the front door he thrust a ten-dollar bill into the taxi driver's hand, and told him please keep the change. The fare on the meter was only $6.90.

Numberless times since the assault, Brendan had tormented himself with the recollection of the innocence, the naïveté, the idiot trust with which he'd originally entered Christensen's house; the wine-warmed pleasure he'd felt, a deluded sense of invulnerability in imagining himself selected out of the entire group of incoming graduate fellows as special . . . favoured by the distinguished composer. What a baby he'd been! Yet Christensen's big broad ruddy face had been lit with what seemed a genuine magnanimity; his hand on Brendan's shoulder as he steered him through the doorway had seemed genuinely avuncular. Rolfe Christensen's gaily drunken hospitality had been of a piece, Brendan had thought, with the hospitality of Maggie Blackburn.

He rang the doorbell. And waited.

He had not been so excited, in a positive sense, in a very long time.

(And who was the killer? Did Nicholas really have evidence? And what had he said about Brendan himself being on tape? Had Christensen taped some of their – encounter? The actual assaults? Could there be a record of Brendan's pleas for mercy, his screams of terror, his sobs, moans? It sickened him to think that Nicholas, or anyone, had heard such a tape; but if the tape existed, now would be the time to destroy it.)

The Christensen house, stately red brick, well-kept, had nonetheless a sepulchral air, for the front rooms were darkened; one might have thought no one was home, except, peering through one of the narrow windows bordering the front door, Brendan could see that the interior, toward the rear, was lit. And he heard, or imagined he heard, voices. Sounds? As of drums?

He tried the doorbell another time, then turned the doorknob and discovered that the door was unlocked; so, his excitement mounting, he entered and made his way along the central hall leading off the foyer, calling, 'Nicholas? It's m-me: it's Brendan.' Nicholas must have been in that impressive room with the cathedral ceiling at the rear of the house that Christensen had referred to as his music studio, for it was from that room the music issued, immediately recognizable as Stravinsky's *Rite of Spring*: that part in which the doomed chosen one is glorified, with lovely piercing notes on flutes and piccolo, and a rhythm that kept one's nerves on edge. It was a piece of music Brendan knew with technical thoroughness, yet it never failed to move him; but he wondered why, at such a time, Nicholas would be playing anything so familiar.

'N-Nicholas? It's Brendan. Are you in – '

Entering the room, which was dimly lit, Brendan was assailed by a smell of physical distress before he saw its cause. For a terrified instant he was unable to comprehend what lay before him; he'd expected to see something so very different: the handsome Nicholas Reickmann alive, rising to greet him, raising a hand, smiling.

Instead, Nicholas lay lifeless upon a kind of *chaise-longue* made of leather and chrome, bound to it with electrical cord. His throat had been savagely cut and there was bright blood everywhere – his clothes were soaked in it, the Moroccan rug beneath him was soaked in it, there were thin streams and a shallow puddle on the hardwood floor close by. It looked as if the room had been hurriedly and carelessly searched: books and records had been swept off shelves, desk drawers had been yanked out, cartons of material were overturned. On the brick wall beside the fireplace the words FAGS DIE had been block-printed in blood.

Brendan sobbed and called out the dead man's name; went to him, touched his shoulder timidly as if to rouse him, and his cheek . . . Nicholas's head lay limp against his left shoulder, his lips were parted in a grimace, his eyes were half-open and only the whites, discoloured, glazed, were visible. It was clear that Nicholas Reickmann, who'd been alive and speaking to Brendan, was dead, and yet . . . could he be dead? *Dead?* The body seemed warm, the face still warm, the blood warm, wet, seeping from the wound in the throat – horrible.

Brendan murmured, 'Oh, God have m-m-mercy. Oh, God – *help.*'

There was a telephone set on the carpet beside the *chaise-longue*, slick with dripping blood. He fumbled for it and the receiver slipped from his fingers; he snatched it up, seeing that he was leaving bloody fingerprints on it, but he had no choice, wiped his hands on his clothing, now breathing hard, audibly, praying under his breath, not quite knowing what he did. He must get help: maybe it wasn't too late to save Nicholas?

His quick-darting eyes saw, but did not quite grasp the significance of, a finely honed steak knife tossed on to a pile of pillows on a sofa close by. It had not occurred to him that Nicholas Reickmann had been what is called *murdered* and that consequently the agent of the murder, the murderer, might be a threat to him, might in fact still be on the premises of the Christensen house.

Brendan could not remember, if he'd ever known, the Forest Park emergency number. Was it the same number in all communities? He was too alone – too much of an isolate – to know.

He'd lived a selfish life and now he must pay. What did it mean, FAGS DIE? He was trying to dial the telephone, dialling O for operator, but his strength was melting from him . . . slowly at first, as in a dreamy cinematic dissolve, then more abruptly, rudely. His consciousness was snuffed out. Brendan Bauer was gone. Falling, he struck his head against the edge of a chrome-legged coffee table. As the pulsing percussive sounds of *The Rite of Spring* continued, as the music plunged toward its cruel, convulsive, dance-to-the-death conclusion, Brendan heard nothing. The dance played itself out without him.

Nineteen

And now, thought Maggie Blackburn, *what must I do?*

On all sides she was being advised not to become further involved with Brendan Bauer, yet she seemed never to doubt that it fell to her, however obliquely, to do something. She was involved already; she *was* responsible. Brendan, who had less than 200 dollars in savings and no possessions of any value, was arraigned on charges of first-degree murder (a capital offence in Connecticut) in the slaying of Nicholas Reickmann and his bail set at a crushing 175,000 dollars; the Bauer family, by way of Brendan's oldest brother, Ryan, who flew unhappily east to deal with the emergency, could afford no more than 4,000 of the 17,500 dollars required for posting bond; naturally it fell to Maggie to provide the remaining 13,500 dollars. And though she wanted her help to Brendan kept a secret, it was very quickly no secret at all.

Nor was it a secret that Maggie was providing an attorney for Brendan too.

Portia telephoned Maggie when she heard, to voice her strong disapproval. 'I know you're very fond of that young man, and if he's truly innocent as he claims it *is* a terrible thing, but the coincidence is really too much, isn't it? First Christensen, and then Reickmann? And Brendan Bauer so involved? And this ugly talk that's going around' – in fact, the talk, wholly unsubstantiated, had been instigated by an anonymous letter mailed from Forest Park to the *New York Times* two mornings after Reickmann's death that 'there is some sort of sex ring here in Forest Park, a gay sex ring involving students' – 'it's all so ugly, Maggie, so horrible. And you've done so much for Brendan already, do you think you should do anything more?'

Maggie Blackburn, downhearted, ran a hand through her short-cropped hair and could think of no adequate reply. I feel sorry for him. I want to help him. I feel . . . guilty for him.

'He *does* have family of his own, doesn't he?' Portia persisted. Her flawless soprano voice had a particular authority over the telephone. 'What on earth would he do, if not for you?'

Maggie said, 'Brendan is in a tragic situation. If you were in his place – '

Portia said, a bit tartly, 'But I'm not in his place. And neither are you.'

'He says – '

'I know what he *says*, but what is the truth? Why are you so convinced he isn't lying?'

' – whoever killed Nicholas Reickmann must have been holding the knife to his throat and forcing him to speak with Brendan over the telephone. And then, as soon as they hung up, and Brendan was on his way – '

'And what of the tape? The blackmail tape, one of the newspapers has called it? To think that Rolfe Christensen went so far as to record the sounds of his . . . behaviour . . . with Brendan and with others! Wouldn't that be a sufficient motive for killing Nicholas, to get the tape back? I mean, if the young man is unbalanced, as people say?'

'Portia, please,' Maggie said, 'he is not unbalanced. He has been going through a difficult time, an unspeakably difficult – '

'Not that Nicholas, our Nicholas, would have blackmailed him or anyone. Of course he wouldn't, he wasn't the type. But Brendan may have misunderstood and been desperate to get the tape back. What a tragedy for us all!' Portia paused, for she was speaking excitedly. Maggie could all but see pinpoints of moisture gleaming on her face. 'Only just imagine, Maggie: a secret society, a ring of some sort, in our midst, without any of us knowing . . . isn't it extraordinary? People are saying that Bill Queller must have been involved. Poor Bill! But most of all, poor Nicholas! And Christensen at the centre, a fat, malicious spider in his web, corrupting young men and boys and daring to keep an archive of his wickedness, like the Marquis de Sade. And then one day he went too far, and misjudged one of his young victims, and – '

'Portia, please: Brendan Bauer is *innocent*.'

' – and everything came tumbling down. And two people are dead, and who knows how many have been affected? And the young man who was driven to such desperation – what a tragedy for *him*.'

Maggie sighed and let her friend talk, for, once started, Portia was capable of aria-like extravagances. She was splendidly overbearing, she was enormously persuasive. And all that she said, of a secret ring, of young Brendan Bauer being driven to commit not one but two murders, of his very madness – these were things virtually everyone in Forest Park was saying, more and more knowledgeably and recklessly as the days passed. The assumption – indeed, the romantic premise – was that Brendan Bauer, though he strenuously denied it, was an agent of retribution, tormented to madness by his abusers: innocently guilty, but guilty nonetheless.

FAGS DIE. The news media had made much of this crude warning.

Certainly the case, as it was officially presented, looked very bad against Brendan Bauer. Had Maggie known nothing of the circumstances involving Brendan with Nicholas on the night of January 16, had he not explained it to her in detail, she might have believed, as so many others did, that the young man found with Nicholas Reickmann's lifeless body, in the very home of the late Rolfe Christensen, must have been the man who killed him. And if he had killed Reickmann, surely he had killed Christensen too? The rumour of a sex ring, a secret society involving young men and boys, some of whom were connected with the Forest Park Conservatory of Music, would seem to give credence to such a belief. (But did such a ring exist? This too Brendan strenuously denied.)

The very circumstances of Brendan's arrest by police seemed unjust: according to his testimony in police headquarters, he had gone to the Christensen house because Nicholas Reickmann had telephoned him, late in the evening of January 16, to insist that he come to see evidence (a diary, Reickmann had promised – but there was no diary amid the clutter of Christensen's music room) pointing to the identity of Christensen's murderer and exonerating Brendan from all suspicion; when he arrived, it was to discover, to his horror, that Reickmann had been killed, had died shortly after speaking with Brendan, his throat savagely slashed with a razor-sharp steak knife (one of a set of expensive knives in Christensen's kitchen); intending to telephone for help, he lost consciousness and fell, injuring the side of his head, and did not revive until some fifteen minutes later, when Forest Park police officers entered the house. (Someone, apparently a man, had telephoned police headquarters to complain of a 'disturbance' at 2283 Littlebrook, at 11.50 p.m. He identified himself only as a neighbour, declined to give his name, and could not afterwards be located by police.)

The killer had drawn Brendan Bauer to the murder scene, and then he had drawn police to Brendan Bauer.

Portia was saying in a warmly urgent voice, 'Please do consider, Maggie. For a week or so? Byron and I have been talking, and others too . . . We feel you really aren't safe over there by yourself.'

Maggie had not been following the drift of her friend's argument. Was Portia inviting her to stay at her house? But why?

'The fact that the "suspect" is out . . . that you've been so involved with him . . . and if he's unbalanced – '

'Portia, he *isn't*. He's upset.'

'And if, as *he* insists, there is another person who has done the killings, why then . . . there is another person who has done the killings. And who knows what he might do next?'

It was Maggie's belief that there was, of course, a pattern to the killings and a single intelligence behind them, yet even in her most fanciful theorizing she could not see how that intelligence could in any way involve her. 'Portia, I'm simply not important enough!'

Said Portia warningly, 'Nicholas must have felt that way too – my God, Maggie, to think that lovely man is *dead*! And we'll never see him again, hear him laugh again, play the clarinet again, he's just – so suddenly – gone. It isn't a time for you to be stubborn.'

Maggie laughed, startled: for how could one defend oneself against a charge of stubbornness without appearing stubborn?

Portia tried to convince Maggie for several more minutes, but Maggie held her ground, for she had work to do, and this was her home, and, truly, she did not feel herself threatened, but by the time the conversation ended Maggie realized she had become badly frightened . . . these little spells had begun to come over her since Nicholas Reickmann's death, small fits of shivering, spells that passed as mysteriously as they came, leaving her, afterwards, both physically weakened and morally resolved not to give in.

Not to give in: to what, exactly, she didn't know.

Though official statements released to the news media by Forest Park police carefully noted that there was no substantial evidence linking the January 16, 1989, murder of Nicholas Reickmann with the December 8, 1988, murder of his friend and Conservatory colleague Rolfe Christensen, at least at this time, thus no certainty that the person who murdered Reickmann had also murdered Christensen, the consensus of belief in the community – and, unofficially, among the police – was that there was only a single killer, and that the young man arrested as a suspect in the Reickmann case would shortly be arrested again as a suspect in the Christensen case.

At his hearing and arraignment in county court, Brendan Bauer entered a plea of not guilty to the charges of first-degree murder being brought against him. His attorney, a Hartford man named Cotler, had warned him not to speak except when speaking was required, but Brendan Bauer, ashen-faced, oddly arrogant, holding his thin body stiff as if, like St Sebastian, he was welcoming a hail of arrows, said, ' "Not guilty" to *both* – I didn't k-kill Nicholas Reickmann, he was my friend, and I didn't k-k-kill Chr-Chr-Chr' – his stammer overcoming him so that a rude hot blush rose into his face and he had to compromise by saying – 'the *o-o-other*.'

Brendan had consented to being represented by a private attorney instead of a public defender only after Maggie and his brother Ryan appealed to him. Not that the Bauers could help with Brendan's legal fees, much; but here was Maggie willing to pay, or willing – for Brendan subsequently insisted upon this arrangement – to lend him the money, in such stages as Mr Cotler required. Despondent in the early hours of his arrest, Brendan had said, 'I *am* d-d-destitute, practically, why not a public d-d-defender? What's the point of a d-d-defence anyway? My life is r-r-r-ruined.'

Maggie had said, sympathetically yet sharply, 'Brendan, that isn't so. You are innocent, and we know you are innocent' – she'd glanced up at the brother, a man in his mid-thirties with a blood-heavy face, disapproving eyes, mouth, jowls, proprietor of a canoe-rental outlet in a small town north of Boise, and saw to her dismay that her sentiment might not be exactly shared – 'and, since you *are* innocent, it will be impossible for the police to prove a case against you.' To Maggie in her excitable, combative state, this truth was self-evident as the glaring white of the snow outside the window.

It was a barred window: they were in Forest Park police head-quarters at the time.

Later, when Brendan was released on his own recognizance and the taciturn brother had flown back to Idaho and Maggie was helping him reorganize his life, Brendan allowed himself to be swayed, or nearly, to Maggie's point of view. It *was* logical, wasn't it? Proof that one has committed a certain act simply cannot be assembled if, in fact, one has not committed that act. And, under US law, it was not enough for a prosecutor to launch a case against a suspect (no matter how circumstantially damning the case) for the suspect to be found guilty: he had to be *found* guilty. 'It's as if, in th-theory, there's this essence called "guilt", and you have to be f-f-found in it,' Brendan said with childlike hope, staring at Maggie. 'And the person who *is* guilty, really guilty, *he* will be f-f-found in it instead; d'you know what I mean?' Maggie could not help but see how the young man's fingers twitched, and she wondered if they moved with a pianist's instinct to strike an invisible but ubiquitous keyboard, as her own sometimes did, or whether – she shivered at the thought – his fingers recalled the stickiness of Nicholas Reickmann's blood.

Maggie said, 'We'll find out who that person is, even if the police can't. I promise!'

With childlike hope herself, or, perhaps, something more than childlike hope, so very strangely, Maggie had a fantasy lately that her father was still alive and she could drive out to Old Westbury to see him, as she'd done for years, but this time to rejuvenate him by laying out the puzzle pieces of this mystery before him, in confidence that, using only his powers of mind – of calculation, deduction, unchecked suspicion – Mr Blackburn could find a way out of their impasse.

(Though possibly he would complain – Maggie could very nearly hear the timbre of his voice – that she had failed to bring him sufficient evidence. *You must do more. Do. More.*)

Brendan continued. 'Oh, Jesus, sometimes I think if I could just t-t-talk to the right person! Get all the words *out*. I don't mean a j-judge, or the damned detectives – they look at me like I'm a m-m-mental case, they just *know* I'm g-guilty – but someone, well,' he said, grinning at Maggie, 'I guess I mean – God? And I could explain everything, and understand it myself, and this would all end, like a bad dream. You know what I m-mean, Maggie?'

Quickly, Maggie Blackburn gave Brendan Bauer's fingers a reassuring, sisterly squeeze.

Yes. She knew what he meant.

Sisterly! So that was how Maggie felt.

She had been an only child. She'd never particularly wanted a brother, so far as she could remember, but, intermittently, as a girl, she'd longed for a sister: for years she'd indulged herself in a fantasy of a twin sister, often imagined her twin sister playing four-hand piano beside her. She'd had murmurous little conversations with the sister, nonsense exchanges: *Hmmm? Hmmm! Yes? No! Right? Left! You? You!* But a brother: no.

Maggie did not tell Brendan of her final, highly disagreeable conversation with his brother Ryan, whom she'd driven to Kennedy Airport on the day following the arraignment. With an expression of furious distaste, Ryan had been discussing the case, and speculating on the outcome, and interrupting himself to say, repeatedly, 'My God! What a disgusting thing! My poor parents! It's an unforgivable shame!' – by which he meant, Maggie supposed, that the shame was not to be forgiven Brendan; until Maggie was moved to say, half-pleading, 'But Brendan *is* innocent, you know. He has been the victim in all this horror.'

Ryan regarded her with a look of contempt. 'A lot of good that does us, Miss Blackburn.'

'What? I don't understand.'

'A lot of good that does *us*, his family,' he said, shaking his head so that his jowls shuddered, 'after he's dirtied our name, and all. It's in the papers back home, you bet. Getting mixed up with men like that . . . queers . . . *fags.*'

'But Brendan was a victim,' Maggie protested. 'He *is* a victim. Don't you feel sorry for him?'

'Oh, we'll support him, and all – he never killed anybody, I'd swear to that. My parents have been talking to him on the phone, haven't they? But, like I say, I feel sorry for *us*. It's an unforgivable shame, what he did.'

'But he didn't do anything,' Maggie said, confused. 'What exactly did he *do*?'

Ryan regarded her with a look of incredulity. 'Dirtied our name, dragged "Bauer" in the dirt. What d'you think he did, made us proud? Jesus!'

They parted without a handshake, and Maggie walked quickly

away, trembling. She was thinking that Brendan Bauer was as without a family as she; the realization depressed her.

For what if, after all, there is only . . . me?

Twenty

He would have to leave his job at Ajax Car Wash, and he would have to move. Again. He dared not go anywhere near the Conservatory campus, for feeling ran high against him; though he was a stranger to virtually all the undergraduates, everyone knew his face from media likenesses, and his name was on everyone's lips: *Brendan Bauer? Brendan Bauer? Brendan Bauer?*

Though the grotesque poisoning death of Rolfe Christensen had sent a shock wave of horror through Forest Park, and a seemingly inexhaustible fund of lurid speculation, there had been, over all, only a respectful show of grief; for the composer had been known by many, admired by some, but genuinely liked by only a select few. Rolfe Christensen had boasted in interviews of preferring envy to affection, and his Wildean bravado had not been misplaced.

By contrast, Nicholas Reickmann had been the object of a good deal of affection. He had been envied and admired and emulated and adored; when news of his violent death first struck the Conservatory campus, on the morning of January 17, students stood about like shell-shock victims. There were public tears, there were public lamentations. There was anger. And that weirdly familiar name leapt about on all sides: *Brendan Bauer? Brendan Bauer? Brendan Bauer? Brendan Bauer murdered Nicholas Reickmann?* (An incident that occurred on January 20 was related by Si Lichtman to Maggie, who thought it dreadful and did not repeat it to Brendan: a young bespectacled man who resembled Brendan had entered a dining hall, and people began to call out,

'There's the murderer!' – 'There's Brendan Bauer!' Only by showing his identification card did the young man escape being mobbed and injured.)

Among the adult residents of Forest Park too there was little sympathy for Brendan Bauer. Those who had not believed him guilty of the Christensen murder, or who had been undecided, now conceded that, yes, he must be the one, a very sick and dangerous young man, a psychopath in disguise as an intelligent, mild-mannered young man with a gift for music. It seemed unjust to even the most liberal-minded that, within twenty-four hours of his arrest, he was free on bail; granted, the bail was crushingly high – 175,000 dollars. But wasn't there a danger of his disappearing? Of murdering a third victim?

Brendan's account of having been summoned to Christensen's house by Nicholas Reickmann struck most observers as absurdly contrived – concocted. It was the alibi of a desperate man, an episode stolen from a Hollywood film. Friends of Reickmann's who were, except for his murderer, the last people to see him alive, Rory Carter and Dabney Sloane, told police that Nicholas had said nothing to them about inviting anyone over after they left; if the name Brendan Bauer had come up during their visit, they did not remember it. (Rory Carter and Dabney Sloane, from New York City, were questioned and cleared by police on the day following the murder: they had been dining in a popular Forest Park restaurant at the estimated time of Nicholas Reickmann's death and had been sighted by a number of people.)

Among Maggie's colleagues there were dismayingly few who shared her faith in Brendan. For some time – a week, ten days – they discussed Nicholas Reickmann's death obsessively, sharing memories of him, bringing fresh news or mild scandal (it seemed that Nicholas of all people had once been married: in his early twenties, to a woman now thirty-three years old, living now in Sacramento and involved in public television production), often working themselves up to tears. For Nicholas with his funky designer clothes and bold-dyed hair, his insincere but beautiful smile, his sloe eyes, had been a sort of golden boy: the kind we delight in imagining invulnerable even to physical decline and decay.

These parties were unwilling to acknowledge, or impatient with acknowledging, the meanings of several mitigating factors reported in the more responsible of the news articles, in the *New York Times*: the testimony of the Forest Park taxi driver who delivered Brendan Bauer to the Christensen house no sooner than 11.45 p.m. – by which time, according to the county coroner's estimate, the victim was almost certainly dead: the laboratory report that Nicholas Reickmann's blood had tested positive for marijuana and alcohol, while Brendan Bauer's blood had tested negatively for both; the fact that Brendan had apparently collapsed from shock while dialling the telephone ... if he'd just killed Nicholas Reickmann, wouldn't it have been in his interest to flee? And why had he taken time to write FAGS DIE on the wall and to play *The Rite of Spring* at so tauntingly high a volume? Christensen's music room had clearly been searched, for things were tossed about, and there were several emptied files and at least two boxes with only part of their contents intact; yet, unless Brendan Bauer had had an accomplice who'd carried such items off the premises, he could hardly have had a hand in the theft. True, the only fingerprints discovered by police (some of them were bloody prints – on the plastic telephone, on the coffee table, on the hardwood floor) matched those of Brendan Bauer; but the handle of the steak knife had been wiped scrupulously clean, and whatever was used to wipe it with, cloth or tissue, had not been found. And the object that was apparently used to momentarily stun Nicholas Reickmann with a blow to the head, so that he could be tied up – a heavy clay ashtray – showed no fingerprints either.

When Maggie pointed these factors out, arguing that they made a genuine case against Brendan unlikely, her listeners nodded thoughtfully yet seemed not to hear. 'He has a look about him, his face, his eyes, the intensity of a fanatic,' Portia insisted. 'You'll see, Maggie; suddenly he'll confess and leave you looking very foolish.' When it became known that Maggie had helped post bond for the accused man and was going to pay his legal fees, a number of friends telephoned to express their concern. Was she being coerced into this, somehow? Did she know what she was doing? And could she afford it, on her salary?

With her close-cropped hair and rapt, urgent but abstract manner, it was Maggie herself who suggested, to some, the single-mindedness of fanaticism. 'Maggie is beginning to resemble', Fritzie Krill wittily observed, 'a Romantic portrait of Joan of Arc: all she needs is a sword.'

Maggie waited, and dreaded, a telephone call from Calvin Gould; but he did not call. Only at a hastily organized early memorial service for Nicholas Reickmann in the chapel did she and Calvin exchange words; Calvin strode to her, took both her hands in his, murmured, 'Maggie – isn't it tragic!' but did not seem at all disapproving of her involvement, or disappointed. Perhaps he did not remember warning her against Brendan? In the exigency of the situation, with numerous media reporters on the Conservatory campus, and the Provost's office very much exposed, and Calvin called upon repeatedly for public comment, he had not time, perhaps, for worrying about Maggie; it was noted, begrudgingly, by Calvin's detractors, that he was handling the scandalous national publicity with surprising skill and tact, just when everyone expected him to go to pieces.

Maggie, looking after him as he left her, at the memorial service, in order to climb to the pulpit to say a few words in memory of Nicholas Reickmann – and very warm, eloquent, sincere words of friendship they were – recalled their meeting in the art museum as if it had happened long ago. Had she misunderstood him? Had she misread the emotion in his face, the pressure of his fingers? She had heard nothing further about Mrs Gould and the mysterious surgical operation; thus she supposed things had gone well. She thought, at least there is one person among us who couldn't possibly have killed Nicholas Reickmann that night: Naomi Gould.

Said Brendan Bauer with studied casualness, on the evening of the windy day Maggie Blackburn helped him move from the Highgate Arms in Waldrop to the Park Garden Apartments in Bridgeport, about eight miles south of Forest Park, on Route 1, 'I . . . never told anyone, last autumn, but that was how he'd t-tied me: with electrical cord. Christensen, I mean. Jesus! it looked like the same c-c-cord.'

Maggie stared uncomprehendingly at Brendan until, in a quick shuddering gesture, he crossed his wrists at chest level in mimicry of being bound.

Maggie whispered, 'Oh, Brendan.'

He said, '*He* used it on me, and whoever k-killed Nicholas used it on *him*. But how did he know? The k-k-killer, I mean.'

'But why didn't you tell anyone, Brendan? You could have told me,' Maggie said. She touched his arm gently and added, 'You did start to tell me, in my house. But then you denied it.'

'I was so . . . ashamed.'

'So you didn't tell anyone about being tied up? By Christensen? You didn't tell the committee?'

'I couldn't! I couldn't find the w-w-words,' Brendan said with a look of distaste. 'Because I . . . he overpowered me just by . . . commanding me. I couldn't fight him, I . . . couldn't get away . . . it was like I was mesmerized. This cord he got from somewhere, out of a drawer or somewhere close by, he wrapped it tight around me, tied my wrists, wound it around my throat . . . pretending he was going to choke me. *Don't provoke me, Bren dan. Don't make me angry, Bren dan.* I was terrified he was going to kill me and . . . I don't really remember what happened, or how long it went on. He got me on my feet, my ankles weren't tied, he pulled me into the bedroom, and . . . and so forth. I wasn't tied up tight all the time, it was just part of the . . . technique. What he did. Was in the habit of doing. And whoever killed Nicholas . . . for some reason he tied him up too. And killed him. *But it wasn't me who did it.*'

It seemed to Maggie that Brendan spoke with far less diffidence now, since his arrest, the arraignment, the ugly publicity. There was a new, perverse strength about him – unless it was desperation. He had told her that, at police headquarters, in the detention cell they'd kept him in when they weren't questioning him, he'd controlled his agitation by doing strenuous exercises: sit-ups, chin-ups, running in place until his body was drenched in sweat and his heart pounded at the point of bursting.

Released on bail, the first thing he'd done was discard the clothes he had been wearing for those approximately twenty-four hours. He'd stood under the shower, he told Maggie, for twenty minutes, wild to get himself clean.

Now he was saying, looking at his hands, his long lanky fingers, as if trying to convince himself, 'It wasn't me who did it. I could never touch another human being with the intention of doing h-h-harm.'

There was a harsh eloquence to his voice but the last word gave him trouble: he had to spit it out.

Maggie was thinking how melancholy, how delimited, the world of the accused: everything scaled down small, dimensions cramped, confining. As if a gifted musician were forced to expend his spirit in the ceaseless reiteration of primary exercises. Over and over again, trying to get the sequence of notes perfect. Trying to placate witnesses, a judge, God.

She said, gently, 'Let me get this clear, Brendan: in September, when you came to speak with me, then when you gave your testimony to the committee at school, you didn't tell anyone about the cord, about being tied up? And when Rolfe Christensen was killed, and the police questioned you – '

'I didn't tell them,' Brendan said. 'I didn't want to give them any more ammunition to use against me.'

'But this time, you *did* tell them? I mean, that there was a connection – '

'No, Maggie. I didn't.'

'You didn't? But – '

'I could have forgotten, couldn't I? How would they ever know, unless you told them? I mean, you're the only person who knows ... about the other. About me being tied too.'

'Shouldn't you have told them, Brendan? This David Miles, he does seem – '

'He *isn't*. He thinks I'm the killer, he thinks I'm a psychopath, he thinks he's got me. If I told him that Christensen had tied me up like that, with that same . . . that same cord . . . he'd know he had me. One more bit of evidence.'

Maggie said doubtfully, 'Do you think so, Brendan?'

'I know so.'

He was breathing hard; his eyes glared out at her from behind his glasses. Earlier that day, before packing for his move, he'd shaved with a shaky hand and there were several stippled nicks on the underside of his jaw, like tiny infuriated pimples. And are you a psychopath, Brendan? Maggie wondered suddenly.

She asked, 'Is there anything else that has happened to you, or because of you, that you haven't told me – or the police – that might have some bearing on this situation?'

Brendan ran both his hands through his hair in a vague, despairing gesture. 'Christ. I don't know.'

'You said you thought Nicholas Reickmann was under duress, when he called you.'

'Not really. Only in retrospect.'

'But he sounded strained, tense – '

'He did. I suppose. But I didn't pick up on it, really, at the time. I was telling the detective, Miles, trying to make him believe me – it's pathetic, isn't it, how we go through our lives trying to make people believe us, especially when we're telling the truth? – I was telling him that, afterwards, yes, sure, afterwards I could *hear* the terror in the poor guy's voice; it was perfectly clear to me what was going on: a maniac, but a maniac he'd probably considered a friend of his, was crouched over him holding a knife to his throat. Right up against the carotid artery, as the coroner said. I can hear this in retrospect but I couldn't hear it at the time. If I had, I might have saved his life. And my own.'

Maggie let this pass. 'Nicholas was friendly to you, you've said? Took you out to dinner a few times?'

'Three times. In town.'

'But there wasn't anything he happened to mention to you,

about Rolfe Christensen, for instance, or Christensen's enemies, that might be helpful?'

'Miles has asked me all these things, and I don't even remember what I said. It's like my brain is filled with holes. Memory is really what it is said to be ... wholly unreliable. I seem to recall that Nicholas joked about Christensen having so many people who would have liked him dead, it would be impossible to do a catalogue of them, impossible to do a thorough investigation; even in Forest Park, there were people, men, who had secret connections with him. Secret connections. I told Miles that, and he's imperturbable, all the police are, or seem that way, turning professional faces on you ... you understand that when they look at you you're a specimen; you aren't *you*. They assume you're lying. And when I'm being questioned closely, by the police, or by you – back in the seminary, certainly – I hear myself saying things that approximate to the truth, or sound truthful; I've long ago forgotten what the truth *is*.'

Maggie was staring at Brendan with a disquieting intentness. 'May I ask you, Brendan – why exactly did you leave the seminary?'

'Didn't I tell you? I ... lost faith.'

'But was there anything specific? Were there any ... incidents?'

Brendan blinked at her, the very emblem of innocence. 'Incidents?'

'Was there any reason for the seminary authorities to ask you to leave, apart from your wanting to leave?'

'I don't believe anyone *asked* me to leave.'

'There was nothing specific? Nothing that *happened*?'

Brendan's face crinkled in disdain; it was clear that he had had quite enough of interrogation. He said, 'I lost my faith, Maggie, that's all. I b-broke the thread of it. It seemed that maybe there *was* God ... but He, or It, is on the far side of an abyss and has nothing to do with me. All that had to do with *me* was music: trying to write it. I would try, and I might fail, but at least it would be *me*. All that other' – he made a comically despairing gesture –

'was just something people told me about, to shore up their own belief, so the hell with it. *The hell with God!* One night after I'd been in the seminary about four months I woke up scared stiff seeing there was n-nothing, just – *n-n-nothing*. I had to get out before something terrible happened.'

'And did . . . something terrible happen?'

'What do you mean, terrible?'

Maggie chose her words carefully. 'Were there any . . . in-cidents? Accidents?'

'Accidents?'

She saw that Brendan was genuinely puzzled and on the edge of being hurt, or offended; so she dropped the subject. She found it difficult to believe that Brendan was lying to her – at least at this moment; but she could hardly believe that Calvin had lied to her previously.

Brendan said, 'Can I ask *you* something, Maggie?'

His tone was both shy and presumptuous.

'Why did you cut your hair?'

Unprepared for such a question, Maggie laughed uneasily and ran a quick self-conscious hand through her hair. The curious thing about having cut it so severely was that, though she'd always worn her hair up, in recent years at least, its absence seemed to leave her neck provocatively exposed.

'Oh, I thought it was time – time for a change.'

'But why? What kind of a change?'

Maggie had no idea. She said with an evasiveness meant to be charming, and not at all evasive, 'Do you think it's too – ugly? Disfiguring? Everyone winces, when they first see it.'

Brendan said gravely, 'No. It's beautiful.'

There was an awkward, almost painful pause, and then they returned to the task at hand, settling Brendan in his new apart-ment – a single-room service apartment, minimally furnished, on the third floor of an elevatorless building in the commercial sec-tion of Bridgeport. Jets from Kennedy Airport passed overhead with dispiriting frequency. (But Brendan had had no choice in moving from Waldrop: not only was his face known to neighbourhood residents, from lurid articles printed in the *Hartford Star* and elsewhere, but his fellow tenants in the Highgate Arms had signed a petition, delivered to the building superintendent, insisting he leave. The word FAG in red spray-paint appeared on his door, and the lock on his mailbox was broken and items stuffed inside of a nature so offensive he declined to tell Maggie what they were. When at Ajax Car Wash Brendan told the manager he thought it would be best for him to quit, the man had said, embarrassed, not meeting Brendan's eye, 'Yes. Right.')

In this lonely place, a place surely inhospitable to music, let alone to the imaginative creation of music, Brendan Bauer meant to be brave; the face he showed Maggie Blackburn was brave and invited no pity. As she prepared to leave (for it was late, after six: she had a rehearsal scheduled for seven with the elusive Bill Queller), Maggie thought, If I were a truly generous woman, I would offer Brendan the guest room in my own house. As Brendan chattered, his eyes lighting upon her, his movements boyishly eager, hopeful, self-effacing, defeated, she wondered if he had had the thought too.

Brendan walked Maggie down the several flights of stairs, out to the kerb, and to her car. He seemed to have something further to tell her even after they had said good night and shaken hands. Did he hope that Maggie might impulsively suggest, as she had sometimes in the past, that they have dinner together; was he frightened, for all he'd already endured, of yet another night alone? Reluctantly, with a look of distaste, he said, 'There is something more, Maggie. About that night. With Christensen. He . . . forced me to say things to him: "I love you" . . . "I want you" . . . things like that.' Brendan bared his teeth in a sudden mocking smile. His eyes shone bright with tears. 'That disgusts you, doesn't it? To save my sk-skin . . . I was willing to say *anything.*'

Maggie was perhaps not quite so surprised at this late revelation, or so disturbed by it, as Brendan seemed to expect. She was thinking of the feminist declaration of Simone de Beauvoir, *One is not born a woman, one becomes one*, transmogrified more plausibly to *One is not born a victim, one becomes one.*

She said quietly, 'It might be better to forget, Brendan, if you can. After all, the man is dead.'

'He isn't dead enough!'

Brendan spoke with such childlike savagery, Maggie was almost moved to laugh.

Still he seemed reluctant to let her go. He leaned on the door of her Volvo as she sat in the driver's seat, key in hand. 'I want to forget, sure. But they have the tape . . . my voice saying things I don't remember . . . "I love you" and "Don't hurt me!" and "Let me go, I won't tell anybody" . . . and screams, and the rest. It's evidence, I guess. It's *me* . . . unmistakably. When they played it, I broke down. Just cried and cried and cried and they were waiting for a confession, I guess, but *I didn't do anything.* Not to either of those men. And whatever is missing from Christensen's archive, a diary, or letters, or other tapes – nobody knows what they are or whom they might implicate. The actual murderer, *he's* safe.'

As if this were the true issue, Maggie said quickly, 'But is that evidence? Admissible evidence? How could it establish anything about your guilt?'

Brendan shrugged. 'I don't know. The one thing I know is, I'm not gay. Whatever the police think, and my family, and – everyone: I am not gay. I am not,' he said defiantly, squinting down at Maggie, 'sexual at all. Is that crazy? Is that sick? I could live without what's called desire. I don't know what I am, only what I'm not. I am a male biologically, I suppose, but I don't think *male*; I never have, really. I'm . . . neuter, nothing . . . just a person.'

So astonished was Maggie by this vehement outburst, she smiled up at her young friend, one of her sudden, dazzling smiles. She said, 'Why, Brendan, the same thing is true of *me*.'

Twenty-one

Of the mysterious incidents that occurred at the Forest Park Conservatory of Music during the academic year 1988-9, none was more mysterious than the disappearance, on the evening of February 12, of the cellist William Queller.

Queller was standing with the pianist Maggie Blackburn, head bowed, expression muted, accepting applause from an audience of approximately three hundred in the Conservatory's concert hall for his technically flawless if somewhat tight performance of the cello part of Beethoven's Sonata in D major for cello and piano, op. 102, no. 2; he stood clutching his beautiful instrument and his bow in a posture of cringing acquiescence, not smiling toward the audience as he customarily did but simply standing there, enduring the waves of seemingly genuine applause, and it was noted by some sharp-eyed observers that a flamelike blush rose up into his face just before he turned abruptly on his heel and walked off, leaving Maggie Blackburn, tall and slender and gracious in her long black velvet dress, glancing startled after him. Queller's exit seemed ungentlemanly: should he not have waited for the pianist and accompanied her offstage?

Maggie's performance at the piano had been technically precise as well, though arguably richer and more subtle in feeling than Queller's cello playing. The Beethoven sonata itself was a riddlesome work: melodic and lushly romantic in part, then again abrasive and markedly 'intellectual'. Heard once, it was the sort of musical piece that required being heard a second time, immediately. Perhaps the cellist Queller, a perfectionist, had been unhappy with his own performance and impatient with the protocol of applause, especially in so musically refined and critical a community as Forest Park; thus he'd walked offstage without a backward glance, unsmiling, cello and bow in hand, bald head gleaming with a film of perspiration ... and must have slipped out of one of the rear exits of the concert hall, unseen.

At least, afterwards, no one could testify to having seen him leave.

The next work on the programme was a Brahms sonata for violin and piano, played by Ardis Manning and Maggie Blackburn and warmly received by the audience – for Ardis Manning was a gifted violinist who played her instrument with an air of sensuous attentiveness, and she and the pianist complemented each other ideally. And then there was a ten-minute intermission; and then there was to be a Mendelssohn trio for violin, cello and piano, except for the embarrassing fact that the cellist Queller was nowhere to be found: not backstage, not in any of the dressing-rooms, not in the men's room, not in any of the corridors of the concert hall, or in the foyer, or in the audience ... After some minutes of unexplained delay, during which a rumour began to circulate through the audience that something had happened to one of the performers (after the murders of Christensen and Reickmann, such rumours commonly circulated in Forest Park), the programme director Stanley Spalding appeared onstage to make the announcement that, due to sudden, changed circumstances, the Mendelssohn trio would not be played that evening but that Ardis Manning and Maggie Blackburn had consented to substitute a Mozart sonata (a brisk virtuoso piece in A major, K. 526, which the two women had presented together several seasons before and had all but memorized). Spalding said not a word about the cellist, and though his affable manner suggested that nothing out of the ordinary had occurred, it was clear that something quite extraordinary had occurred and that Spalding himself did not know what it was.

The evening's concert had been designated as a benefit performance for a scholarship fund just established in memory of

Nicholas Reickmann: tickets were priced fairly high, for a local Conservatory production. Thus Bill Queller's unexplained departure was felt to be the more rude, for even if he'd been taken suddenly ill, he could have informed someone.

Under duress, the violinist and the pianist acquitted themselves admirably, and the Mozart piece received a gratifying amount of applause. But at the reception following, both women were perceived to look distinctly troubled. Students gathered about them to ask worriedly, 'Where did Mr Queller go? Is he sick?' Friends and colleagues inquired, 'Where on earth did Bill go? Didn't he *say* anything to you?' Maggie was thinking that Bill might have been annoyed with her, for the way she'd played the adagio movement of the Beethoven sonata, or distressed with the cramped style of his own playing. He had not been satisfied with their several rehearsals and had said half-jokingly that perhaps they should postpone the performance again – 'out of respect for poor Nicky, at least.' But it was unlike Bill to behave so impulsively and so publicly. No matter his weaknesses and biases as a man, he was a thoroughly professional musician. Something was certainly wrong.

Several friends, Maggie among them, tried to contact Bill Queller that evening, but his telephone rang unanswered. Nor was his car in the driveway of his home. Nor did he appear next morning for an eleven o'clock class he was scheduled to teach. By this time rumours were fierce: Bill Queller, longtime friend of Rolfe Christensen, friend too of Nicholas Reickmann, had fled Forest Park out of terror of being arrested for their murders or out of terror of being the next to die; or had he fled Forest Park out of shame for being a member of the 'gay sex ring'? Days passed, and no one had word of him, and calls were made to relatives of his, who professed to know nothing of his whereabouts; and on the Wednesday following the Sunday of his disappearance, police detectives again appeared on the Conservatory campus, making inquiries into Bill Queller's life – his friends, his acquaintances, his work, his habits, his talk of real or imagined enemies, his plans for the future, his connections with the late

Christensen and the late Reickmann. No one knew where he had gone except that he had not closed his bank account, nor had he stopped by his home on Sunday evening to take any belongings with him. He had simply gone. He had disappeared.

Twenty-two

'What do you make of Maggie Blackburn these days?'

'I don't know: what do *you* make of her?'

Amid that prolonged winter of shocks and surprises in Forest Park it was a minor theme, but a persistent one, that Maggie Blackburn, whom friends and colleagues would have sworn they knew, knew thoroughly, with perhaps more certainty than they knew themselves, had, subtly yet unmistakably, 'changed'.

It was observed that Maggie, always so patient, so agreeable, so self-effacing, had become quite abruptly a woman with an air of secret determination; she was never rude, or even impolite, but she was frequently in a hurry, thus hadn't time to take on, as she'd always so uncomplainingly done, others' problems and responsibilities. When Katherine Nash, also a piano instructor at the Conservatory, was away for two weeks in mid-February, performing in the South-west, Maggie deeply regretted being unable to take on a single one of her piano pupils; when Fritzie Krill invited her to give her unofficial annual and unpaid lecture in his popular course, 'The Opera', Maggie deeply regretted being otherwise engaged at that time – in fact, out of town. When the dean's office called to arrange for emergency meetings of one or another committee, or to conscript faculty members for new committees, Maggie deeply regretted being unavailable and could not be swayed from her decision. She made up her mind, unequivocally, that she would not oversee the Conservatory's ambitious summer session. She disappointed Portia MacLeod, who had been counting on her to help organize a reception for two hundred guests following a recital the soprano was giving in March at the Brooklyn Academy of Music, as, so often in the past, Maggie had helped organize such events, with unfailing energy and good humour. 'Don't you at least intend to be *involved*, Maggie?' Portia demanded, rather hurt, and Maggie replied, in her new tone of regret and finality, 'Portia, you must know I *am* involved – with other things.'

And while there could be little doubt in Forest Park as to the nature of the things with which, this winter, Maggie Blackburn was involved, no one, not even Brendan Bauer, could have guessed at the depth of her involvement.

She compiled lists, she wrote letters to strangers, she made bold telephone calls. She travelled, mainly at weekends. She questioned her friends in Forest Park, her acquaintances, her colleagues, anyone and everyone, trying not to seem too obviously a person under a spell; rather, more, a community-minded woman with an interest in seeking out the truth.

Which was: the truth about who had killed Rolfe Christensen, and who had killed Nicholas Reickmann.

She supposed there must be a single murderer. But, one night, mulling over the mystery, she seemed to hear her father's voice admonishing her: *There might be a single murderer; there might be more than a single murderer.*

When, compiling her lists, Maggie was reluctant to include certain names – Bill Queller, Si Lichtman, many another – it seemed that the admonitory voice sounded most impatiently: *Suspect everyone. It is guilt that should be assumed, not innocence.*

How ironic, she thought, Father is more alive now, more living, in me, than he was when . . . when he'd been alive.

And Maggie began to weep, helplessly.

She had never grieved for her father, really. She had never, in a way, known her father, any more than he had known her. Maggie had forever operated from a position of heedless trust, Mr Blackburn from a position of mistrust.

Truth is unsparing.
  Truth is pitiless.
  Truth does not 'exist' but must be made to reveal itself.

First-degree murder, with which Brendan Bauer had been charged in criminal court, was a capital offence in the State of Connecticut. This meant, not automatic sentencing if a jury found for the prosecution, but a second trial, a 'penalty-phase' trial, for the purpose of determining whether the crime was grave enough (usually involving an 'outrageously or wantonly vile' intention) to justify execution. The means of execution was electrocution.

Brendan smiled a ghastly smile and said, with the sort of adolescent humour that makes adults flinch, 'It *is* "cruel and unusual punishment", Maggie – they say smoke comes out of the top of your head.'

Maggie said, quickly, 'Of course nothing of the kind will ever happen to you. Mr Cotler is convinced . . . there really isn't any evidence . . . if the district attorney presents the case to a grand jury . . . and even if the worst happened . . . I mean, you went to trial, and were found guilty . . . there are always appeals.'

'Oh, sure,' Brendan Bauer said, yawning. 'The ultimate appeal is to the empty blue sky. See it up there, waiting?'

Maggie Blackburn went to Detective Sergeant David Miles to confer, demanding of this seemingly mild-mannered policeman what the actual evidence was, that justified this nightmare of a 'case' hanging over the head of an innocent young man. Of course, Miles would tell her very little; and what he told her, Maggie already knew from newspaper accounts. She said, 'But it's so unfair! It's so unjust!'

Miles said, bemusedly, 'You've taken this up, Miss Blackburn, as if your own life were involved and not the suspect's.'

Maggie said angrily, 'But it *is*.'

She came away at least with a hopeful sense that, forensic reports being negative thus far – that is, hair and blood samples submitted by Brendan Bauer had yielded 'no conclusive evidence' linking him to Nicholas Reickmann's death – the police might be obliged, in time, to drop the charges against Brendan.

She came away too with Detective Sergeant Miles's card, which contained his telephone number at police headquarters, and upon which, in pencil, he'd jotted down his home number. 'If for any reason you want to talk to me, Miss Blackburn,' the policeman said, regarding her with an unreadable look, 'don't hesitate to call. And if you ever believe you're in danger – *please call*. At any hour of the day or night.'

(This card Maggie tacked to the cork bulletin board beside her kitchen telephone, amid a miscellany of similar cards, telephone numbers on scraps of paper, postcards and memos. She did not want to think what sort of danger David Miles might mean or from what quarter it might come. She succeeded in not thinking of it at all.)

Weeks before the evening of the recital, when Bill Queller astonished the Forest Park community by so pointedly walking out of its collective life, Maggie had known that he was a disturbed man. Several times he had suggested that they postpone or cancel their programme, and when Maggie showed signs of reluctantly agreeing he said, ironically, 'And then what? Once you've given in to defeat, what *then*?'

Maggie was not personally frightened of Bill Queller; though she understood that he might be considered a prime suspect in the Christensen murder (on the night of Reickmann's death, according to David Miles, Queller had been visiting friends in New York City and had not returned to Forest Park until after midnight), she did not seriously believe him capable of such an act. When they met to rehearse, he was depressed rather than aggressive; his anxiety was transmogrified into a fastidious attentiveness to musical notes, a fierce compulsion to play and play again, until single passages were 'perfect'.

When Ardis Manning was present and they were practising the Mendelssohn trio, Bill Queller was generally quiet; said nothing out of the ordinary. When he was alone with Maggie, practising the more demanding and elusive Beethoven sonata, he frequently sighed and laughed to himself, wiping his damp face and fixing Maggie with an inscrutable stare. He said mysteriously, '*I* am the cello, *you* are the piano, these notes are the thoughts passing through the dead Beethoven's mind.' Another time: 'I see people watching, I can virtually hear their thoughts. But how dare they think such thoughts about *me*.' It was on the occasion of their final rehearsal, on the afternoon of Saturday, February 11, in Maggie's living-room.

Seeing Maggie's startled look Bill Queller continued, 'This terrible rumour, these malicious lies. "Gay sex ring." My life is ruined.'

Maggie said quickly, 'Oh, but Bill, really I don't think – '

'*Ruined.*'

Bill Queller was wearing inappropriately youthful chino pants that fit his stocky figure snugly, and a pullover velour shirt in green. His plump, soft, lined face appeared pink not from health, or even from exertion, but from masses of tiny capillaries burst beneath the surface of his skin. His eyelids were red-rimmed and puffy. When Maggie tried to speak, to placate him, he waved her silent. 'D'you know I blame Rolfe for all this? His legacy. That vile selfish man. If he had not persisted in his . . . behaviour . . . if he had not done what it seems he did to that poor boy what's-his-name . . . it would not have been done to *him* what was done to him. Oral vengeance. "Chocolate-covered truffles" indeed. And poor Nicky, poor dear sweet Nicky, would be alive at this minute.'

Maggie, sitting at the piano, regarding the cellist with sympathetic yet wondering eyes, said, hesitantly, 'Do you . . . have any idea *who* . . . ?'

Bill Queller laughed and waved at Maggie with his bow, as if she were a particularly obtuse child.

'Do I have any idea *who*? My dear Maggie, we are *legion*.'

'What do you mean?'

'A vile crude selfish man who yet did not deserve . . . such a fate. For he *could* be so winning, indeed he'd . . . *won* . . . many hearts. Many . . . loyalties. D'you know Cal Gould himself dedicated one of his early books to R.C.? Granted, the men were scarcely on speaking terms later. D'you know I once nursed' – and here Bill named a distinguished musician, American, recently deceased, of the generation of Aaron Copland – 'back from utter despair, a suicide attempt, in the 1950s, as a result of Rolfe's fickle behaviour? "How could you, Rolfe!" I said to him. "That poor man!" And Rolfe said, "I am not a charity – am I?" and I must confess I dissolved in laughter.' Bill wiped his face another time, sighing, panting, as if preparing to leave Maggie's house. (Though they had not finished their rehearsal.) 'Like Shakespeare's Falstaff, he had the gift of inspiring in others, not wit exactly, but a startling response to *his* wit. You laughed at cruel things because, presto! they were not cruel but *fun-ny*.'

Maggie did not know how to respond. She saw here an opportunity for some discreet questioning but was overcome suddenly by shyness, or caution. Though the cellist appeared in a benign mood Maggie sensed how precariously close he was to rage.

'Shall we continue with the second movement?' Maggie asked tentatively. When there was no reply, she asked, as if inspired, 'Would you like some coffee, Bill?' And Queller said at once, 'Oh, yes, dear, a lovely idea – but *no*: a drink maybe,' and Maggie rose from the piano like any hostess. 'Wine, or – ?' and Bill said, 'Scotch, my dear. As long as you're going about it. Scotch, straight. Maggie Blackburn, you are *such* a dear . . . a gem . . . like few of your kind.'

Maggie laughed, stung, at this ambiguous remark and went to fetch a drink for her guest, who remained in the living-room, humming and clucking to himself, running his bow lightly across the strings of his cello. Is he the murderer? she wondered, again.

'Blackmail was his trump card, but alas his downfall as well,' Bill Queller said, taking the glass of Scotch from Maggie and drinking at once, with a deep shuddering sigh. 'Not that I know from personal experience because I do not. Our relationship was in no way coercive, for I liked him and he did not like me well enough to wish me to capitulate to him against my will . . . if you

208

follow my meaning, Maggie, which I sense you do not.'

'Blackmail?'

'Black*mails*. Partly out of necessity, for his career was always "in crisis", and partly *pour le sport*.'

'Rolfe Christensen was blackmailing people?'

Bill Queller wagged a warning finger and laughed and said, 'Try for instance Si Lichtman, not *me*. I was perhaps not pretty enough to – um, qualify.' He was on his feet, preparing to leave. He finished his drink in a single swallow and pursed his lips as if he were tasting something vile and seized hold of Maggie's hand and said in a new, earnest voice, '*You* don't judge, Maggie? You've been so kind to your young friend what's-his-name, it requires a truly generous heart, and he *is* . . . oh I'm certain! . . . quite blameless. *I* am fifty-six years old: my heart is not merely dried out but positively *salted*. All I have left is my music, my lovely cello, and my . . . I'd like to say *pride* but I must mean *shame*. My public, irrefragable *shame*.'

Embarrassed, Maggie murmured, 'Oh, Bill, please, I really don't think – '

Tartly, Bill Queller said, 'Nor do you, dear Maggie, *know*.'

Squeezing her hand just a trifle too hard.

On his way out of Maggie's house Bill said, 'I know you won't repeat this, dear, especially not to . . . what *is* his name – the detective, the one with the unfortunate skin – but sometimes I can't remember if I did either of the . . . acts. Sometimes as in a dream where you both *know* and *don't know*, d'you understand? . . . it seems that I bought the chocolates myself, and – um, the rest; and I (I who cannot bear even to glance at rare roast beef lying on a dinner plate!) seem to have taken a butcher's knife, or some sort of knife, to poor Nicky Reickmann whom . . . I adored. It is all so confusing, isn't it? But you, dear Maggie: *you* don't judge. Do you?'

At the door, seeing the expression on Maggie's face, the cellist relented in his ebullience and assured her that they would perform 'splendidly' the next day; she was not to fret. 'No matter the disintegration within I promise to be "Queller" on the outside,' he said, squeezing Maggie's hand, again rather hard, and looking her frankly in the eyes. 'These public rituals are our sole opportunities, after all, to redeem ourselves – don't you agree?'

If Maggie had known that the dedication – *To R.C.: with infinite thanks* – was there, at the front of Calvin Gould's 1977 study of Schumann, *The Romantic Lyre*, she had not remembered it. Though she kept Calvin's several books prominently displayed on a shelf in her living-room, and though they were books which, in fact, she did consult frequently.

And yet it means nothing, probably, she thought.

Said Si Lichtman in his nasal, languorous voice, choosing his words with such care that they sounded faintly contemptuous and pausing frequently to pick bits of tobacco, or imagined bits of tobacco, off his tongue, 'Shall I be frank? For once? Yes he *did*. He *did* exert a kind of . . . pressure. And now he's dead I should feel some relief but I don't, quite. Maybe I will, but I don't, yet. I suppose it's because so much is unresolved, and though the police have arrested Brendan Bauer, and very likely the poor young man *did* commit both murders, there doesn't seem actually to be any . . . resolution. It's like a deliberately thwarted recapitulation, in a symphony, let's say, and where there should be a release of tension, a reaffirmation of an earlier key, there is, instead, parody . . . the curse of our modernist times. But to explain Christensen, or to try: most normal people aspire to be liked, even loved; admired, generally. It isn't simply vanity or pride, it's a genuine, healthy, human emotion. But not Rolfe Christensen. He preferred being *dis*liked, since it gave him a sense of power. If, for instance, someone was drawn to him – as many were, of course, especially when he was younger: not I, but others – he took a sadistic pleasure in deliberately thwarting the impulse. Why should I submit to your notion of me? he seemed to be asking. I'm more powerful than you; I can't be controlled by *you*. He took a positive relish in disembowelling the weak; I believe he actually identified with Wagner, though he professed to scorn German influences. What a monster! And yet he had . . . has . . . his defenders: not I, but others.'

It was the Tuesday following the Sunday of Bill Queller's disappearance. Maggie was in Lichtman's office at the Conservatory, where she'd gone to ask her colleague pointedly about Rolfe Christensen and blackmail; Lichtman had hesitated only a moment before beginning to speak. Yes, he knew something of Christensen and blackmail, but Maggie must promise not to repeat what he said.

'Yes,' said Maggie. 'I promise.'

'I gather that Bill told you . . . certain things? I didn't belong to their circle; I'm not even certain there *was* a circle. Rolfe wanted power in opposition to normal human attachments. But he kept his victims . . . if that isn't too strong a word . . . unconnected with one another. For instance, in my case – did Bill tell you? Did Bill *know*? – it was a quite accidental discovery of something I'd written that bore an awkward resemblance to something by another baroque specialist. I had a postdoctorate fellowship, I was working on Bach manuscripts, I might have been careless . . . or desperate . . . and failed to attribute sources as I should have done. In retrospect, after eighteen years, I don't truly think it was very important, but at the time I hadn't tenure; at the time I was extremely vulnerable, and even so much as a suspicion of plagiarism would have ruined my academic career. Composers, of course, especially composers like Christensen, coming at a time when musical inspiration seems to have all but dried up, borrow. But for a music historian, standards are different, purer, and Christensen knew he had me. Ah, he had me!

'I was twenty-eight when, out of playfulness almost, Christensen began this . . . persecution; I'm forty-six now. We had a mutual acquaintance – in fact, a mentor of mine at Princeton' – Lichtman named a prominent baroque scholar, now retired – 'and there was the perennial threat that Christensen would tell him about my alleged plagiarism if I didn't cooperate with him in various ways. (*Not* erotically. I do believe I would have murdered him, if he'd tried to force me into *that*.) It's difficult for me to explain how Christensen's persecution of me was almost good-natured at times, as if it were a sort of mutual joke, a secret rapport; he'd arrange to have drinks with me and go into one of his lyric speeches about how he deserved greater homage from the younger generation of music critics; it was adulation Christensen wanted, enormous respect, for the man truly believed himself a genius. "I don't want to settle for posthumous fame," he actually said, once. Rolfe Christensen, that charlatan! Admittedly, he had some talent, but he squandered it, fussy little self-conscious neoclassical pieces, the sort of thing Prokofiev did in 1917, then moved away from. Christensen was always so fearful of criticism, so fawning with people he perceived as having power . . . though absolutely vicious about them, behind their backs.

'It was I (and, Maggie, you must never tell anyone!) who was instrumental in getting Christensen his precious Pulitzer Prize, I was one of the three judges on the music committee that year and he put extraordinary pressure on me, and I hadn't any choice, really, or so it seemed . . . being a "prominent" musicologist, after all, from the prestigious Forest Park Conservatory, with a reputation that might be damaged by the slightest suspicion of impropriety. For though I now had tenure, I now had a professional reputation to guard. For this favour, the Pulitzer, Christensen was absurdly grateful. It changed his public image overnight; he became respectable, he became *the* American composer in certain circles. Suddenly he was receiving commissions, he was chairing award-giving panels in Washington, he was invited to the White House. Very quickly, of course, for such is our capacity for self-delusion, Christensen came to believe that he'd won the prize because he deserved it . . . even as he knew, with a part of his mind, that he'd won it solely because of me, Si Lichtman, a man who thoroughly detested him!

'Not long afterwards, he lost his teaching job at Stanford, the result of some sort of sordid entanglement with a young music student, and began to put pressure on us to hire him here, as composer-in-residence. "I want a position at Forest Park, I deserve a position at Forest Park," he said. "There's no one in America who deserves that position more than Rolfe Christensen," he actually shouted at me over the phone. And so, eventually, Rolfe Christensen did get appointed here. I didn't push hard for the appointment but I didn't oppose it either. Christensen would have known if I had; he would have done his best to ruin me. Well: he came here, as you well know; he tried to behave himself with our students and spent a good deal of time in Manhattan, where he had an apartment in SoHo; the trustees and their wives, the wealthy benefactors and their wives, were all quite charmed by Christensen – he showed his very best face to them, which is, more or less, all that such people require. Until the time of the Bauer incident, when he seems to have lost control entirely, Christensen was no worse and no better than many another prominent artist in a similar position anywhere. You pay the big man, the big name, to be on your faculty, for publicity's sake, and naturally he does very little in terms of actual teaching; might in fact be on leave every other year or travelling much of the time. The real work of teaching is done by others, as we all know. Do we know!'

There was a pause. Lichtman said, squinting at Maggie Blackburn through a haze of cigarette smoke, 'Maggie, you look so sad . . . or pained. You did ask me, after all, and so I'm telling you. Things I've never wanted to tell my wife, for shame. But if you didn't want to hear, why did you ask?'

Put so forcibly, the question was like a mild rebuke.

'I . . . I did want to hear, Si. Of course.'

Maggie's eyes were stinging from the smoke of Lichtman's cigarette.

Is this man the murderer? was not a question one might reasonably pose in terms of Si Lichtman, the highly regarded baroque specialist, the amateur harpsichordist, the good, decent, reliable colleague with the kindly smile, yet the speech he'd just made, in a self-mocking yet somewhat aggressive voice, filled Maggie with a sensation of regret and dismay; very nearly, in its way, with a kind of horror. For the research Maggie had been

213

involved in recently, a species of detection, the writing of letters to friends, associates, former colleagues, and students of the late Rolfe Christensen, telephone calls made around the country and even to London, to solicit a sense of the man's position in the world of music, had suggested to her that there might well be a network of a kind in the profession to which she'd devoted herself, for love: a way in which, secretly, as if in an elaborate game, men systematically protected one another, promoted one another, lied about one another, gave awards, prizes, academic appointments to one another – while, frequently, detesting one another. How was it possible!

One man, self-described as a former friend of Rolfe Christensen's but an ongoing acolyte, said, with the assurance that Maggie would keep his identity secret, 'Friends come and go, but enemies accumulate. You wouldn't want Rolfe Christensen as an enemy.'

(Since Nicholas Reickmann's murder and Brendan Bauer's arrest, Maggie had compiled lists: lists of names, some familiar to her, some remotely familiar, others entirely unknown. All were related in some significant way to Rolfe Christensen; some to both Christensen and Reickmann. There was an A list, there was a B list, there was a C list; there was a Forest Park list, a New York City-SoHo list, an Interlaken list, an Aspen list, a Salzburg list, a London list, a Clarkson-School-of-the-Arts-Summer-'83 list – places with which, over the course of his lengthy and varied career, the composer had been associated.)

As Lichtman spoke, trusting her, Maggie halfway wondered if, in turn, she might trust him: might show him her lists, solicit his opinion . . . But, no: Si's name is among the names of suspects, she thought, on more than one list. He would never forgive me.

Instead, Maggie heard herself ask a question she had not intended to ask. 'Was Calvin Gould centrally involved in bringing Rolfe Christensen here?'

It was a question to which Maggie already knew the answer. 'Yes, of course,' Lichtman said. 'As Provost, naturally. As Cal was – and is – involved in any high-ranking appointment.'

'What I mean is, do you think Calvin might have been involved with Christensen in . . . the way you were? That he might have been blackmailed?'

Lichtman had lit up another cigarette and now exhaled smoke in derisory streams from his nostrils. Unhesitatingly, he said, 'Oh, I doubt it. Cal Gould? Nahhhhh.'

'You don't think so.'

'I don't, no. Cal just isn't' – and here Lichtman paused to pick a bit of tobacco, or an imagined bit of tobacco, off his tongue – 'the type. Not that pusillanimous, not that passive; not, you know, the victim type.'

'But neither do you seem, Si, the "victim type".'

Maggie had not intended to flatter Si Lichtman, still less to sexually flatter him, for the remark seemed to her merely a statement of fact; but Lichtman, long-faced, with big discoloured horsy teeth, kindly crinkles about his eyes, smiled broadly at her, and sighed, and said, after a moment, enigmatically, 'And neither do you, Maggie Blackburn.'

The remark would strike Maggie, afterwards, as a blend of the aggressive and the flirtatious, but she let it pass now, for she was in her zeal, hardly less than Detective Sergeant David Miles or the late Mr Blackburn, not to be deflected from her line of inquiry. She leaned forward in her chair, facing Si Lichtman across his desk, and said, in a low, rapid, rather breathless voice, 'Calvin Gould wasn't Provost yet, actually, when Rolfe Christensen was appointed here. But was he active in arranging the appointment? Do you remember?'

Lichtman frowned, and fussed with his pack of cigarettes, and said, 'That was – how long ago? – eleven years, twelve? Yes, I'm sure Cal was active; he has always been what's called *active*. He gave up piano, and he seems to have given up serious musical scholarship, because they weren't active enough for him. That is why he was promoted so rapidly and why he'll be our next President, despite his . . . well, let's say his awkward domestic life; his handicap, if it *is* a handicap, in not having a conventional wife and helpmate, like dear Mrs Babcock. Still,' Lichtman said, with a look of distaste, as if being forced to see, from this perspective, his own position, 'Cal Gould just isn't the type. He isn't a coward. I can't imagine him, an ex-marine, enduring that kind of pressure from someone like Christensen, acquiescing to that kind of coercion. It was shame, sheer shame, I mean the fear of public shame, that kept me under his thumb all those years; no other reason. I might not strike you, Maggie, as a victim, and I hope I don't strike others that way, including my wife and children, but I am, I suppose, a moral coward about my professional reputation, my standing among my peers, the way my students perceive me – that sort of thing. It's harder for men, I think, than for women: women may think of themselves as "women", aliens of a kind in masculine territory; but men never think of themselves as "men", only as what is given, the norm, the *normal*. Thus to maintain one's precious, precarious ego in a field of so many other combative egos is sometimes exhausting.' Lichtman laughed suddenly, baring his teeth in a grimace of a smile. He said, 'Maggie, you *do* look pained. Surely none of this is surprising, really?'

Maggie thought, Yes, in fact it is.

She thought, in dismay, Yes. It *is*.

Yet she perceived that Si Lichtman, perhaps unconsciously, meant to deflect her from her line of inquiry; so, after a suitable pause, she continued. 'But why would Calvin have been active in bringing Rolfe Christensen, with his controversial reputation, to Forest Park? Calvin is genuinely devoted to the school; he is truly impassioned about it; of all our colleagues he works the longest hours. It can't be just personal ambition. And why did Calvin protect Christensen last autumn, when everyone was prepared for the school to fire Christensen, and when, in fact' – Maggie's heart pained her: how could she be uttering such disloyal things about the man she respected so much, whom indeed she loved, and who had almost singlehandedly brought her to Forest Park, then had overseen the advancement of her career – 'he disliked him intensely?'

Lichtman stared at Maggie as if seeing her for the first time, and not quite sure whether he liked what he saw. With a negligent shrug of his shoulders, he said, 'Oh, politics. Christensen was a name; the school wanted a name; Cal, as Provost at least, has to be concerned with public relations – billionaire donors above all. And it was Woodbridge, I'm sure, who swayed the committee into keeping Christensen. His brilliantly petty lawyerly mind.'

Maggie persisted, for indeed this part of the Christensen case had always perplexed her. 'But when I first spoke with Calvin, in his office, the morning after Brendan Bauer came to me with his account of being raped, Calvin's reaction was immediate – he was angry, he was disgusted, he was incensed. His response was absolutely genuine. He hadn't any thought of public relations or scandal, only sympathy for Brendan Bauer; but later, after the committee began to meet, he seemed to have changed his mind. As Brendan said, he seemed to be protecting Rolfe Christensen. He counselled Brendan not to press criminal charges.'

Lichtman said, an edge to his voice, 'Cal is an ambitious man; he doesn't want trouble. I'm sure it was Woodbridge who coerced the committee into its transparently political, cowardly decision. You know how lawyers are: it's all a game to them, essentially.' He bared his oversized teeth in a grin. 'What are you leading to, with your suggestion that Cal was involved with Rolfe Christensen? Are you suggesting that he killed him? *Cal*, of all people?'

Quickly, Maggie said, 'Of course not. But if Calvin had been somehow involved – in a way or ways we don't know about – he might know who did kill him, or have some idea. He might . . .'

Maggie's voice trailed off into ineffectual silence.

She would not tell Lichtman that Calvin Gould had dedicated one of his books 'to R.C.: with infinite thanks'; or that, though Calvin had said he'd been a student at Interlaken the summer following Rolfe Christensen's position there, in 1967, he had in fact been a student *during* Christensen's residence, in 1966; or that, at the end of the season, there had been a fire of mysterious origin in one of the local hotels – suspected arson, though the arsonist was never found. It all seemed so preposterous, suddenly, the very contemplation of it left her dazed and bewildered.

Maggie rose to leave, and Lichtman hurriedly stubbed out his cigarette and walked her to the door. He said, 'Would you like to meet again, Maggie, to discuss this? Shall I call you?' Maggie murmured a vague unencouraging reply, for her colleague had been staring at her rather intently these past several minutes, and she did not, in fact, think he had anything further to tell her. He seemed to understand, for, at the door, he said, with a lightly ironic smile, 'I liked you so much better, Maggie, with your hair.'

Twenty-three

And is that too a sign? And, if so, what does it mean?

His necktie was a handsome pale green with small stylized birds embossed upon it, parrots perhaps, in darker green: it looked like silk, it looked like high fashion, it looked familiar.

How happily he was chattering about the Bridgeport Nautilus Health Club in which he now worked, in a shopping mall less than ten minutes from his apartment: he was allowed to use the machines himself every day, when the club closed; he was composing music virtually all the time, at least in his head; he felt stronger, healthier, better – so very much better than he'd felt in memory – 'More like a human being with a body, than just a kind of vaporous idea inside a body.' He did look strong, and he did look healthy. His colour was good. His fair brown hair was brushed back from his forehead in a way flattering to his narrow face; his new glasses, chunky black plastic frames, gave him a look of maturity and intelligence. He smiled often and ate his food hungrily. He stammered infrequently.

Brendan was wearing a sports shirt and a dull-grey jacket and that splendid silkish necktie. Seated across from him in the restaurant booth, Maggie found herself staring at the necktie as if it were a clue of some kind, there to be decoded.

They were having dinner together, at Brendan's invitation, for the first time in weeks: in a small warmly lit Italian restaurant in Brendan's new neighbourhood, in a booth at the rear, sharing a tall bottle of red wine and eating pasta. At least, Brendan was eating. Maggie, who was very tired, made an effort to eat but drank her wine rather gratefully. *A sign, amid so many. And, if so, what does it mean?*

Because Maggie had been away for a long weekend, on one of her fact-finding trips, it had not been until the evening of Monday, February 20, that Brendan was able to contact her. His voice over the telephone had been restrained, but Maggie could hear at once a boyish excitement quivering beneath it.

'Hello, Maggie! I've been trying to get you! Where have you *been*?'

His words, and their reproachful tone, struck her as unnervingly familiar.

The news he bore her was, on the face of it at least, very good news: Mr Cotler had learned on Friday that the district attorney's office was 'dissatisfied' with the case the Forest Park police had thus far assembled against Brendan Bauer and had decided not to present it to the county grand jury for the March session.

'So – why don't we celebrate? I'd like to take you out to dinner, Maggie,' Brendan said extravagantly, 'a belated Valentine's Day dinner.'

Said Maggie doubtfully, 'Isn't it premature to celebrate?'

Said Brendan, not to be daunted, ' "Better premature than not at all" – that's my philosophy, now.'

So they met the following evening at Luigi's, a local restaurant within walking distance of Brendan's new apartment. Throughout the meal the young man's mood was sunny, even ebullient; Maggie supposed it was a form of mild hysteria, a reaction against so many weeks of suppressed emotion. Such moods swept upon her too, often when she was playing the piano or lecturing to her class of eighty students, but, like a spurt of adrenalin, they were short-lived and left her, afterwards, with an acute sense of loneliness.

Brendan was eating pasta and sipping wine and chattering about one or another experimental composer whose work he'd been studying, and about new work of his own ('pointillist, mathematical, with quotes from Shostakovich's Fifth Symphony'); he told Maggie he was becoming acquainted with some of his neighbours and with the town in general, and it wasn't nearly so demoralizing as he'd anticipated. 'Bridgeport is a real place,' he said, 'not like Forest Park, which is, you know, only a sort of rarified idea. Bridgeport is even, with the jets passing overhead, sort of *musical*.'

And he liked his apartment well enough, and he liked his job at the health club very well, and – and so on. Maggie gazed at him with a sisterly fondness edged with exasperation. Didn't he know that the corners of his mouth were stained with tomato sauce and, if he weren't more careful, he would end up staining his handsome new necktie?

'Where were you all weekend, Maggie?' Brendan asked. Then, hesitantly, 'You look a little tired.'

Maggie, who was certainly tired yet who certainly did not appreciate being told she looked tired, made an effort to smile; but felt so suddenly sad, so inexpressibly sad, she felt her face stiffen. She said, 'Oh, nowhere.'

'Yes – but *where*?'

Brendan Bauer, warmed by wine, was being playfully impetuous.

'I'd rather not say.'

'Was it about – the case?'

Oh, everything is about the case! Maggie wanted to exclaim, but said instead, 'I'll tell you another time.'

'You look as if – well – you lost your best friend, or maybe' – here Brendan paused and seemed about to stammer: Maggie had grown to recognize the almost imperceptible dip of the chin, the zipperish pursing of the mouth – 'gosh, I don't know: your heart is broken, sort of?' He began to blush and pushed his chunky-framed glasses up on his nose. 'Not that it's any of my business, I know it *isn't*.'

Maggie had stopped eating but had not stopped drinking. The wine was going pleasantly to her head. Alcohol stirred in her a warm yet remote, comforting yet ambivalent, erotic sensation that in turn stirred memories she might wish untouched. She was thinking that no man had touched her, no man had kissed her, since Matt Springer of how many months ago, a man whose face she recalled vividly at illogical moments but could not recall when she tried. Yes, she was sad. And yes, her heart was broken. But she said, to placate Brendan and to deflect his line of inquiry, 'This certainly is a very nice restaurant: you were right.'

Brendan said, again with that little dip of his chin, 'I . . . I called Portia MacLeod on Sunday, to see if she knew where you were. She said you'd gone somewhere up in New England but she didn't know why, exactly; she thought it was some music colloquium. I guess it wasn't?'

Maggie said, drawing her fingertips over her eyelids, 'I told you, Brendan, I'd rather not talk about it.'

'But if it's because of the case, because of *me* – I feel so damned *burdensome*.'

This remark, which might have evoked riotous laughter if Maggie were a little drunker, Maggie let pass.

'Oh, no. Not at all. Please don't feel that way. It's all in the interests of – justice.'

'But are you actually talking with people, trying to find out things?'

Maggie shook her head, no; she didn't care to discuss it.

She had been asking so many questions lately, some of them of strangers, she had nearly forgotten how unpleasant it is to be interrogated.

How like being forced to submit to someone dragging a comb through your snarled hair.

Since her conversation with Si Lichtman the previous week, Maggie had pressed forward, with both zeal and a mounting sense of dread, in what she would have been embarrassed to call her investigation. She had indeed flown to Maine: to Bangor, where her ten-passenger plane had landed in a snowstorm and from which it had departed in a blizzard. *Am I, Maggie Blackburn, the person who is doing such things? And what will come of it?* She recalled her father saying, as, at the nursing home, he'd stooped over one of his intricate jigsaw puzzles, frowning and sucking his teeth noisily, 'I won't be able to sleep if I don't finish up this damned thing.'

Brendan saw that Maggie was becoming annoyed with him; thus he retreated to safer topics. He told her that Mr Cotler had learned that, among Nicholas Reickmann's possessions, one of his relatives, who'd come to Forest Park to empty out his apartment, had discovered not one but apparently several threatening letters – from men who believed themselves ill-treated by Reickmann or who were provoked to desperation by Reickmann's real or imagined seduction of lovers of their own. 'So the case against me, which is the case they've charged me with, doesn't look so air-tight to the police now,' Brendan said almost complacently.

Maggie tried to smile at this news, even as she dismissed its relevance. She was certain now that Nicholas Reickmann had been murdered solely because he was Rolfe Christensen's literary executor; he had been murdered because the murderer, one of those blackmailed by Christensen, had wanted the incriminating evidence destroyed and had decided to destroy the luckless executor too, in case he'd discovered it. And how, if one of Nicholas Reickmann's enemies had wanted to kill him, had the man known Reickmann would be at Christensen's house that evening?

Their plates were taken away, and Brendan gallantly began to pour the remainder of the wine into Maggie's glass, but she put her hand over it to prevent him. She was already dangerously sleepy, and she had to drive home. She wanted suddenly to be gone from Brendan Bauer, to whom she felt bizarrely attracted, at least in her wine-muddled state, and from whom she felt, morally, rather revulsed – for in his childlike relief at being temporarily free of pressure from the police, Brendan seemed not to care, or even to know, that, though charges of first-degree murder against him might be dropped the true murderer still existed.

Existed, and might well murder again.

As they prepared to leave the restaurant, putting on their coats, Maggie said, 'Your necktie, Brendan; I've been admiring it. Is it new?'

Brendan Bauer glanced down at the tie as if seeing it for the first time. 'Oh, God, I forgot I was wearing this!' he said, concerned. 'It's beautiful, isn't it? It's a necktie of Nicholas Reickmann's, actually. Poor Nicholas! The last time I saw him, he'd taken me out to dinner in Forest Park, at that little Indian restaurant on South Main Street, and for some reason I couldn't figure out at the time, he suddenly unknotted his necktie – this tie – and gave it to me. I was very surprised of course. Nicholas made a charming joke of it, didn't want to embarrass me I guess, pretending he wanted to exchange neckties with me – I was wearing that ugly old leather necktie of mine; I can't imagine why I ever thought it was interesting – so Nicholas gave me his. I've never worn it before tonight; I never had any occasion that warranted it.'

Seeing Maggie's look of surprise, or more than surprise, Brendan said quickly, 'Later, I gave some thought to what Nicholas had meant by the gesture, and I think it was this: he felt guilty, and he damn well should have felt guilty, for, you know, letting Rolfe Christensen drive me home from your party that night – just watching the two of us walk to Christensen's car and making no move to interfere. Saying not a word. Nicholas never apologized, of course, or even brought up the subject, but I'm sure that was it. He knew he was partly responsible for what happened to me – for the hell I'd been going through, for months – and so he gave me his fancy French necktie: *as if that were a just compensation.*'

Brendan Bauer brushed at his eyes; his mouth was trembling. Seeing how Maggie continued to stare at him, and at the necktie, he said, less vehemently, 'It *is* spectacular, isn't it? Poor Nicholas! The only drawback is, I don't have anything to wear with it – it makes the rest of me look so shabby and sad.'

Still Maggie did not respond, still she stood dumbly staring, as if the necktie, the handsome necktie, quite transfixed her. There was a question to be answered, but Maggie could not think what it was until Brendan Bauer repeated with innocent enthusiasm, a little too insistently, 'But it *is* spectacular, isn't it?' And Maggie Blackburn felt constrained to say, simply, 'Yes.'

Twenty-four

Driving home, ascending gradually, to Forest Park and to Acacia Drive, Maggie Blackburn said aloud, to no purpose, 'Yes.' By this time her cheeks were streaked frankly with tears.

Entering her nearly darkened house – there was a light burning in the kitchen at the rear, there was a light burning upstairs in her bedroom, with the hope of discouraging burglars – Maggie imagined, for a moment, she heard a faint happy quizzical chattering: canaries? But there were no canaries of course. And walking through the kitchen, through the darkened living-room and to the foot of the stairs, she imagined, for a moment, that someone had just now preceded her, an intruder, male, whose presence had roughly parted the air: but there was no one of course.

On midwinter mornings flooded with sunlight, the world outside her windows brittle and hard-edged with ice, Maggie often thought, waking, *How good to be alive!* – before the memory of the murders, and her involvement with them, swept over her. But at night, when the house was silent except for the rattling vibrating noises of the old furnace and the wind outside in the trees, she had no such comfort. *Here you are, Maggie: and where is here?*

She had brought back with her from Bangor, from, specifically, the drab fluorescent-lit office of the Clerk of Public Records of Brewer County, Maine, a pea-sized throbbing behind the eyes, not migraine but somewhere beyond migraine, a sensation to which no name she knew could be assigned. After her dinner with Brendan in the romantically lit Luigi's, an episode of about an hour and a half, the sensation began to swell.

She'd worn, that evening, as she'd worn to the Conservatory that day, a pair of grey tweed trousers that fitted her loosely, a beige cashmere jacket somewhat worn at the elbows, a turtleneck sweater of so etiolated a colour it might have been grey, or beige, or off-white: still, she was shivering. She was shivering steadily. The tender nape of her neck felt particularly exposed.

Mr Blackburn glanced up sharply as Maggie stood in a doorway blinking away tears. His damp baleful eyes. The fury of his elderly disappointment. Didn't you suspect everyone, as I told you? – anyone?

It was 9.35 p.m., not late, but Maggie decided to go to bed.

It was only 9.35 p.m. on February 20, 1989, an hour and a date to be remembered, perhaps recorded, but Maggie hadn't the energy; she was going to bed.

At the foot of the stairs she stood, one hand on the railing, head bowed. Had Brendan Bauer killed both men? – or just one? But which one?

Neither. He was incapable of such a thing.

Neither. He was telling the truth and had always told the truth.

For instance, when Maggie Blackburn had summoned up, out of who knows where, some measure of courage, audacity, impudence, to telephone Precious Blood Seminary in St Louis, Missouri, and to speak with Father Novick, the Rector, asking him about one of his former seminarians, Brendan Bauer – had there been incidents associated with the young man, a fire of suspicious origin shortly before he left – she had been assured that nothing out of the ordinary had happened, nothing that Father Novick could recall. Brendan Bauer had simply decided, as a statistically predictable percentage of novices did each year, that he had no true vocation for the priesthood; thus he'd asked to leave, and that was all.

Perhaps Father Novick was lying.

But Father Novick was not lying.

How do you know?

Because I know.

But how?

Because I know.

If Father Novick was not lying, and Brendan Bauer was not lying, then who was lying? – and why?

Maggie Blackburn had brought home work, a sheaf of student papers to correct, a lecture ('Bartók and Stravinsky') to complete, but she was too exhausted, she was too confused, too sick at heart; she was going to bed. For after all, no one had broken in to her house during her absence; it was deathly silent as always.

Then, two days later, the confrontation for which she'd been waiting occurred.

Nine-fifteen, a quiet weekday, Maggie was sitting on her sofa listening to a savagely bright and brilliant recording of Glenn Gould playing Bach, one she'd heard many times before of course and knew well, and when the knocker to her front door sounded – once, twice, a third time – polite but distinct raps – she rose without hesitation to go to the door, to answer it. Her manner suggested that nothing was out of the ordinary, since nothing was out of the ordinary . . . was it?

If Father Novick was not lying, and Brendan Bauer was not lying, then who was lying? – and why?

'Hello, Maggie! Am I . . . interrupting?'

'Oh no, Calvin. Certainly not. I – '

'Is it too late for . . . ?'

'Please come in.'

'On my way home . . . happened to be driving by . . . saw your light . . .'

'Please come in, Calvin, let me take your – '

'I realized that you and I haven't spoken together for quite a while.'

'May I take your coat?'

'You're certain it isn't too . . . ?'

'Of course not, no.'

'It has been a long time, hasn't it? Maggie?'

'Y-yes. It has.'

With his usual athletic briskness Calvin Gould removed his topcoat but did not in fact hand it over; he simply laid it, with no fuss, over a chair in the foyer. Since, as he said, he wouldn't be staying long.

They moved into the warmly lit living-room where the white piano gleamed, dazzling the eye, and Maggie Blackburn, blinking back moisture, saw the piano, and her own living-room, as if for the first time.

On the stereo, Glenn Gould was executing three-part inventions. So fierce and so elegant, in other circumstances Maggie and Calvin, both pianists, would have stood transfixed; in these, Maggie was moved to turn off the stereo. And the music was gone, as if for ever.

A profound and riddlesome silence washed over them.

Calvin Gould sighed, and flexed his fingers, and said, marvelling, 'Ah! My namesake, isn't it? – that lovely lovely touch.' He paused, smiling into a corner of the room. Then he looked at Maggie, and his smile deepened. 'It *is*, isn't it?'

Maggie seemed not to understand. She was blinking rapidly; she too was smiling.

'Glenn Gould, I mean?'

'Oh, yes, Glenn Gould.'

'That inimitable touch.'

So they talked about Glenn Gould for some minutes, and about Bach. That is, Calvin did most of the talking; but Maggie could be perceived as nodding in agreement, listening intently. Calvin remarked that Bach had always been, for him, for the depth of winter: that was the time he most played Bach and had done so since adolescence.

And Bach was, said Calvin, for difficult phases of the soul – thus he was playing Bach, these days.

When, that is, he had time.

Maggie was nodding, yes, yes.

Her eyes appeared enlarged, perhaps because the day before she'd had her hair cut again, and again it was cropped severely short, both along the sides and at the back.

Maggie was wearing an old black sweater and an old pair of slacks. No shoes or bedroom slippers, only warm woollen socks, also black. Clearly, it would be supposed, should something happen to her, that she had not been expecting a visitor at this hour – there were student papers from Music 305 scattered on her sofa and coffee table, there was the cup of camomile tea she had been sipping when the knocker on her front door sounded, all with a look of a Renoir or a Bonnard interior disturbed, its female inhabitant mysteriously missing.

Ever the most gracious of hostesses, Maggie asked her visitor would he care for something to drink. Coffee, wine, beer, Scotch?

Not seeming to hear, Calvin observed that it was a painful thing, a dangerous thing almost, for a pianist not to play the piano every day without fail. 'It's as if you lose touch with your very soul.'

His words were sad, but his voice was forthright, even exuberant.

Maggie nodded yes. Oh, yes.

She asked him a second time if he would care for something to drink, and this time he heard her and said, 'No, thank you, Maggie, I can only stay a few minutes; it *is* late.'

Calvin asked Maggie how she was, how the semester was going for her, how she was bearing up under the strain, and they talked for a while of these matters, and of the police investigation, and of Brendan Bauer, though, again, Calvin did most of the talking, moving about the living-room restlessly as he spoke, smiling and glancing around and flexing, still unconsciously, his long powerful pianist's fingers. His stretch must have been well above an octave – ten keys, even eleven.

Calvin was wearing one of his attractive, expensive, but unmemorable suits. Grey pinstripe, or navy blue. A necktie of some muted shade, nothing at all like Nicholas Reickmann's splendid ties. The skin across his cheekbones looked tight, and his eyes were ringed, as if thoughtfully, in shadow. When Maggie had gone to the door to let him in she'd seen that his breath was steaming faintly from the cold, and there was the curious illusion now, in her living-room, that his breath was still steaming faintly.

229

But of course that was an illusion. Maggie's living-room was cosily warm.

Still, Maggie was shivering.

She might have wished she was wearing shoes.

Calvin conversationally examined some of the piano music on Maggie's piano, struck a chord or two, murmured something flattering about the tone, and, reverting to the subject of Bach, said, 'It was *The Well-tempered Clavier* you were playing from, Maggie, when I first heard you. When we first met.'

Maggie said softly, 'Yes.'

'Do you remember? *I* remember.'

Maggie nodded, wordlessly. Examining some photostatted sheets of music on the piano, Calvin didn't notice.

Maggie cleared her throat like any slightly nervous hostess and asked her guest would he like to sit down? And Calvin smiled at her, perhaps not hearing, and something both urgent and apprehensive shone for an instant in his eyes; and he reverted to the subject of Brendan Bauer . . . who Calvin was obliged to believe had committed both murders even as Maggie was obliged to believe he had committed neither, her belief predicated solely upon emotion, not logic or hard evidence. Calvin asked, 'How *is* Brendan? I haven't spoken with him in weeks,' and Maggie said, 'I . . . think he's fine,' and Calvin said, 'You see him frequently, Maggie, don't you?' and Maggie said, faltering, 'Not frequently, exactly . . . he's living in Bridgeport now,' and Calvin laughed and said, 'But that's hardly far away!' and Maggie said, 'It's been a terrible strain for him,' and Calvin said emphatically, 'It's been a terrible strain for us all. And, my God, poor Nicky!'

An expression of extreme repugnance crossed his handsome face.

Though she was very distracted, Maggie could see that her friend's youth had left him some time this winter: his eyes were those of a man of middle age, and his greying-black hair, so crisply brushed back from his forehead, had begun quite visibly to recede. He looked years older than the man with whom she had spoken, so enigmatically, yet with such an undercurrent of feeling, in the New Haven museum only six weeks before this evening. Only a week before Nicholas Reickmann's death.

Maggie asked her guest a second time would he like to sit down, and this time Calvin heard her and said quickly, glancing at his wristwatch, 'No, thanks, Maggie, you're very sweet but I just dropped by for a minute or two . . . wanted to see how you were . . . *are*. But you're fine, I guess? You're all right?'

'I'm all right.'

'A little on edge . . .'

'Yes.'

'You seem to have really extended yourself, in helping him. Brendan Bauer, I mean.'

'He hasn't anyone else. His own family – '

'Yes, I'd heard . . .'

'A nightmare. If the charges are kept at first-degree murder – '

'Yes, but these capital offences are always negotiated, and in Bauer's case – white male, middle-class, student, no prior history . . .'

'But he's innocent.'

'. . . statutory mitigating factors his lawyer can argue, such as "defendant under unusual and substantial duress" . . . "victim solicited, participated in, or consented to the conduct which resulted in his death" – you hired a good lawyer for him, I heard?'

'*But he's innocent.*'

'No district attorney would ever press for the death penalty, not for Brendan Bauer.'

Calvin had been moving about Maggie's living-room, speaking almost vehemently, as if for ears other than merely Maggie's. 'He's lucky, after all . . . Bauer . . . he must think of himself as damned lucky *he* didn't die. When that madman had him, I mean. Tied up like that. Electrical cord, wasn't it? Like poor Nicky, too. Of course, what had been done to him, or almost done, he'd done to Nicky . . . I mean, Nicholas. That's the horror of such things. Such perversions. They sink into the bloodstream . . . like malaria, or AIDS. Doesn't he ever express that sentiment? Bauer, I mean? That, for all the hell he's gone

231

through, he's damned lucky to be alive?'

Maggie seemed not to have heard, she simply stood, staring, one hand rising involuntarily to her chest . . . where her heart, which had begun beating quickly when the knocking sounded at her door, was beating now very quickly indeed.

'Or doesn't he confide in you to that degree? Aren't you . . . after all . . . that close?'

Calvin had approached Maggie and was looking at her searchingly, with the eyes almost of a jealous lover.

Maggie managed to whisper, 'No. We're not close.'

'No? You're not?'

'No.'

'People seem to think you are.'

'No.'

Maggie's terror might have shone in her face, in her slack parted lips and dilated eyes, except, perhaps . . . except she was a professional performer after all, with ways of feigning calm.

She licked her lips and made a wan feminine gesture, a gesture of accommodation. 'I suppose you're right, Calvin.'

Still he was looking at her searchingly, undecided.

'I know I'm right, Maggie.'

By this time neither had any idea what they were talking about, and Maggie would understand later that Calvin had come to her house truly not knowing what to think, what to say, still less what to do; he'd been, in his agitation that was in fact a sort of calm, improvising, as one might at the piano, directed not by logic but by intuition.

In any case it seemed that a crisis had been reached and had passed, for Calvin sighed, smiling at Maggie, and moved in the direction of the door – saying it *was* late, he *was* damned sorry to have barged in upon her. And Maggie followed him into the hall. And Maggie heard herself murmur breathless words assuring her visitor that he had not barged in upon her, certainly not; really, he might have stayed for a drink, he was welcome at any time . . . blushing for the wrongness, and the stupidity, of such a remark; though Calvin hadn't evidently heard.

'Well, Maggie! Good night.'

'Good night, Calvin.'

'You *do* have a lovely little house here. Your life . . . it's lovely, too. Isn't it?'

Maggie laughed, confused, not required to reply to such a question, and Calvin Gould took up his topcoat but didn't trouble to put it on; his car was parked at the kerb close by. At the door he lingered, reluctant to leave yet needing to leave, looking at Maggie Blackburn again closely, with a kind of inchoate and melancholy desire, saying, 'Let's try to keep in contact, shall we? Of everyone in Forest Park you mean the most to me, Maggie.'

Maggie was gazing at Calvin with wide damp dilated eyes: like, perhaps, any young or youngish unmarried woman surprised in the solitude of her home by any man for whom she has felt a decided erotic attraction and has believed, or has imagined, that this attraction might be reciprocated. Calvin took up Maggie's hand as if to shake it in parting, but simply held it instead, and at his touch she came perilously close to crying out and did indeed shrink backwards, but surely, masculine as Calvin was, and forceful, and aggressive, he might merely have interpreted such a reaction as a sexually repressed woman's sexual fright.

Calvin Gould amended, 'Next to my wife, I should say. Of everyone in Forest Park . . . everyone *else* . . . you mean the most to me, Maggie.'

Maggie Blackburn murmured, 'Do I?'

'But your fingers are so cold . . . you must have low blood pressure, Maggie. Like Naomi.'

'I . . . I think I do.'

'Do you faint easily?'

'No.'

'You've never fainted?'

'I don't think so . . . I don't remember.'

'Yet you seem so breathless now. So frightened of something.'

'I . . . I'm not frightened.'

'Of me?'

233

'No.'

'Not of me?'

'Well . . . yes . . . a little, yes.'

'There's no reason, you know. You know that.'

'Yes, Calvin.'

'You *do* know it . . . don't you?'

'Yes, Calvin.'

'Because I'm enormously fond of you. Because I wish you well . . . I'd never harm you.'

'I . . . I know.'

'Somehow it has happened, over the years, that I don't have many friends. Friends I can trust. But I feel that I can trust you, Maggie, can't I?'

'Yes, Calvin. Of course.'

'And you can trust me.'

'Yes.'

'You need a friend, Maggie . . . in a time like this.'

'Yes.'

'When we don't know what will happen next. Who will be . . . touched, next.'

Maggie nodded, wordless.

'*Her* fingers, and her toes too – Naomi's, I mean – get icy-cold at times, if the temperature drops only a few degrees. It's caused by low blood pressure, but the doctors say there isn't much to be done. She gets lightheaded occasionally, but, like you, she rarely faints. You say you rarely faint?'

'Yes. I mean no. I rarely faint.'

'Yet you seem so frightened, right now.'

'I . . . I'm not really.'

'You don't want me to kiss you, I guess?'

'I – '

'Just once?'

'I don't – '

Calvin Gould framed Maggie Blackburn's face deftly in his hands and kissed her, just once, on the lips.

'Your lips are cold; you *are* frightened of me,' Calvin said, apologetically. 'I'd never force myself on you, Maggie, please believe me. If you'd like me to leave . . .'

Maggie's heartbeat was so gigantic, she was in terror he would feel it and know.

'. . . of course I'll leave.'

'Yes, I think . . .'

'If you want . . . ?'

'. . . think you should, Calvin.'

'I should? Now?'

'Yes. Please.'

Maggie's voice quivered on the edge of dissolution.

But this too Calvin might attribute to her womanly apprehension of him as a man, for surely there was a powerful sexual attraction between them.

Calvin's camel's-hair coat was draped over his arm, and his hand was on the doorknob. Was he leaving, so soon after having arrived? But why wasn't he leaving? Maggie Blackburn saw that he smiled at her with his mouth in a way to inspire confidence, it was a smile familiar to her from her most shameless fantasies, yet his mind worked rapidly and coldly trying to determine what she knew, or if she knew or even suspected anything; what he'd meant to say, coming here as he had, with so transparently feeble an excuse . . . for there was no purpose to Calvin Gould's driving on Acacia Drive at this hour or any hour, it certainly was not a route to bear him home from the Forest Park Conservatory of Music. Maggie looked into the face of a man who was at that very moment trying to determine what he'd meant to say, or to do, by coming to her. For clearly it was improvisation. And his breath smelled faintly of alcohol.

He said, not accusingly so much as merely quizzically, 'I hear you've been asking questions about me, Maggie.'

'I . . . I have?'

In panic she thought, He knows I've been to Maine, I've seen the birth record.

But it was not that, for of course Calvin could not know about that; it was something else, something lesser, yet that this incident, small as it was and surely insignificant, easily explained away, excited his suspicion – was that not revealing of his state of mind? his shrewdness, finely honed as a knife? Hand still on the doorknob as if he'd been halted in his very movement out the door, Calvin was telling Maggie that his secretary Barbara Matlock happened to remark to him today, this afternoon, that she and Maggie had met in a store in town and got to talking – 'And you were asking about Naomi's operation last month? How well had it gone, and how serious was it?'

'I . . . I was hoping that – '

'But you'd already asked about the operation, Maggie, hadn't you? Back in January?'

'I . . . I did?'

'Didn't you? Of me?'

Maggie's heart was beating to suffocation; she simply could not speak.

'Unless that was someone else,' Calvin said thoughtfully. 'Maybe I've confused you with another woman friend.'

'Yes.'

'Well. Naomi has made a complete recovery. I gather Barbara told you the surgery wasn't major, it was elective, but on the whole, over the course of her life, Naomi's health hasn't been consistently good. So it upsets her, and I suppose I should say it upsets me, to learn that people are talking about us behind our backs, even when they mean to be sympathetic.' He paused, regarding Maggie doubtfully. 'Even when, like you, Maggie, they obviously have friendly motives.'

'I . . . I see.'

But suddenly the ordeal was over. Calvin opened the door, stepped out into the freezing night air, said, 'Good night, Maggie – thanks,' as if nothing were out of the ordinary; and Maggie called after him in a voice thinner than she might have wished, but adequate for the occasion, 'Good night, Calvin.'

She could see his breath faintly steaming as he hurried out to the kerb, to his car.

It could not have required more than a few seconds for Maggie Blackburn to walk from her front door through the little foyer, through the dining-room, and into the kitchen, where there was a telephone and, on her cork bulletin board, the little white card bearing Detective Sergeant David Miles's telephone numbers: but these seconds seemed to require a good deal of effort, an exertion of will, muscular coordination, neurological strain. She was very close to fainting – she was close to physical collapse.

And yet the danger was past; Calvin Gould had gone.

She'd locked the door behind him. She was safe. She had David Miles's home telephone number and would call him, and explain . . . though precisely what she must explain she didn't, in her state of anxiety, quite know.

Maggie had initially thought, when they were together in the living-room, that Calvin had let slip the remark about the electrical cord in order to gauge its effect upon her, because of course no one except Brendan Bauer was supposed to know of his having been tied up at all by Rolfe Christensen, let alone with electrical cord; but it seemed more plausible, on second thought, that the slip had been accidental – Calvin simply had not known that that detail had never entered any public record of the Christensen assault, whether made to the Conservatory committee, of which he'd been a member, or the Forest Park police. Unfortunately, David Miles knew nothing about it either.

The reason Calvin had come to see her, revealed only at the door, had been to determine why Maggie had made inquiries regarding Naomi Gould, the woman he called his wife – which testified to the heightened paranoia the man must be feeling. To suspect Maggie of suspecting him, or him and his 'wife', how desperate he must be! – how dangerous!

Even so, Maggie tried to console herself: *Calvin wouldn't hurt you. He wouldn't hurt you.*

He had kissed her, hadn't he? – but his lips were cold, hard, without love, a kind of interrogation, and his fingers framing her face had been vicelike, tight enough to cause discomfort. *How many times you'd dreamt of that man kissing you – and so he has! Poor*

237

fool!

Maggie shuddered. It would have been so easy for Calvin's hands to drop to her throat, and squeeze, and squeeze, and squeeze the life out of her.

In the kitchen a single muted bulb burned above the electric stove, but Maggie did not want to switch the brighter overhead light on, reasoning that, should Calvin be somehow observing her, he could not see her clearly, or her actions . . . though at the same time she knew, or was fairly certain, that Calvin had driven away in his car and that she was safe. *What can I tell David Miles? What sense will any of this make?* She had the detective's card in her fingers but her fingers had lost nearly all sensation, and the card fell to the floor and she stooped clumsily to pick it up . . . a wave of dizziness struck her . . . and the music in her head was, so unexpectedly, a blast of Charles Ives, that din of rival musics, Sunday brass bands, the unlovely cacophony of the outside world. Maggie fumbled for the card and snatched it up, panting . . . wondering if perhaps she'd imagined everything, and Calvin Gould who was her friend had simply dropped by for the purpose he'd told her, to see how she was, and how she was bearing up under the strain. Already she was forgetting what he'd said about Brendan having been tied up, tied with electrical cord, and even if she wasn't forgetting perhaps there was a rational explanation for his knowing, perhaps in fact without informing her Brendan had told the committee or had told Calvin in private and had afterwards forgotten . . . what then? how would it seem if Maggie Blackburn called the police, in a semi-hysterical state, and accused Calvin Gould, the Provost of the Forest Park Conservatory of Music, of murder?

And how would it seem if she revealed the fact, astonishing in itself but not, in itself, incriminating, that the woman with whom Calvin Gould lived, and whom he presented to the world as his wife, was not his wife but his sister – his twin sister, baptized Caroline Gould?

For so Maggie had discovered on her trip to Bangor, Maine, where Calvin Gould had been born. The fact had not aroused her suspicion so much as confirmed it, for she'd known, or had guessed, that 'Naomi' was related by something far deeper than a mere marital bond to Calvin Gould.

But what of this can I tell David Miles? What sense will any of it make?

These minutes, Maggie Blackburn stood indecisively, the detective's card in her fingers. She stood in her dim-lit kitchen in front of the telephone on the wall, staring into space, thinking, or trying to think. She knew that Calvin Gould was a murderer but in what did her 'knowledge' consist, seeing the fact in his eyes, when he'd allowed her to look deeply, intimately, into them, as into a lover's eyes? Yet at the same time she could not seriously believe that the man was a murderer – could she?

If you ever think you're in danger, please call.

Maggie Blackburn had decided to telephone David Miles when, to her surprise, the telephone began ringing; she took up the receiver hoping it might – somehow – be help; but there came instead that high, nasal, breathless voice, that so familiar voice. 'Hello, M-Maggie? This is Brendan' – overloud and anxious in her ear, and boyishly emboldened as if with drink. 'I'm calling to say that I . . . I love you, Maggie, and I want to be with you . . . spend the rest of my life with you. I know I'm not worthy of you . . . no one is . . . but I would try to be a better man, Maggie . . . I promise. I . . . I know this is unexpected, you're probably . . . shocked . . . but I hope you aren't offended. Maggie, I've never been in love before, *I'm so miserable and so happy*!'

Maggie heard the sounds of her young friend's earnest words, rather than their specific sense, blazing past her like sparks.

'Maggie? Are you . . . all right? Did I upset you?'

Maggie said quickly, 'I can't talk at the moment, Brendan. I . . . I'm sorry.'

'You aren't angry with me, are you?' He paused, and Maggie could hear him swallowing hard in an effort to forestall a spasm of stammering. 'Maggie, I . . . love you.'

Even as Brendan spoke, repeating what he'd said to a woman who scarcely heard him, and, hearing him, could feel only a commingling of dismay and exasperation, there was a sound at the door: the kitchen door, which opened out into the rear of Maggie Blackburn's garage: where it seemed suddenly, someone was standing, peering into the kitchen.

Maggie stared, helpless.

It was Calvin Gould: at the door, rapping on the windowpane, three distinct raps with his bare knuckles.

'Sorry, Brendan, I . . . can't talk now, I . . . someone is here, a . . . visitor.'

'But Maggie – '

Maggie quickly hung up. For there was Calvin Gould at her rear door, asking to be let in. Again.

And had she any choice but to open the door and let him in?

She went to the door, unresisting. She might have been reasoning that, given the social circumstances of her relationship with Calvin, there could be no reason for her to refuse to open this door for him. Thus, if she refused, her odd behaviour would have to be interpreted as springing from a new, previously un-examined premise. After all, Calvin was enormously fond of Maggie: hadn't he told her so? Hadn't he kissed her? He might simply have left his gloves behind, might have forgotten to tell her something of a professional nature.

She might have been reasoning too – for so the stiff staring ex-pression on her face suggested – that, should she refuse to open the door, should she run panicked into another part of the house, upstairs for instance, to her bedroom where there was a tele-phone, Calvin would simply break the window, reach inside, and let himself in.

So Maggie Blackburn, of her own volition, opened a door for the second time that night to Calvin Gould – and knew, as the man stepped inside, in the instant before he kicked the door shut and gripped her shoulders and began to shake her violently, that she had made a mistake.

'Maggie! Damn you! *You!*'

Twenty-five

In the aftermath of having seen a production of Bartók's *Blue-beard's Castle*, at the age of nineteen, Maggie Blackburn had endured a night of terrifying dreams, vivid in memory even after fifteen years: she had been trapped, like Bluebeard's importunate young bride, Judith, in a hideously protracted and indefinable drama, a drama of her own instigation seemingly, yet beyond her control; the very substance of the air she breathed had turned gelatinous, music made material. So the nightmare of her several hours with Calvin Gould in the late evening of February 22, 1989, was similarly protracted and indefinable, a drama to be explicated only in retrospect when it would be perceived that, for Calvin Gould, the dilemma lay in indecision: in not knowing whom he should kill, Maggie or himself or both; or whether in fact he was compelled by circumstances to kill another person at all.

Repeatedly he said, baffled, angry, 'So you know, don't you. You know, somehow . . . but how?'

And: 'If I could trust you! But I can't trust you . . . can I? Can I trust you, Maggie?'

And: '*No one can prove anything*. Not about Naomi, and not about me. But why is it *you*? Of all people . . . why *you*?'

He was mad; or, if not mad, maddened: a man accustomed to supreme control of his life, now provoked beyond endurance.

Pacing about Maggie's living-room flexing and unflexing his fingers, regarding her with bright dilated eyes. He muttered to himself and to her; his hair was dishevelled, his shirt collar open;

he appeared drunk – yet bitterly calm, beneath his distraction. 'You *did* go up to Maine, didn't you? I'd heard that and I could hardly believe it! *You*! Maggie Blackburn! Of all people! Forcing me to – do what I have to do!'

For the first half-hour or so Maggie protested in tears that she didn't know what Calvin meant, had no idea to what he was referring – the murders? – but why did he imagine she suspected him? Yet, clearly, Calvin could see the terror and guilt in her face; and she trembled almost convulsively, hunched in a corner of her sofa, believing herself doomed. Until at last, exhausted, she burst into tears, and Calvin stood over her, where he'd pushed her roughly down, and he took up both her hands in his, saying, with almost a lover's solicitude, 'So you acknowledge it, then: you know I killed both men,' and Maggie, sobbing helplessly, beyond all pretence by this time, even if the effort might prolong or even save her life, said, 'Not both. Not *you*.'

She would think afterwards that, on that evening, she had made no blunder that was not in a sense one with the blunder of that first glass of wine drunk at her own party months before, in this house, thus lulling her suspicion, deadening her judgement, yet stoking her romantic yearning and stimulating her to drink a second glass, and a third . . . harmless in themselves except, in retrospect, to blame for that hour's dereliction of moral duty with its repercussions for ever afterwards: as, in her mind's eye, Rolfe Christensen once again walked with young Brendan Bauer out of her front door, hand on his shoulder, face ruddy with high spirits, appetite. And so, a dreamlike sequence of events, rapid in summary, like playing cards rippling out of a shuffled deck, bringing Maggie Blackburn to this impasse of February 22, 1989, in her own living-room, and the frighteningly laconic, even affable confession Calvin Gould was making to her of having poisoned Rolfe Christensen, a crime which, in fact, he had not committed, by way of explaining the necessary murder of Nicholas Reickmann, which he had.

'I was seventeen. That summer at Interlaken. And I knew

nothing. I may have heard of the word "homosexual" but I knew nothing. In my family no one would ever have spoken of anything so . . . physical. In fact, no one spoke of love. It would have been acutely embarrassing . . . it *is*. I was attending a private high school in Bangor, a boys' school, since my parents were trying to separate my sister and me as much as they could . . . I'd had about nine years of piano lessons by then and everyone thought I was extremely talented . . . you know how small-city musical circles are. Yes, *you* must know. I seem to have thought I was pretty good, I knew I wanted a musical career but I couldn't gauge how talented I was, really, or whether I had the nerves for it, and I never did know since it all ended . . . *He* ended it: my hope to be a concert pianist. There I was one July afternoon playing Liszt in a young pianists' competition at Interlaken, where I had a summer scholarship for some absurd sum – three hundred dollars, I think – but it was enormous to me, and I'd never been so frightened and so excited, and there *he* was, Rolfe Christensen himself, the composer, the man everyone deferred to, and somehow I was named first in the competition; I'd played Liszt's *Funé-railles* as if my life depended upon it. I can't imagine what I sounded like, so many years ago. But *he* claimed to admire my playing. Oh, *he* was filled with praise . . . all sorts of amazing words. He would arrange for me to have a scholarship to Juilliard if I wanted one, just a snap of his fingers and I'd be in. I was simply in awe of the man. I was in a fever of . . . of awe.

'At the age of seventeen I was very shy, but arrogant too. Shy with others and arrogant in private. I had to think exaggerated thoughts about myself in order to avoid thinking the other . . . low, vicious, angry thoughts. Because there was always my sister, my twin, for whom things hadn't turned out well.

'So it was summer, and Interlaken, hundreds of miles from home, and there were so many talented young musicians, so many I should have been jealous of, and intimidated by, but Rolfe Christensen liked *me*, took *me* out to dinner, talked with *me* as if I were someone important. And one night in town we had champagne, there was something to celebrate so we celebrated it with champagne, and there we were back at his hotel room, and . . . and I didn't remember afterwards exactly what happened except it was something physical and shameful and . . . and irrevocable. And it was going to happen again.

'And afterwards, Christensen had this strange power over me. Not just the threat of telling others . . . though there was always that threat, up to the day of the man's death and in fact beyond his death . . . but another kind of power too: the power of forcing a victim into complicity. That was the true shame of it. *It was as if he'd turned me into a woman.*

'I lost control, just once. Started a fire. The last week of the summer session. I'd never done anything like that before in my life . . . but it had to be done. Not because I hoped to kill him but I had to let him know I was capable of killing him any time I wanted. And that impressed him, that scared him. Always afterwards he would allude to that night, the fire in the hotel, the fire trucks, the excitement . . . all because of *him*. "It's for life, Calvin," he'd say. "It's a sacred bond neither of us can break." He had this diary he kept – he'd showed it to me. And what he wrote in it, about me. We were never really lovers again after that summer because he was afraid of me – I was too fierce for him, he said – but he kept in touch with me, travelled to see me for years afterwards, when I was in college at Syracuse and afterwards . . . he said he'd never let me go. "I never let any of you go, Calvin, you are part of my living immortality." It made me almost physically ill, the way he spoke to me in this mocking singsong when he was drunk. At Syracuse he'd telephone. "Cal vin," he'd say, "do you know what I'm doing to you now, Cal vin Gould? And now? And *now* . . . ?" I didn't dare hang up. I hated him, the pig, but I didn't dare hang up. He had such power over me, I didn't dare make an enemy of him.

'He had many lovers, of course. He always had lovers. But he hung on to them all, or nearly, because he was terrified of dying. He did truly live in awe of music, of great musicians and transcendent geniuses like Mozart, he knew he was inferior to such greatness but all of his life, I mean on the surface of his life, he denied it . . . played the role of the man of genius himself. So he needed his protégés as collaborators. He needed us too to reward now and then, to get scholarships for, special grants, awards, jobs. A network of young men. Young men gradually growing up. He was a pig, he was loathsome and vicious, but he was kindly too . . . he needed that too, to complete himself; he thought of himself as a legend in the making. After I arranged for him to come to Forest Park, the one thing I'd vowed I would never do, give in to his wheedling and his threats and his cajoling, after that, when he was settled in here and damned grateful to be settled in, he told me I had earned my place in the legend of his life and that his biographers would speak of me in glowing terms.

'When he did what he did to Brendan Bauer, and when he boasted of it afterwards to me, I knew he had to die. And so he died. *Fags die.* And Nicky too – he didn't deserve it but he got in the way. Too bad!'

Calvin Gould laughed suddenly. During this long monologue he'd dragged a chair to a position in front of Maggie Blackburn; he was sitting with his elbows on his knees, leaning forward. He spoke harshly, yet with satisfaction; with the air of a man tasting his words and taking pleasure in their bitterness. Maggie stared at him, wondering if he were mad. And what madness was, if it could be so logically stated.

Maggie's features were thin, sharp, pointed; her skin was waxy-white and translucent, her eyes glazed. She might have been perceived as a woman of delicate sensibility whom extreme fright had drained of appropriate emotion. Nor did her black sweater, her nondescript dark slacks, her feet in black woollen socks seem appropriate to the occasion.

Calvin said, with an impatient gesture, as if embarrassed, 'Your mouth, Maggie: it's bleeding. Wipe it.'

In the kitchen when they'd struggled briefly, rather more blundering together in surprise and alarm than truly struggling, Calvin must have struck Maggie a blow to the mouth without knowing what he did, nor could Maggie have remembered being struck. Now, touching her lips, she was confused seeing blood on her fingers.

She thought, *I don't want to die.*

It seemed to her inescapable: *If he touches me again he won't be able to stop. He'll kill me.*

Then the telephone began ringing, and Calvin got to his feet at once, as alerted as if someone were at the door. 'Better answer it, Maggie,' he said, yanking her up from the sofa, 'and tell whoever it is you can't talk now.'

His strong fingers closed about her upper arm, Calvin Gould walked Maggie Blackburn briskly into her kitchen, and when she lifted the receiver to her ear, murmuring, 'Yes? Hello?' he brought his head against hers so that he could hear the voice at the other end of the line. *How close. How familiar. How like a lover, such intimacy.* He cradled Maggie's head tightly in the crook of his arm; his forearm straining against her throat gave her a sensation of mild strangulation.

The caller was Brendan Bauer. Of course.

And the young man was upset, of course; in a state of intense excitement; sounding anxious and solicitous and, unless Maggie imagined it, a little drunk. Maggie told him in a surprisingly level voice that she couldn't talk at the moment, it was late, they could talk in the morning, and Brendan seemed to accept this, but asked, before hanging up, 'Are you angry with me, Maggie? Did I say something I shouldn't have said?' and Maggie said, 'No, no, Brendan' – on the verge of tears – 'why can't you let me alone!'

Brendan murmured something abject and apologetic and then the line was dead.

Calvin Gould hung up the receiver.

They returned to the living-room, to the lighted corner of the room, this time with a bottle of Scotch and two glasses, for Calvin needed a drink, he said, a drink to steady his nerves. He asked Maggie if she and Brendan Bauer were lovers, and Maggie shook her head no, of course they were not lovers, and Calvin said, well, love can be one-sided, maybe it's best that way – 'One-sided: like a mirror showing only your face.' And he laughed, drawing his lips back from his teeth, mirthlessly but loudly.

He splashed a generous amount of Scotch into each of the glasses and gave one to Maggie.

He said, 'I'm one of Forest Park's secret drinkers, did you know? But of course not: I'm *secret*.'

He swallowed a mouthful of Scotch, and sighed, and smiled at Maggie, and said, 'It's best that way. As much secret as you can.'

Maggie turned a face to her captor that was too pale, stark, gaunt to be a face of beauty. She had a look both attentive and dazed. Slowly, the little blood bead began to form again on her lower lip, and this time Calvin tossed her a crumpled hand- kerchief – a white linen handkerchief embossed with the initials *CSG* – which she was reluctant to soil. 'Use it. Keep it. I don't need it,' Calvin said indifferently.

This white linen handkerchief, stained with her own blood, Maggie Blackburn would keep for the remainder of her life. *How like lovers, such intimacy.*

It might have been recognized by a neutral witness that Calvin Gould was in a crisis of indecision: he sat, but was continually shifting about in his chair; he drank, but quickly, with an ex- pression of distaste. Within minutes his voice became slurred. 'If I could trust you, Maggie . . . but I can't. Like with Nicky. It was too late, with him . . . He knew, he'd read the diary . . . He promised me he'd never tell anyone, never so much as hint of it to anyone; he begged me, poor Nicky, just to take the diary and the letters and anything I wanted and destroy them and no one would know – and I wanted to believe him; I was sympathetic – but it's too painful a life, it wears you down, knowing there are people who have power over you. It's easier to make an end of it, somehow.'

Quietly Maggie said, 'I hope you won't hurt me, Calvin. You know I've always been your – '

'I don't have any friends. No one knows who I am.'

'I've always been . . . sympathetic . . .'

Calvin said, grimacing, 'You wouldn't be, though, dear Maggie: if you knew. The way I killed Nicky, for instance.'

There was a brief chill silence.

'I hadn't wanted to kill him, I liked him . . . very much. He was a form of myself, I'd thought. When I went to Christensen's house that night to see him it was . . . like this. Like this visit with you. I went to talk with Nicky Reickmann and to see what might happen. In fact, Nicky had invited me over. He was absolutely trusting. He was a truly generous man. I suppose he felt a certain kinship with me in the matter of Christensen, though our experiences were hardly comparable since I was seventeen years old when Christensen seduced me and Nicky Reickmann was an adult, fully experienced man who wasn't seduced at all but agreed to some sort of transaction, or series of transactions, for the advancement of his career . . . and it worked, for Christensen kept his promises, most of the time: that was part of his legend. His "immortality". So it was a total surprise to Nicky, a profound shock, that I turned out to want more than just the evidence to destroy; I wanted the witness to the fact of the evidence dead. He swore he would tell no one and I believed him, actually . . . but that wasn't enough. I didn't want anyone to know. And anyone who knew, I wanted dead.'

Calvin paused, and looked at Maggie, who was staring at him with an expression of hopelessness, and said, with a shrug of his shoulders, 'I'm not happy with the way things have turned out but I hadn't any choice. Once you begin a certain action it's necessary to complete it . . . bring it to an end. So you become an actor, and you yourself are watching. A performer. Watching your hands. At a distance. It's prescribed beforehand . . . someone else has written it. I don't believe that up until the very moment I cut his throat Nicky Reickmann truly thought it would happen, that anyone as "nice" as Calvin Gould could do anything so brutal to him, and it may be that he died not believing it. He'd been so cooperative, talking Brendan Bauer into coming to Christensen's house, doing exactly as I instructed him; he must have known there was a purpose to my request, but he didn't allow himself to wonder what it was. And then of course it was too late. I killed my friend the way you'd slaughter an animal: it's a matter of hydraulics almost: how to get the life out of the living organism with as much dispatch as possible.'

Calvin poured another several inches of Scotch into his glass. He said, '*You're* not drinking, Maggie. Not keeping me company.'

Maggie was holding the glass in both hands, and both hands were resting in her lap. For otherwise her severe trembling might have spilled the liquid.

In his slurred, pitying voice, Calvin went on. 'What am I going to do with you, Maggie? Or with us? We might go for a ride together tonight ... d'you think? There've been times in my life, my life and my sister's, when I'd about made up my mind to bring things to an end; driving along a highway, a kind of crazy elation would come over me. How easy to die, to let speed accomplish it for you! And the death isn't ruled suicide, merely accident. I've come close, and the peculiar thing is, my close calls weren't related in any way I could determine to anything upsetting in my life at the time; for instance when I was promoted to Provost here, and everyone was congratulating me, and I felt optimistic about the future, right about that time I thought, *This is your opportunity to escape, no one would ever guess*. But I didn't do it. I hung on. There's something contemptible, isn't there, about hanging on ... I don't blame you for looking at me in disgust.'

Quickly Maggie said, 'I ... I'm not – '

'You are exactly as you appear to be, and always have been; and I ... I'm something very different. "He is as repulsive as Rolfe Christensen," you're thinking.'

'No, Calvin, I – '

Calvin leaned forward suddenly, as if playfully, and touched Maggie: circled her left wrist with his fingers, forefinger and thumb. 'Every time I've seen you play the piano I've wanted to do that. How fine-boned you are ... you don't have the necessary strength, do you, for pressing your own advantage. Or for playing the piano really passionately, as it sometimes needs to be played. I remember your telling me when we first met that you'd decided to withdraw from the Van Cliburn competition – you hated that kind of competing, you said. And I thought, She doesn't have the strength for it, that's all. Whereas I had the strength but not the

249

talent. Or the faith in myself.'

Stooping before Maggie, so very unexpectedly, yet matter-of-factly, Calvin Gould circled his forefinger and thumb around Maggie's ankle as well. And she sat very still, gazing down at Calvin's damp face, his eyes that were rimmed with black, his mouth that seemed quizzical, working. Now he might kill her, now he might do anything at all with her, any action on his part was permissible; she could only hope – as perhaps Nicholas Reickmann had hoped – for mercy.

He said, squinting up at her, his eyes faintly bloodshot, '*Why* did you intrude, Maggie? Why did you check up on me? How did you know it might be – *me*?' He sighed and settled back on his chair, glass raised to the level of his grinning teeth. 'I wish you hadn't.'

Maggie said slowly, for her words were in fact a revelation to her, 'I seemed to know that the deaths had to do with you, Calvin. Because of inconsistencies in things you said, and things you did … nothing that would have meant much to anyone who didn't know you. But I knew that something was wrong. I knew. And I couldn't accept that you were responsible because I was in love with you.'

Calvin laughed and said, aggressively, 'Oh, you were? You think you were? But only because you didn't know me, Maggie.'

'The woman you called your wife, whom I'd always thought was your wife, of course, as everyone did … is someone I've been aware of for years. Because, as I said, I was in love with you.' Maggie paused and dabbed at her mouth with the stained white handkerchief. In her queer emotionless state, which was perhaps a state of absolute resignation, as before death, she still could not bring herself to look up at Calvin Gould at this moment, for her words seemed to her not embarrassing, merely piteous. 'So I thought of her, of "Naomi Gould". Even when I didn't want to think of her, I thought of her; I was mildly obsessed by her. Why her and not me? I would think. Why had she the unimaginable good fortune to be your wife when she didn't, so far as I could judge, seem to appreciate you, at least in any public way, while I . . . I hadn't anything? I had my work, and my life, but I hadn't you. Then, when he was questioning me, David Miles remarked that poison is a method of killing that people who couldn't bear witnessing violence might choose, because they don't have to see their victims die; and it struck me – it was a bizarre, terrifying thought – that I might have done such a thing myself. And suddenly I was thinking of her. Of that woman, Naomi Gould. But I don't know why.'

Calvin said, flatly, 'Nor do I. She had nothing to do with any of this.'

'After Nicholas died – '

'She didn't, you know. She had nothing to do with any of this.'

'After Nicholas died, it came back to me how explicit you'd been about your wife having surgery. She'd been scheduled for that day, she would have been in the hospital that night, the night Nicholas was killed. It came to me then, and again I don't know why – the thought wasn't serious, really, just something that flew into my head – that "Naomi Gould" was the only one of us who has an alibi that is unshakeable. And this made me wonder why "Naomi Gould" would need an alibi, or why someone might imagine she would need one. And it occurred to me that if she had sent the poisoned chocolates to Rolfe Christensen, with or without your knowing, at the time of the second murder you could protect her by . . . by arranging things as you did.'

'My sister knew nothing about any of this, I assure you. *I* sent the poisoned chocolates, and *I* cut Nicholas Reickmann's throat.' Calvin shifted impatiently in his chair. 'I hope you haven't told anyone else about this, Maggie.'

Yet Maggie persisted. 'And the person who bought the chocolates was a woman, according to the sales clerk in the store; or a man who might have been in disguise as a woman. That couldn't have been you, Calvin. You could never have disguised yourself as a woman.'

The word 'Calvin' hung oddly, almost musically, in the air. It seemed to have acquired an elegiac tone.

Calvin said, 'What of Brendan Bauer, the obvious suspect?

What of Bill Queller? *He's* gone.'

Maggie said, 'I never suspected Brendan but I did suspect Bill Queller, for a while. But it was your behaviour that – '

'Being gone,' Calvin said with a grunting sort of laugh, 'as he is, Queller is maybe the guilty party, after all. And not me. And maybe the man will stay gone.'

Maggie looked searchingly at Calvin, but his expression was unreadable.

He can't have killed him too! she thought.

She said, faltering, 'I didn't want to think these things. About "Naomi". About you. I tried not to think them. Just as I'd never wanted, all these years, to be so . . . obsessive about the woman I believed to be your wife. I told myself I wasn't jealous or envious. I told myself I had my own life to live. And it was . . . it *is* . . . a happy life. But I couldn't seem to help it. Thinking about you and her. And then I would see her sometimes, accidentally, and it was always an experience that was disorienting . . . because, see-ing her, the woman I believed to be your wife, it wasn't that I was reminded of you so much as that, seeing her, I was *seeing* you. In a woman's shape.'

Calvin said, smiling, though without mirth, his eyes cold, 'Yet we don't look that much alike, my sister and me. Not any longer.'

Maggie said, 'No. You don't. Superficially, you don't. You aren't identical twins, of course; you don't really look alike, I know. But I happened to see the two of you together when you were leaving the museum that day, I was standing at a first-floor window looking down, and there was something about your bone structures, your profiles, the way you held your heads, the way you were walking, and the way you seemed to be oblivious of each other, as if you hadn't any need to communicate. It went through me like an electric shock, seeing you . . . even though I didn't know what I'd seen. And tried immediately to put it out of my mind.'

Calvin said, almost jeeringly, 'Did you! It's too bad you didn't succeed.'

Maggie sat for a moment, silent. She was gripping the glass of

252

Scotch so hard that her knuckles drained of blood.

She was thinking, Is there nothing I can do, no way of escaping him? Tricking him, overpowering him, appealing to his sense of . . . But she did not know to what, in Calvin Gould, she might appeal. The horror was, she did not know the man at all.

Hesitantly she asked, 'What happened to your sister, Calvin? To make her so . . .'

'So strange, so unsocial? It didn't exactly happen,' Calvin said, shifting restlessly in his chair, 'I caused it. I tried to kill her, when we were twelve years old. Of course,' he said quickly, squinting at Maggie, 'I didn't know what I'd done at the time. Caroline knew, but I didn't. She always knows, and I never do. That's been the pattern of our twinness all our lives.

'Not that I know about twinness. I don't! I'm not morbid-minded. That isn't my nature. Caroline made a study of twinness but I never did, I wasn't interested, I'm not morbid-minded, ask anyone who knows me. I'm a professional man; I move from A to B to C with my eye on X, Y, Z. To Caroline, being twins was something sacred and inviolable, which is why she loathed anyone who came between us if she knew about him or her . . . if she even sensed the fact of another presence. But I was different. I am different. I set out to be normal and *I am normal*. As you say, we're not identical twins. Hardly! At the most, we're sister and brother. I'm older than Caroline, I'm much larger and stronger physically, and better coordinated; I have different character traits and talents . . . of course. My personality is the antithesis of hers. *I don't believe she has any personality at all*.

'I've been – I've tried to be – a man of action, a man of the world. When I was nineteen, I enlisted in the marines . . . though that didn't work out as I'd hoped. (They gave me an honourable discharge.) When I was twenty-six I was married to a beautiful young woman named Naomi, part English and part Malaysian . . . though that didn't work out either as I'd hoped. I met my wife in Rome, the year I had a fellowship to the American Academy there, and we travelled for fifteen months, in Italy, Greece, northern Africa, Turkey; then something went wrong between us, she fell in love with another man, or in any case disappeared with another man, into Afghanistan. She might be living today or she might be dead. I'd heard she'd died of a drug overdose, but I don't know. I made inquiries but not extensively. I came back home because by this time my parents were dead and my sister was hospitalized and I thought I'd take care of her until she was better and I could straighten out my own life professionally . . . Why are you looking at me so strangely, Maggie? Do I surprise you?'

Calvin Gould smiled his bitter, satisfied smile.

Maggie said, perplexed, 'You *were* married . . . ? To a woman named Naomi?'

'And maybe I still am, I don't know,' Calvin said carelessly. 'There is no connection between my life in the United States and my life with her, back in the 1970s; we were only together fifteen months. We weren't, I suppose you might say, compatible. Sexually adjusted. She was headstrong and very independent, very experienced, and I was . . . rather shy . . . stricken . . . feeling always inadequate . . . because of what had happened to me, what had been done to me. Hadn't I been made into a woman? It seemed to me that a real woman could tell and would be disgusted. But I don't know. I never knew. Possibly my marriage would have disintegrated anyway. My wife didn't take fidelity very seriously . . .

'I came back to the States. I was desperate to re-establish my professional career as a musicologist, a theorist, and a teacher of music; if I couldn't be a performer I wanted to devote myself to music anyway; and I was feeling guilty about my sister, who seemed to have had a breakdown, some sort of nervous collapse, around the time of my marriage. It was my intention to get her out of the hospital and take care of her until she was well . . . but it didn't quite work out that way because Caroline never got what might be called "well". We moved around a good deal, at first. I had a job in San Francisco, then in London, then in Boston, then here. It seemed to have happened, and I don't know why, that my sister Caroline became my wife Naomi. It must have been my conscious decision, but I truly don't remember making it.' Calvin Gould smiled and pressed the rim of his glass against his forehead. His face was lightly coated in perspiration glinting like mica; his skin, normally olive-dark, was of the hue and the texture of bread dough. 'I suppose I wanted to be . . . protected. I couldn't marry and couldn't be expected to marry if I already had a wife; *she* couldn't marry and couldn't be expected to marry if she already had a husband. How effortless, how inevitable it seemed. There was a sense of destiny to it.'

Maggie said faintly, 'That's . . . extraordinary.'

Calvin laughed. 'Yet it felt ordinary. Both my parents had died, and we hadn't any relatives to speak of, at least no one who would know of our lives away from Maine, or care. And my professional colleagues would hardly be suspicious: why would they? People are trusting, if they like you. They believe nearly anything if it's plausible. "Naomi Gould" was a woman who had had some health problems, that was all – no conventional faculty wife, but not exactly an embarrassment. It might have been that, over the years, I deeply resented my life and resented her – my twin – but it was my destiny, and I accepted it. Until last autumn, when things began to go bad.'

Maggie asked, 'And why was that? Why last autumn?'

'You know. *Him.* What he'd done to Bauer, and . . . all the upset. And I was at the centre of things. What an irony! It was the past being replayed, and instead of Calvin Gould there was Brendan Bauer, and I . . . I began to get . . . distracted. And he came to me – Christensen, I mean – he actually came to me to boast of it. To boast! The pig! He talked of his "little adventure" as if he thought I would be impressed, or amused, or, who knows, sexually aroused . . . but he was frightened too, because he knew he'd gone too far this time. (So I knew about everything: I knew about the tape he'd recorded and the electrical cord. I knew things Brendan Bauer himself had apparently forgotten.) About all this, the Christensen affair, I never spoke to my sister . . . but somehow she knew. She knew what I felt. She knew about him from the past, though I'd never told her exactly what had happened to me in Interlaken, and she seemed to know about Brendan Bauer. My emotional life is somehow connected with Caroline, it's as if we are a single person, a single organism, sharing a nervous system, memory, instincts . . . but nothing else. We don't know each other, really. She's jealous of my work, my colleagues, my friends; she resents anything that isn't her. I hate the connection between us, I've always hated it . . . but there it is. I couldn't escape her if I wanted to, and she couldn't escape me. As long as we're both . . .' Calvin's voice trailed off, as if thought, or strength, had failed him.

Maggie said, 'Your sister . . . where is she now?'

'Now? She's at home. Waiting.'

Maggie tasted cold. 'Waiting . . . for what?'

One of Calvin's eyelids was distinctly lower than the other. He was drunk, or nearly; Maggie had never seen him in such a state and did not know if this made him more, or less, dangerous. Yet he seemed, as he spoke, to be appealing to her, staring at her as he was with an expression of pity, sympathy, regret. Could he bring himself to kill her? After so exposing himself to her? Maggie raised her glass of Scotch shakily to her lips and forced herself to take a small swallow. *It is precisely because he has exposed himself to you that he will kill you. As he killed Nicholas Reickmann.*

Calvin Gould, suddenly restless, got to his feet. He swayed for a moment, then regained his balance. Maggie's eye had been drawn, during his monologue, to a vase on her piano; a beautiful milk-glass heirloom vase about fifteen inches high, thicker than it appeared, and heavier. In her desperation that was a kind of calm, Maggie wondered if she might leap for the vase, take it up, strike Calvin Gould with it . . . knock him unconscious . . . and so escape, to the house next door. But was this a realistic hope? If she failed to strike Calvin unconscious with the first blow, he would simply overpower her; he might be unable to stop until he hurt her very badly indeed. She guessed that he was preparing to commit an act of extreme desperation himself, without quite knowing, at the moment, what it might be. Did she have the strength to hit him that hard with the vase? And what if the vase merely shattered? And had she truly the will to strike him, to hurt another person, even in the defence of her own life?

Calvin said, 'You . . . said you were in love with me, Maggie? Did you mean it?'

Maggie said, 'Yes. I meant it.'

'But you didn't know me.'

'I . . . I loved the person I knew. I knew you, certainly, in a way.'

'But it was a deluded way.'

Maggie shook her head, her eyes welling suddenly with tears.

'I don't want to hurt you: if only I could trust you.'

'Calvin, please, you can – '

'But she would know, too. And she's jealous.'

'You can trust me.'

'No, you'd turn me in. As soon as I let you go, as soon as . . . this ended . . . you'd run to the telephone, or next door to the neighbours . . . of course.' Calvin had begun to pace about the room again, flexing and unflexing his fingers. When his back was turned for a moment Maggie steeled herself and made a quick, tentative move . . . but he whipped back immediately towards her, like an athlete so keenly attuned to his reflexes he has no need of thinking, or even of seeing in the usual way.

Maggie's heart was beating so violently, with the rush of adrenalin and hope, she came very near to fainting.

Gravely, Calvin Gould said, looming over her, 'We might both go for a drive. That would be an answer.'

Maggie could not speak.

'A way of making an end.' Calvin contemplated her. 'And *she* would be left then, and . . . and I wouldn't know of her. Not a thing of her . . . after forty years! Everything erased! You know, my parents hadn't wanted children at all. We were born by accident. My mother was forty-one, my father was fifty-three, they were eccentric people, strong-willed, opinionated, both of them were hypochondriacs but also often ill . . . my mother always insisted she didn't know how the pregnancy had happened; she had been blameless herself. That was her word, "blameless".' Calvin laughed as if genuinely amused. 'When Caroline and I were very small, both our parents confused us, the one for the other, and it had a strange effect upon us . . . made us wild, euphoric. You can't know, if you don't have a twin, what happiness it is – it's something you can virtually taste – to be mistaken for someone else, and to be in two places at once.' Calvin laughed again. Spittle gleamed at the corners of his mouth. 'Both my parents, our parents, were fearful of us, but especially my father. He was a truly eccentric man: he had money but never spent it; he owned a small insurance company in Bangor and was convinced his clients and his office staff were trying to cheat him; much of the time he and my mother weren't on speaking terms, and he slept in his office downtown. Caroline and I conspired against them even before we could talk. Before we were out of the crib. Those fools, those *idiots*! Trying to control *us*! We were both energetic and rebellious, but Caroline had a condition, I think, what's diagnosed today as hyperkinesis; sugar would set her off, she'd run wild, fly into temper tantrums, smash things, hit and kick and cry uncontrollably . . . once, in fourth grade, she even attacked our teacher. During these spells she was a furious little animal, but at other times she could be . . . almost tractable. And smart. And watchful, and shrewd. Of the two of us it should have been Caroline who grew up . . . superior.'

Calvin paused, grimacing. Maggie, wanting him to keep talking, asked, hesitantly, 'Was she musical, like you?'

Calvin didn't reply for so long that Maggie thought he hadn't heard her question. Then he said, slowly, 'Caroline did have musical talent. In fact she had perfect pitch – which I don't. Maybe she still does, I don't know. When we were both very small, three or four years old, she seemed more talented than I, singing and dancing and sitting at the piano; but when we began lessons, at the age of ten, Caroline was too restless to practise scales and too impatient with mistakes; she'd fly into a rage . . . she simply lacked the discipline. So she stopped taking lessons. And resented my continuing. Sometimes when I was playing the piano Caroline would rush into the room laughing and strike the keyboard with her fists ... My parents must have known that there was something seriously wrong with her, but to my knowledge they never took her to a specialist. Our family doctor dismissed her behaviour, which he hadn't, in any case, witnessed, as high-strung or spoiled.

'I was desperate to detach myself from my sister, but I didn't know how to do it until I was older. I wouldn't have understood that that was what I wanted: detachment. To be *my*self, not our two selves. And we were drawn together, of course; there was a sort of crazed outlaw happiness between us, like a grass fire burning wild, because we were united against other people: our parents most of all, but also our classmates, our teachers. Anything I was feeling, without knowing what I felt, *she* would feel too ... and know how to kindle it in me. I suppose there has been nothing in my adult life, certainly not my marriage, to compare with it ... But by the time we were twelve I was drawing away from her, or trying to, and she felt it and resented it; she was always trying to lure me back into childish behaviour, with our secret language, our codes and signals, our hiding places, our games. We played in the woods out behind our house, in abandoned buildings, in vacant lots.

'One day Caroline dared me to follow her up on to the tin roof of an old canning factory about a mile from our house; she was taunting "*Cal*-vin, *Cal*-vin" almost the way Christensen would do a few years later, I wanted to leave her there and go back without her but somehow I couldn't; I was afraid to leave her though I was afraid to follow her too; I climbed up on to the roof after her and crawled along on my hands and knees; I remember the sun blinding me, and Caroline walking erect, or nearly, and I yelled something at her, and started after her, and she stepped back off the roof ... and fell. She screamed, and fell, and I thought she must be dead. I climbed down to the ground and tried to wake her: she'd struck her head and was bleeding; it looked as if her shoulder was broken; I was terrified she was dying but at the same time I suspected she was only pretending. "Come on, Caroline, wake up," I said, "God damn you, wake *up*.' But she didn't wake up. So finally I ran towards home to get help. My head was pounding and I couldn't see very well; there was a sort of red haze over my vision. I was running but I was running slower and slower. Then I was being wakened, where I'd passed out on someone's lawn . . . a woman found me. By the time an ambulance came for my sister she'd been unconscious almost an hour.

'She had to have emergency neurosurgery to remove a blood clot in her brain. A year later she had another operation. She had to relearn everything: walking, feeding and dressing herself, speech, reading. She has never really learned to write but she can draw and paint . . . to a degree. She isn't autistic and she isn't schizophrenic but she sometimes sees and hears things no one else does; and, conversely – or perversely – she doesn't always see and hear things others do. I can shout into her face and she won't hear. Or I can say nothing at all, I can lock myself away in my own room, and she will hear . . . she'll know. Sometimes I'm convinced she knows everything about me, things I don't know myself. For years she attended a school for the "mentally handi-capped", as they're called; she has been hospitalized a dozen times; and though she is capable of normal behaviour today, anyone talking with her can sense almost immediately that there's something not quite right about her . . . it's the way she enun-ciates her words, the way she holds her head, the alignment of her eyes. People are frightened of her without knowing why, but . . . *I know why*.' Calvin laughed. He had been speaking with in-creasing belligerence.

He was standing, swaying on his feet, glaring not at but towards Maggie Blackburn, who sat in a corner of the sofa, tense, coiled, steeled against him. He said, 'I hate people staring at her, I hate the thoughts they think. About her, and about me. D'you hear? I hate your goddamned pity. *All of you*.'

Maggie said quickly, 'I don't pity you, Calvin. I don't pity either of you.'

For the past several minutes she had been listening transfixed to Calvin Gould's words, even as, with another part of her mind, she understood that time was running out for her.

Calvin didn't hear; or, hearing, paid no heed. He said, his voice rising, 'You should never have intruded. You betrayed me. Saying you loved me – and you betrayed me! Did you think I would ever incriminate *her*?' He spoke wildly, in disgust and anger; his words, though incoherent, were perfectly intelligible. 'She had nothing to do with it. With either. No one can prove she did. I killed them both. *I killed them both.*'

It could have been no more than a fraction of a second that he was turned away, not quite facing Maggie; and in that instant Maggie, long poised to make her desperate leap, did leap, across an abyss of several feet – seizing the heavy white vase in both hands and swinging it in a clumsy arc, managing to strike Calvin Gould a stunning blow to the side of the head. Taken wholly by surprise, Calvin cried out like a stricken animal, and stumbled, and began to fall; Maggie dropped the vase and ran, ran out of the living-room and into the front hall, her legs dazed beneath her, her feet in their woollen socks skidding on the hardwood floor, and then she was at the door and outside, in the freezing air that did not impede her but seemed to bear her aloft, drawing breath to scream *except in the radiance of terror she was unable to scream* and the man in close pursuit grabbed hold of her and pulled her back, yanking her it seemed out of the very air and throwing her off her feet with no more effort than if she were a life-sized rag doll, and even as she fell he began to strike her with his fists, in a delirium which Maggie could recall afterwards only in fragments like a crudely cut film in which 'Maggie Blackburn' performed at a distance, unable to scream even now, as if paralysed, nor could she hear the sounds her assailant uttered, words of anguish, despair, rage as he dragged her back into the house and struck her several more blows, not with his fists now but with the flat of his hand, stooping over her, panting into her face.

But Maggie did not see him. Maggie had ceased seeing.

Twenty-six

I killed them both. One for personal reasons, the other for reasons of expediency.

Otherwise, lacking this note, his death might have been reconstructed as 'accidental'.

Twenty-seven

From a distance, Maggie Blackburn heard her name being called.

It was a melancholy hollow sound, as of a voice echoing in a deep well.

For hours she had lain unresisting, neither conscious nor unconscious, awaiting the next, the fatal, blow. She did not know that she had suffered a head concussion, as it would be called; nor even that she was bleeding from facial cuts; the music in her head had retreated, shrunk, to a dim buzzing core, barely audible. And now she heard her name being called. And she was too exhausted to respond.

Yet she opened her eyes, which were strangely swollen, the lashes crusted with blood, and she saw, through a haze of tears, a face so familiar as to require no act of naming: a youthful face, forehead lined, eyeglasses glittering, set in an expression of extreme concern.

'M-Maggie? Oh, my God – Maggie?'

He knelt beside her. He lifted her awkwardly in his arms.

It was 7.20 a.m. on February 23, 1989, a wintry morning, sunless, glaring with white. Brendan Bauer had taken a taxi to Maggie Blackburn's house because she had failed to answer his several telephone calls, the first of which he'd made at 6.30. He rang the front doorbell, there was no answer, so he opened the door, which was unlocked, and discovered Maggie in her blood-splattered black sweater and slacks, shoeless, arms flung outward, lying unconscious just inside the front door.

By the time the ambulance arrived, Calvin Gould had been dead for nearly six hours and Brendan Bauer was no longer a suspect in a murder case. But neither Brendan Bauer nor Maggie Blackburn would know that fact until later in the day.

As for Maggie: as soon as Brendan arrived and knelt over her, to wake her, she understood that she had not died. Now he was here, he would take care of her; she felt the unanticipated strength of his arms, she heard the desperation in his voice. And she shut her eyes in sheer gratitude. Floating.

She was never to articulate the thought that, had Calvin Gould meant to seriously harm her, Brendan Bauer would have arrived hours too late.

Dear Brendan!

Epilogue

By late September, seven months after the death of Calvin Gould on an icy stretch of Route 1 north of Forest Park, in the early hours of February 23, the amazed talk in and about the Forest Park Conservatory of Music was of a new, though hardly equivalent, surprise: the young graduate student and composer Brendan Bauer had not only accompanied Maggie Blackburn to Minneapolis, Minnesota, where Maggie had accepted an associate professorship in the Music Department of the University of Minnesota, but was believed to be living in Maggie's very house.

How was this possible? Were the two lovers? Or was the arrangement merely expedient, of mutual benefit?

Portia MacLeod, who would have claimed to be Maggie Blackburn's closest friend and the person of all the world who might lay claim to Maggie's confidence, expressed an air of hurt as well as simple astonishment. 'Living . . . in your house? The house you've just rented? But what does that mean, Maggie?' she asked.

'I don't know that it means anything, Portia,' Maggie said. The friends were speaking over the telephone: Maggie was twelve hundred miles away now, living in a residential section of Minneapolis contiguous with the university. 'Except what it is.'

And that coolly ambiguous reply Portia was left to interpret for herself, and to bear about Forest Park, to proffer for interpretation.

As it happened, Maggie Blackburn had not died. But only

because Calvin Gould had decided not to kill her.

This fact, on its surface so self-evident, otherwise so obscure, Maggie often contemplated. And when she was not actively contemplating it she was yet aware of it, as one is aware of one's breath, one's heartbeat, the pulsing of one's blood. That rhythmic beat that is life, indefinable.

So in a way (though Maggie could not speak of this to anyone) she was forever in Calvin's debt . . . though her fine, delicate skin bore tiny scars, particularly about her eyes, as a result of the beating he'd inflicted upon her.

Perhaps the man had been mad, at the last. He had certainly been a killer.

But he had not killed her.

In the end he must have decided, Maggie thought, to choose me over her. *Her* waiting for him in their house.

Within forty-eight hours of Calvin Gould's suicide, while Maggie was still on the critical list in the Forest Park Medical Centre, it was known through the community that the woman whom everyone had accepted as Naomi Gould, Calvin Gould's wife, was in fact Caroline Gould, Calvin Gould's twin sister, who had a history of neurological and emotional disorders dating back to childhood . . . and though the immediate speculation followed that perhaps this eccentric woman might have been involved in one of both of the murders, no proof was ever offered; if police questioned Caroline Gould, their findings were never made public. As soon as Caroline learned of her brother Calvin's death she had become, it was said, totally incapacitated: in a state of delusional mania, alternating with periods of suicidal depression; the unhappy woman was likely to be hospitalized for the rest of her life.

So Calvin has punished both himself and his twin, Maggie thought.

He had his revenge. And he'd escaped.

'Why didn't you telephone me sooner, if you suspected him?'

'I . . . didn't want to appear excitable, "hysterical".'

'But you must have known, if you'd discovered he'd lied to throw suspicion on Brendan Bauer, there would have had to be a reason. And you'd gone to Bangor, you'd done some investigating – '

'Yes but I was – I wanted it secret.'

'Why "secret"? At the risk of being killed?'

'Because though I knew Calvin was involved I couldn't bear to think that – he was involved. And his sister – '

Detective Sergeant David Miles stared at Maggie Blackburn in her hospital bed at the Medical Centre. Too sedated to entirely assess that look, still less to gauge how, in her battered disoriented state, she might appear to him, Maggie tried to smile, stretched her swollen lips, and murmured, as if shyly, or stubbornly, 'I had to trust my own judgement.'

Miles said, 'Your judgement was really quite sound. It's your sentiment that interfered.'

Maggie decided not to tell David Miles of her suspicion, or was it in fact a certainty, that Caroline Gould, and not Calvin Gould, had sent the poisoned chocolates to Rolfe Christensen. Hadn't Calvin all but admitted it, in his zeal to protect her? *I killed them both. I killed them both. I killed them both.*

As the detective was leaving, Maggie called out, managing again a painful smile, 'Mr Miles, may I ask one thing? – if it isn't too embarrassing?'

'Yes?'

'Did you ever suspect – me? I mean, of Rolfe Christensen's death.'

With an equanimity that reminded Maggie of her father, in the days of his prime, David Miles said, 'Yes of course. But not as strongly as we'd suspected Bauer.'

'We might have been accomplices, though. Brendan and me.'

'Yes, we'd thought of that too.'

' "Poison is the weapon of choice, Miss Blackburn, for people like you" – I remember your saying that to me,' Maggie said. ' "For that type of personality that can't bear violence." '

David Miles frowned, considering. 'Did I say that? Those words? Really? To you? It doesn't sound like me at all.'

Maggie felt a clutch of fear suddenly. 'Then who does it sound like?' she asked.

If Caroline Gould was in fact the poisoner, the first of the Forest Park murderers, the twin whose act propelled the other twin to act, there was never any evidence to support such a theory: no potassium cyanide, for instance, found on the property owned by Calvin Gould; no incriminating diary of Rolfe Christensen's, or other items taken from his house. Not even wrapping paper, wrapping tape, string. If any such evidence had existed it had naturally been destroyed.

Nor could there be any proof connecting the purchase of the gourmet chocolates with Caroline Gould; any more than there was proof connecting the murder of Nicholas Reickmann with Calvin Gould – except for Calvin's thoughtful confession, so neatly prepared, so carefully signed, in an envelope left on his desk in the Provost's office. *I killed them both.*

And there was the remark he'd made to Maggie, angrily, hopefully. *So you acknowledge it, then: you know that I killed both men.*

In fact, the distraught Caroline Gould insisted, in periods of relative lucidity, in the hospital, that she *had* killed – 'ten, twenty, fifty people' – many of them back in Maine. Excitedly, she'd named names: among the alleged victims were her mother and father (who had died of cancer and heart disease respectively, years ago) and her brother Calvin, whose vehicular death had been described to her as 'accidental'.

Such confessions were attributed to the woman's mental state, of course. For it was an undisputed medical fact, Caroline Gould had suffered a psychotic collapse.

And there remained the mystery, in some ways the most puzzling mystery of all, of Bill Queller's disappearance.

'Do you think – Calvin killed him too?'

'Do you think – he killed himself?'

'Is it possible for a man to – simply disappear?'

So everyone speculated, except Maggie Blackburn, who had lost her taste for such speculation, as, so very abruptly, she'd lost her taste for what might be called criminal detection.

Calvin had hinted, hadn't he, that he might have been responsible for Bill's vanishing; yet it did not seem to Maggie that Calvin could have coerced Bill to walk out of the concert hall that evening as he'd done, so dramatically, so irrevocably. One minute enduring waves of applause for a performance in which he hadn't much pride, the next minute turning and walking out. For ever. As if, with an impatient flick of someone's wrist, a radio or a stereo had been switched off, its musical notes rudely silenced.

Gradually, people ceased speculating about Bill Queller: his fate had been eclipsed by the more desperate fates of others. Maggie, who had liked Bill, and admired him, came to feel, guiltily, that in some obscure way she had failed him.

I am the cello, you are the piano, these notes are the thoughts passing through the dead Beethoven's mind.

*

'I must leave.'

Yes, Maggie was grateful to be alive, and, apart from the scattering of tiny scars on her face, she bore no trace of the beating she'd suffered. Yet she knew within days of the attack, and the ensuing publicity and scandal, that she would have to leave Forest Park.

Where she'd been so happy, for nearly seven years.

So hopeful.

There were too many memories for her, memories cruelly overlaid upon her most innocent daily routines: driving to the Conservatory campus, parking her car in the usual lot, crossing the quadrangle to her office building ... where, one March morning, Maggie realized that her face was contorted with grief and her hands were shaking uncontrollably. Another time, apparently unable to get out of her car, she woke from a sort of trance to discover herself sitting behind the wheel, a full hour

269

after having driven into the parking lot. The episode frightened her. It was likely that certain of her colleagues had noticed her there sitting stony-faced and staring, perhaps some had even waved to her, called out hello ... without her knowing. Her physical being had been there but where had *she* been?

I don't want to have a breakdown, Maggie thought, like *her*.

Like a low-grade fever the thought began to burn in her: she must leave Forest Park.

She must escape from not only the persistent thought of Calvin Gould but the denial of that thought; the suppression of her deep unhappiness and dismay at having lost the man irrevocably ... even as she knew such a sentiment was grotesque.

Sensing her state of mind, or nerves – for Maggie had become, in the eyes of her friends, a victim, requiring solicitude – the Dean of the Faculty Peter Fisher took her to lunch one day in late March, to make her an unexpected proposal of a year's leave at full salary: she might go abroad, travel, give piano recitals, immerse herself again in her music ... try to forget. And the MacLeods, who were planning to spend several weeks in Florence in June, invited her to accompany them as their guest: 'And when we get back, why don't you sell your house and buy another,' Portia said, 'that's what *I* would do.'

Portia meant: because you were terrorized in that house.

Because, there, Calvin Gould beat you into insensibility.

Maggie politely thanked these friends, and others, for their kindness; she had a sense of their monitoring her behaviour and apparent welfare behind her back and reporting about her to one another. Yet she had to leave. She felt she had no choice. Now the fever had taken hold, it began to burn like passion.

Like the majority of her colleagues, Maggie Blackburn frequently received offers from other teaching institutions inquiring into the possibility of her taking another position elsewhere. In the past, she had always declined; but she'd been attracted to the University of Minnesota for personal as well as academic reasons since the chairman of the Music Department there was a former teacher of hers from the Boston Conservatory, whom she admired very much; and, of course, there was her family connection with Minneapolis-St Paul, long neglected. She had not been back to that part of the country since the death of one of her aunts, a decade before. Suddenly, she felt excitement: would it not be like going home, to move back to Minnesota? Yet, at the same time, as in a fairy tale, might it not be like beginning her life anew?

So, to the astonishment of her friends and colleagues in Forest Park, Maggie discreetly reactivated the invitation from the chairman at Minnesota and by the first of May had accepted the offer of an associate professorship in the department; by the first of June she'd sold her house on Acacia Drive; by the first of September she was preparing to move to Minnesota. And Brendan Bauer, Maggie's frequent companion, had managed somehow, with characteristic resourcefulness, to acquire a teaching assistantship in the department . . . so he too was leaving Forest Park.

Leaving, with Maggie Blackburn?

But what did that mean?

As soon as Brendan learned of Maggie's plans for leaving Forest Park, before, even, Maggie had accepted the offer from the University of Minnesota, he'd come to her and said earnestly, 'I want to go with you – don't say no, Maggie!' He snatched up her hand in both his hands and kissed it: these days, where Maggie Blackburn was concerned, Brendan was given to impulsive gestures.

Since charges of first-degree murder against him had been dropped by Forest Park authorities, Brendan Bauer was a new man, or nearly. In repose, his face shifted to an expression of equanimity; the majority of the time, his speech was clear of any impediment; he was, to Maggie's eye not very successfully, even growing a beard. Seeing him at a distance or hearing him play her piano, Maggie felt a sense of satisfaction, as if, in a way, the young man were her accomplishment. She thought of how crudely his family had treated him, how little faith they'd had in him, and what shame they'd felt, and it was impressed upon her that he had no family really, unless it was Maggie Blackburn herself.

Yet she insisted, 'I don't believe I can ever love you, Brendan,' and Brendan would agree almost too readily.

'Oh, that's all right, Maggie – I can love *you*.'

And Maggie would say doubtfully, 'But – is that enough?' adding quickly, 'Of course I'm very fond of you.' And, further, 'I suppose it's the case now, you've become my closest friend.'

And Brendan would say, 'And you're my only friend, Maggie – the only friend I truly *want*.'

Maggie Blackburn could not bring herself, finally, to say no to Brendan Bauer's plea to take him with her to Minneapolis.

There, in that new setting, the two were considered a couple . . . but what sort of couple, precisely? They were not married, evidently, but were they lovers? Since Maggie Blackburn was a tenured professor, a woman in her mid- or early thirties, and Brendan Bauer was a graduate student who looked much younger, it seemed probable, to some observers, that they were professional colleagues, linked by way of a common interest in music. In which case, Brendan might be renting a room in Maggie's house and sharing household expenses, living *in* her house but not living *with* her.

Then again, they often displayed affection for each other, of a kind. So perhaps in fact they were lovers.

On the subject of Brendan Bauer, Maggie Blackburn's new circle of friends were divided: some considered the young composer bright, charming and talented; others considered him brash, impetuous and argumentative. Like many composers of his generation he disdained older conventional musical forms, but unlike most of these young composers, in academic circles at least, he did not hesitate to express his opinions. When Maggie suggested that he be more diplomatic, Brendan said, surprised, 'But shouldn't I tell the truth, Maggie?'

In Minneapolis, Maggie Blackburn and Brendan Bauer lived on a residential street called Aspen, in a two-storey house of stone, stucco and wood, undistinguished among its neighbours.

Maggie's metallic-grey Volvo was frequently in the driveway; both she and Brendan drove it. Residents of Aspen Street, before being formally introduced to Maggie Blackburn or Brendan Bauer, were led to assume, by the couple's relative ages and a glancing similarity between them – height, body type, skin tone, manner – that the two might be sister and brother.

One Saturday afternoon in early October Maggie Blackburn in an old shirt and slacks was shelving books in the living-room of the Aspen Street house when Brendan Bauer, who had been out doing errands, entered the house through the kitchen and called out playfully, 'Maggie – look what I've found!'

He strode through the doorway bearing aloft, as if in triumph, Maggie's bamboo birdcage, into which he'd placed two newly purchased canaries: a red-factor male and an American female with pale yellow feathers. The birds were excited, flying from perch to perch, emitting small sharp questioning cries. When Maggie saw the cage and the birds she stood staring and could not speak, and Brendan asked, anxiously, 'You *do* like them, Maggie, don't you? Aren't they beautiful? And just like the ones you – lost?'

The new house, into which Maggie Blackburn and Brendan Bauer had only just completed moving and in which they were not yet entirely settled, was no larger than Maggie's former house in Forest Park, but its individual rooms seemed more capacious; the ceilings a few inches higher, the windows admitting more light. In the dining-room area, which opened into the living-room, a plate-glass window overlooked a tangled bed of dahlias and chrysanthemums; it faced south and west, flooded with autumnal sunshine.

Brendan asked again if Maggie liked the canaries, and this time Maggie said, 'Oh, *yes*.'

The male canary was a brilliant flame-orange, the female a creamy yellow, shading, in her tail feathers, into white; they continued fluttering excitedly from perch to perch. Observing them, now from close up, Maggie was moved to think that nothing in

273

her life ever changed except to shift, as if by subterranean stealth or grace, from one moment of wonder to the next.

Brendan Bauer, his thin face glowing with pleasure, brought the bamboo cage to the dining-room window, to position it. 'Shall we hang it here, Maggie, or here?'

'In the sun,' Maggie Blackburn said, 'where it's always been.'